THE
UNIVERSE
OF
REALMS
OMNIBUS

BOOK 2

WORKS BY TY'RON W. C. ROBINSON II

BOOKS/SHORT STORIES

DARK TITAN UNIVERSE SAGA

MAIN SERIES
Dark Titan Knights
The Resistance Protocol
Tales of the Scattered
Tales of the Numinous
Day of Octagon
Crossbreed
Heaven's Called
The Oranos Imperative
Underworld

SPIN-OFFS
In A Glass of Dawn: The Casebook of
Travis Vail
Maveth: Bloodsport
The Curse of The Mutant-Thing
Trail of Vengeance
War of The Thunder Gods

ONE-SHOTS
Maveth, The Death-Bringer
Mystery of The Mutant-Thing
Shade & Switchblade
Retribution of Cain
The Mythologists
Ambush Bot
Kang-Zhu
Cheeseburger Man
Tessa Balthazar
Elite 5

COLLECTIONS
Dark Titan Omnibus: Volume 1
Dark Titan Omnibus: Volume 2
Dark Titan One-Shot Collection
Dark Titan One-Shot Collection II

THE HAUNTED CITY SAGA
The Legendary Warslinger: The Haunted City I
Battle of Astolat: A Haunted City Prequel (KOBO Exclusive)
Redemption of the Lost: The Haunted City II
Helper's Hand: A Haunted City One-Shot

SYMBOLUM VENATORES
Symbolum Venatores: The Gabriel Kane Collection
Hod: A Symbolum Venatores Book
Symbolum Venatores: War of The Two Kingdoms
Symbolum Venatores: Elrad's Chronicles

EVERWAR UNIVERSE
EverWar Universe: Knights & Lords

PRODIGIOUS WORLDS
Mark Porter of Argoron
Raiders of Vanok
Praxus of Lithonia

FRIGHTENED! SERIES
Frightened!: The Beginning

INSTINCTS SERIES
Lost in Shadows: Remastered

CHEVAH MYTHOS
The Eleventh Hour; A Chevah Mythos Story

THE HORDE TRILOGY
The Horde

DARK TITAN'S THE DEAD DAYS
Accounts of The Dead Days

OTHER BOOKS
The Book of The Elect
The Extended Age Omnibus
The Supreme Pursuer: Darkness of the Hunt and Other Stories
Massacre in the Dusk
Venture Into Horror: Tales of the Supernatural
The Universe of Realms Omnibus: Book 1

THE DARK TITAN AUDIO EXPERIENCE PODCAST
Season 1: Introductions
Season 2: In a Glass of Dawn
Season 2.5: Accounts of The Dead Days
Season 3: Battle For Astolat
Season 4: Hallow Sword: Cursed

DARK TITAN

THE
UNIVERSE
OF
REALMS
OMNIBUS

BOOK 2

TY'RON W. C. ROBINSON II

CONTENTS

FRIGHTENED!: THE BEGINNING

THE GHOST OF THE HOUND

A man is walking through a cemetery past midnight. He's only carrying a flashlight and a piece of paper. He scans the cemetery grounds as if he's searching for something. As he walks through the cemetery, he hears something in the distant, around the covered bushes near a tombstone. He glances toward the bushes. The bushes rustle. He starts moving his head around.

"Is someone there?" The man uttered.

He receives no response and decides to walk over near the tombstone to check for himself.

"If someone is over there, I suggest you come out this instant or else."

He suddenly hears a groan coming from near the tombstone. The man stopped and stood quietly.

"Time's a wasting right now. I'm on a very important mission here and I do not want to be disturbed."

He moved his flashlight slowly and pointed it towards the tombstone and the bushes.

"Guess nothing isn't here after all. I could possibly check tomorrow night."

The man sets his sights on leaving the cemetery. He suddenly hears the sound of low breathing coming from behind him. Moving cautiously, he slowly turns around sees himself staring into the red eyes of a huge black dog.

"It can't be real. You can't be real!"

The large dog lunges toward the man and stands over him as the man SCREAMS in fear.

Police officers and officials are walking around the cemetery as the coroner takes the body of the man toward the van. The police continue to search the perimeter for any traces that could lead to the culprit. They only find the man's stack of papers. One officer looks at it and sees the information about the Ghost Hound. The officer turned to his associate officer.

"I don't know what to say." An officer said. "Just take this in for further investigation."

"Yes sir."

The associate officer takes the stack of papers and walks way toward the police car. The leading officer looks down the drips of blood that are laying on the grass. He shakes his head.

Inside the living room is Carl, 12, who's reading about the news on the internet and he hears the news on the TV speaking about the cemetery. He looks up at the TV and grabs the remote, turning the volume up. He now focuses his attention toward the TV.

"We're here currently at the cemetery where a man was found murdered from severe bites and claw marks on his throat and chest. The police have found no trace of what could've done the murder. The investigation is still ongoing and no one is allowed to approach the marked off area of the cemetery. If they do, they will be fined or arrested."

Carl looked at TV and shook his head.

"I'm curious as to what happened there."

Coming down the stairs is Carl's mother, Brenda. She approaches Carl as he sits on the couch. She taps his shoulder and he turns toward her.

"Come on. Time to head to school."

"Yes ma'am."

Carl closes his laptop and places it into his backpack and turns off the TV. He walks to the front door and opens it as his mother walks behind him through the door. She closes the door behind her.

Children and teenagers are being dropped off at the school as other kids walks around the school's front campus. Brenda stops the car in front of the school. Carl grabs his backpack.

"Make sure you have a good day."

"I'll do my best."

Carl opens the car door and steps out of the car. He closes the car door as his mother waves to him. He waves back as she drives away.

Carl turns and walks into the school.

Carl approaches his science classroom. He turns to his left, passing by numerous students as he entered the classroom.

Carl walks toward his desk as someone from behind touches his shoulder. He turns around and it's his friend, Eric, 12. They shake hands as they approach the desks.

"I have to tell you something."

"What is it?" Carl wondered.

"I'm not sure if you heard about what happened at the cemetery."

"You're talking about the murder on the news this morning?"

"Yes, that's exactly what I'm talking about." Eric said. "I think we should go into the cemetery after school.

"But, the area is closed off to the public. If we were to enter it, we could pay a fine or even be arrested."

"I suggest that we head in their tonight. Nobody will be there to see us. We won't get into any trouble."

"My parents won't let me stay out that late."

"How about right after school." Eric suggested. "We head over there and after we can head back home."

Carl pauses and looks over at the nearby window. He turned to Eric. Smiling.

"I'm for it." Carl replied.

"Alright! Looks like we're doing some detective work ourselves."

As they continue to speak and laugh, a girl approaches them and sits at the desk in front of Eric. Stacy is her name. Eric taps her on the shoulder. She turns around and looks at Eric.

"Hey, guess what, Stacy."

"What is it this time?" She asked.

"Me and Carl are detectives now."

Stacy had a confused look on her face as she glanced at Carl, who pointed toward Eric.

"He'll explain everything." Carl gestured toward Eric.

Eric leaned over closer to Stacy. Acting as if what he's about to say is top secret.

"Look, I don't know if you heard this morning about what happened at the cemetery, but me and Carl are going over there after school to do our own investigation."

Stacy shook her head.

"You realize that if you two are caught, you could be arrested."

"That's what I told him." Carl mentioned. "But, I want to know what happened there."

"Well, Carl gets the picture. How about you?"

Stacy sighed.

"I'll only tag alone. Just because it sounds like a interesting case."

Eric raises his hand toward Stacy. Looking for a high-five. Stacy shakes her head. Disagreeing with Eric as she turns around facing the front of the class. He turns toward Carl. Carl gives Eric a high-five. The science teacher, Ms. Lawrence, walks through the door and stands by her desk.

"Very well, students." said Ms. Lawrence. "I hope all of you have done your homework. So, please place it on your desk for me to see."

Carl looks around at the other students as he searches through his backpack for his homework. Thinking to himself, he realizes that he forgot the homework at home. Eric turns to Carl, noticing him moving quickly through his bag.

"What's the problem?" Eric asked.

"Forgot my homework at home. It shouldn't be a problem I hope."

She starts walking through the aisle in between the desks, scanning each student's desk for their homework. She approaches Carl and Eric's desks. She looks at Eric, shaking her head.

"May I ask about your homework, Mr. Hughes?"

"I had some important things I had to do, and I forgot about it."

"I sort of doubt that. You just decided not to do it."

Eric shrugged.

"You caught me. But, I'll do the next homework. I assure you."

"I'll wait and see."

She turns to Carl and looks at his desk. Only seeing an open notebook and two pencils sitting beside it. She looks Carl in the eyes as he does the same.

"I take it you and Eric had important things to do other than your homework."

"No ma'am." Carl said. "I did the homework. I just forgot it at home. I was watching the news this morning and forgot to grab it."

Ms. Lawrence held up her right hand.

"Wait. You're telling me that a twelve-year old boy such as yourself was watching the news this morning?"

"Yes ma'am. I was focused on the report that discussed the cemetery murder."

"Very interesting. So, what do you think killed that man?"

"I personally believe it was the Ghost Hound." Carl said.

"The Ghost Hound?"

"Yes ma'am. He was carrying stacks of paper that contained information about a Ghost Hound that lived in the cemetery."

"You do understand ghost hounds don't exist."

"Well, the man believed so and he's currently deceased."

A pause from Ms. Lawrence. Carl stared.

"Besides the belief of ghost hounds, I'll tell you this. I'll let you bring in your homework tomorrow morning." Ms. Lawrence said. "Only because you paid close attention to the news."

"Thanks."

"I'm only allowing it because not many students pay attention to the news in this day."

She returned to her desk and starts teaching to the class. Eric looked over to Carl with a questioning look on his face. Carl looked at him.

"What?" Carl said.

"I paid attention to the news as well. Should've just thrown it out there."

"I wouldn't hold it too close. Just bring it in tomorrow. Right now, we should focus on the cemetery and finding out about this ghost hound."

"I agree."

They turn, facing the teacher in front of the class.

School is over as Carl, Eric, and Stacy walk out of the front entrance as they see their parents' car waiting for them. Carl turned around, facing Eric and Stacy.

"As soon as we're all in our rooms, we'll contact each other and head for the cemetery."

"Sure thing." Eric said.

5

"See you two at the graveyard." Stacy said.

Stacy walks to her parents' car. Carl and Eric to the same.

Carl enters his room and places his backpack onto his bed. He takes out the laptop and sits it on his desk. Opening it up, he glances at the daily news and discovers that the cemetery has been slightly opened.

"This is great."

Carl grabbed his phone, texting Eric and Stacy the details of his discovery.

Inside the cemetery, Carl waited for Eric and Stacy to arrive. He glances at his watch and hears footsteps. He looked up and Eric approaches him.

"I see you made it." Eric said.

"I couldn't miss this. I'm excited to find out what we can find."

Eric looks around the area. Glancing and scouting. Carl looks around as well.

"Seen Stacy anywhere?"

"No. She probably opted out."

"I did not opt out."

Carl and Eric turn to their left and see Stacy walking toward them.

"I'm right here. So, let's do this."

Stacy walks past Carl and Eric as she approaches the entrance to the cemetery. They follow behind her. Stacy stands by the entrance and slowly opens the gate. As they walk through the gate, they notice the surroundings feel uncomfortable. Eric looks around.

"I didn't expect it to feel this way."

"Don't worry about it." Carl said. "As soon as we find what we're looking for, we'll be out of here."

They continue to walk until Carl spots the yellow police tape circling the spot where the man was found. He points toward it.

"There it is."

"Well, well. So, what's the next step in all of this?" Eric asked.

"We go and look for ourselves."

"While the two of you do your search, I'll stay on the lookout for anyone in a police uniform." Stacy said.

"Sounds good to me."

"Please pay attention, Stacy. Close attention."

"I have it under control. Nothing to worry about.

Carl and Eric approach the yellow tape. Carl raises up the tape as he and Eric step into the perimeter. They start searching the ground for any type of evidence. Eric looks down and notices the dried blood on the grass.

"There's the blood."

Carl looks over and sees it.

"I see it. There has to be something else here that can give us more of a lead."

Carl continues walking around the perimeter. Quickly, they heard the sound of footsteps approach at a pace. Eric looks over. He sees Stacy approaching them.

"Stacy, I thought you were supposed to be on watch."

"We have a slight problem."

Carl looked toward Stacy and sees a man walking behind her. He stops behind her, holding a shovel in his hand. He looks at Eric and Carl. Shaking his head slowly.

They have now met the Caretaker. The guardian of the cemetery and its nearby church.

"Seems you three aren't supposed to be here."

"We were just about to leave." Eric said, holding his hands up. "No problems here."

"No, you weren't. You were checking out that area where the man was found. Didn't you notice the yellow tape?"

"Yes sir." Carl said. "But, we figured that we should have a look for ourselves. You see we're detectives in training."

"Be that as it may. I suggest the three of you leave this place before sunset. Unless you want to be the next victims of the Ghost Hound."

Carl paused. Eric and Stacy glanced at each other.

"What do you mean victims of the Ghost Hound?" Stacy asked.

"I've said too much already. Now, you three should leave. Go home, you parents must be worrying about your whereabouts."

The Caretaker walks away, heading toward the nearby church. Carl watched him leave. Eric turns toward Carl, so does Stacy.

"I think we should ask him more questions about this Ghost Hound." Carl questioned.

"I don't know about that." Eric said. "You seen the way he approached us and the way he talked. We should just leave."

"I agree with Eric for once on this one." Stacy said.

"Well, I don't agree with either of you. I'm going over there and asking more questions."

Carl walks toward the church. Eric and Stacy stay still and look at each other.

"We should just follow him." Eric gestured. "Get some interesting answers."

"Ugh. Yeah. Let's hope we don't become the next victims."

They followed Carl toward the church.

Carl runs into the old and beaten church. He sees the Caretaker sweeping the middle aisle towards the front. Carl walks toward him. He stops sweeping and turns, facing Carl. He stops walking.

"Tell me why you're in here. Looking for deliverance?"

"I'm not here for deliverance. I'm here to ask you more questions concerning the Ghost Hound."

The Caretaker holds his head down. Nodding. He looks up at Carl, seeing Eric and Stacy behind him.

"Well, what would you like to know about the Ghost Hound?"

"Where does it come from and why is it only seen in this cemetery?"

"The Ghost Hound is seen across the world. Whether its cemeteries, highways, forests, even in some public locations. There's more than one Ghost Hound."

"Wait, you're telling us that there are more of those things?" Eric asked.

"I am. Thousands more at best."

"How would you know about all of this?" Stacy asked.

The Caretaker walks toward Stacy. He looks at her. Taking off his gray hat and leaning toward her. He points toward his left eye, which is damaged.

"You see my left eye."

"My goodness. What happened?"

"This is the mark of a Ghost Hound. Attacked during a night shift. I managed to survive, but barely. Later I seen a whole pack of those things roaming across the fields.

"How big are they?" Carl asked.

"Huge. Very large beasts. It would take almost a dozen people to lift one off another human being. Which is the reason that wandering man did not survive.

"So, how did you survive?"

"With the faith of a higher power. Guided me through the fight and saved my life after. I owe it all I could possibly give."

"So, there's a slight chance that the Ghost Hound could appear tonight?" Carl asked curiously.

"It's always out there after midnight. Don't get any ideas of trying to see one up close. Because you won't like it."

"It won't be a problem. We know how to take care of ourselves."

"Hopefully, you have a higher power to protect you on this nonsensical quest."

Carl looks at the Caretaker's neck. Seeing the necklace, which resembled a star.

"One more quick question."

"What is it?" The Caretaker said.

"That necklace you're wearing. What is it?"

The Caretaker holds the necklace and looks down toward it. He looks at Carl.

"Something that I've had possession of for a very long time."

"Oh. Alright. Thanks for the questions."

The Caretaker nodded with a smirk.

"Anytime, son."

They leave the church as the Caretaker goes back to sweeping the floors. They start walking through the cemetery, heading for the exit.

"So, what's the plan?" Eric asked. "We come back tonight or another day?"

We'll come back tonight." Carl answered. "See this Ghost Hound or Hounds for ourselves."

Carl sits at his desk, reasserting on the internet about the Ghost Hound. He fins certain web sites that have information on the Ghost Hound, though the name of the hound is known as the Hellhound. He glances down to the bottom right corner of the laptop. Looking at the time. He gets up from his desk and leaves his room.

Carl walks down the stairs into the living room where his mother and father are dressed up in casual suits. Carl glances at them.

"You two are dressed nicely."

"That's because your father and I are going out tonight."

"Figured a Wednesday night would do us some good." Robert, Carl's father said. "Somewhere you were going, son?"

"I was going to go over to Eric's house, play some video games."

"Are you sure you're going over to his house to play video games?"

"Because the last time you went over to his house, you two were playing pranks on the entire neighborhood."

"No pranks this time." Carl laughed. "I promise you."

"Robert, don't worry. Carl will be just fine. He won't play any jokes on the neighborhood again. He's learned his lesson from last time."

Robert nods. He grabs the keys to his car from the counter and he walks toward the front door with Brenda. He looks back at Carl.

"Just take care while we're out."

"I will."

They leave out the door. Carl waits to hear the car engine. **VROOM!**, He hears the engine and grabs his phone from his pocket. He texts Eric and Stacy. He runs back upstairs to his room. Carl runs into his room and grabs the papers that were laying out of the printer. The papers contained information on the Ghost Hound.

Carl exits his home. He locks the door behind him as he starts walking down the street toward Eric's house. Without notice, Eric jumps up behind the bushes. Scaring Carl a bit. He turns to him and sees Eric with a flashlight.

"See you're all set up and ready."

"Same goes to you."

Carl looks around the neighborhood.

"What about Stacy?"

"She's just leaving her home. She'll meet us at the cemetery."

"Great. Let's start our search."

Carl and Eric reach the cemetery. Carl looks around for Stacy, doesn't see her. Eric looks around.

"She told me she would be here before us."

"Apparently, she was wrong."

They hear footsteps behind them. Carl turns and sees Stacy.

"Why do the two of you always accuse me of being wrong?"

"Usually, you are. Good thing you made it. Now, we can start."

Eric stands still. He rubs his arms as if he's cold and suddenly feels a presence nearby. He turns toward Carl and Stacy. They notice the sign of fear in Eric's face.

"Eric, what's the matter?"

"It's here. The Ghost Hound is here."

Carl looks around. Stacy does the same. Carl walks toward Eric.

"Where? I don't see it."

"It's here. I can feel it. You don't feel it? The surprising cold atmosphere? The shivering?"

"No. But, I take it you are."

"Yeah." Stacy said. "You're shaking."

"Every last bit of it." Eric said. "I think it preys on who's afraid the most. Shame it's myself."

"We're going to find this Ghost Hound and we'll all be just fine." Carl said. "You'll see tomorrow."

"Yeah, Nothing to worry about with us here at your side."

"Good thing I have great friends who have my back."

"Always. Same goes here."

"OK, guys. Can we just go ahead and find this thing before our parents realize we're out longer than what we said?"

Carl and Eric nodded.

"Sure thing." Eric said.

"Of course." Carl replied.

Carl opens the front gate to the cemetery. The door creaks open. As the walk through the cemetery, Eric looks around at the graves. Holding his flashlight closely.

"So, if any of us see this thing, who's running first?"

"You." Stacy said.

"Yeah. Already told you I was afraid."

"Just try to stay calm and hold your ground."

Carl hears Eric shivering and turns around. Seeing the light from his flashlight shivering. Eric looks at Carl and stops shivering.

"You'll be just fine."

They keep walking through the cemetery. Passing by large amounts of graves. Stacy looks further and notices a fog.

"Guys, head's up. A fog's approaching."

"Oh no." Eric said with fear in his voice. "It's here."

"Perfect. It's what it needs to manifest."

The fog slowly covers them up and gets thicker as they walk further inside of it. Eric waves his flashlight around to have a better look. RRRRR. A growl is heard and they each look in front of each other in the midst of the fog. Carl notices a smell in the fog. He sniffs.

"You guys smell that?"

Eric and Stacy sniff. They smell it as well.

"Yeah. What is it? I have never smelled something like that before.

"It's sulfur. You know where sulfur is usually followed by?"

They spot a formed object approaching them. They saw the four legs and its black fur. Its head raises up from under the fog. Its red eyes stare deeply at them. Its sharp teeth are hungry. They are looking at the Ghost Hound. It barks once and Eric takes off. As he runs the other direction, the Hound jumps in front of him and stares. It barks again as Eric backs up toward Carl and Stacy.

"Well, it's here." Eric said. "So, mission accomplished?"

"Would you shut it." Stacy said.

Eric quiets down. The Hound circles them, sniffs each of them before facing Carl. They are appalled by the Hound's massive size, near the equivalent of a small bull. The Hound snatches the papers out of Carl's hands and tears them to shreds.

"We're not bad people."

"You're talking to it now." Eric noticed.

"Please, the two of you just stay quiet."

The Hound inches closer to Carl, extending his hand toward the Hound's head. Reaching to pet it. Stacy looked over.

"What are you doing, Carl?!"

"Hey, don't touch that!" Eric yelled.

Carl glances at Stacy and Eric before looking back at the Hound. Its staying still and staring into Carl's eyes. He goes to pet it. He looks up and notices the fog slowly returning. The Hound looked back, seeing the fog. It turned to Carl and slowly backed up toward the fog. The fog consumes the Hound as it passes by.

"Carl, where did it go?" Stacy asked.

"I don't know."

They look behind the fog and see the Caretaker standing still with a shovel in hand. Stacy turns to Carl as Eric waves.

"Well, what do you know. We're caught."

Carl holds his hands up. Eric points at Carl.

"You three don't have to worry." The Caretaker said. "I won't tell a single soul.

Stacy exhales heavily. Eric wipes his forehead.

"Where did the Hound go?" Carl asked.

"It took off as soon as the fog returned. They tend to do that on different occasions."

"I can say that we've seen it and know it exist."

"I'll rather not see it again." Eric gestured. "You've seen how huge it was."

"Maybe what they say is right after all." Stacy said. "Most of what we see is only a fragment of what is really there."

"Believe me when I say that many who walk among the earth today haven't' seen anything yet."

"You won't have to worry." Eric said sincerely. "We believe you."

Carl looks at his watch and notices the time. Past ten.

"I think it's time we all head back home."

"Good point." Stacy said. "Before our parents come out and kill us."

They leave the cemetery. The Caretaker watches on.

"You three take good care of yourselves."

Carl turned toward the Caretaker and nodded with respect.

"We will."

Carl went to turn back around, the Caretaker had vanished. Nowhere to be seen in the area. Stacy and Eric turn around and neither see him.

"Wasn't he just here." Stacy asked.

"Can we just go on home now." Eric begged.

Carl stood speechless for the moment.

"Yeah." Carl uttered calmly with confusion. "Yeah, we're going home."

They leave the cemetery. Behind them in the field, the grass slowly blows as a black paw stands on top of the grass. Settling. A low growl is sounded.

Carl and Eric walk through the hallway, heading to their science class. They turn a left and enter the door. They walk into the classroom as many students are sitting down and preparing their notebooks and paper. Carl and Eric sit next to each other as Stacy enters the classroom and sits next to Eric.

"What a strange weekend it's been." Stacy said.

"No doubt about that."

Ms. Lawrence approaches Carl. He looks at her and nodded. However, her face was still. Her mind was on something.

"Remember what I said about your previous homework?

"Oh. Yes ma'am."

Carl reaches into his backpack and pulls out his homework. He hands it to her. She looks at it and smiles toward him.

"Good thing you remembered."

"How could I forget."

Ms. Lawrence smiles and returns to her desk. Carl glances out through the classroom window and sees something moving across the bushes. He raises his head to peek over. He sees something black moving through. It shows itself. it is the Ghost Hound. Carl is speechless. The Ghost Hound walks and behind it are seven more. A whole pack of Ghost Hounds. Carl glances at Eric and sees him talking to Stacy. He looks back outside and sees the last Hound. It stops and turns to the window, staring at Carl. He stares back and notices the dog's collar. It's the necklace that the Caretaker wore.

"The Caretaker?" Carl whispered to himself.

The Hound nods to Carl, he does the same as he watches the Hound catch up to the pack and they slowly disappear. Carl turns to the front of the class. Smiling. Stacy looks over toward him. Seeing him smiling.

"Hey, what are you smiling about?"

"Oh, nothing. Just nothing."

He looks back out through the window. Smile still on his face.

THE TRAIL OF BIGFOOT

A group of campers are sitting by a fire near their tents. They talk with one another while looking around the area surrounding him.

"Hey, you guys realize that we're in the same forest as the Bigfoot?"

"Yeah. We do." The young woman said.

"So, I have a plan. You can call it a dare if you wish. But, why don't we go out and search for Bigfoot ourselves."

The camp is silent. The campers look at each other before staring at the male camper. One of the other male campers stands up and walks over to the camper. He sits beside him.

"Why don't you go out there and find Bigfoot. Just imagine how much attention and fame you could receive."

The campers smile. Thinking on the possibilities which would come if encountering a Bigfoot.

"I like the way you're talking."

The camper stands up and grabs one of the flashlights sitting by one of the tents. He looked back at the camp and heads into the forest. The rest of the campers looked at each other with a little doubt in their faces.

Within the forest itself, the camper continues walking with a large smile on his face. The fame and fortune on his mind as he started moving in excitement.

"I'm going to find you a Bigfoot. Believe me, I surely will."

While he walked through the forest, he hears what sounds like branches cracking on the ground as if their being stepped on. He stopped walking and stood still. He turns around seeing if any of the campers had followed him into the forest to scare him.

"Alright, guys. Don't try to make this a joke."

More rustling sounds come from the tree nearby. The camper

becomes more terrified as to which he cannot see. The rustling continues as the camper makes a 360-degree turn, looking around himself. After a few seconds, the rustling stopped, and everything went silent. All the camper can hear are his friends talking amongst themselves back at the site. He releases a small sigh and wipes his forehead.

"Thought someone was playing a trick on me. Just my imagination."

He turned around to walk back to his camp and from behind him comes a long hairy arm with brown hair. The arm snatches the camper's shirt and pulls him with great strength. The camper falls onto his back and tries his hardest to get up and run, but, the arm grabs his leg and knocks him onto the ground. He claws his way trying to hold on to something as the arm pulls him deeper into the abyss of the forest.

"HELP!!! I NEED HELP!!! SOMEBODY PLEASE HELP ME!!!"

His cries for help can barely be heard by his other camping friends as he is pulled into the darkness of the forest as his screams immediately stop.

A young boy holds a rifle in his hand as an older man stands behind him. The young boy is Matt and the older man is his Uncle Charles. Both of them are wearing camouflage uniforms to blend in with the trees. Charles is teaching Matt how to use the rifle for hunting. Matt tries to hold the rifle tightly.

"Just remember what I told you before, nephew. Be steady and relax your arms."

"Relax my arms and be steady."

"That's right. Just do what I said, and you'll do good. Now, there must be some buck around here."

"Maybe someone has already come by and scared them off?"

"No chance that happened. There are too many deer out here to count at times and we shouldn't miss out on this."

Matt stared through the bushes in front of him and spots movement. His eyes bulge as he steadies the rifle.

"Uncle, there's a deer. Over there."

Charles reaches for his binoculars and looks. He sees the deer in front of him. An adult deer.

"About time one of them big bucks showed up." said Charles. "Are you ready to do

this, Matt?"

"I am ready to do this."

"Show me what you can do, nephew."

Matt holds the rifle tight and relaxes himself. Taking a few deep breaths as Charles watches on. The deer still standing in his previous position. He places his finger on the trigger and takes one last breath. FIRE! Matt fires the shot and hits the deer in its side. Both Matt and Charles see the deer fall to the ground and both jump up with excitement.

"That's what I'm talking about." Charles said proudly. "That's how you take a shot."

"I'm surprised I did it. I took down a deer."

"You did great. Now, let's go grab the thing and take it back home so we can have some food on our table."

Charles gives Matt a high-five as they walk over to the deer. Charles grabs the deer by his hind legs as Matt holds it by its front legs. They take the deer back to their truck and place it in the back. They enter the truck and Charles drives away from the forest.

Charles drives the truck as Matt sits in the passenger's seat with a big smile on his face. Charles looks over at Matt.

"I am truly excited to see you continue this on, nephew."

"It was great. I've never felt anything like that."

"The power of the rifle or making your first hunt?"

"I would have to say both."

Charles notices the radio broadcast and turns up the volume to listen. He hears a reporter talking.

"We have reports of a hairy beast that appears to be lurking around the woods of our area and officials say those who live near the woods need to caution themselves when stepping outside of their homes."

"What kind of hairy beast are they talking about, Uncle?"

"I'm not too sure at the moment."

The Radio Reporter continued to speak.

"From what we've uncovered by the reports, the descriptions of the hairy

beast resemble that of the legendary Bigfoot."

Matt turned his head over toward Charles with a shocking awe on his face.

"Bigfoot, they say, huh."

"Do you believe that we could go out one day and search for it ourselves? Like we do our hunting?"

"I would say one day we could go out and look for Bigfoot. Should be an exciting event."

The truck drives down the road.

Charles pulls the truck up to his cabin-style country home on the outskirts of the city. Matt gets out of the truck and heads inside the home as Charles follows him.

Matt walked over to his left and placed the rifle back into the gun shelf sitting on the right side of the wall. Charles walked over and placed his rifle into the shelf and closed it. He locks it after. They hear someone knocking on their door and Charles walks over to answer it.

"See who this is at the door."

Charles opened the door and sees his neighbor, Arnold, with his daughter Bridgette. He invites them in. Peter a friend of Matt's runs toward the door to get Charles' attention. Charles smiles as Peter entered the home. Knowing who he was.

"Well, how are you folks doing on this day?"

"No problems coming upon us today, Charles." said Arnold. "Bridgette wanted to come over to see Matt. Guess the Peter fellow there is also a friend of your nephew."

"He comes around every so often." Charles said. "A close friend of Matt's. So, why did you decide to visit me today?"

"I was curious to know if you heard about the Bigfoot sighting that took place in these woods?"

"I heard about it this morning on the radio. What happened now? Something else come up about the beast?"

"There was also a missing person's report that was published, and the campers claim their friend had to have been taken by Bigfoot. Though, they aren't sure on that matter. The police are already on it and have brought in a huntsman to capture the beast."

"A huntsman?" Charles said with confusion in his voice.

"The Forest Ranger has been going around the nearby homes to warn them about the search and the beast itself."

"No ranger has come over to my place today."

A few knocks are heard from the door as Charles gets out of his chair to walk toward the door. He opens the door and it's the Forest Ranger, wearing a brown buttoned-down shirt with light brown slacks and combat boots. He wears his black sunglasses.

"May I help you good sir?"

"I'm the Forest Ranger and I've been going around the nearby homes to give a warning to the people about these woods."

"I'm aware about what's transpired in the woods, sir. No need to tell me about the whole thing."

"It is my duty to give you the information needed about what we're doing in this forest. We have an investigation on a missing person as well as a Bigfoot sighting. Since you live near the forest, we will have your land watched by our officials for searching the person and or the Bigfoot creature."

Charles cocked his head as he stared toward the Ranger.

"You mean to tell me that my home and I are going to be watched until you end your search party?"

"That is correct, sir." The Ranger stated.

"Well, for you and your party to know, I don't approve of this. This makes you guys spying on my property and myself. Including my nephew who is here for the weekend."

The Ranger stood still, keeping his eyes locked on Charles.

"You have no say so on this matter, sir. I bid you a good day."

The Ranger steps off the porch and gets into his jeep and drove off Charles' property. Charles shuts the door as Arnold stands up and approaches him.

"I take it you didn't like what he said."

"You do understand that this is spying at its finest."

"We can do nothing about it, my friend. It is in their hands now."

Matt and Peter sit and look at ways to hunt and study astrology. They hear a knock at the door.

"Come in." Matt said.

Bridgette walks into the room and sits next to Matt and Peter. She sees them studying astrology and looking up hunting tips on the internet.

"This can't be all you guys continue to do on a daily basis?"

"We also play video games, watch a little TV, and gaze at the stars with the telescope." Peter added.

"On a daily basis at most."

"I thought you would be looking at the Bigfoot sighting that took place over here."

"I heard about it on the radio this morning. I talked with my uncle to see if we could go and search for it."

"Take it from me, friend. Bigfoot cannot exist. There are so many scientific studies that indicate it can't exist."

"Maybe sometimes they receive the wrong calculations."

"No. Science always gets it correct when doing a strict search and study. Same goes for mathematics. Numbers do not lie."

Bridgette gave Peter a smartly look as she turned her attention toward Matt, who's changed from studying hunting to Bigfoot sightings on his computer.

"Well, we could find out for sure by searching the beast ourselves." Matt said.

"I don't think that would be possible. Considering the amount of police that are scattered throughout the forest. We could be caught and in trouble."

"We don't go in the daytime. Most Bigfoot sightings occur when night falls. So, we can go out tonight and do our own investigation."

"A distinctive and thorough investigation would work just fine." Peter said. We'll need flashlights and equipment to get this going."

Matt looks at Peter and gives him a high-five. They turn to Bridgette, who only stares at them. She sighs and gives them both a high-five.

"I'll do it." She said. "Just for the sake of making history."

"If anyone is making any kind of history. It would be me."

"We'll see who will be making history when we find the Bigfoot ourselves and prove its existence."

The police scatter the woods looking for the missing person and the Bigfoot. The Forest Ranger arrives on the scene and approaches one of the leading officers.

"Any luck on the missing person?"

"No luck at all." An officer answered. "Do you really want us to search for this Bigfoot creature?"

"We have someone for that task already. You're only needed for the missing person."

The officer giggles and smirks at the Ranger.

"You can't possibly be serious when you say that you have someone who will search these woods for a Bigfoot. We know the thing is make-believe."

"Have you ever encountered the creature yourself, officer?"

"You have to be joking around with me on this one, Ranger. There is no such thing as a Bigfoot. Like I just said, it's all make-believe. Same thing goes for ghosts, warlocks, dragons, and even ghost hounds. Which that investigation itself was a complete cover-up."

"I only asked if you've seen the Bigfoot. I didn't ask for your belief in the supernatural. That leads me to believe that you've never seen the beast. Therefore, worry yourself on the missing person and the Huntsman will deal with the beast."

The Officer shows a confused look on his face as he squinted his eyes a bit.

"I'm sorry. But, did you just say a Huntsman will be searching for Bigfoot?"

Yes. He's one of our best guys to work with on search hunts."

A camouflage jeep pulls up on the side of the road, facing the woods. The Ranger and Officer turn around to see black combat boots step out of the jeep as the driver walks around the vehicle to enter the forest.

"There he is now, officer." The Ranger pointed.

The officer looks and sees that the man is the Huntsman. Wearing all camouflage to blend in with the forest and is carrying a machete in hand. He approaches the Ranger and they shake hands.

"Good to have you back here, Huntsman."

"No issue. I'm just here to do my duty. Now, where's this Bigfoot that you speak of."

The Huntsman walks into the woods, passing by and walking

through the number of scattered officers searching.

"He looks like a tough kind of guy."

"He's one of the best." The Ranger declared. "Very simple to understand."

Matt sits in his room with Peter and they discuss possible plans to sneak into the woods without being caught by the police. They look at a map that shows the entire location of the map.

"Do you think it's possible that we could come in through that way?" Matt asked, pointing at the map.

"I doubt we could enter through there." Peter replied. "I would only assume that more police would be on that side of the woods rather than this side. Just a guess."

"How do you suggest we convince my uncle to let us out into the woods for the night?"

"He wouldn't let you go into those woods on your own. Let alone with me by your side. He would want to enter the woods too."

"Why don't we go and ask him."

"It's worth a shot."

Matt gets up from the chairs and leaves his room. Peter follows him.

Matt comes down the steps with Peter following. He sees his uncle sitting down on the couch watching the TV. Charles glances at Matt and Peter as they approach him.

"What are you two boys planning on now?"

"What gives you the perception that we have something planned?" Peter asked cautiously.

"You two never come around together unless you're preparing to do something. What are you preparing to do?"

"We hope to go into the forest tonight to search for the Bigfoot." Matt said.

Charles looks at Matt with his eyebrows raised. Peter turns his head.

"You understand that the law is out there searching for a missing person and they're watching every home around the forest. Going out there would get you in some deep trouble."

"Not to worry, Uncle. We found a way of getting into the forest without being caught by the police."

Charles sat on the couch, thinking. Matt and Peter glanced over at each other before turning their attention back to Charles. He stood up and walked to the door. He grabbed his jacket and put it on. He reached over for his cap and placed it on his head. He walked over to the gun shelf and took out his rifle. He walked to the door before turning toward Matt and Peter.

"I'm not letting you two going out there alone with the law and a beast."

"Wait till Bridgette finds out about this."

Charles turned quickly toward Peter.

"Bridgette is involved in your little scheme too?! Does her father know about this?"

"No, Uncle. He does not know about any of this."

"Where is she now?" Charles asked. "Is she already in the woods waiting for you two to show up?"

"Yes sir." Peter answered. "She went ahead to get a better look at the entrance for us.

"Let's go. I'll tell her father about this and see what he has to say."

Bridgette waits at the entrance of the forest waiting for Matt and Peter to arrive. She stands behind a tree to avoid passing cars.

"Where are you two boys?"

Charles drives his truck with Matt and Peter in the passenger's area. Peter looks around the forest to find Bridgette.

"She should be around here somewhere." Peter said.

"Are you sure, Peter?"

"He's right, Uncle. She should be around this area here."

Charles stops the truck on the side of the road and gets out of the truck. Matt and Peter exit the truck and Peter starts walking into the woods.

"Bridgette, are you here?" Peter yelled.

"Bridgette, are you over here?" Matt yelled. "Hello?"

They hear something rustling in the trees in front of them. Peter startles with Matt inching closer to the trees. Charles takes out his rifle and slowly walks toward the trees in front of Matt. The rustling stops and Bridgette reveals herself. The group sighs in relief.

"What did you expect it would be? The Bigfoot itself."

"Very funny." Matt said.

"It could have been more frightening if it was Bigfoot. Peter added.

"Enough horsing around." said Charles. "Let's get this all over with."

They enter the forest together, staying close toward one another.

While Matt, Bridgette, Peter, and Charles walk through the dark forest, they hear sounds of people speaking amongst themselves. In the distance, Peter notices lights ahead of them. He points toward them.

"Anyone else see those lights ahead?"

"Stay close." Charles said. "No telling who that could be.?

"It could be the police." Bridgette said.

"That's what I was getting to. Just try to stay quiet and avoid those lights up there."

They walk slowly to avoid the lights in front of them. They make a slight right turn into the forest, going an opposite direction from the lights.

On the other end of the forest, the Huntsman searches for the Bigfoot. He walks through the bushes and trees, slicing them apart with his machete. He releases a small smirk while walking through.

"Where is this Bigfoot?" He wondered.

He took out a communicator and began to speak.

"Do you mind if I ask where the last location of this creature was?"

On the other end of the talkie is the Forest Ranger. Whom responded to the Huntsman's question.

Not too far from where you're currently location, Huntsman. Continue forward and you should come right up on it.

"I appreciate it." Huntsman said.

The Huntsman continues walking forward. He catches a swift stench in the air. He exhales and covers his face.

"That stench. What is it?"

He kept walking forward as the smell began to grow more enticing toward him.

Walking through, Matt catches the same stench in the air. He covers his nose as the stench reaches Charles, Bridgette, and Peter.

"What is that smell?" Matt asked.

"It smells like something died around here." Peter replied.

"Maybe it's that missing person they were searching for." Bridgette suggested.

"No." Charles said. "I recognize that stench from anywhere."

"Where is it coming from, Uncle?"

"We're getting closer. Very close."

They continue walking and the stench increases. As they walked closer to the stench, they hear a sudden rustle in front of them. As if something or someone is walking through the forest next to them.

Continuing from the other end of the forest, The Huntsman begins power walking as the stench becomes stronger. He covers his face from inhaling the stench that smells of a foul animal or a dead animal. As the Huntsman walks, he steps on a pair of berries that are laying on the ground. He reaches down and rubs the crushed berries with his fingers and sniffs.

"I suspect I'm getting closer to my prize."

Matt, Charles, Peter, and Bridgette continue going deeper into the forest as the stench consumes their entire location. All four of them cover their faces, mainly their noses and mouths from the stench.

"I've never smelled a stench quite like this." Peter said. "It is strong."

"That's the stench of a Bigfoot, my people. We are nearing its presence. Watch your every location and movement. Keep quiet as possible."

As they continued walking, they suddenly hear a distant roar. The roar sounded like an animal that is not known to man, yet so loud that nearly the entire forest would be able to hear it. The Huntsman stopped in his tracks as he listened to the roar.

"What kind of beast are you?"

As each side continue to get closer to the area where the roar is coming from, Matt looks over to his left and sees the Huntsman walking in their direction, going the same route as they were. Peter takes a glance over and also sees the Huntsman. He points toward him.

"May I ask who that man is over there?"

Charles looked over to where Peter pointed and saw the Huntsman. He immediately recognized the man.

"Quick! Hide!"

They all scatter and hide within the bushes and behind the trees as the Huntsman walks right into their location. The Huntsman knows that someone is also in the forest with him besides the police and the Forest Ranger. Yet, he knows they're on the other side of the forest. He sniffs and whistle with a low tone.

"Now, I am aware that I'm not alone in this part of the forest. So, I suggest you teenagers or cryptid fanatics please leave at once or suffer a greater fate than going to jail.

They stay silent as they glance over at the Huntsman, who's standing in the middle of the location they were previously standing. He circles around to see every direction around him.

"Very well. I give you this one warning. Do not and I repeat this, do not get in my way unless you want to disappear from off the grid."

The Huntsman turns around and continues getting closer to the roar, that is still ongoing. As he walks away, Matt comes out from behind the bushes and so does the rest of them.

"What's the current plan, Uncle?"

"We keep going with our plan."

"Wait, didn't you just hear what that man said." Bridgette said. "If he sees us, he's going to rid of us."

"You're paranoid, Bridgette." Peter responded. "He was only talking out of overconfidence. He just wanted to frighten us."

"We keep moving. But incredibly quiet. We have to avoid the Huntsman at all cost."

"Sure thing." Matt said.

The Forest Ranger continues to sit outside of the forest in his jeep as more police continue searching for the missing person. The Ranger takes out the talkie and speaks into it.

"Huntsman. Do you hear me? Please speak."

The Huntsman answers on the talkie.

"I hear you clear as the night sky, Ranger. What have you gotten for me?"

"I just need to check on your search to see how it was going. We heard a roar out there and wondered if you encountered what caused it?"

"I am on the pursuit as I speak with you. Though, I will tell you that we have some human visitors in the forest with us and they're awfully close to my location."

"I'll send some officers to your location and they'll smoke them out."

"There's no need for that, Ranger. I can handle the visitors just as I will handle this Bigfoot."

"Very well. Continue doing your work and we'll get back to you."

"Well when it's done."

The Ranger places his talkie down on the passenger seat and looks out of the door window at the officers going in and out of the forest.

The Huntsman continues walking as Matt and the others slowly and quietly follow behind him. The Huntsman looks down and sees a large amount of leaves and broken branches on the ground. Formed to look as if something was living in the location.

"It seems that I've stepped right into your territory, beast. Now, where are you?"

Matt and the others arrive at the location and hide in a small space from the Huntsman. They look around and see the leaves and branches that surround the location.

"Look at how the area is designed." Matt noticed. 'Do you think the Bigfoot could be

living here?"

"This is its lair and we're stepping right onto its territory." Charles said. "We need to be careful on this one."

The Huntsman circles the area and scouts through the nearby trees and bushes. He passed by Matt and the others during his search. He walks and stands directly in the middle of the area.

"Very well, now." The Huntsman proclaimed. "I know you're somewhere close, beast. Now, I demand that you show yourself to me and I will be out of my way."

The Huntsman looks around and can only hear silence as the forest is quiet. **CRACK!** The Huntsman turns around and starts to hear branches being stepped on coming from within the dark part of the forest and is slowly approaching the area. The Huntsman smiles and stands his ground with his right hand behind his back. Matt and the others look and hear the branches cracking.

"Come on! You wretched beast! I do not have all night to wait for your arrival."

A spider slowly crawls onto Peter's shirt. Bridgette turned and noticed it. She pointed toward it.

"Peter, there's a spider on your shirt."

"Don't be ridiculous." Peter gestured with a smirk.

Matt glanced over to Peter and saw the spider.

"There is a spider on your shoulder, Peter."

Peter slowly looked over on his right shoulder and seen the spider being still. Peter shrieked and jumped out of the bushes and right into the sight of the Huntsman. The Huntsman smiles.

"Well, what have we here tonight. A young teenage boy out in the dark forest alone? It cannot be so."

Matt, Charles, and Bridgette step out from behind the bushes and stand beside Peter, staring at the Huntsman.

"Oh. We have the whole crew here don't we. Two young boys, a young girl, and a old man to guide them. Seems you haven't done your job guiding them."

"The way I choose the guide them is none of your concern, Huntsman." Charles said.

"You know who I am and why I'm here."

"You don't belong here. I suggest you leave the forest while you still can."

"What exactly could you do to me. Hit me with your cane?!"

"I'll hit you with something."

Charles reached back and brought out his rifle. He aims it directly at the Huntsman. The Huntsman smiles as his eyes get bigger.

"The old man threatens to shoot someone who's here to help his area."

"We don't need your help here. We can take care of ourselves."

"Not according to what I've heard about from the recent news that surrounds this land. A camper goes missing, a bigfoot sighting. Tell me, does that sound life a safe environment to live in or not?"

"I don't care what you think of it. You don't live in this area."

"If that's how you truly feel. Looks as if I have no choice but to do this and I won't be sorry for it."

The Huntsman throws a small knife at Charles and the knife pierces him in the shoulder. He yells as he falls to the ground. The rifle falls off his shoulders and onto the ground next to him.

"UNCLE!!!" Matt screamed.

Matt knelt at his uncle, who is in pain form the knife. Peter and Bridgette kneeled toward Charles. The Huntsman only stands and gives out a low giggle.

"I said I wouldn't be sorry for what I was about to do. Now, if you teenagers would step out of the way. I need to find my prize."

Another loud roar is heard from within the forest and its right next to the location where the Huntsman is currently standing. His faced twists as he smiled, and his eyes become even bigger than previously.

"Now, it's time to get down to business."

They all hear the loud, thumping footsteps approaching them. They all look over into the shadow covered area of the forest and out comes a tall, brutish figure. Covered from head to toe in dark brown fur. Its yellowish-red eyes stare deeply toward the Huntsman. The Bigfoot had arrived.

"FINALLY! I've come into contact with the legendary Bigfoot. Now, I
shall take you down and end your reign of terror!"

The Bigfoot roars at the Huntsman as he reaches to his side and pulls out his machete. Matt glances over and seen the machete.

"No!" Matt yelled.

The Huntsman and Bigfoot circle each other in a stare down. The Bigfoot growls toward the Huntsman as he only smiles and begins to laugh in a sinister way.

"Ready to die?" The Huntsman asked with a grin.

The Bigfoot roars at the Huntsman as he lunges toward the Bigfoot. The Huntsman struggles with the Bigfoot. Matt looks down at his uncle's rifle and picks it up.

The Huntsman continues fighting the Bigfoot, trying to get an open area to slice at the Bigfoot. The Bigfoot shoves the Huntsman back.

"Seems that I underestimated your great strength. However, it won't be enough to stop me!"

The Huntsman waves the machete and it slices the right leg of the Bigfoot. The Bigfoot groaned in pain as it fell to one knee. The Huntsman laughs as he stands over the kneeled Bigfoot.

"Now, I will finish you off and I will claim your fame."

The Huntsman raises up the machete over the Bigfoot's head. He prepares for the final kill. ***BAM!*** A gunshot is heard, and the Huntsman falls backwards. He notices that something is wrong. He looks down at his chest and sees himself bleeding from a gunshot. He turns his head toward his right and sees Matt holding the rifle. He knows that Matt shot him.

"Looks like I've claimed your fame."

The Huntsman smirks and dies. The Bigfoot gains the strength to stand on its two feet. It looks down at the Huntsman's body and roars. Matt and the others sit still as the Bigfoot looked over toward them. The Bigfoot stared in the eyes of Matt and they begin to hear rustling in the woods coming toward them. Sounds like a mass of people running over toward the area.

"We have to go now." Charles said.

Matt and Peter help Charles up as they leave the area. Matt looks back and only sees the hairy back of the Bigfoot walking away deep into the shadows of the forest.

After leaving, the police arrive along with the Forest Ranger. He looks down and sees the Huntsman laying on the ground.

"Search this entire area! Immediately!

The Forest Ranger only stands still, looking down at the body of the Huntsman.

Matt, Peter, and Bridgette sit in the living room of the home, watching the TV and on the internet by use of the laptop. In the kitchen sits Charles, who's shoulder is bandaged up and next to him is Arnold and his wife.

"Looks like you'll be ok."

"I've been through much worse."

Matt focused heavily on the TV and the news broadcast comes up about the Huntsman being found dead in the woods and how there were not sightings of the Bigfoot. Charles glanced over and walked toward Matt. He sat next to him on the couch.

"Don't worry yourself about it. You did what had to be done. To protect

not only, me, but your friends, yourself, and even the Bigfoot."

"I understand Uncle. Thanks for the practice."

"I knew it would come in handy someday."

The land from Charles' home to Arnold's home and to the other residents' homes is clear and peaceful during the night. The forest itself, quiet and still. Yet, deep within the forest, the roar sounded off once more.

THE SNOWMAN OF ANTARCTICA

There are a group of adventurers walking though the iced and snowy grounds of Antarctica. While they walk through the lands, they take a second to gaze around the area. Seeing nothing but ice and snow on the grounds and nearby hills covered in snow.

"What do you think this land would look like if there were no ice?"

"It would be nothing but water. We wouldn't even be standing on top of this ice right now."

They glance around even more. Picturing the icy lands as nothing but water in the sea.

"I wonder how many animals actually live out here. Besides the polar bears of course."

"Why don't you go take a walk and see if you can find any animals."

"You know what. That is exactly what I'll do. Don't wait up for me."

The Adventurer goes walking solo through the lands. The rest of the Adventurers continue to gaze and walk their pathway. After walking a few miles, The Adventurer reaches the point to where he can only see his fellow teammates from a distance. He waves his arm up to see if they can spot him and they apparently do not see him.

"I know they can see me from up here."

He continues walking until he finds himself in front of an entrance to a cave. His mind now amazed and emotions uncontrollable.

"There's a cave. A cave made of ice and snow completely. Wait till the others see this."

He decides to approach the cave entrance, unaware of what could be living inside. All he can see is pure darkness in the cave.

He slowly begins to take a step into the cave, hearing his voice beginning to echo through. He goes deeper into the cave and trips over an object. He gets up and uses his flashlight to see what the object was and it's a metallic box with German writing on the top with a peculiar, yet historical symbol.

"Nazis here in Antarctica? This must have been their escape base during WW2."

While looking at the box, a low growl is heard from deep within the cave. Getting the Adventurer's attention. He raises his flashlight up. Shaking.

"This must be the bears' home."

The growl intensifies as the Adventurer decides to leave the cave. He runs toward the entrance as he hears something running behind him. Not looking back he ran as fast as he

can.

He exits the cave but is snatched on his jacket by a snow-covered hand and pulled back into the darkness of the cave. Screaming for help as his voice slowly fades away.

An airplane comes into Antarctica. After making its stop, a pair of people exit the plan, tourists and a man named Roger, with his daughter, Mary They look around for someone and a man approaches them with a smile on his face. Stanley.

"About time you showed up, brother."

"Hey, we were in a plane. It takes a matter of time."

Stanley turned to Mary with a smile.

"Welcome to Antarctica, young lady."

"May I ask where my mother is?"

"She's currently in the base doing her work as usual." Stanley answered. "Come with me and we can see her."

"Sure."

Roger and Mary walked with Stanley to his jeep.

Stanley drove, Roger sat in the passenger's seat. Mary sat quietly in the back gazing out the window, seeing the icy grounds and mountains.

"All of Antarctica looks like this?" Mary asked.

"Majority of it of course. Icy mountains, icy landscape, icy buildings. No telling what else is here."

"I heard about the missing adventurer." Roger said. "Any

information as to what happened?"

"No idea besides he was with some fellow colleagues before he took a solo walk from the group and went to what they believed to be a cave."

"A cave?" Mary said. "What lives in it?"

"We don't know." Stanley answered. "Funny thing is we never knew about a cave being nearby. The colleagues said it appeared to be made completely of ice and snow."

"The whole thing?"

"Yes. Surprised something of that kind could stand up like that this entire time. Even without any of us knowing it even existed."

"Maybe a snowman built it."

Roger chuckled.

"No telling in today's time."

"I know. Strange things happening all across the world. From Ghost Hounds to what I read about a Bigfoot in the wilderness. A lot of stuff is taking place."

"Maybe we'll see something unexplainable while we're here, Mary."

"I would like to see a snowman." Mary said. "A living, breathing snowman."

They arrived at the base. Exiting the jeep and walking towards the building.

Entering the base, Roger and Mary see over a dozen people, men and women going to and from and studying the ice and the landscape of Antarctica. Others are monitoring the airplane takeoffs.

"I can say that I'm appalled at what I'm looking at right now."

"The majority of the public have no idea this place even exists."

"So, everyone here is doing research on Antarctica?"

"Yes. Everyone you see here."

Roger looked ahead, spotting a young boy sitting at a desk nearby. He pointed.

"Including that young boy over there?"

Stanley looked, seeing the boy.

"That's Lucas, he's one of the workers' son."

Lucas, a young fifteen-year-old sat at a desk looking at the computer monitor showing lava underneath the frozen grounds of

Antarctica. Roger, Mary, and Stanley approach him.

"Lucas, I would like you to meet Roger and his daughter, Mary."

"Nice to meet you." Lucas said.

"Same here." Roger replied.

"So, what do you do here?" Mary wondered.

"I usually monitor the computer showing the volcano that's underneath the ice."

"A volcano underneath the ground?" Mary said with excitement. "Really?"

"Yeah. See right here."

Lucas allows Mary to see the monitor showing the lava underneath the ice. Roger turned to Stanley.

"Where are his parents?"

"Somewhere in here. They don't go too far unless it's a precaution."

A woman approaches them. Smiling. She is Patricia, Roger's wife, and Mary's mother.

"Hi, Patricia."

Roger and Patricia give each other a kiss and hug.

"Surprised you decided to come all the way out here."

I did it for Mary and to see you again, of course."

Mary looked and saw her mother. She went over and hugged her.

"I've missed you."

"I've missed you too, baby. How's everything back at home."

"It's the same way you left it."

"Not a spot nor scratch?"

"Not a spot nor a scratch." Mary replied.

Roger smiled. Taking in the moment between mother and daughter.

"I see you've meet Lucas. He's a nice boy."

"Can I stay here with him?"

"Sure."

"We'll leave you guys to your monitoring as Stanley would like to show me something." Roger said.

Roger and Stanley head another direction as Patricia returns to her area.

Another airplane landed at the airport of Ross Island. This is a smaller plane and the door opens and out comes a man dressed in military gear. He is Alexander Strakova, a Russian General.

"Nice to see you here again, General Strakova." A security guard greeted.

"The same I give to you."

Strakova looks at the area and walks toward the jeep waiting for him.

Lucas changed the screen on the monitor, revealing a cave. Showing they've placed a camera not too far from the entrance. Mary looked on.

"That's the ice cave?"

"Yeah. So far they've said that nothing has come out or went into it."

"No animals?"

"None so far." Lucas answered.

"Would it be funny if a snowman had come out of the cave?"

"That would be something I would like to see."

"Do you think they could exist?"

Anything is possible.

They sit and watch the monitor and from the entrance of the ice cave, they notice something moving around. Peculiar looking figure. Grabbing their attention, they locked their eyes onto the screen, watching the live footage.

"You saw that?"

"Yeah. It is a shadow. But a shadow to what?"

They continue to watch as the shadow becomes darker as it hits the light. They see what exits the cave and are baffled. A tall figure with wooden legs and arms and a body and head made of snow.

"It's a snowman!"

"Figured they were real."

They leave the desk and go searching for Roger, Stanley, and Patricia. They bump a few people on the way.

"Sorry. Sorry." Lucas said with respect.

"Coming through with some important news." Mary added.

Alexander walked through the military base a few miles from the researching base where Roger and Mary are present. The military base is filled army tanks, jeeps, even a helicopter. Alexander walks toward a desk where a soldier is sitting. The soldier glanced up, seeing Alexander approaching.

"General Strakova."

"Good soldier. How has the time been here in this icy land?"

"Warm and most of the time chilly."

"What have you found?"

"We're detected some strange occurrences near the cave."

"Ah. Very well. Proceed as planned."

"Yes sir."

The soldiers headed out toward the cave as Lucas and Mary found Roger, Stanley, and Patricia in another room.

"We've got something to tell you." Lucas said.

"Tell us what?" Roger said."

"You have to believe us."

"OK, we believe you." Patricia replied. "What did you guys see?"

"Uhh, we saw a snowman in the cave."

"At the cave?" Roger asked. "Why were you two out there?"

"We weren't." Lucas said. "We saw it on camera and came to tell you."

Roger turned to Patricia. She looked around and saw the soldiers heading outside to the cave. She and Roger immediately followed the soldiers. Lucas and Mary followed quietly to avoid being seen by the soldiers and the parents.

Roger saw the soldiers and quickly stepped in front of them.

"Step aside." A soldier said.

"You're heading to the cave?"

"We were given orders to enter the cave and find the source."

Roger stepped back, realizing what the source truly was.

"You can't. if you kill it, you'll end up destroying something of history and nature."

"Not our problem. Now, step aside."

Roger paused and stepped aside as the soldiers went down the hallway and to the outside. Patricia followed as Roger told her they must find a way to stop them from attacking the snowman. Lucas and Mary continued following. Meanwhile, General Strakova was already standing outside at the cave once the soldiers arrived. They saluted as he approached them.

"What is inside this cave is valuable to our nation. We must retrieve it by any means. We don't know the full intent of the source. But, we do not we can capture it."

Roger and Patricia arrived outside, seeing Strakova instructing the soldiers. They went forward while Lucas and Mary stayed by the door to avoid being seen. Roger passed the soldiers, approaching Strakova.

"Why are two scientists out here?"

"General, don't destroy what is inside the cave. It's unbelievably valuable."

"I know it's valuable. Valuable to the Russian government."

"General, the thing inside the cave," Patricia added. "we don't know what it's capable of."

"I understand your words. That is why my men are out here. To make sure such an action does not take place. Not on our end anyway."

Strakova stepped forward to the cave entrance. He sighed.

"We need to find a way of bringing it out. Bring the fire."

Several soldiers brought forth fire and tossed it into the cave. Within seconds, the cave lighted up with fire and immediately, a loud roar sounded off from within the cave. Roger and Patricia were still. Strakova grinned. Lucas and Mary stayed quiet at the doorway, watching. The soldiers did not move. Nor did their faces change expression. The ground shook as the intensity came closer. Strakova stepped forward to the cave after each shock. After three shocks, they saw what was inside the cave and it baffled the minds of Roger and Patricia. Lucas and Mary saw it as well. The soldiers did not move, but they were terrified. Strakova grinned, looking up at the snowman.

"What is this?!" Strakova said.

"It's incredible." Roger said.

"How's it possible?" Patricia questioned.

Strakova stared at the snowman. Nodding with a smile.

"If you can understand what I am saying, then good. You are to come with us. Now."

The snowman did not say a word. Only stared at Strakova. It looked up toward the soldiers and turned to Roger and Patricia. Facing Strakova once again. It groaned before turning away to return to the cave. Strakova was insulted as he pulled out his gun and fired a shot at the snowman's feet.

"You will obey my word, creature!"

"General, stop." Roger said.

"Do not instruct me on what to do, scientist. I will deal with this thing according to our rules."

The snowman turned around toward them and roared as it rushed toward Strakova, attacking him. The soldiers retailed with rounds of fire. The snowman melted the incoming blows and shook the ground, causing a small avalanche above the cave to fall upon them. The snowman looked down at Strakova and grabbed his leg, dragging him into the cave. Roger stepped forward, but Patricia stopped him.

"There's nothing we can do."

All they could hear was Strakova's scream as it faded into the darkness of the cave. They turned around to see Lucas, Mary, and Stanley waiting at the door. Sometime after once they left Antarctica. More military presence was brought forth as they began a deeper investigation to the cave and the surrounding areas. Upon further discovery, they found traces of snow layered with unusual DNA, signifying the snowman isn't the only one of its kind living in the caves of Antarctica.

AT THE SIGHT OF TROLLS

Within the Town Park there stands a territorial bridge. Many people who crossed the bridge only do so to reach the other side. However, there was a day where a park stranger had entered the park late one night, seeking to get himself some rest from a long day. He sat down at the bench near the lights. The park was quiet, until he heard a slight laugh come from behind him. He stood up from the bench and turned around, seeing the bridge. He walked over to the bridge, standing in the middle and looking down into the cavern beneath.

"Is anyone there?" The stranger asked.

There was no response, except for the laughter once more. The stranger was at a loss and he went to return to the bench before finding himself staring at a figure on the other end of the bridge. The stranger stepped forward to see who the stranger could be and before he could see their faces, he let out a loud scream. The next day, the park was surrounded with investigators who've found the stranger in a state of panic. Frozen solid. He continued to mummer about trolls who lived under the bridge of the park.

Afterwards, once the park was clear of the investigators and the stranger, civilians were able to return. One day, there was a young girl named Angelica with her friend James. Their parents were also in the park. Angelica and James played hide-and-seek with some of their friends, Stana and Chris. While finding somewhere to hide, James ran over toward the bridge and thought it was a good idea to hide underneath it. James crawled down the small ditch, it was damp from the water which flowed through it. Once James was on the ground, he saw the entrance to a cave right under the bridge. Intrigued, he walked closer. When he took the first step forward, he heard a groan come from the cave.

"Hello?" James said, echoing in the cave.

The groan returned to him, this time louder than before. The groan suddenly became laughter and frightened James as he crawled back up to the bridge. Right when he reached the top, he gazed down to the cave and saw a figure staring at him. The figure had green skin and was covered in fur. Its nose was large as were the eyes. James screamed at the sight of the creature and ran to his friends, stopping the game.

"There's a monster under the bridge!" James told them.

"What monster?" Angelica asked.

"It's under the bridge. It has green skin and lots of hair."

"You're kidding." Stana said. "There can't be a monster out here. People would know."

"Not if the monster lived deep underground." Angelica referenced. "James, where did this monster come from?"

"It came from the cave under the bridge."

"There's a cave under the bridge?" Chris asked.

"Yeah."

James led Angelica, Stana, and Chris down into the ditch under the bridge and they saw the entrance to the cave. They were astounded by the sight of it. James stayed back while Chris and Stana moved forward, yelling words into the cave and hearing their echoes. Angelica turned around, seeing James was still scared by what he saw. She walked over to him calmly comforting her friend.

"Look, we don't have to stay here. We can tell our parents to take us home."

"No. No." James said. "I'm not afraid. I just want to know what the monster is."

"Are you sure?"

"I'm sure."

"Hey, did you go inside the cave?" Chris asked James.

"No. I only stopped at the front. Didn't go in because I heard the sound of the monster coming from the inside."

"We should go in there." Stana said. "See this monster for ourselves."

"Hey, you think the monster had something to do with that man who was found?" Chris referenced.

"I'm not sure about that." Angelica said. "If that was the case, the police would've closed this area by now."

"They didn't find the monster. I'm positive they don't know about this cave."

"Chris has a point." Stana said. "We'll only know if James is correct if we go in the cave and see for ourselves."

"But, neither of us have a flashlight." Angelica said. "How else are we supposed to see inside a dark cave?"

"Hey, use your phone."

"My phone?" Angelica said, pulling out her phone.

"Use the flashlight on that."

"But that'll run the battery down."

"We should get back." James mentioned. "Our parents are probably looking for us."

"You're just scared. That's all." Chris said. "Angelica, are you coming with us?"

Angelica looked at the cave, turning to James. She shook her head.

"Come back and tell us what you find."

Chris scoffed at Angelica's decision and mocked James' fear.

"Suit yourselves." Chris turned to Stana. "Coming with?"

"Of course."

Chris took out his own phone and turned on the flashlight as he and Stana entered the cave. Angelica and James waited to see what they would find. Inside the cave itself was cold and watery. Much of the water was dripping from the top of the cave and the stench of it was like a river. Mud covered the ground. Chris moved the light around, seeing nothing but mud and bugs. Stana hated bugs. Hearing the crunch sound underneath her feet gave her a reason to panic. Chris calmed her as they walked further into the cave.

After about three steps, they saw the cave had grew and was larger than the entrance showed. The cave presented to them three other pathways. Chris took one and Stana took the other. Stana used her own phone for a light source. Down Chris' path, he stumbled upon dried bones. Stana's path led her to finding what looked like beds made of bark. Now, for the third path, Chris and Stana went together and down the path, they discovered hair on the ground. It looked as if it was shredded off. The hair resembled a human's hair, but was too dark and too large to be from a person. When they looked closer at the hair, a groan came from deeper in the path and they ran. Finding their way out as they could hear footsteps quickly moving behind them. Once they made it back to the entrance, James saw the terror on their faces as they went back up to the bridge.

"What's wrong?" Angelica asked.

"There's something in there." Chris said. "Something with lots of hair."

"Did you see it?"

"No." Stana answered. "But, it chased us out."

They made their way back to the top while James stared at the cave, hearing the groaning in his mind repeating itself. Angelica looked at him, seeing him fixed upon the cave.

"James, let's go."

James followed them to the top and they returned to their game. After two hours, their parents called them, telling them it's time to head home. Chris and Stana had already left with their parents while Angelica and James were preparing to leave. Just as they entered the vehicles, James looked out the window and saw the monster standing on the bridge. He rolled down the window, getting Angelica's attention. She saw him as he pointed to the bridge. She looked and saw the monster herself.

"Mom." Angelica said.

"What is it?"

"You see that thing on the bridge?"

"What thing?"

Angelica's mother looked out and saw nothing but the bridge. She turned toward her daughter with confusion.

"What are you talking about?"

Angelica looked out, still seeing the monster.

"You don't see it?"

"I only see the bridge." She replied.

Angelica sighed. She looked over to James and shook her head. James did the same. They both looked, seeing the monster standing on the bridge with a large grin on its face. Almost human-like. As the left the park, Angelica asked her mother what type of monsters live under bridges and she told her daughter, "Trolls, my dear."

A CLOAK DARKLY

After a day of school, Scott walked home. He and his two friends, Frank and Evelyn went their separate ways. While on the walk, Scott stumbled across a pawn shop. Strange to him, there was no shop in the area before. Scott had always taken the same route from school to home. Yet, on this day, there was a pawn shop. The shop looked old and foreign with many objects hanging on the windows and above the doors. Scott was hesitant to enter the shop. However, curiosity got the best of him, never seeing such a place like it. Scott shrugged his shoulders and went into the pawn shop.

Inside, Scott saw a variety of items. From bikes to hover boards, animal trophies, jewelry, and a lot of other items people would search for. While walking over and looking at the hover boards, which is something Scott had always dreamed of having, the Merchant appeared from behind the counter, seeing Scott. The merchant had wavy hair and a long black beard. His clothes looked as it they were from another time-period. On the side of his face were tattoos. One was of a hammer with lightning coming from within.

"Young one." The Merchant said, startling Scott.

"Oh. I'm sorry."

"No need to apologize. I didn't hear you come in."

"The bell rung when I opened the door."

"Did it now." The Merchant said. "Hmm. Must be my hearing is all."

"I have to ask you, sir. When did this place open?"

"Truthfully, it's always been here."

"I've never seen it before. I take the route here from school."

The Merchant nodded.

"I see. So, tell me, young one, what brought you into my shop of goods?"

"I was curious. Never seen a place like it."

"It's only a pawn shop. People come in to sell what they have and to purchase what they don't have. It's a simple matter."

"People come here and sell you what they have?"

"Yes. In return, they get paid or they get something else. Something of higher value. Or lower. Depends on their interest."

"Well, I don't have anything to sell."

"No need. I saw you gazing over at the hover boards. I can tell you want one."

"I do. But, my parents said I'm not ready for one yet."

The Merchant rubbed his chin and pointed after a thought entered his mind.

"Wait here. I have something you might be interested in."

Scott waited as the Merchant went to the back of the shop. After a minute, the Merchant returned with a large box, a chest it seemed to be as he sat it down on the counter. Scott approached the counter, looking at the box. It was old and rugged. On the sides it had some ancient writing upon it. Scott pointed toward the writing.

"What is that?"

"It's from a place called Scandinavia. The language of the old ones."

The Merchant opened the box and pulled out what was inside. Scott looked and saw it for himself as the Merchant came around the counter to show him the full item.

"Is that a jacket?" Scott asked.

"Oh no." The Merchant said. "It's a cloak."

"A cloak. Like a long coat basically."

"Yes. And it appears it's your size."

The Merchant handed the cloak over to Scott and he examined it. The cloak was dark black with a glowing blue within. The cloak was long enough to cover Scott's feet and it had a hood, capable of covering Scott's head to where only his nose and mouth could be seen from a distance.

"Go ahead and try it on." The Merchant said.

"Really?"

"Yeah sure."

Scott put on the cloak and the Merchant nodded with a smile. "It fits you perfectly."

"Yeah. It does." Scott said. "It's as if it was made for me."

"Some have said that about clothing before."

Scott removed the hood, reaching down into his pocket. The Merchant knew what he was doing and stopped him.

"No need to use your money for the cloak. Take it for free."

"For free?"

"Yeah. Our conversation was payment enough. The cloak is in goods hands with you."

"Thank you."

"Take care now."

Scott left the pawn shop and made it home. While at home, Scott examined the cloak in his room, looking at it in the mirror and flipping the hood around. Scott took it off and placed it in the closer before heading to bed. While sleeping, the cloak hanging in the closet was glowing. The colors were blue like the sky, yet darker. Little streaks of lightning emitted from within the cloak.

The following day, Scott woke up and could smell electricity coming from the closet. He went and looked, seeing nothing but the cloak. He thought for a second and grabbed it, placing it in his backpack. He got dressed and left for school. Little did Scott know, the cloak overnight had burnt some of his clothes. At the school, Scott met up with Frank and Evelyn. During lunch break, he showed them the cloak. No one had noticed due to its coat-like appearance and it is in the middle of winter.

"Where did you get this?" Frank asked.

"At the pawn shop."

"What shop?" Evelyn asked. "I've never heard of a pawn shop around here."

'It was on the way home. I never saw it before. But, it was there."

"And you got this cloak from the shop?"

"Yeah."

"How much was it?" Frank wondered. "It looks like it cost a lot of money."

"Actually, the owner gave it to me for free."

"You're kidding?" Evelyn chuckled. "For free? You must've done something nice for the guy."

"He said it was my size and it is."

Frank looked closer at the cloak's sleeves, seeing some of the same writing on them as it was on the box. He pointed them out to Scott and Evelyn.

"Hey, what are those?"

"They look like some ancient language." Evelyn said. "Probably Old English I'm assuming."

"You're assuming?" Scott said.

"Yeah. Why? Do you know what language it is?"

"The owner told me it was an old language. He said it was from Scandinavia."

"Scandinavia?" Frank said with confusion.

"Wait. Like Vikings." Evelyn said. "The language they used in Norway."

"How do you know so much about the Vikings?" Scott wondered. "We've never heard you talk about them before."

"It was on TV. My father watches a lot of stuff about them. Even bought some books on their history."

"So, put it on." Frank told Scott.

Scott stood up from the table and put on the cloak. Everything was in place, including the hood. Frank and Evelyn could only see his nose and mouth. Scott stood out and extended his arms.

"How does it look?"

"It looks cool." Frank said.

"It does fit you perfectly."

From behind Scott came three guys, each one taller than Scott, Frank, and Evelyn. They looked at the cloak and started to mock Scott on his dress. They laughed at him and made fun of the cloak. Frank stood up for Scott and was shoved to the floor by one of the guys. Evelyn stood up from the table, yelling at them to stop and leave them be. They refused and started to poke at Scott. Scott didn't move. Evelyn did notice how Scott started to shiver. She looked at his hands and they were sparking with lightning.

"What is that?" She whispered.

Frank raised up from the floor, seeing Scott's hands.

"Scott, are you alright."

The guys continued poking until Scott turned toward them and stretched out his hands, blasting the three guys with large lightning bolts. The guys went flying across the cafeteria, startling the other students and teachers. The three guys stumbled to get to their feet as Scott walked toward them, lightning sparking from his hands and feet. The cloak gave off an energy of electricity. Even Scott's eyes started to glow blue from the lightning.

"Something's wrong." Evelyn said to Frank.

"What do we do?"

"We try to calm him down. Just be careful."

They ran toward Scott and tried to reason with him, but he didn't listen. It's not because he's ignoring them. The cloak's power is starting to consume Scott due to his inner anger. He continued shooting lighting at the three guys as they ran out of the cafeteria. The whole area is in a state of panic as people try to hide from Scott while Evelyn and Frank attempt to calm him down. Evelyn stopped and thought.

"We need to get the cloak off of him."

"How are we doing to do that?" Frank asked.

"I take one arm. You take the other."

"Alright then."

They ran to both sides of Scott and grabbed the sleeves. Pulling them backwards to get Scott's arms free from the cloak. Scott grunted, pulling his arms forward and causing his friends to slip on the ground. Scott continued walking forward, chasing the three guys. Evelyn sighed as she stood up.

"Leaving me no choice." She said as she ran behind him and pulled back the hood.

Scott stopped in his tracks. His eyes looked dazed as he removed the cloak before turning around to his friends. He saw they were breathing heavily and didn't understand why.

"It's ok." Evelyn said. "Just put that cloak in your bag before anyone sees your face."

"I saw his face." A voice said from behind her.

She and Frank turned around to see Principal Armstrong standing by. His arms were crossed as he looked at the three of them. Armstrong commanded for Scott to see him in his office while Evelyn and Frank return to their classes. Scott followed Armstrong into his office and sat down at the desk.

"First off, such actions like that would require an expulsion. However, from what I saw, you had no control over your actions, did you?"

"I don't remember any of it." Scott said calmly.

"What do you remember?"

"I remember putting on the cloak and showing it to my friends. After that, those three guys came over and bullied us. That's all I remember until I turned around to see my friends standing behind me. And you, of course."

"I see. How old are you, by the way?"

"I'm ten. Ten and a half."

"Ten and a half." Armstrong nodded. "I have to ask. Do your parents know about that cloak?"

"No. I never told them where I got it. They haven't seen it either."

"Where did you get it?"

"From the pawn shop on my way home."

"Pawn shop?" Armstrong questioned. "There's no pawn shop in this area."

Scott was confused. So was Armstrong. He gestured with his hands, wanting to see the cloak. Scott was afraid and Armstrong calmed him down. Stating the didn't have to put it on. Scott opened his bag, revealing the cloak in full to the principal. Immediately, Armstrong saw the runes on the sleeves.

"And you got this from a pawn shop?"

"Yes sir. The owner gave it to me for free."

The Principal nodded. "First off, tell me, did this owner give you a name?"

"No sir. He didn't."

"What did he look like? Describe him to me."

He looked like a regular man. Except for the long beard and tattoos."

"Tattoos. What kind of tattoos?"

"There was one on his face. A hammer with lightning."

"Hammer with lightning." Armstrong said. "It all makes sense."

"What makes sense, Principal Armstrong?" Scott questioned.

"The cloak belonged to a druid during the Viking Age."

"A druid?" Scott said. "I'm not understanding what a druid is."

"A druid in Viking culture is like a magician of sorts. They worshipped the gods of the Norse myths."

"Gods? Like what kind?"

"Odin, Thor, and suchlike. Now, this cloak belonged to a druid. It explains why you were shooting lighting from your hands. It also explains why it was lightning in the first place and the owner with the hammer tattoo."

"I'm not understanding, sir."

"The owner was Thor himself. This cloak had to have belonged to a druid he was close to. Or Odin."

"Well, if this belonged to Thor or any of them, I don't want it anymore."

"Here's your solution, Scott. Return the cloak. If you can. If you cannot, send it somewhere to a place where no one will be able to find it. Do you understand?"

"Yes sir."

"Good."

Scott left the office, returning to his friends before school ended. They told him to get rid of the cloak, as it brought a dark energy around him. Scott understood and once he left school, he took the same route as always and saw the pawn shop once more. He entered without haste and placed the cloak on the counter as the Merchant approached.

"I don't want it." Scott said. "You can keep it."

The Merchant grabbed the cloak. He looked at it and turned to Scott.

"It didn't work for you?"

"It worked a little too much."

The Merchant nodded.

"Understood. Anything else you want?"

"No thanks. I have enough."

"Nice seeing you again." The Merchant said.

Scott nodded as he left the shop. The Merchant returned the cloak to the box, which was in fact a chest of Norse magic. He folded the cloak and put it in the box, shutting the lid and locking it. The Merchant then, looked out the windows, seeing no one. He stood in the middle of the shop and extended his hand. The thunder roared from above as something was charging toward his hand and all Scott could hear while walking home was the thunder from above and it began to rain. He turned around, seeing the pawn shop disappearing in a bright light. Scott looked again and the shop was gone. Like it never existed. Scott ran home and never spoke again about the cloak.

THE BEAST AMONG US

A camping trip was set for the school's weekend field trip. On this trip were twelve students and four teachers. One of the primary students on the trip was Felicity. She and her three friends, Lydia, Nora, and Tara were all prepared for the trip. This trip was planned for several weeks, giving the students the proper amount of time to prepare themselves. Now, the location of their camping site was deep in the woods. Not too far out from the main roads, but far enough from homes which were around the area.

When they arrived at the site, they saw four cabins. They were for the teachers. The students had their tents to sleep in. once, they arrived and everyone exited the bus, the teachers began explaining to them what they will do throughout this two-day trip. They were to learn outdoor activities such as making fires, first-aid, fishing, and more. One student by the name of Pietro knew of these tasks and could do them on his own since he lives out in the wilderness unlike his student counterparts. When the tasks had begun, the students were led into groups of four with each teacher. The teachers taught them in the individual classes they had. Pietro did not partake in the classes. The teachers were already aware of his background. While learning first-aid, Felicity noticed Pietro looking out in the forest. She saw he was focused on something. As she finished her part, she approached him while gazing out to the trees.

"You look like you're trying to see something."

"We're not alone out here." Pietro said. "There's something here. Lurking in the trees."

"Like what? A bear or something?"

"There are bears out here. As well as mountain lions."

"Seriously?"

"But, that's not what I'm sensing. It's something else. Something scarier."

"Well, be sure to tell the teachers about it."

"I already tried. They said I'm making stuff up."

Felicity sighed as she looked over, seeing her friends waving toward her. She nodded and waved back as Pietro continued staring in the woods. She saw it in his eyes. He senses something and its close to the camp. She patted Pietro on the shoulder with a smile.

"I believe you."

"Thank you." Pietro replied with a nod.

"Just one more thing." Felicity noted. "Make sure to warn me if something does come this way. I want to be prepared."

"I will."

Felicity went and returned to her friends who had just started the class of making fires. Pietro sat down, staring into the woods. After several hours, the sun started to set, and the students had set up their tents. The teachers prepared their cabins. The cabins themselves were only walking distance from the tents. Nine feet from the tents was a small pond, which they used for fishing. Felicity had her tent set up, sharing it with Lydia while Nora and Tara shared a tent of their own. Both tents sat next to each other. Pietro's tent was close to the students and furthest from the cabins. Pietro sat at the campfire with the other students, still listening out into the forest. Felicity looked out, seeing Pietro was still focused on what was within the forest, yet he was calm. There was no fear on his face. He didn't even shiver in terror. Pietro is used to the wilderness, but there was nothing ordinary which could have him in complete focus.

That night, when all were asleep, Pietro was awoken by the sound of something dragging on the ground. The sound of snapping branches caught his attention. He sat up quietly and listened. What Pietro saw was a silhouette of something walking past his tent, leaving the direction of the camp. The silhouette stood upright like a human, yet had a tail. A hairy tail.

The next morning, Pietro told the teachers what he saw the previous night and they brushed it off as a bear simply passing through the camp. They were glad no students were harmed or attacked. Pietro knew they would not understand and kept his focus on the wilderness.

Felicity saw him and approached him again.

"I saw you talking to the teachers. What happened?"

"There was something in our camp last night. It woke me up. I heard the branches of the trees snapping."

"Did you see what it was?"

"Only its shadow. It didn't look like an ordinary animal."

Well, I'm curious. What did it look like to you?"

"Truthfully, it stood on two legs. Just like us. Except it had a tail. Not a long one. But a hairy one."

"I don't know any animal that fits that description. Felicity added. "I've only heard of stories on movies about animals like that."

"I think it was a werewolf." Pietro said. "That's my theory."

"A werewolf?" Felicity joked. "You cannot be serious. Werewolves don't exist. Otherwise, people would know."

"Not all people know how to start fires on their own or fish, do they?"

"Fair point." Felicity nodded. "I have an idea."

"I'm listening." Pietro said.

"How about we tag along for the night. Find out what this animal really is."

"I'm not sure the teachers will allow us to stay up all night. Especially together."

"After they enter their cabins for the night. The two of us can go out into the woods and find the animal. What do you say?"

Pietro nodded in agreement with Felicity's idea. Following nightfall, Felicity left her tent as the others were asleep. She looked out and saw Pietro outside of his tent, looking out into the woods. He had a flashlight in hand. As well as a knife. Felicity approached him, pointing at the knife.

"Where did you get that?"

"I brought it with me." Pietro replied. "We're out here in the wilderness. Someone has to come prepared."

"So, are you ready?"

"I am. Let's get going."

Felicity and Pietro headed out into the wilderness. They were out searching for the animal and the environment was silent. Only the wind whistling across the trees could be heard. The moon's light shined upon them, giving them enough light to search the forest. The flashlight was a bonus item in case the areas became darker. Pietro was calm and collective while Felicity showed slight signs of fear and uncertainty. Pietro saw the fear upon her and sighed.

"You'll be alright out here."

"I know. It's just I've never been out in the woods like this. Especially during the night."

"You never been out past dark before?" Pietro asked.

"Not this late."

"How old are you?"

"I'm fourteen."

"And your parents allowed you to stay out a night one time?"

"It was a friend's sleepover."

"Which friend?"

"Lydia. We're like sisters. Nora and Tara are my besties."

"You didn't tell them about what we're doing right now did you?"

"No. I told no one."

"That's good."

"But what if we see something out here? We should let them know."

"I'll rather not do that."

"Why not?"

"I don't want to scare the camp. The teachers don't believe me anyway. Telling them won't do much good."

They continued walking and the smell of water caught Pietro's nose. He moved faster and quieter with Felicity following him. Tracing down the stench, Pietro discovered a lake and next to it was a cave. Felicity saw the cave and how the entrance was large.

"You think a bear might live in there?" Felicity whispered.

"Probably."

Pietro circled the cave and peeked inside with the flashlight and he saw something large, immediately he moved from the entrance and returned to the trees where Felicity was waiting. She saw the terror in his eyes as he crouched down.

"Stay quiet." Pietro told her."

She stayed quiet as they heard footsteps coming from the cave. They looked and waited to see what it could be and after the fifth step, they saw the animal which was inside the cave. Pietro's eyes widen and Felicity was afraid. The creature was on all fours and had to be at least two-to-four feet tall.

"Is that a bear?" Felicity whispered.

The animal walked further out toward the lake and Pietro saw the tail. He knew it was the animal which walked through the camp to night before.

"No." Pietro replied. "I don't think that's a bear."

"Bears don't have tails." Felicity said. "Not like that. The only kind of animal that has a tail like that are wolves."

"Exactly." Pietro replied. "We're looking at a werewolf."

The animal went and drank water from the lake, grunting. Felicity took a step back and stepped on some branches. The animal's head turned around quickly toward them.

"Oh no." She said.

The animal stood up on its hind legs, reaching seven feet in height. Sniffing the surroundings. Pietro grabbed Felicity by the arm and took off running. The animal howled and went after them. They ran as fast as they could, hearing the pouncing of the animal's feet behind them. After a minute, they made it back to the camp and the animal's sound was gone. They turned around to look and didn't see the animal. Taking a moment to calm themselves, one of the teachers walked out of the cabin, seeing the two students and approached them.

"What are you two doing up?"

"We were just examining the forest." Felicity said.

"That's all." Pietro added.

"No bother. Go to your tents. Now. Get some sleep."

They went and slept. The next day, the students were all set for their final day out in the wilderness while Pietro and Felicity talked with each other about the animal. Felicity wondered if they should tell everyone while Pietro suggested they keep the information to themselves. While they talked, Lydia approached them.

"What are you guys doing?"

"Just talking." Felicity said.

"Right." Lydia joked. "Talking about what?"

"The woods." Pietro said.

"The woods?"

"Yeah." Felicity said.

"I'm not believing you."

Felicity turned to Pietro and he shook his head. Felicity couldn't hold it in any longer and she told Lydia about what she and Pietro saw the night before. Lydia laughed it off until Pietro gave her more detail about the animal. Lydia's first thought was to tell the teachers, but Felicity stopped her.

"They have to know." Lydia said.

"Yes. They won't believe us anyway."

'How are you sure?"

"Because I already tried to tell them." Pietro said.

"When?"

"The first day we came out here."

Lydia nodded. "So, what are you going to do for tonight?"

"What do you mean?" Felicity asked.

"It's our last night our here. We leave in the morning."

"You want to see the werewolf for yourself, don't you?" Pietro said.

"Only to see if it's real."

Felicity looked at Pietro and he simply nodded with a sigh. They agreed to bring Lydia along for one last look. Once the night had come, they went out again with Lydia, taking the same path as before.

Upon returning to the lake, they noticed the cave was quiet as was their surroundings. It startled Pietro. He knew something was wrong. A low-pitched growl mumbled from the bushes near the lake. Pietro looked out and saw the eyes. Piercing glaring white eyes. No pupils. He pointed as Felicity and Lydia saw the eyes.

"What is that?" Lydia asked.

The animal bolted from the bushes and rushed toward them. They saw the animal in full as it ran toward Lydia. Pietro shoved her out of the animal's path and started slashing the animal with his knife. He yelled for Felicity and Lydia to run and they did. Pietro distracted the animal long enough to find an escape. Felicity and Lydia returned to the campsite with Pietro following several minutes after.

"What are we going to do?!" Lydia screamed, startling the entire camp.

Pietro sighed. "Great."

The teachers exited their cabins as the students started coming out of their tents. Lydia pointed out to the woods. Yelling about the werewolf. Pietro and Felicity tried to calm her down, but they could not. The teachers immediately shut it down and told the students to return to their tents. The following morning as everyone packed their gear and got onto the bus. Pietro took one more look out into the woods and saw the animal once again, running through the trees. He pointed and felicity looked, seeing the animal as well. The bus started and left the campsite. Along the way, Pietro saw a sign on the side of the road that simply read, "*Bray Road*".

PREY ON THE FEARFUL

There was once a young girl named Julie. Her parents had moved into a suburban neighborhood during the early autumn season. While they set up their new home and decorated with all types of furniture and artwork, Julie had encountered a peculiar friend who was around the neighborhood. The friend said his name was Heth and he was a good friend throughout the neighborhood. Everyone knew of him and his family. As Halloween came closer, the neighborhood was completely decorated in much Halloween décor. Floating skeletons, pumpkins, ghosts, and even monsters were se up in the yards. Others had Halloween decorations on their doors and windows. Heth had come to Julie's home to visit. The two were almost inseparable. Beside the fact of the other children who lived in the neighborhood. Heth was friendly with all of them.

"So, what are you dressing up as for Halloween?" Julie asked Heth.

"I'm going as a spirit."

"A spirit? You mean a ghost?"

"In a sense. I dress up as a spirit every Halloween."

"Well, what kind of spirit or ghost? One that haunts houses? Perhaps, you're the kind that terrorizes people into giving you their candy?"

"They can keep the candy. I usually get something other than sweets."

"I'm curious. Tell me."

"I prefer to gain people's fear."

"Their fear?" Julie said. "Oh! You like scaring people."

"Yes. It makes things feel perfect. Especially at this time of the year."

"Then, what do you dress as? A regular ghost covered in white?"

"I wear mostly a black robe. My mask resembles a scarecrow."

"So, you're basically a hidden scarecrow? Nice concept."

"Just wait till we go trick-or-treating. You'll see what I mean when people's fear does good."

After some weeks had passed, the children gathered in their costumes. They were dressed in a variety of characters. Some were superheroes. Others were monsters, cowboys, wizards. Julie was dressed as an elf queen. Heth appeared before all of them, wearing exactly what he told Julie. The boys in the crowd saw Heth's mask and they yelled. Saying the mask was clever and terrifying. Heth looked over to Julie and nodded with a smirk. The children went house-to-house, trick-or-treating. The parents of the homes enjoyed seeing them in their costumes.

'I see this one is dressed as the Nano Man." One father said. "Great choice."

Heth walked with Julie and some of the other children in the neighborhood to each of the homes. Heth looked out further into the neighborhood, seeing a dark shroud of mist in the air. He told Julie and the others he'll return. Julie asked where he was going.

"Just going to get something."

Heth left the group and followed the mist. The dark mist led Heth near the end of the neighborhood and into the part of the woods next to the suburbs. Heth went into the woods as the mist moved in deeper. Heth walked through the bushes and trees to catch the mist and when there was an opened space, the mist was gone. Heth looked around for the mist and did not see anything. Not even a shadow from its presence. He chose to leave the woods and return to the suburb. Once, he made that decision, he was stuck in the presence of a figure. The figure appeared human yet was made up of the mist itself. Heth stumbled in his steps, backing away from the figure.

"What are you?" He asked.

"What am I?" The figure echoed. "I am what you sought to do this night."

"I don't know what you mean."

"Yes, you do. You desire to scare the children out here. To frighten their parents as well. Fear is what you seek after this night. Not treats to eat."

"How do you know all of this?" Heth asked with fear in his voice.

"I am the spirit which you've chosen to imitate."

"What? I do not understand. How can I be dressed as you? I'm just dressed as a regular spirit."

"No, you are not. You are going around in my appearance. I am the Spirit of Fear itself."

"No way." Heth said. "That's not possible. You can't be real. It's all just a story told to us to keep us in line with our parents' rules."

"You're not listening. I was around when your parents were children and their parents before them. I've been around this world for many years and will continue to be around. I have been given orders to obey. Rules to follow. Just like you and the others."

"You're telling me even you, a ghost, has to follow rules?"

"Everything follows rules. It's how the world works."

Heth calmed himself down and took a moment to breathe. The spirit was kind enough to allow Heth to relax. Not wanting to terrify him any longer. The spirit commanded Heth to return to Julie and the others and join in on the fun of the evening. Heth agreed and went to leave. Before he went further out, the spirit called to him.

"Before you go, remember these words. For the actions you are partaking in have dire consequences. Such actions you cannot understand at this moment in time. Your age isn't ready enough for such reveals. But, I will tell you this. In the future, when you are of age, all shall be revealed unto you. You will begin to learn much about the world and its history."

"Why is that?" Heth wondered. "What of the others? Shouldn't they have the right to know those kinds of things too?"

"They will. In due time. I can only tell you of what you will encounter. Because it is this moment here that was set in motion by your path."

Heth nodded and went away as the spirit evaporated and vanished from his sight. Heth returned to Julie and the others. She noticed something strange about him.

"You're OK?" She asked.

"I'm fine. So, what has happened since my little break?"

"Well, I've collected so much candy that I won't be able to eat it all alone."

"Do you mind if you can share some with me?" Heth asked.

"Of course!"

For the rest of the night, Heth and Julie hung out with the other children of the neighborhood. Seeing what they all have collected on their trick-or-treat hunts. The amount of candy they collected was very vast in numbers. Heth realized he no longer wanted to scare them or anyone else. He just wanted to spend time with his friends. While they laughed and talked with themselves, the spirit was hovering over the neighborhood. Its eyes were centered on Heth and kindly turned toward Julie. The spirit nodded, showing a faint glowing smile on its face. The spirit disappeared as the moon was over the neighborhood on that Halloween night.

A HOWL IN SIGHT

Out the Midwest, there was a family. Their plan was to settle in a small town and live a quiet life. The father worked as a mechanic while the mother was a chase keeper at home. They had three children. Two daughters and a son. One day when the family was together at home, their daughter noticed a pack of wolves outside of their home in the field. A family of wolves.

"Look!' She said to her parents.

Her parents looked outside the window, seeing the wolves. They quickly panicked and told the children to remain inside as the father went out to scare the wolves away. The father yelled at the pack and they fled from his presence. One wolf in particular, turned back, facing the father and glanced over to the windows, seeing the daughter. The wolf nodded and ran away. The father returned inside and the family was calm. Later during the night, the daughter began hearing the sounds of howling coming from outside. She arose from her bed and walked toward the window. Outside, she saw the same wolf standing on a boulder in the field, howling at the moon.

The next day, the family was visited by another family who lived out in the area as well. They were of Native American descent and they spoke with the family. The daughter had become friends with their daughter. She had told them about the wolves and they responded by saying the wolves are known to reside in the area. They've been in the region for centuries. After the families fellowshipped, the wolves were seen again later that night. This time both daughters saw the wolves and the same one as before nodded toward them as it left. The same wolf went atop the boulder and howled once again.

The wolves never stopped passing through the field of the home. The daughter eventually befriended them and every night the wolf would howl at the moon and occasionally the daughter would repeat after it. Still, to this day, as the daughter grew older, she still sees the same wolves passing through. They're just a howl in sight.

THE SHOCKER IN HIDING

Sightings occurred throughout a small town of a strange electrical occurrence shorting out the energy of the town. The officials searched the town to find any evidence of an attack or disturbance. No thunderstorms have touched the town in weeks. No weather issues of any kind nor any electrical issues that may have gone past their notice. Within the town, the civilians had their own theories as to what may be interfering with the electricity. Some believed it to be the number of technologies the people have in their homes. Others referred to solar flares. A few made mention of UFOs.

There were two children who were aware of the ongoing situation. Flora and Wesley. They were friends within their local school. Flora had researched the events taking place and traced them to a nearby TNT warehouse near the outskirts of the town. Wesley attempted to find a way to travel to the warehouse, however his parents would not agree. Calling Flora's theory only a child's fairy tale. Flora had told her parents about the theories and they concluded that the power lines must be repaired or restructured to secure proper electricity throughout the town.

One day at home, Flora's brother, Toby had arrived from his workplace and she had told him all she knew concerning the electricity and the warehouse. Toby, always the critical thinker, took Flora's words seriously as well as her theories. Toby had an idea.

"We need to go to the warehouse?" Flora said.

"And you want me to drive you there?" Toby asked.

"Well, mom and dad won't do it. You're the only option I have."

"What about Wesley's parents? His father works in the electric department. I'm sure he can find a way to get you there."

"That's the thing. His parents do not believe in the theories. Wesley is depending on you taking us."

"So, I'm taking the both of you out to a warehouse in the outskirts?"

"How else are we able to get there? Plus, we need supervision. Just in case our parents find out."

Toby took in his sister's words and grinned.

"Fine. I will take you both there."

"Yes!" Flora yelled.

"It's only there and back. Nowhere else. Got it?"

"Got it."

Flora contacted Wesley and told him the details. Wesley was excited for the chance. The next day, which was a Sunday, Toby and Flora went out and picked up Wesley from his home. They traveled out to the warehouse. A deserted place. The building was out-of-work for many years. Far from ten years in detail. The forest had begun to overtake the building with trees growing from within the warehouse.

"Now, what do you believe that's here to connect to the electrical issues?" Toby questioned his sister.

"Whatever is causing the electricity to go on and off is coming from this warehouse. The maps showed the pathway of the electricity's tracks."

"It had tracks?" Wesley said.

"That was on the map. You didn't see it."

"No."

"The blue lines on the map across the buildings and the poles. That's the tracks."

Wesley was given the map by Flora and he saw the tracks. He nodded and looked around the warehouse. Seeing how the wood is creaking from the forest's wind. Toby walked around the building. Shrugging his shoulders in confusion.

"I'm not sure what you expected to find here."

"There's something here. The tracks are the evidence."

Wesley investigated the warehouse from the broken-down wall and with a quick flash, he saw a strange figure pass through the building. He yelled and pointed.

"Something's in there."

"Something?" Flora asked. "Like what?"

"I don't know. But, it moved fast. Extremely fast."

"Was it an animal?" Toby asked. "Like a fox or a deer?"

"No." Wesley said. "I don't know. Didn't get a good look at it."

Toby nodded, turning toward the warehouse's wall and he stepped forward. Wesley was surely afraid as Flora turned to her brother.

"What are you doing?"

"I'm going to see what he saw in here. Only way to know for sure."

"Then, I'm coming with you."

"What?" Wesley said. "Toby can handle himself."

"I appreciate that, young one. Flora, I'll be fine. I'll go in and see whatever it was that Wesley saw. Afterwards, I'll come back out and give you the details. After that, we head home."

"I'm going in too." Flora said.

Toby turned to Wesley and pointed.

"You're staying out here or are you coming with?"

Wesley paused and sighed. Following them into the warehouse. Within the building was nothing but dust, grass, and dirt. Small sounds of birds chirping could be heard from above. Must be a set of nests within the building according to Toby. Flora reached into her pocket, pulling out a flashlight. Toby saw the light and scoffed.

"You came prepared."

"I had to."

"Did you bring more?" Wesley added. "I'm just curious."

Flora reached into her jacket pocket, handing Wesley another flashlight. Toby nodded, taking out his phone.

"That's cool."

They searched the warehouse for any sign of animals that may be running around the area. Only seeing birds passing through and nothing on the ground, Toby called it a day. Stating it was time to leave and return home. Flora did a search of her own, she could feel a strange occurrence of energy in the air. She looked around the warehouse, feeling it on her arms. She turned to Wesley, seeing his hair standing up.

"Your hair." She pointed.

Wesley touched his hair, feeling it standing upright on his head.

Toby's hair was also standing upright. He patted it down, but it continued to rise. Wesley's hair did the same. Flora's hair was also staring to stand up.

"What is happening?" Toby wondered. "Why's our hair standing up on its own?"

"It's static electricity." Flora replied.

"Something's here." Wesley said quietly. "Something is in here with us."

Toby nodded, feeling very uneasy in the warehouse. He lowered his phone as the energy started to affect it. The flashlights were also blinking on and off, causing fear to cover Wesley. Flora was not afraid and nor was Toby. Toby was cautious, preferably for his sister and Wesley's sakes.

"I think it's time we get going now." Toby said. "Follow me out of here."

They headed out of the warehouse and as they were leaving, a quick and bright flash of light passed them by. Directly in front of them. They paused and were startled. Wesley breathed heavily.

"That's it." He said.

"What's it?" Flora asked.

"That's what I saw."

"Yep." Toby said. "It's time we get out of here."

They arrive outside and enter Toby's car. He drove off from the warehouse and back on the road. While on the road, Wesley looked back and saw the same flash of light behind them. He pointed and yelled. Toby looked at his mirror, seeing the light himself. Flora also saw it as it chased them down the road.

"What is that thing?!" Wesley yelled.

"It looks like a ball of light." Toby replied.

"It's not. Flora added. "It's what's been causing the electrical shortages."

The light reached the car and lunged on the top, scratching the windows with claws on its hands. The screeching sound across the windows terrified them as Toby drove faster. Wesley only screamed as the light reached down toward his side of the car, revealing its face through the window. A face of lightning. No eyes. No nose. Just a mouth. Within the mouth was a red light. Red electricity sparking.

"Go faster!" Wesley yelled.

"I'm going as fast as possible." Toby replied.

Flora looked ahead of them, seeing the low tree branch. She pointed it out to her brother. Toby looked and saw it. He nodded. Knowing what to do. Then, Toby pressed his foot on the pedal and the car moved faster toward the branch. Wesley ducked his head as they drove under the branch and the light creature was pulled from the car, now tangled in the branch.

Later, Wesley was sent home. Toby and Flora returned home and kept all the details of the encounter to themselves. Upon nightfall, the electricity flickered across the town. Causing the townspeople to go out and search for the source. While the town searched for the cause, Toby and Flora spotted something hovering in the air. Wesley was in his room, seeing the same thing.

"It's back," Flora said.

The civilians caught the glimpse of the flying creature, to which the power lines began showing lightning bolts circulating them and rising into the air toward the figure. The light figure screeched loud over the town, letting them know it exists and wants the power source.

"What are we going to do?" Flora asked her brother.

"We're going to stop that thing." Toby replied. "One way or another."

Toby grabbed his keys and went outside with Flora following. They picked up Wesley from his home and went out into the downtown district to confront the light creature. The town went into a panic as the creature began siphoning out the electricity. Flora, Toby, and Wesley did whatever was possible to slow the creature down. Until one older man took out a water hose, approaching the creature.

"Hey!" The old man yelled. "Get on outta here!"

The water flew out and sprayed the creature completely. The water caused the light creature to tremble and it flew off into the night sky.

"That was it?" Wesley said.

"I don't think it's completely gone." Flora said.

"No." Toby replied. "It'll be back. Someday."

"And what are we going to do then?" Wesley asked.

"We'll be ready for it."

THE ROC ABOVE US

During a small walk in the Tuwaiq Mountains in Saudi Arabia, a man and his three sons were out looking at the landscape of the area. Seeing the desert canyon and the ways of the desert that lead toward the city of Riyadh, where they are from. As they made their walks, one of the sons looked ahead, seeing something in the sky. He pointed it out, getting his father's attention.

"Abu, what is that?"

"What are you talking of?" The father asked, looking ahead.

He keened his eyes and saw what had appeared to be a large object in the sky. The object was heading in their direction and the father told the sons to stand back as the object was coming closer. They turned around and went toward the narrow canyon to avoid being seen by the object. Once, hey entered the canyon, the winds picked up and the sands rose from the ground, covering the area in a small, yet dense sandstorm. The sons were calm, as was their father. Above them, they could hear rushing sounds. One of the sons believed it to be a plane flying over as the sounds were the engines. However, the father knew better and listened closely to the sound.

"That is not a plane." The father told his son. "It's something else."

They waited in the canyon as the sand fell to the ground and the winds had ceased. Rising from the canyon and back above the ground, the father looked out and saw that the ground was pushed around by the wind with such a strong force. It mesmerized him and his sons were curious. No plane could have moved the sands as it were. The younger son looked ahead of them in the other direction and he saw what he could not believe. Pulling his father's robe.

"What is it, son?"

"That."

The father looked up and saw what his son was staring at. A large bird, resembling an eagle. The bird was feasting on a prey it captured before entering the mountains. The father stepped back, telling his sons to remain quiet. The bird stood at the height of a forty-foot building. The wings were massive, and the talons were large and sharp. Sharp enough to crack the rocks of the mountains.

"*Abu*, what are we going to do?" The son asked.

"Be quiet and follow me."

The father made his move to get from the view of the bird as it feasted. Returning to their camels, the father made his way to reach the city of Riyadh.

Once arriving, he began telling the people about the large bird he saw in the mountains. Most of them assumed he only saw a large eagle. However, there was one man standing by who heard the man's full story. He approached him and his sons. Telling them in detail what the bird was and where it had come from. The father was curious with the stranger's detailed description of the bird.

"Tell me how you know so much about this bird?"

"I've seen one before." the stranger said. "They've been around for centuries."

"What are they?" The son asked.

"They're called by several names across our lands. Here, we refer to them simply as *Rukhs*. Some call them *Rocs*."

"I remember now." The father said. "My grandfather would tell me stories of such creatures. Flying across the Arabian deserts. Encountering with explorers and sailors alike. I never thought the creatures could actually exist."

"Well, my friend, I'm here to tell you they do. Now, there is no need to be afraid of the creature. Unless it decides on coming to this city to cause chaos."

"We felt the winds when it flew over us." Another son said. "It created a sandstorm."

The stranger grinned.

"That was the storm we saw? I didn't know."

"But, what about the people here?"

"What of them, good man?" The stranger asked.

"They must know. We have to tell them. To get someone to go out there and make sure the bird doesn't reach the city."

The stranger told the father to silence himself to avoid further suspicion by the bystanders who were going about their business in the marketplace. The sons were quiet yet interested in the bird's history and characteristics. The stranger nodded silently.

"My people and I will handle the bird. You and your sons should head home. Unless you have business to attend."

"We'll be heading home soon. Just after I get some things."

"Understood, good sir. Don't worry about this city or the bird. Who I work with, we handle matters like this. We have dealt with other creatures such as the Rukh. Many whom the population will scoff at if you utter the names to them."

"There's more creatures out there?" The father asked.

"Plenty more. However, go about your business and leave the bird to me."

"I will."

"Also, don't go around telling others about the bird or our discussion. The quieter everything operates, the better for it all."

The father was taken aback by the words of the stranger. He leaned in closer.

"Why all of this secrecy?"

"Honestly. It's better for everyone. Better for Riyadh."

The father took in the words of the stranger and nodded. The father left with his sons and went about his other duties for the day. The stranger went into a building where he began telling several others about the bird's presence in the mountains. They listened and took in the words of the stranger.

Later that night, they went out into the desert and found the bird sleeping. Immediately, they went and attacked the creature. Seeking to kill it. The bird screeched in the night and fought back, spanning its wings, and creating the wind. The sandstorm returned and eventually overtook the stranger and his colleagues.

The following day, the father found out the stranger and his colleagues were found in the desert underneath the sand. The sons wanted to go back out to see if they would catch another glimpse of the bird. The father agreed and once they were out in the mountains again, the Roc flew past them to where they saw the creature in full. Its golden feathers, fire-red eyes, and increasing winds. The sons savored the moment as the bird flew from them. The father was startled, yet calm. They returned home and told the mother about their encounter.

"Umm, the Roc was above us." The youngest son said.

BEWARE THE BOOGEYMAN

One night when Jimmy was fast asleep, he found himself in a strange dream. The dream revolved around a strange figure following him in a forest. The forest was glowing with neon-blue light and the grounds were covered in leaves and small branches. Jimmy walked through the forest, hearing laughter, talking, and screams coming from all across the forest. Yet, the figure still followed him down the trail.

"Why are you following me?" Jimmy turned and asked.

Upon turning around, there was no one in his sight, but Jimmy could hear the laughter from the unseen force around him. From that moment, Jimmy ran further through the forest. Seeing nothing but trees in his sights as the laughter followed him and intensified. Jimmy continued running and eventually found himself at an edge of a cliff. Jimmy sighed and heard creeping footsteps behind him. Jimmy breathed in and exhaled before turning around. Once Jimmy turned, the unseen force rushed toward him, waking him up from his sleep.

The next day, Jimmy told his parents about his dream. His father suggested he stop watching scary movies before going to sleep. His mother only said it was something he had eaten before going to bed. Jimmy arrived at school and told his friends of the dream. They claimed the unseen force to have been the Boogeyman. Jimmy had never heard of the Boogeyman before. He questioned his friends about the unseen force. They told him the Boogeyman creeps into the dreams of those he wishes. His main goal is to terrify those who are asleep and to cause a great disturbance upon them. Waking them up late at night from their sleep, only to leave them in a state of fear.

Jimmy took some time to himself and began researching the Boogeyman's history and folktales from across various parts of the world. After finding enough sources, Jimmy decided to keep his mind focused when he sleeps to prepare for the Boogeyman. Later that night once Jimmy fell asleep, he found himself in the forest again and could hear the same laughter as before. Jimmy stood still, looking around the forest.

"I know who you are. Come out and face me."

The laughter grew and in front of Jimmy appeared from the ground a dark black mist. The mist arose from the ground, standing on two legs of its own. Jimmy watched as it morphed into what almost looked like a human. A thin frail human. It had the facial appearance of an old man, wearing torn pants and a ripped shirt.

"You have found me." The mist spoke.

"I know who you are." Jimmy replied. "You're him. The Boogeyman."

"That's right! I am he who haunts the visions of the night!"

"Why have you chosen to invade my dreams? To cause me to fear the night and the darkness around me?"

"Because you were next on my list."

"Your list?"

"Yes. I have a list of every person in the world. I set out a time and season to invade their dreams to deliver fear into their minds. However, you out of so many few have found a way to counter my tactics."

"I did some research. Nothing major."

"Ah. You're a student. You put in the work to accomplish your goal."

"I want you to leave my dreams."

"Is that what you genuinely want? Is that what you truly desire? Dreams of peace, love, and honor?"

"It's better than running in a dark forest in fear of your life. Even if it's only a dream."

"And leave everyone else alone."

The Boogeyman scoffed at Jimmy's words and shook his head in shame as the whistling of the wind moved throughout the forest. The faint sounds of crickets and even birds chirping echoed throughout the neon lighted area.

"Leave everyone be? I cannot do such a task. I was designed to invade dreams. It is my purpose. My calling."

"Wait. You were made to invade people's dreams? To scare them? On purpose?!"

"Yes. That is why I am here speaking with you. Otherwise, I would've never invaded your dreams or the dreams of all the others. Both past and future."

"Who made you?"

The Boogeyman grinned.

"If you only knew."

"I want to know." Jimmy demanded. "Who made you?"

"You're a little too young for those answers. However, in times to come, may be find what you are asking of. It will suit you better in those times rather than the present moment."

"You're saying my age isn't appropriate enough for an answer?"

"You're only twelve. Let's say, when you reach eighteen or nineteen, these answers may make sense o you. Otherwise, you'll have to be much older. But, your age does not apply to such revelations. Only your mind, eyes, and ears."

"But I want to know."

"You have the heart of a student. You search out what is right, and you seek what is true. You may be one of them who discovers so much more in your future."

'My future is what I will make of it."

"You will see if that is the truth. Time will tell of these matters."

The Boogeyman's attention was quickly pulled into another section of the forest. Jimmy did not understand what was happening as the Boogeyman began to move away in fear. Jimmy looked in the direction of the Boogeyman's sight, seeing nothing but the darkness of the forest. The Boogeyman stepped back with his eyes widely opening. Fear could be seen on his face. It startled Jimmy.

"This is not possible." The Boogeyman said.

"What are you talking about?" Jimmy questioned." What's not possible?"

"He's found me. He's found me."

"Who's found you?"

The Boogeyman took off in the other direction as a chilly wind blew toward Jimmy and within the rustling wind, Jimmy saw a figure.

The figure was cloaked in black and violet. Its face was pale as snow. Its hair was black as the night sky and its eyes were glowing blue within the darkness. Jimmy was frozen solid in his place as the figure looked over to him and nodded.

"Wake." The figure said.

Jimmy awoke from the dream, seeing the sunlight piercing through the window curtains. He went over to his desk and started writing all he saw and heard while in the dream. To keep it as a remembrance of what is to come and what will be revealed. In jimmy's studies, he found that even though the Boogeyman brings terror to those who are sleep, there is another who sends a much deeper fear into the heart of the Boogeyman himself.

THE TOWER OF NO RETURN

Three friends by the names of Kurt, Anastasia, and George have decided to go on a short adventure into the Midwest. Each of them reached the age of eighteen, their goal was simply to have an adventure. A small one once more. When they traveled out into the Midwest, they quickly went out into the desert regions of the land. Kurt had a love for the desert, resembling a place of ancient times. Anastasia was more interested in the architecture of nature's history. George was only there for the peace and quiet. A better place in his mind to stay rather than the cities.

"Can you imagine who lived here in times past." Kurt said.

"They have to have lived in caves out here." Anastasia added.

"You're sure about that?" George asked. "Caves? Are you sure they're any of them out here?"

"There has to be."

They went out and searched for caves. Finding none. Anastasia suggested they'll go and look the next day with Kurt and George agreeing. They ate and slept in their tents in the middle of nowhere. George usually stayed out of his tent, gazing up at the sky, looking at the stars. During the night, George heard a strange humming sound moving in the air. He unzipped his tent and took a small look into the sky. He saw nothing, but the humming was still present. George didn't understand what it could possibly be, and the humming stopped. As if it had never passed by. George shrugged his shoulders and went back into his tent to sleep.

The next day, upon waking up, George had told them about the humming sound he heard the night before. Kurt said it might've been just a plane flying over. Anastasia had the theory of the humming coming from beneath the ground. Tremors perhaps. George was sure of either of their answers. After eating breakfast, they went out and searched for the caves. Walking along further than the previous day, they only found one cave and it was small. Anastasia saw some paintings on the walls of the cave. Depicting beings with large eyes and wings. Their bodies appeared human, but they were not humans.

"What are those things?" Kurt asked.

"I do not know." Anastasia replied. "They look like some sorts of strange beings. Not sure where they're from."

"They look like aliens." George added. "Look at the human figures under them. They look as if they're bowing down to them."

Kurt looked closer, seeing the stick-figured humans bowing before the strange beings. Anastasia took a closer look as well, seeing the oval-shaped eyes of the beings. She didn't understand what they could be or where they might have come from.

"If these paintings are in this cave," Anastasia said, "perhaps, there are other caves out here with similar paintings."

"It's possible." Kurt said. "We just have to keep looking."

"Well, there's still some time until sunset. So, let's go see what we find next."

They continued walking through the desert regions, now entering the massive area of mountains and canyons. There, Anastasia knew immediately there were caves in the area. Kurt loved the scenery of the land. George savored the silence that was around them. While they walked into the canyons, they found another cave. A little bigger than the previous one, but this one had paintings of its own. Anastasia looked at the paintings, quickly realizing they aren't related to the first cave.

"What does it show?" Kurt asked.

"It shows just one guy." Anastasia said. "He's wearing what looks like Old West clothing. The duster. The hat. He's even carrying a sword on his back."

"A sword." George said. "Are you sure you're right about that?"

"I am. Take a look."

They saw the painting and it was exactly what she said. What was in front of the figure was a city. A dark city. They didn't understand what it meant, and Anastasia wrote it down in her notebook. She had done the same with the first cave. They also took photos of the paintings in both caves. They continued going throughout the canyons, finding more caves and seeing more paintings. One had a painting of a tower. A tall tower detailed in black with a white highlight surrounding it. Another cave had a painting of a war between flying figures and what appeared to be robots. Another cave had paintings that resembled a kingdom in Ancient Egypt only with a slight detail of a glowing sword.

"What is all of this?" Kurt asked. "This isn't what we were taught in school."

"No." Anastasia replied. "This is something else. Something that has been kept hidden for an exceedingly long time."

"Then, it's a good thing we found all of this." George added. "That way, we can keep the photos and information around us. Share it with those who are interested in this kind of stuff."

"Everyone should know about this." Anastasia said. "The world should know."

"I don't think that's a good idea." Kurt said. "If the world finds out about all of these caves, people will never get the chance to see them."

"You're saying you want to keep all of this to ourselves?"

"Just for the time being." Kurt replied. "It won't hurt anyone."

"Better to tell those who are in these fields rather than everyone who doesn't care." George added.

Anastasia understood their words and she knew them well. She sighed. Agreeing with them. Afterwards, they returned to their camp as the sun began to set. During the night, the humming sound returned with George coming out of his tent to find a tall tower sitting in the distance from their campsite. He went and woke up Kurt and Anastasia. Telling them of what's standing outside. They exited their tents, hearing the humming sound as well to find a tall tower in their presence.

"That's the tower from the cave painting." Anastasia noted. "The actual tower."

"What should we do?" Kurt asked.

"I have an idea." George replied. "But, I'm not sure you're up to it."

"You want to go to it, don't you?"

"Only way to know what it may be."

"Then, you go first." Kurt said. "Tell us what you see when you come back."

"You're serious?" George said. "You're not coming with?"

"I'm not too keen on approaching a strange tower that appeared out of nowhere."

"Go." Anastasia said. "See what is there and come back with the results."

"I will."

George went and walked toward the tower. The humming sound intensified as it came closer. Cover his eyes from the bright lights surrounding the tower. He saw the door and opened it. Within, George saw several different lands. One of water, another of a vast desert, one of a large city, and another in what looked to be another planet. George listened as the humming sound began changing sound. George nodded, looking back at Kurt and Anastasia.

"I'll be back!" George yelled as he entered the door.

Once the door had closed behind George, the tower vanished with a bright boom of light. The humming was gone. Kurt and Anastasia searched for George the entire night until sunrise.

Later in the following day, they went and searched for George. What they had found was the first cave painting had changed. Kurt looked and saw what Anastasia pointed out.

"Is that George?"

It was at that moment wherever George had ended up, he's in a place far from their own and the tower could be one of no return for those who entered its door.

LOST IN SHADOWS: REMASTERED

<u>CHAPTER 1</u>

New Haven Detective and U.S. Marshal Preston Maddox drives down a pair of narrow streets as he's on the search for Jonny Cartel, one of the top drug lords of New Haven, Connecticut. Preston, who's wearing his casual suit attire, drives through the quiet streets of New Haven. He turns a corner that heads toward Orange Avenue, around the West River.

"I take it he's around this area. Somewhere."

He turned a corner, which was leading him into a dark pathway. On the other side of the street is a small warehouse covered in rusted panels. Preston drove closer to the warehouse and spotted a white van on the left side. Preston noticed a group of guys standing by the van, wearing all black with their faces barely covered, stacking what appears to be bags of marijuana and cocaine in the back. Preston also noticed a black SUV beside the van with one man coming out, wearing a white suit with slick hair.

"There's the son of a bitch." Preston said as he sees Jonny Cartel.

Preston slowly put the car in park and turned off the vehicle. He exited out of the car and began walking toward the scene. As he walked closer, one of the men spotted him and started yelling. The other men looked up and see Preston. Jonny turned and stared at Preston. Preston does the same.

"Well, looks like the Instinct has found me." Jonny said. "What's the next step, Detective? I hope you're not here for a license plate or sticker check on my SUV here."

"I'm here to take your worthless self to prison. Unless you have another option of a location you'll like to take you?"

Jonny laughed as he looked toward his men. They laughed along with him, until Preston glared at them. Jonny turned back to Preston, looking at his clothes before keeping his attention focused on Preston.

"Look here, I got an hour before I leave for Miami. So, do me a favor, Maddox. Get a change in style of clothes for once. This whole intimidation approach isn't quite working for you when you're wearing only slacks and a casual jacket."

"I appreciate your generosity in the apparel department, Cartel. Though, I can care less on how you perceive someone's clothing. Anyway, that's not why I'm here and you know why I'm here standing before you and your pack of goons."

"OK, so what can I do to change your mind? Hmm? Give you some profit on the side? Hand you one of my nice fine women to keep you company for the time being?"

"I can care less about your greenbacks or your filthy whores you have stashed back at your place."

Preston held his ground quietly.

"I'm giving you a few choices to make. Either you can come with me, get in my car and I'll ship you off to prison or we can have ourselves a classic standoff where you and most of your men here are killed on the spot. Your decision, not mine."

Jonny stood quietly, not making a sound. Only staring at Preston. Preston kept his eyes locked on Cartel, not making any facial expressions of any kind.

"Tongue turned to lead, Cartel?"

Jonny walked toward the van. He tells his men to pack up whatever they had in their hands and told them to leave the area. The men toss whatever they have into the van and they drive it off into the darkness of street. Preston and Jonny are the only two men at the warehouse.

"Alright, Maddox. Now you have a choice to make and make it right for yourself."

"OK. What are these choices you have in mind for myself that would make me accept them and leave you here to continue your pathetic way?'

Jonny moved his right hand to his side, revealing a revolver under the side of his jacket. Preston noticed it and looked up at Jonny.

"You sure you want to play this little round? I told you already. You want to go that route, you'll end up dead and possibly some of your men too."

"There is no other way around all of this. Now, you can choose your choice. Either you can go ahead and leave this area and don't make a second thought or I could just shoot you on the spot and leave your body to rot."

"So, if I choose the first one, I assume I'll live. If I take the second option, you're going to put one in me. Is that how this is going here?"

"You're smarter than how you dress yourself, Marshal."

"Funny. The decisions you've just gave me are similar to the choices that you gave to that woman I suppose."

Jonny stood frozen still, having what appeared to be a confused and worried look on his face. He shook his head before staying still.

"I'm afraid I don't know what you're talking about, Marshal."

"The woman, whose body was found in the river a few weeks ago. I know you're aware of the case. Only her torso was found floating in the water. Her lower body was discovered across town at some cannibal site where they were partially eating off of it. They eat mostly the thighs and some of the calves. Other than that, they still left some over for anyone to share."

"Holy shit Holy shit! God damn it! If you knew how she behaved and how she acted, you would know deep down that she deserved it, *Instinct*!."

"No, I don't know why. Probably will never figure out why you had her killed and fed to cannibals. But, overall, why did she deserve it? Is it because she didn't have enough federal reserve notes to pay her remaining price off?"

"She was nothing but a traitorous whore. Sneaking behind my back, working for that Ray Colby guy from Jersey since he just opened ship down here in my town. My town! That kind of shit doesn't play fair in my world of business, Maddox and you understand that don't you."

"I do. But, its none of my concern how you run your business. My concern is stopping your business and putting you in a cell or maybe six feet under."

Jonny started to shake, he held up the revolver, pointed at Preston. Preston stood still, starting at Cartel.

"You know what, I've just had enough of this! I have a plane to catch, Marshal. Big business meeting tomorrow. So, if you'll excuse me."

Jonny started walking toward the SUV. Preston stood his ground, with his right hand to his side. Jonny, still pointing the revolver, gets to the driver's seat of the SUV. Preston stared at Jonny with his hand still to his side. Jonny paused and shut the door as he started stomping toward Preston with the revolver.

"You take one step, you son of a bitch and I'm going to blow your fucking brains out all over this place, Instinct!"

"I wouldn't try that, Cartel. You wouldn't want to make a big mistake by killing a United States Marshal and ruining your world of business for a very long time to come. Even if you have a plane to catch for a supposed big business meeting. I'm sure your other clients and partners will understand what you've been through and will find a way for their business to continue in their eyes before they're caught on their own soil."

"I'll spell this out for you once and only this once. The only way I'll ever lose this business is OVER MY COLD, DECAYING, CORPSE!!!"

Preston pulled out his gun and fired shots toward Jonny in the chest a consecutive three times. Jonny slowly fell to the ground, dropping the revolver in the process. Preston walked toward Jonny, who's trying to reach for revolver while lying on the concrete pavement., Preston kicked it away from Jonny's hand. Jonny bled from his chest as his blood flowed around his body, soaking his suit.

"From the look of you on the ground holding your chest, you didn't listen to my warning, Cartel. I told you not to try anything like that."

"It doesn't matter, Marshal. Maybe I deserved to die. Maybe this is where my journey ends and all. But, soon, there will come a time where you are on the opposite end of a gunshot such as this and you'll be on the ground gasping for your breath. When the day comes that it happens, you'll know what's to come afterwards."

"I highly doubt your kind and strong prophetic words." Preston said with a smile. "But, whenever that day does arrive, I'll be in this same position and the other will be in the position that you're currently lying in."

Preston reached into his pocket, pulling out his black and silver Blackberry. He dialed 9-1-1. The phone started ringing and the 9-1-1 Operator is on the other end.

"9-1-1. Please state your immediate emergency."

"This is Preston Maddox. U.S. Marshal and secondary detective over at the New Haven Detective and Marshal Agency. I've called because I'm currently standing around the West River, close to Orange Avenue at a warehouse. I need an ambulance and a coroner right away."

"An ambulance is on its way, Marshal. Should I assist backup as well?"

"No need for that ma'am. Just the ambulance and coroner will do just fine. I appreciate it and thank you."

He hung up and placed the smartphone back into his pocket. He walked over to Jonny. He kneeled in front of him as Cartel continued to gasp for his breath.

"Don't worry, Jonny. Ambulance is on its way. They'll do what they can for your sake."

"What about the coroner? Don't think I didn't hear that part."

"That's just in case you die here. Which is the most probability."

"Just go to hell, Marshal. Go to hell and burn for the rest of your eternal days."

Jonny's head cocked over as he exhaled his last breath. Jonny died on the spot as Preston only stared at his deceased body. He nodded and walked back to his car, leaving Jonny on the ground for the ambulance to find.

In a suburban neighborhood lies many homes of which families and friends live among each other. One of the homes has its lights on and inside of the home's kitchen is a forty-year old mother washing the dishes as her sixteen-year-old daughter sat in the living room in front of a fireplace watching the TV.

"What are you watching over there?"

"Just some random show. Nothing much on tonight, so I figured I would just watch something that grabbed my interest."

"Seems to me how you're pretty quiet over there that you're either in deep of the show or your bored by it."

"It's interesting so far, mom."

The daughter turned and looked toward the door. Hearing a tapping sound coming from outside. Noticing that the room is quiet except for the TV and her mother washing the dishes. She sat up from off the couch and walked slowly close to the door to see if the sound was coming from outside. The sound started again, this time alerting the mother. She looked over and turned to her daughter, who continued to approach the door.

"What was that outside?"

"I'm not sure. Sound like its right next to the door. Do you want me to go ahead and check it out?"

"Since you're already on your feet, I suggest you could. Just be cautious. There's no telling what that sound could be. Especially in a city like this."

The sound faded away as the daughter inched closer to the door. The mother continued washing the dishes as she glanced over toward her daughter and looked at what was playing on the TV. Hearing no sound, she looked at her daughter.

"Everything alright over there? You seem to be a little nervous?"

"I'm doing fine. Just taking precautions, that's all."

The daughter placed her hand on the doorknob and slowly turned the knob. Opening the door slightly, it gives a chilling creak as she opened the door. Upon seeing nothing or no one by the door, she releases a sigh of relief. The mother walked over toward the living room, seeing her daughter looking out the door and she went back to the kitchen.

"Haley, is everything alright? What are you doing?"

"I'm-"

As she responded to her mother, a hand covered by a black glove quickly reached in from the open creak on the left side of the door. The hand snatched Haley by her jaw and held her mouth shut. She tried to release a scream to gain her mother's attention. Hearing a series of bumping sounds coming from the front, the mother dried her hands and walked out of the kitchen.

"What in the hell are you doing in here?"

She stood in a frozen state as she saw Haley fighting off the black glove. Haley trued kicking out of the door at the individual's body, but the black glove held Haley tightly and slammed her head into the wall. Her mother stood covering her mouth with tears beginning to flow from her eyes.

"Oh my god. Haley, I'm coming."

As she took a step, another black glove reached out from behind her as it appeared the individual came through the back door nearby the kitchen. The intervals entered the home, their bodies appeared to be fit, wearing all black with their faces covered with solid black masks, to where even their eyes aren't revealed. The two individuals throw Haley and her mother against the walls and begin to pummel them to the floor. Both scream for help as they're being beaten.

CHAPTER 2

Officers arrived at a suburb home in the New Haven neighborhoods. They are heading through, going back and forth in and out of the home. An ambulance and coroner arrived on the scene as well. The paramedics entered the home with a stretcher, as do the coroner. A black car pulled up and out came Preston. He walked toward a fellow officer. The officer turned and was immediately what some would call star struck.

"U.S. Marshal and fellow New Haven detective, Preston Maddox." The Officer said. "It's an honor to meet you."

"It's an honor to meet you as well. So, what's the situation here, officer?"

"We received a call from one of the neighbors that something suspicious was occurring late last night at this house. From what we know, there were two females, one adult, the other, teenager. It seems that they were both murdered."

"Just being curious here, but, how were they murdered."

"I'll show you.' the Officer said. 'Follow me."

Preston followed the officer into the home. Inside, the home looked like your typical standard suburb home. A nice leather couch in the living room with a flat-screen TV, a beautiful kitchen with nice shiny tiles on the floor. The home currently filled and surrounded with officers, coroner, and forensic scientists. Preston looked inside the kitchen, to the left and seen the adult woman lying on the tile floor with her head severed.

Preston turned and said to the officer, "So, this is the mother. Couldn't really tell from a distance."

"Yes sir, the teenager is in the laundry room. Follow me,

Marshal."

They walked into the laundry room, which is on the left side of the kitchen. Preston looked inside and noticed something red leaking from the dryer. He looked over to the officer and pointed to the dryer.

"Wait. Hold on a quick second. Please do not tell me that she's in there?" He asked.

"Marshal, I'm afraid she is." the officer said.

Another officer walked in and opened the dryer. The door widely opened as an arm flopped out, covered and dripping with blood. They looked inside and see that the teenage girl was shoved into the dryer and stayed inside while it was operating, in which tossed her around and killed her in the process. Preston and the officer left the laundry room, returned outside to their cars.

They walked out of the front door as Preston turned to the officer.

"What was the relationship between the adult and teenager?"

"They were mother and daughter. It was just them in the house at the time. The mother divorced a few months back and took the daughter with her."

"Should we contact the father of the daughter regarding this incident?"

The officer turned and looked toward Preston and said, "I think its best we do that after we get the bodies out of the house."

Preston walked toward his car, but the officer called him back, he walked over to him. The officer looked at little nervous, as if he's about to ask a unusual question.

"Marshal, I have a question to ask you." The officer said enthusiastically.

"Go for it, officer"

"Why do they call you "*The Instinct*" exactly? I never understood the reason for it."

Preston smiled, rubbing his chin and turning his head, looking in another direction. He exhaled slowly before turning and looked at the officer with a mild smile.

"Look at it this way, everyone has instincts in their own sense of perception. It's what makes us do what we do. I just tend to use it all the time. If not most of the time. No hesitation in place of my career. I don't second guess, unless it's confuses the living hell out of me."

"I've always been curious of why you're called that. It must be cool to have a nickname in this line of work."

"Not exactly. From my perspective, nicknames today are now overrated. Don't have any sense of meaning to them."

"Really?" said a voice from behind Preston.

Preston turned and saw his boss, Eldon Ross, the chief commissioner of the New Haven Marshal and Detective Agency. Eldon is a man in his early fifties, wearing a button-down shirt with a nice tie and slacks. Eldon looked at Preston with a glare as he turned to the officer.

"You really believe what Preston's telling you, officer? Because if you are, that just makes you nothing but a rookie in this field."

"Well, sir, he's the Instinct." The officer said without hesitation. "I meant to say, yes sir."

"The Instinct. The only thing Preston could possibly be is a hard-headed guy who doesn't listen to the instructions he's given. Instead, he makes up his own schedule of work and does what he wants whenever he wants. Try convincing me that he's using his gut to make those decisions."

"Eldon, what have I done this time for you to arrive here like this and call me out?"

"You know what you did. So, don't play those childlike games with me, Maddox. Your little incident from last night is quickly spreading around the entire agency and somewhat across the city. This isn't going to go well for you, me, or the agency."

"Eldon, let me explain the situation to you. A few weeks ago, I gave Cartel a choice to leave New Haven or he would meet us end by my hand. After those weeks had passed, I confronted him at one of his hiding spots, smuggling drugs. We talked for a bit as I gave him a short amount of time to leave and he made his decision right there. Besides, I've been on his trail for a few months now and it was getting tiresome."

Eldon shrugged his shoulders. "Yeah right. What else you have in terms of defense? Did you plan on talking him to death?"

"It was self-defense as well." Preston said. "He pulled first, and I fired the first shot. Which was the last shot before I called the police and coroner."

Eldon looked down and around the area as he rubbed his bald head. Glancing at the officers exiting the home. He looked at Preston. "Ok, once you're back at the office, we'll discuss all of this thoroughly and we'll find some way to get through your mess. alright."

"I'll see you back at the office, Eldon." Preston said as Eldon walked away from the area.

The officer walked over to Preston and said, "Jonny Cartel? The elite crime boss, Jonny Cartel."

"What about Cartel is getting you hyped up right now?"

"So, you really shot Jonny Cartel? You killed the bastard. How did it feel accomplishing it?"

Preston stared at the officer. He showed a faint smile before walking away.

"Something just had to be done about the man. That's all I can possibly say on the matter."

Preston walked to his car, gets inside and leaves the neighborhood, going to the Agency Office.

CHAPTER 3

Preston arrived at the New Haven Marshal and Detective Agency. He walked into the front doors. Preston looked around and spotted everyone staring at him. Preston walked to the elevator and pressed the button. He stood waiting for the elevator door to open, so he can leave the lobby. One gentleman, wearing a grey suit walked by and looked at Preston. He does the same.

"Is there a problem, sir?" Preston said.

The gentleman turned his head and continued walking. Preston smiled as the elevator beeped and its door opened. He walked in and pressed the button for the third floor. The elevator door closed. He reached to the third floor and sees Eldon waiting for him in the head office. Preston walked toward the office as he passed by other detectives in their offices solving their own cases. Eldon sat behind his desk, surfing through the internet. He heard a knock on the door.

"Come on in, Preston."

Preston opened the door and walked in. "How did you know it was me that was walking through?"

"I can sense you from the elevator. Anyone can tell if you're in the building or not"

Preston smiled. "Funny. I'm sure you could. What did you need to talk to me about exactly?"

Eldon turned to Preston from the computer screen and looked at him with a gaze. Preston glanced his eyes a bit across the office.

"The reason why you're here Preston is because of the actions you took by killing Jonny Cartel. You know what you did was a big mistake?"

"Are you sure it was a mistake. Because from my point of view, the man had to be stopped one way or another."

"Well, this agency doesn't go by your point of view, it goes by its Chief's point of view. Meaning me."

"I got that well enough."

"So, because of your actions. With a lot of thought and right timing as well. I've decided that you need someone to watch what you're doing on these cases."

"Wait a minute. Just hold on a second. What exactly do you mean someone will be looking out for me? Are you implying a suggestion that I might have a partner?"

"Yes, Preston. That's exactly what I'm suggesting. Look, this is how I see it. You shot Jonny Cartel out in the open with no hesitation. So, if you were to come across someone with a similar history, you would do the same to them. If not worse."

"Of course, that's the way I do my job. Besides, Eldon, I already told you that it was self-defense. Cartel pulled out his weapon first, he also threatened to kill me. So, what else was I supposed to do."

"You could've called backup you know."

"Call backup?" Preston said. "It wasn't that big of a deal. We were the only two there after he commanded his guys to leave."

Eldon leaned back in his chair, rocking in it to relax himself and feel comfortable. "So, overall, what's the big problem about having a partner?"

"My last partner worked on both sides of the law and to make it even crazier, the guy was a snitch."

"A snitch you say. Good thing your new partner only works on one side of the law. Our side of the law and I'll also add that she's very good at what she does anyway."

"Wait. She?" Preston said with a raised voice.

"Well, of course, Preston. Your new partner is a she. There's not a problem is there?"

Eldon looked at the door and waved his hand, signaled someone to come in. The individual walked in and stood by the door, just a few inches from where Preston sat. He hasn't looked behind him yet to see his new partner.

"Preston, here's your new partner. In the flesh I should say."

"Preston smirked. "Really. Let me get a good look at her."

Preston turned and sees his new partner. He looked at her from head to toe. She had nice straight blonde hair that reached near her shoulders and she wore a pair of blue jeans with a white buttoned-down shirt and a brown leather jacket to go with it. Preston smiled at her. She showed no emotion toward him, but only gave him a significant stare. As if she had no trust in him of any measure. Preston turned back to Eldon, smirking.

"This beautiful young woman is Emily Weston. A fellow United States Marshal and Detective from Newark in the state of New Jersey."

Preston turned again. "It's a pleasure to meet you, Ms. Weston."

"Same here." Emily said. "You look different than what I've heard."

"Do tell what you've heard about me. I'm sure the tales were pleasant enough to share to everyone, meaning me, myself, and I."

"Just that your what they call an angry man whose hell bent on claiming justice and changing the ways of civilization as we know it. Using your gun as the holy grail."

Preston laughed as Eldon chucked a bit. Emily stayed quiet with only a face with no emotion of any kind. Preston stopped laughing and noticed Emily's face. Eldon gave one more chuckle before glancing at Emily.

Emily is in her late twenties and her confidence gave her the shine of a woman who stood independent, able to get the job done. She looked toward Eldon.

"I've heard quite enough information about the murders that occurred in the neighborhood last night. I was only wondering how the investigation is currently operating?"

"The investigation is currently ongoing." said Eldon. "But, since you asked about it, you and Preston can go to the neighborhood and asks some of the neighbors about anything unusual that occurred that night."

"That's interesting enough to hear."

Preston looked at them both with a grin. Thinking to himself if he should give some words toward them. As the words near his tongue, he decides otherwise not to speak them.

"Um, pardon me, Eldon, I was planning on going over to a location where I know some answers could be currently available."

"That's Great. Even a better idea I could add to that. Since you brought it up and you apparently want some company, why don't you go ahead and take Emily with you on this."

"She can't go with me on this one." Preston said while smiling. "Besides, she's a well-established novice here in New Haven and no offense to her, but, I don't play well with others when it comes to the law and my tasks."

Emily turned to Preston and stared him in the eyes like a predator inching for a bite toward its prey.

"I could say the same about myself. In Newark, I did most of my work alone and had some help in some cases. So, look Preston, unlike some of the women that you've come across and met in your days, I'm not one of them. Nor do I fit in their caliber in any way, shape, or form. I'm just a woman that gets the job done whenever I can, however I can. With or without your assistance."

"Really?" Preston said. "You're saying you're some type of new breed of female detective. I'm sure I could dig up something from your past back in Jersey that could shake you up a bit."

"Not exactly. You'll hardly find anything on me that could lead to your gloating habits."

Emily turned to Eldon and asked for the address to the murder location. Eldon gave her the file of the location. She walked out of the office. Preston stood up and watched as Emily walked to the elevator. She turned to Eldon. Eldon is smirking at Preston.

"Listen, just try to work with her Preston." Eldon said. "Just try, please."

"Sure thing, I'll try. But, I won't like it." Preston said.

Preston left the office as Eldon goes back to the computer, still smiling about Preston's attitude toward Emily. Preston is outside as Emily waited for him at his car. Preston slowly walked towards the car. He sees Emily standing by the passenger's seat. He pointed at her and the car.

"Mind if I ask where's your car?"

"I thought I'll ride with you if you don't mind me." Emily said. "Don't want to waste gas on mine. You should be alright with that I presume."

Preston looked with a glint and said, "You have a nice valid point there."

Preston took out the keys and unlocked the car. Emily sits on the passenger's side as Preston sits into the driver's seat. He started the car and they left the office, driving to the neighborhood.

"Though, I hope you're standing next to the car when I unlock it. So, that way I won't drive off without you and you can call on a cab to pick you up and drop you off."

As they drove down the streets, Emily turned and stared outside her window at all the locations around the area that they've passed by. Preston noticed and slightly turned toward her direction and watched her as she glanced the surrounding locations. Many vehicles are passing by as Preston entered onto the freeway. The number of passing and surrounding vehicles gives Emily a questioning though.

"Looking for something out there?" Preston asked. "You seem very on point looking at these places is all."

"No. I just never knew that New Haven was this crowded." Emily said. "Though it would be much smaller than what I'm currently seeing."

"We have our moments. Some days are good while the rest are bad. We get through it all. So, what brought you here to begin with?"

"Things became quiet around Newark, so I began looking for another location to work. Later, the agency began recruiting and some of the new detectives went to Newark and I was moved here."

"By the look on your face and the tone in your voice, you don't sound to happy about your transfer. Are you happy?"

"Honestly, I didn't expect to come here." Emily said. "I'm one of the best US Marshals in this country, so I believed they would send me to bigger places like New York, L.A., Miami, Las Vegas, Houston. Just somewhere big."

Preston smiled.

"Very soon, Ms. Weston, you'll realize that New Haven is

bigger than it looks to be."

Emily looked. "Can't wait for that."

Currently at the New Haven Airport is Billy Bronson, a scruffy, scrawny, slim man who's wearing a flannel shirt with jeans and a denim jacket, also wearing a baseball cap. He walked towards the tunnel, seeing a lot of passengers walking in and out. He stood at the tunnel, scouted the area looking for someone. He caught someone from a distance and started straining his eyes to get a better look.

"Please let that be him." Billy said.

He finally sees the individual he's come to pick up. Billy walked over to him.

"There's my guy!"

The individual is known as Hoyt Bennett, a man in his late thirties, whose slim with bold features and hair that looked as if it's never been washed or combed. He's also wearing a long-sleeved buttoned shirt with jeans and black dress shoes. Hoyt walked over to Billy, smiling.

"Well, isn't it the great Billy Bronson. We meet once again in this crazy nonstop lifetime of ours."

"Hoyt Bennett. How long has it been, pal?"

They shook hands as Hoyt hugged Billy and patted him on the back. Billy decided to do the same. Hoyt picked up his bags as they walked through the airport.

"How have things been in New Haven since my little departure?"

"You know how this place works. The same old situation with the same old people. Sometimes, even new folks that comes across these ways."

"Billy, I'll say this. It's time to get things going since I'm back in town."

"How so? What do you have planned already?"

"In short words, Billy, it's time to blow some shit up."

Hoyt continued to smile as he started walking toward the exit doors of the airport Billy slowly followed him outside. Shaking his head in uncertainly as to what's being planned in Hoyt's head.

CHAPTER 4

Preston and Emily arrived in the neighborhood. Preston parked the car in front of a blue and white wooden house that's across the street from the murder house. They exit out of the car and walked toward the front door, going up the short steps. Preston knocked on the door. They hear someone on the other side of the door.

"Who's there." said a voice from inside.

Emily said, "The US-" Immediately, Preston cuts her off from speaking to the individual on the other side of the door.

"The US Marshal and Detective Agency."

Preston said. "We were hoping you could speak with us about the murder that occurred across from your home."

The door opened and an African American male is on the other side. He allowed Preston and Emily inside of his home to discuss the murder.

"We would just like to-" Preston said, before Emily cuts him off and smiled toward him.

"We would like to only speak with you, sir. About the incident."

"Come in." the man said.

Preston and Emily walked into the neighbor's home as the door closed. Preston glared at Emily.

"How's it feel to be on the other end?" Emily asked.

Emily walked into the living room as Preston stared at her.

"She's learning." Preston said as he walks inside behind her.

In the countryside of New Haven, Coover and Rusty Bronson, the two older brothers of Billy Bronson sit inside their small home. They are sitting around the kitchen table, counting loads of cash. Coover sniffed the cash as Rusty continued counting.

"Why are you sniffing the money?" Rusty asked. "You know how many germs and possible diseases have touch and rubbed against those dollars."

"It's a sign of good fortune, brother." Coover said. "I wouldn't give two shit loads of coke to avoid the smell of a pack of paper."

"Now, Coover, you need to make sure that no one knows what we've currently have up our sleeves." Rusty said.

"What do you mean? What's up our sleeves?"

"The plans? You remember? The plans that we're supposed to follow courtesy of our boss?" Rusty said.

"Oh, yeah. I haven't forgotten that." Coover said. "Speaking of plans, you heard about that double homicide that happened in that neighborhood area?"

"Of course. What's the big fuss about it."

"It had to be fun you know. Killing those two bitches. A mother and a daughter. It's like a double birthday gift to me."

"Yeah. You have your ways with that distorted mind of yours, little brother. Hopefully, you won't have to put it to great use when a particular time comes along."

Rusty grabbed several stacks of money and started placing half of the money into a brown leather suitcase. Coover, on the other hand, started placing some of the money in his jacket pockets.

"You can keep doing what you're doing, Coover. We need to deliver the rest of this money to the boss?" Rusty said. "He wants it as soon as possible."

"You want to deliver it now?" Coover said. "While it's still in the early hours of the day."

"Why else would we wait. Because you're too lazy to get off your ass for a change to do a proper delivery."

"I got you, brother. Lazy my ass. I can get a large amount of jobs completed whenever the situation fits perfectly."

They get up from the table and started walking towards the

front door. They walk outside towards their grey F-250 truck. Rusty placed the suitcase in the back of the truck, covering it with a black sheet made of cloth. Coover opened the door and sat in the passenger's seat. Rusty walks to the side of the truck and gets into the truck and started driving down the pathway.

Back at the neighborhood, Preston and Emily continued speaking with the African American man about the double murders across the street. They are sitting in the living room. Preston and Emily on the blue couch and the neighbor sitting in a wooden chair.

Preston told the neighbor, "We're here on business, sir and because of that we would like to ask you if you've seen or heard anything about the murders that occurred last night across from you."

"Well, officer, I came home around 11:50 and went straight into bed." the Neighbor said. "Though, I did see a black van with two individuals. They were wearing black as well, from head to toe. They came from the back of the van."

"So, is that all you saw before you went to bed?" Emily asked.

"Yes ma'am. I thought they were just stopping by or playing a trick on someone. That's what it looked like to me."

"Another question, if I may." Preston said. "Did you catch the license plate on the back of the van?"

"No, sir. It was too dark for me to see." The neighbor said.

"Are you sure it was too dark, or you just didn't want to look?" Emily asked.

"Excuse me, but, are you assuming that I knew what they were up to?" The neighbor asked.

"No, I'm just assuming that you saw something unusual and you don't want us to know about it." Emily said.

"Sir, with all due respect, she's my new partner and she's new to the town." Preston said. "She hasn't learned much since being here for a short time, so, don't mind her."

Emily gave Preston a deep glare. He sat quietly and gave her a smile. She turned her attention towards the neighbor.

"I'll tell you this, officer. You should get rid of this bitch and find yourself a much more worthy partner." The neighbor said.

Emily gets up from the couch and stood over the neighbor. Preston also stood up and started tapping her on the shoulder to get her attention. Which, he does. Emily gave him another glaring look.

"What?" Emily asked him.

"Just sit back down. We're here on business." Preston said.

Emily continued to stare at Preston. He's silent as a beeping sound is heard. It's Preston's blackberry. He pulled it out of his jacket pocket and answered it. On the other side of the phone is Eldon.

"Maddox." Preston said.

"Preston, I need you and Emily to get back to the office as soon as you can." Eldon said. "We have more things to discuss."

"We'll be there." Preston said.

Preston hung up the phone and placed it back into his pocket. He looked over at the neighbor and told him that it was nice meeting him and thanked him for his cooperation. The neighbor thanked him back and they left the house and get into the car, heading back to the office.

"Where are we going?" Emily asked.

"Eldon needs us back at the office. Something's come up I suppose."

Meanwhile, at a local bar in town, Hoyt and Billy are sitting at the bar, drinking shots of whiskey. Hoyt drinks his and puts the glass down. Billy tried to drink his glass, but can't bear the taste of it. Hoyt watches him calmly as he tried drinking the glass of whiskey.

"I sense there's a problem, Billy?" Hoyt asked. "You can't take a shot of whiskey?"

"Sorry, Hoyt. It's just too strong for me." Billy said.

Hoyt looked toward the female bartender, he gets her attention and pointed to the bottle of vodka on the shelf. She grabbed the bottle and placed it in front of Hoyt.

"Please pour my good friend here a glass of this wonderful vodka you have here." Hoyt said to the bartender. "From our he's looking, he could surely use it right now."

"I'm not sure about that, Hoyt." Billy said. "Vodka isn't my type of drink."

The bartender poured the vodka into another glass and she handed it to Hoyt. He took the glass and turned to Billy. Billy glanced at him, then glanced at the glass. Hoyt smiled.

"You are a twenty-eight-year-old man that working for the local trucking company and now, your closest friend has finally made his return home. The best thing you could do right now is have a decent drink with him."

Billy looked at Hoyt and turned his attention toward the glass. He took the glass and held it up. Hoyt kept his smile as he watched Billy with the glass in hand.

"Hoyt, if it's for your hometown return and to have you here safe and sound, I guess I'll drink to that." Billy said as he drank the vodka from the glass.

Billy's facial expression changed after drinking the vodka and looked as if Billy smelled manure close to his nose after drinking. Hoyt looked at him and smirked. Hoyt's expression showed he became proud that his friend decided to have something like vodka to drink for a change. Hoyt is now happy and turned to the bartender.

"Dear sweetheart, another round, please" Hoyt said. "My friend and I are going to have some fun around here. This is what I'm talking about."

CHAPTER 5

At the city bank, Coover and Rusty parked, wearing all black with their faces covered with ski masks. Rusty gets out of the truck, while Coover stayed inside to watch the area. Rusty went ahead and walked into the bank. Once he entered the bank, seeing the people setting deposits and some even cashing their checks, Rusty started shouting in a high grumpy voice for everyone to get down. The people in the bank get down and hide under tables and around walls. Rusty is carrying a brown gym bag on his left side and a magnum gun in his right. He walks toward the counter and slams the bag onto the counter and points the gun at the banker.

"Alright, little smart boy. Start placing the money in the bag right now!" Rusty yelled. "Come on, you asshole, we don't have much time to spare with your slow packing speed."

The banker is highly afraid and started placing tons of money inside the bag. The people watched in fear. Another banker, whose hiding behind another counter, pulled out a shotgun. He placed the shotgun in gear and stood up, pointed it at Rusty. Rusty sees him and the shotgun goes off, Rusty ducked quickly to avoid the shot. Rusty ran over to the banker and shot him in the head as blood splattered across the golden-brown wall. The remaining civilians run out of the bank to avoid being shot themselves. Coover, still in the truck, sees the number of people running out of the bank. He used the door mirror to see if one of them could be Rusty.

Rusty is still inside the bank, collecting the remaining amount of money on the counter. He looked at the banker and asked him if he was done. The banker confirmed that he was finished as Rusty ran out of the bank, heading for the truck. People continue to be scattered around the entire interior and exterior of the bank. Rusty tossed the bag in the back of the truck. He turned and waved his hand toward Coover.

"Coover! Now's the time." Rusty yelled. "Load the damn thing, will you."

"Right away, brother."

He exited out of the truck, carrying a rocket launcher on his right shoulder. Coover slowly aimed the launcher toward the front of the bank and fired it. The rocket soared through the midair as it smashed itself into the bank, causing it to explode. Fire rises from the shot as they get back into the truck and drive off, leaving the bank in a sea of flames.

Preston and Emily arrived back to the agency. They walked toward Eldon's office and inside they noticed Eldon in the boardroom, speaking with a young man. The young man is wearing a red shirt with brown slacks. They walked into the boardroom and Eldon sees them.

"I see you've made it." Eldon said. "I take it there were no problems speaking with the witness."

"No problems there in that situation. So, you called. I guess there's a situation that we should know or something in that area?"

"A mighty situation. Mainly for you and your concern for New Haven. I thought you should know that your old friend is back in town." Eldon said.

"What old friend?"

"You remember that Bennett fellow, don't you?"

"Which one? The older brother or the younger brother?"

"Can't figure out which one. The two of you were friends at one point before both of you went on different paths in life."

Preston looked confused. "You mean Hoyt? Hoyt Bennett? The Hoyt that was sent to DC because of his previous actions in this town."

"Yes, apparently, Hoyt's back in town and he was last seen at the airport." Eldon said.

"What's the big deal with this Hoyt Bennett?" Emily said. "Terrible individual?"

"Hoyt is a highly-known criminal that has caused major chaos across this city. Apparently, he was caught and sent to prison in Washington D.C. But, now it seems that he's been released and he's back in town." Eldon said.

"After a while, me and Hoyt were great friends. Until I left for bigger things and he stayed and dove into obstacles that allowed himself to gain the attention of the law. After a series of events that featured banks, churches, and stores blowing up, he was arrested and sent to DC."

"So, there's no telling what he'll do next." Emily said.

"I'll visit the bar to check up." Preston told Eldon. "I have a feeling he'll be there."

"Ok. If you truly feel that's the case here."

Preston looked behind Eldon, seeing the young man. Preston pointed at him and looked toward Eldon. Eldon only glanced at Preston before centering his full attention toward him.

"While I'm at it, may I ask who's the young man over there? He looks like a kid. You're brining in kids now, Eldon?"

"He's not a kid. He's only in his early twenties. No big deal."

"Early twenties you say. To me, the boy looks like he's in his mid to late teens. You're sure you got the age correct?"

"I'm positive, Preston. Just don't bother the fellow."

Eldon turned and allowed the young man to walk forward. He walked with a sense of determination.

"Preston, Emily, this is Cody Aries. A young man who's highly trained in this field. He will be operating here from now on along with us in the agency."

"Highly trained you say?" said Preston.

"Yes sir, Marshal." Cody said toward Preston. "I'm a highly trained marksman and I've been training for years."

"Really. You're looking at the same here."

"I trained in sniper. Near and far distance from the target."

"That's an impressive feat. But, firing shots from afar is not my cup of Joe."

Emily walked forward and extended her hand to Cody. They shook hands and smiled toward one another. Emily welcomed him to the agency. Cody said it's a nice honor to meet the other marshals.

Eldon walked over to Preston as Emily and Cody spoke with one another.

"So, what were you and Emily doing before you came here?" Eldon said. "If I may have the privilege of asking the two of you."

"We visited the murder neighborhood and spoke with the neighbor who lived across the street from the home." Preston said. "He spoke to us and gave some information regarding the murder victims as well as the supposed murderers."

"Ok. Get any information?" Eldon said. "On who the culprits could be?"

"Not exactly. Though, he did mention a black van with two individuals wearing black. He couldn't see any faces sense they were wearing masks. I believe ski masks for certain."

"Did you get the license plate numbers?" Eldon said. "Did he see it?"

"No. He said it was too dark for him to see." Preston said. "Only saw silhouettes of the two culprits and light reflecting off the van they got into."

"We'll be on the lookout for any black vans with two individuals." Eldon said. "Especially if they fit the size descriptions that were given to us by other neighbors in the area that spotted them."

"Sure. Speaking of looking out, it my break time." Preston said. "So, if you don't mind me."

Preston left the boardroom as Emily and Cody continued speaking with one another. Eldon prepared to leave the boardroom, but Preston walked back in. Beginning to speak to Eldon.

"Oh, one more thing while I'm standing here."

"Ok, Preston. What is it?"

Preston looked at Emily and pointed toward her. She looked at him and so does Eldon.

"Not on me or any of my own thoughts. I'll just have to say you're going to have to do something with her. From my point of view in this field, she's a bad cause."

"I would say the same about you." Emily said. "No need of going over to Eldon to talk him into releasing me from the agency."

"Very well, Watson. It was nice meeting you, Cody."

Cody waved to Preston as he left the room. Emily looked over at Eldon. He shrugged his shoulders and left the room.

"Don't mind Preston. He loves to talk bad about others before they can get a word out about himself."

Hoyt and Billy are still at the bar, though it seems that Billy is drunk from the distorted look on his face. Hoyt smiled as he sees how happy Billy appears to be from drinking the amount of alcohol.

"Billy, how are you feeling right now?" Hoyt asked. "You look like you're feeling fine."

"Better than those murder victims from last night that's for damn sure."

The word *murder* caught Hoyt's derived attention. He wanted to hear more about the murder. So, he inched closer to Billy and turned toward him, beginning to ask more questions about more details involving the murders.

"What do you mean murders?"

"I forgot to tell you while we were leaving the airport. Probably couldn't talk about it there because the TSA and other officials would've arrested both of us as suspected terrorists. But, a mother and daughter were found murdered this morning. But, the murder occurred sometime around last night0. Possibly after midnight."

"May I ask how they were murdered? There had to have been some description on the bodies."

"You sure you want to know? Because it's very graphic in nature, the two bodies. I mean completely graphic. It could make your stomach turn circles."

"Just tell me how the bodies looked, Billy."

"Ok. Fine. The mother's head was severed completely from the body and the daughter was found contorted inside an operating dryer."

"Good lord. Do they know who the murderers are? Are there any traces toward them? Any significant features of any kind?"

"Not, not as of now." Billy said. "Though, though, that Marshal agency group now have a hot female detective on the case along with that Preston guy."

"Preston? Sounds familiar to me. What's this Preston guy's last name?"

"Um… *Maddrops, Maddcocks, Maddtops.* Something along that category. Not sure on what it actually was."

"Madd? Its *Maddox.*"

Billy turned and looked at Hoyt with a confused gaze. Billy shook his head as Hoyt only stared.

"Ok? Its Maddox. So, what's the big deal about this guy anyway? Is he a cold case or a no-good asshole?"

"The big deal about him, Billy, my good friend is I know Maddox very well. We have a large past with each other and since he's still here, I've just conjured up an idea that will shake the foundation of New Haven as we know it. It will cause Maddox to go insane."

"What is it, this idea of yours that will shake up the city and that Maddox fellow?"

"I'll tell you once we leave. We can't risk the chance of someone hearing what we're talking about in this place. There's no telling what could happen if someone were to hear it."

"Well, let's leave now and you can tell me in the truck. If that's how you really feel about this situation."

Hoyt stood up from the barstool and handed the bartender a one-ounce silver eagle. She took it and looked at Hoyt.

"May I ask what this is?"

"Just a little something to remember me by sweetheart."

Hoyt blew her a kiss and gave her a wink. She smiled and walked to the back. Hoyt and Billy left the bar.

Back in the countryside of town, Coover and Rusty are at their home. They counted the money that was stolen from the bank. The money was scattered across a wooden table with a couple of dollars falling on the floor. Coover looked at Rusty with a concerned look. Rusty looked at Coover. "What's the look for?"

"Are we giving all the money to the boss?" Coover said. "Because, I would like to keep some it to buy someone equipment for our projects."

"No." Rusty said. "There's no way I'm doing that. The money in the suitcase will go to him. The money from the bank belongs to us."

"Good. That's good." Coover said. "Oh, you have any possible idea where "Little bro" might be?"

"He's probably handling something for mama." Rusty said. "She loved him the most you know."

"Yeah, she really cared a lot for him." Coover said. "What does that say about the two of us."

A knock on the door is heard and Coover goes to answer it. He opened the door and it's their boss, Ray Colby, a crime lord originally from New Jersey, wearing his black suit with a red shirt. Rusty comes from the kitchen to greet him.

"Mr. Colby, sir." Rusty said. "We didn't expect you to be here."

"I'm here for my money." Colby said. "Now, do you have it for me?"

"Yes sir, we do." Rusty said.

Rusty walked toward the kitchen and rolls out the suitcase. He opened the case for Colby, revealed to him the money inside. Colby smiled and looked at the two brothers. He patted them on their shoulders as he stood up and walked toward the front door.

"You boys are doing a fine job." Colby said. "Don't let that go to your heads or you won't be having a job."

"We try our best, boss." Coover said.

"Sure, you do." Colby said as he left their home.

CHAPTER 6

Hoyt and Billy are sitting on the outskirts of town inside of a small cabin-like house surrounding by a few trees that stood up in the backyard. The front yard is covered with small bushes and short grass. Inside the house are mounted heads of deer on the walls and stuffed bears in the corners. Billy looked at the surroundings and turned to Hoyt.

"Hoyt, what's in this place if I may ask you?"

"This place, my good friend, was one of my old hideouts we had to keep ourselves from the law in any circumstance. It's just a little something I left behind before they were carried off to D.C. Fun times this place was."

"From the look of this place, it damn sure looks as if some rough-ass hunter appeared to be living in here. No offense, Hoyt, but, you're not exactly a hunter."

"I haven't hunted in quite a long time. Though, this cabin here, it belonged to my brother Darren. I guess you could consider him a rough-ass hunter. Seeing as he was always the one going out and catch us some deer, fish, elk. Hell, even one time, he brought home a total of eight squirrels for us to eat since he couldn't find any deer to track."

"Sounds like a good brother to me."

"Speaking of him, how's he been with me being absent and such?"

"From what I understand, he's still working in the mechanic areas across town. Stays to himself as usual."

"That is my brother's way of living a peaceful life. I rather not bother him in such a time we're in."

Hoyt walked toward the kitchen area, where he noticed a small closet. He walked to the closet and pulled out a key. Billy walked around the home, looking at its details left and right. Billy walked over to where Hoyt was located.

"So, the law couldn't find you here? In this little shack."

"No, they could not. The damn officials couldn't even find a trace that lead here."

They later hear a knock on the door. Before they could turn around to see who it was, they suddenly hear a voice coming from the door.

"It seems that streak has come to an end." The voice said. "If you catch that kind of clear understanding."

Hoyt and Billy turn around, seeing Preston standing in the doorway. Hoyt looked and started smirking. Billy started to shiver as if he's afraid of Preston, due to him being a US Marshal and a homicide detective.

"Of all the people who are involved with law enforcement, there would be only one of them that could possibly find me. It's been a long time hasn't it, Preston? How come you didn't show up at the airport for my arrival or should I say, my comeback to the city?"

"Didn't know you were returning to New Haven. Could care less if you didn't."

"Funny sense of humor. You should've checked your calendar, my dear friend if you really wanted to know when it was taking place. I assumed someone like you should've had the knowledge that I would return to the city that made me famous. Due to my past experiences."

"I knew you would. Just didn't think you'll be back this soon." Preston said. "So, why is it that they let you out of prison so early? Good behavior? Good assistance with the mop up crew?"

"I did my time and they released me in the right manner." Hoyt said. "Though, it did influence me of what to do with my life once I returned to the rightful place that I call home."

"The rightful place you call home? Interesting question I have and will love to ask at this peculiar time. How did your time behind bars influence you to be more of a smart-ass rather than a dumb-ass? I figured that someone who was locked up for quite a long time would have better thinking skills rather that going back into your history to what sent you into your rightful home called a prison."

Hoyt laughed as he continued the conversation by saying, "A smart-ass. Though, that's what I am, but, I thought that I could help out with the double homicide that occurred in that neighborhood last night."

"Who told you about that?" Preston asked. "I take it you've already been around the city."

"Oh, Billy here, told me about the situation."

Preston looked over to Billy and pointed at him and looked back to Hoyt. Preston turned back to Billy. Preston smiled as Billy continued to be in fear of him.

"Billy? As in Billy Bronson? Of the Bronson Brothers?"

"Yes sir, fellow Marshal detective or whatever you're supposed to be in the law enforcement. That is who I am." Billy said with a tremble in his voice.

Preston turned back to Hoyt, who said, "He told me about it while we were having a drink at the bar earlier."

"So, that explains the smell of vodka on your breath." Preston said. "I knew you were up to something. You and alcohol don't mix very well, Hoyt."

"Neither, do you and I." Hoyt said. "Though, we were friends long ago, that is until you went off to college and I just stayed here and became a crime lord."

"And after that you were caught and sent to prison in D.C." Preston said. "Yeah, we all get the back-story here."

"Yeah, we all do." Hoyt said. "But, it would seem you're here only because you have me as a suspect involving the murder case. Otherwise, why would you be here."

"I'll put it to you this way, Hoyt." Preston said. "If I find out that you had anything to do with the double homicides or you have any information regarding them, you my friend, will be in some deep shit."

Hoyt laughed and said, "Wow, still using those same old lines from high school, I see."

"Yeah, they still come in use." Preston said.

Hoyt walked back into the kitchen, going back to the closet. He looked back at Preston.

"Now, if you'll excuse us, we have some business to conduct. So, if you please leave."

Preston smiled as he walked toward the door. He opened the door and put one foot out before telling Hoyt it was nice seeing him. Hoyt said the same to Preston as he left the home. Hoyt pulled out the key once again and finally opened the closet. Billy stands behind him, watching as Hoyt pulls out a large black leather box, roughly thirty-six to forty inches.

"Whoa. What's in that box, Hoyt?"

"The solution to our new cause. Wait till you see what's in here."

Hoyt opened the box and he sees what's inside. He began to smile as Billy walked over and looked at what's lying inside of the box. Billy turned to Hoyt in shock as he asked him, "Hey, Hoyt. Is that what I think it is?"

Hoyt pulled out the object that's laying inside the box and holds it up in his hands. Billy starts backing up to avoid being hit by the object.

"Billy, it's time that we blow some shit up." Hoyt said as he looked down at his hands, revealing a grenade launcher. Hoyt looked up toward Billy and released a great smile.

CHAPTER 7

It is now within the evening across New Haven as Preston headed out to eat at a seafood restaurant. He walked in and went up to the counter, where a waitress was waiting. He scouted the restaurant himself to find a perfect table for himself. He smiled at the waitress.

"How many, sir?" the Waitress said.

"Just one, ma'am." Preston said.

The waitress walked Preston to his table, and he gets a glass of water and orders a Shrimp Alfredo Pasta with a salad. The waitress left the table and Preston looked around the restaurant. Seeing lots of people eating in the restaurant and talking with each other, he spotted someone in the distance. He sees a woman that looks highly familiar to him and he realized that it's his ex-wife, Karen Rogers. She turned and saw him, to which he waved at her and she done the same. Preston turned again and saw his ex-wife coming toward him.

"Karen?" Preston said.

"Hi, Preston." Karen said. "It's good to see you once again."

"Same here." Preston said. "Good to see you as well."

"So, how's life been treating you?" Karen said.

"You know, good days and bad days always come and go." Preston said. "How about you and your life so far?"

"Things have been going quite well for me and my husband."

"Hopefully its going well."

Preston looked behind Karen and saw a man approaching them, wearing a smooth grey suit with black tie. He rubbed his hand over his head as he walked toward them and looked as if he knew one of them. Karen turned and noticed him. She called him over to the table. He stopped at the table, smiling as he placed his arm around Karen's shoulders. Preston looked at him.

"From the arm trick, I take it you're the husband that she just mentioned?"

"I'm Richard, Richard Rogers." he said. "You look a little familiar. Have we met at some place?"

"Not that I can think of at the top of a hat."

"This is my husband, Preston." Karen said. "Just wanted you two to finally meet one another."

"I understand. It truly is an honor to finally meet you, honestly. So, what is your occupation exactly. If you don't mind me asking. Just curious is all."

"I run a car dealership. It keeps me in the excitement mood. One day I'll own my own dealership and potentially a car manufacturing business."

"He just loves cars. He's told me how he wants to start a vintage car collection, but, doesn't have enough of the money to afford it. Though, he's getting there. Hopefully, he'll have his collection and be proud of what he's done."

"Well, hopefully, it finds a way to get there and collect all the vehicles he wishes for."

Preston looked at Richard and introduced himself to him and they shook hands. Richard tells Karen that they have to go, to which Karen said bye to Preston, he does the same as he watched them leave the restaurant.

At a 7-Eleven, Emily stopped at a gas station, refilling the gas in her white Lincoln. Once she finished pumping the gas, she walked into the station and paid the cashier. The cashier noticed Emily's badge on the side of her hip. He glanced at her before she turned toward him.

"Something wrong?" She said.

"No ma'am. I was just looking at your badge right there. So, I take it you're a cop or something?"

"US Marshal and a homicide detective."

"Two occupations with different circumstances and outcomes. Marshals are in the big leagues compared to homicide detectives."

"I suppose you could say it that way."

She paid off the gas, nodded to the cashier and walked out of the station. As she walked back to her car, she noticed a black van parked in a shadowed area across from the gas station. She entered the car and sat for a few seconds. Trying to see if anyone will come out of the van. Though, no one did as the van stayed still and she drove off the station grounds.

During the night, Coover and Rusty arrived at a warehouse in the outskirts of New Haven. They walked inside and see four sets of steel tables merged into one with over a dozen men in suits inside.

The men sitting down at the tables are crime lords and the men standing behind them are their thugs, carrying AKs and shotguns. Rusty looked around the warehouse.

"Have any of you seen Colby around here?"

"I'm right here." said Colby walking toward them from the back entrance of the warehouse.

"Colby, we need to speak with you." Rusty said.

"About what?" Colby said. "Is it something involving the money?"

"Yes sir." Coover said. "We just need to have a word with you."

Colby walked toward the end of the table and sits. He told Coover and Rusty to sit as well. They find their sets of chairs and sit as well. The other crime lords stared at them, as if why should they be here. Rusty glared at each of them and turned his attention toward Colby.

"Me and my brother here, boss, are just wondering about our extra share with your upcoming event." Rusty said. "We're just curious about the situation is all."

"The upcoming event will be announced soon." Colby said. "As for now, you two should be concerning yourselves with the Marshals. Since, they'll discover it was the two of you, who committed those murders."

Coover stood up, staring at Colby, "What do you mean the Marshals?! They've already got some suspects in line and we aren't any of them."

"Sure, you aren't, Coover." Colby said. "But, I do believe that you will be soon enough. Just make one mistake and they'll find you."

"I'm sure you heard that Hoyt Bennett is back in town." Rusty said.

"Hoyt Bennett has finally returned, so you say." Colby said. "Well, this is great. He can be a major asset in my event. That is unless he backs out somehow."

"What do you want us to do?" Rusty asked. "Find him and bring him in for you?"

"Or we could just kill him for you." Coover said. "Which ever one you prefer, boss."

"No need for that in this situation. Just concern yourselves about your own business this time around." Colby said. "I'll deal with Hoyt Bennett."

Coover and Rusty left the warehouse as Colby began speaking with the other crime lords in the room. His assistant closed the main door into the office area, other assistants closed the entire warehouse.

Preston headed back to his apartment during the late night. He gets there and realized that the door is unlocked. From his point of view, someone unlocked the door and went in. He pulled out his handgun and kicked in the door. He looked to his left and saw a woman sitting at his table. She is Italian, has beautiful black hair and seductive green eyes. She slowly drinks from a glass of wine from Preston's pantry.

"Carla." Preston said. "What the hell are you doing in my apartment?"

"Hello, Preston." Carla said. "It's been a very long time."

"Yes, it has." Preston said. "Again, what are you doing in my apartment? I don't recall handing you a key."

"Sit down and I will tell you how I came into entering your apartment."

Preston sat at the table and stared at Carla Garcia, his ex-girlfriend of six years. She stared at him as she continued drinking the wine. Preston only stared at her as she drank. Thinning to himself of why she's currently in his apartment.

"I told the complex owner that I lived in this apartment and forgot the key. So, he gave me one and that's how I ended up in your apartment. Funny stuff, huh."

"I don't find anything funny about someone receiving a key to an apartment that they don't live in or pay the bill for."

"You seem surprised, Preston." Carla said. "I kind of figured you would be. Seeing me here and all."

"What exactly did you think how I would react seeing you here." Preston said. "I wasn't expecting you, at all. Especially inside my apartment to which were you do not reside."

"You know I've always done unexpected things." Carla said. "You should remember all those times."

"I do remember those times." Preston said. "But, you would've learned not to do those things after the times. One of these days, it will get you killed."

"I'm sure I would survive it, if you were still by my side." Carla said. "Are you still on my side?"

Preston leaned in. "What exactly are you doing here, Carla?"

"Excuse me, is that the way to say hello, I'm only here to surprise you." Carla said. "Figured you would love this surprise."

Carla took out another glass and poured wine inside. She passed it to Preston, who took a sip out of the glass. As if a glass of wine would pull him out of concentration.

"How would you coming here, not surprise me." Preston said smiling. "As I told you, I don't recall you living here."

"Oh, I almost forgot. I did hear about the incident that occurred between you and Jonny Cartel and the double homicide." Carla said. "It's flowing all around the city. You're not too far from being considered a fugitive with all this on your record."

"I did what needed to be done." Preston said. "I gave him a warning and he didn't take it. So, I had to put him down. Besides, Cartel was a fugitive in his own right of action."

"Now, that's something I wouldn't expect from you, Preston."

123

Carla said. "One day, it will come to pass that you'll be on the other side of the chase."

"I take it you never got to understand me very well, Carla." Preston said. "As a matter of fact, you've never known me very well."

"Oh, is that so." Carla said smiling. "Let me remind you of how you taught me some of your detective skills and some of your tricks. That was really our relationship. You're giving me free lessons on how to do the things of the law."

Preston smiled, "So, you're going to try to use my tricks against me? Is that the real reason why you're here? Some sort of information, you're trying to gain from me?"

"Not exactly, baby." Carla said. "Though, I can tell you that I plan to use them to my advantage when the right situation arises."

"Really." Preston said as he put his glass down on the table. "Because, I remember you always having to use your looks to your advantage to gain whatever you wanted."

"Which is why you're going to teach me the rest of your techniques." Carla said. "I believe I'll need them for whatever comes my way in the near future."

Preston stared at Carla as she does the same. Preston smiled and said, "I don't think so."

Carla put down her glass and gets up from the chair. Preston looked her, as she's wearing all red. She walked behind him and started massaging his shoulders. Preston doesn't do anything, though he's facial expressions shows that he's not liking it. She started rubbing him on his chest. He turned and looked at her.

"You know this isn't going to work." Preston said. "Don't even think it will in your little warped mind."

"Aw, it worked before remember." Carla said. "It worked all the time to be exact."

Carla sat on Preston's lap and begins kissing him. He starts kissing her back and he holds her in his arms tightly and lays her onto his bed. They continue kissing and go to the point of taking each other's clothes off. Now, they are only in their underwear as they continue kissing and she moans as Preston rubs his hand up Carla's thigh. They are both enjoying this moment as they continue to do so.

Then, they go under the bed sheets.

Driving a small pickup truck is Hoyt with Billy in the passenger's seat. They drove toward a small building, appeared to be made of brick. it's a jailhouse. Hoyt stopped the truck and looked around the area. Billy stayed inside and began to worry. He looked over at Hoyt and said, "Why here? Why this place?"

"Billy, this is a small jailhouse, where only the minors are concerned to go." Hoyt said. "I figure its best just to put them out of their misery."

Hoyt gets out of the truck and walked toward the back. Hoyt opened the black box from the back and pulled out the grenade launcher. He walked in front of the truck and pointed the launcher towards the jailhouse. Billy noticed a small group of guards at the front door.

"Hoyt, you can't be serious about this!" Billy said. "Hoyt?!"

"These are the moments that create legends, Billy." Hoyt said. "Now, we will become the legends ourselves."

One of the guards noticed Hoyt and pointed at him. Hoyt aimed the launcher and yelled, "INCOMING CALL!" and fired the launcher. The grenade flew into a window and exploded the entire jailhouse. The guards inside are killed by falling debris and the building is up in flames, instantly killing anyone who was inside. Hoyt smiled.

"Hoyt, let's go!" Billy yelled. "Come on, Hoyt!"

"Step one, accomplished." Hoyt said.

Hoyt placed the launcher in the back of the truck and drove away from the scene as the jailhouse is consumed in flames. Hoyt laughed and smiled as he drove away from the area.

CHAPTER 8

Preston woke up from the night he didn't expect. He looked around and noticed that Carla is gone. He put on his clothes and searched the room and found his notes stolen. He knew that Carla took the notes from his room. The notes contained most of Preston's skills and tricks that he's used and currently using in his field of work.

"Shit." Preston said. "Goddamn. Shit."

He grabbed his keys and left for the office.

At another location, inside a mobile home, Billy sat still until he heard a knock at the door. He opened the door and its Hoyt. Hoyt walked in to discuss the recent attack on the jailhouse. Billy is still shaken up by the event and Hoyt tries to discuss the reason for blowing up the jailhouse.

"Hoyt, I just don't understand why that location." Billy said. "Of all locations that could've been chosen."

"Look, I know that it must've freaked you out from the start." Hoyt said. But, from watching that, just imagine what else we can accomplish together. By doing this, we can set boundaries across New Haven and later beyond Connecticut itself."

"I see your point there, but, I don't think I can continue going on like this." Billy said. "Who knows what could happen next. I could be arrested or even shot at."

Hoyt looked at him, "What do you mean, Billy? You're in the business of a lifetime. For God's sake, in this line of work, you get arrested, you get shot, you get stabbed. Hell, in some occasions, you get raped, molested and mutilated. Now, we don't need to deal with your feelings and emotions on this line of work."

"I'm just saying that it's difficult for me to do these things when the Marshal guy knows who I am, and I can't imagine what could happen next." Billy said. "I could go to jail or worse."

"You shouldn't worry about my old friend, Preston." Hoyt said. "That's his instinct to search and find, from all angles. It's in his blood, but, he will never get the opportunity to catch you. That is if you're on my side."

"I'm always on your side, Hoyt." Billy said. "Always."

Hoyt smiled, "That's good to know, because I'll need you for our next task at hand."

"Which is what?" Billy asked.

"I hear from a few anonymous sources that Colby and his crime lord buddies of New Haven gather together at a warehouse on the outskirts of town."

"So, how do we find the warehouse?" Billy asked. "If that's where they are exactly?"

"I already know the warehouse's location. I used to work in there." Hoyt said. "It was once used for a trucking company, until the company closed it down and moved over to China. Now, it's the place where all drug lords hang out and talk amongst each other. The perfect opportunity to get rid of the garbage that fills this city with disgust and hatred amongst its people."

"So, when do we strike and are we using the grenade launcher again?" Billy asked.

"We will be using a launcher alright." Hoyt said smiling. "We strike within the next two days. When the building is packed."

Preston walked into the office and sees Eldon, Emily, and Cody inside of his office. He walked toward the door and went inside.

"Preston, good to see you here up and early." Eldon said. "From the look of your face and body language, you look like you have a rough night."

"Kind of." Preston said. "It was a little rough and edgy for me. What's the situation today?"

"A city bank was robbed and blown to shit yesterday." Eldon said. "Later that night, a jailhouse was blown up. So, we will be going to these two locations today to get evidence and information. We'll go ahead and start with the bank first."

"Alright. Are there any suspects involved with these cases?" Preston asked. "Or am I jumping the front gun here."

"You're jumping the gun here. Though we have no ideas right now." Eldon said. "But, there is a banker who's waiting for us at the bank scene. He could give us answers."

Preston looked. "Great, I'll meet you guys there and we'll discuss everything on the sites."

They left the office and head to their cars. Preston noticed Emily's white Lincoln. She looked at him and he smiled. Cody gets into the jeep with Eldon. They all drove down the street, making a left turn towards the City Bank. Few minutes later, they arrived at the bank scene, looked at the building covered with a black charcoal appearance. They get out of their vehicles and started walking toward the bank. Eldon looked around for Preston, yet, he's nowhere to be seen.

"Where's Preston?" Eldon said.

"He's probably running late to the sites as usual." Emily said. "As always from what I hear in the office."

Cody looked to his left and saw Preston's car heading their direction. He pointed him out.

"Preston's right there." Cody said. "I think so. That's his car isn't it."

Preston arrived at the scene and noticed Eldon and Emily staring at him. He smiled at both of them as he exited out of his car. He looked again at Emily's white Lincoln. She turned to him.

"A white Lincoln, nice." Preston said. "Surprised you had the profit to purchase one."

"It gets me around." Emily said. "And I save my money unlike others who spend it on things they don't need."

"Still, it's a very nice car." Preston said. "Though, it isn't black like mine."

Eldon turned to Preston. Shook his head as Preston only grinned slightly.

128

"Preston. Don't start any of this bullshit while we're here on business, please. Now let's get this going on this job."

Eldon walked around the bank's locations. Cody and Emily followed him. Preston stood and smirked before he started looking around the area. They noticed all the damage caused from the explosion. Burnt brick walls, windows blown out with huge holes on circling the entire bank. Preston continued looking around the bank for clues. They were not allowed to enter the bank, due to being cleaned out by other officials across New Haven. Cody recognized the damage and approached Eldon.

"From the look of the building, only a high-powered weapon could've caused this much damage." Cody said.

"What are you getting at, Cody?" Eldon asked. "You believe that a larger weapon was used on this place?"

"Some kind of launcher, perhaps." Cody said. "From what I can tell."

Emily walked over to Eldon. "A grenade launcher? Are you sure?"

"No, he's not sure." Preston said. "It was a rocket launcher."

Eldon walked over to Preston, who's standing next to a strap on the ground with a cap. Eldon smiled and turned to Preston.

"Excellent work, Preston." Eldon said. "I have to say I'm impressed by just little work you did finding this."

"Well, you know, I just try my best." Preston said. "Besides, it was just lying there. So, it was in my inclination to point it out for you."

Eldon walked over to Cody and he followed. Eldon told Cody to put the strap into the evidence bag for further investigation and fingerprint analysis. Cody took the strap and placed it inside the bag and walked toward the jeep. Preston turned to Emily.

"I believe it's your turn now."

"Chief, what's that over there?" Emily asked.

"Well, what is it." Eldon said. "I need some description of what's your seeing."

Emily walked over to the area and discovered a wallet. She opened the wallet and noticed it belonged to a banker who worked at the bank who possibly ran out with the civilians during the robbery. Emily waved her hand toward Cody, signaling him to come over to her.

"It's a wallet." Emily said. "Appears it belonged to one of the bankers who worked here. We could check his address and phone to see if he's still alive or dead."

"Let me have a look at it." Eldon said.

Preston walked over to them, "A wallet? You sure it isn't just a notepad or something less important?"

Eldon opened the wallet and finds the information on its owner. He smiled and turned to Emily.

"Great work, Emily." Eldon said. "Impressive work you guys are doing. It must be my lucky day."

He handed the wallet to Cody, who put it inside a plastic bag and walked to the jeep with Eldon. Emily smiled and turned to Preston, who glared at her.

"What?" Preston asked. "You've come to gloat now?"

"No." Emily said. "I'm just telling you to try a little harder if you want to impress me."

Eldon and Cody get back into the jeep as Eldon told Preston and Emily that they're heading toward the jailhouse next. They left as Emily and Preston leave.

Across the street, in a neighborhood, a burgundy Nissan. Inside are two men, one Caucasian and the other of African descent. They are wearing nice suits and ties. They sit inside the Nissan as they watched Preston and Emily leave the bank scene. The Caucasian looked at the African.

"So, what are we waiting for?" The Caucasian said. "Let's just go over there and blow them all to smithereens and be done with the job."

"As much as I would love to, we can't do that. We have to wait on Ray's word."

"I don't know about you, man. But, I'm starting to wonder if Ray has no idea what he's putting his men through. Just think about it, while we're here, watching the area, the Detective Agency have those two Marshals snooping around."

"What's your point, man?" The African asked. "You don't like what Ray has planned for them?"

"What he has planned seems to be just good and dandy. But, just think about it for a second. One of those marshals is the female from Jersey. You've heard what the guys have said about her. Telling us she's very skilled in marksmanship." the Caucasian said. "The other is that "Instincts" guy who shot Jonny Cartel not too long ago and has already cost us a lot of profit."

"You're speaking of Emily Weston and Preston Maddox. What about them makes it important for us to kill them right now?"

"I just think that Ray should look closer into this." the Caucasian said. "Just to keep a heads up on it before they come busting down his doors and taking us all to prison."

"I'll have a talk with Ray about it and see what he says." the African said. "I'll also ask him about the two marshals. From my time working with him, I know for a fact if he knows the female Marshal."

"Really. Never knew that."

"They have a long history with one another. They were the two most known people in the law area. Whenever someone talked about the law, they were both mentioned."

"That's what I'm talking about. Seems like we should be the ones to end that long feud."

"We'll wait on Ray's word to see if that will be the case."

Coover and Rusty sit inside a diner where they are having a meeting with Ray. He walked in and they sit at the table. Ray is accompanied with two bodyguards, one on his left and another on his right. He sat at the table as the bodyguards stood, guarding the area. Ray looked at Coover and Rusty.

"Glad you could make it, boys." Ray said. "It's nice to see you. So, how's everyone in your neck of the woods?"

"They're doing fine." Coover said. "Everyone's minding their own business. They have no clue to what's going on."

"No problems there, boss." Rusty said. "So, what's the situation you have for us at hand?"

"I heard about the jailhouse that was blown to pieces last night and I also heard from a reliable source that your brother, Billy was there with Hoyt Bennett."

"Seriously." Coover said. "Little young' Billy's teaming up with Hoyt now?"

"According to my knowledge, seems so." Ray said. "So, I'll let the two of you speak with your brother and find a way to tell him that he's on the wrong side of this chess board."

"We'll talk with him, boss." Rusty said. "We will. You have no worries there."

"I hope so, Rusty." Ray said. "Because, I don't want to have to kill him and later have your mother on my trails. I know for a fact what she would do if any of her sons were killed."

"You don't have to worry about our mother." Rusty said. "Once we speak with Billy and tell him about the means, he'll join our side and leave Hoyt to die alone."

"That's great to hear." Ray said. "Well, nice meeting you here."

Ray commanded his guards to leave behind him as Coover and Rusty sat at the table, plotting an idea to pull Billy away from Hoyt. They watch as Ray leaves the diner and they leave as well. Coover leaves with a mug of coffee for some odd reason.

Preston, Emily, Eldon, and Cody arrived at the jailhouse scene and see that's it much more damaged than the bank. Half of the building had completely been turned to rubble with debris covering the ground around it. Other officials are at the scene as well, including United States Marshal Darius Conway, an African-American man. Eldon walked over to him and they shake hands.

"It's good to see you again, Conway." Eldon said. "It's been a long time since you've come across the office."

"Yes sir. It has." Darius said. "Been on some business across the country and now I'm back to work here."

"So, what's the incident here?" Eldon asked. "Any leads you've gathered?"

"Well, according to one witness, they saw a truck drive up and stop in the street." Darius said. "Two men were inside, one of them got out of the truck and went to the back and pulled out a grenade launcher. He pointed it toward the building and blew the jailhouse up, killing everyone inside and the guards up front."

"Any suspects so far?" Eldon asked. "Anyone who seen the shooter and his companion?"

"None have come up yet." Darius said. "But, according to the witness I spoke with, the shooter yelled out, "Incoming Call" before he fired the launcher. So, I hope we'll receive some news very soon."

Preston looked around the area and walked over toward Eldon and Darius. Preston told Darius to excuse him and Eldon, so he could ask him about the scene.

"So, what did Darius tell you about the incident?" Preston asked.

"It seems that a grenade launcher was the cause of this." Eldon said.

"A grenade launcher?" Preston asked. "You can tell what was used on this place just by looking at it?"

"It appears so due to the amount of debris that's here." Eldon said. "First, the bank gets blown up by a rocket launcher. Now, a jailhouse is blown up by a grenade launcher. It seems that this is being done by the same individuals."

"No, not the same." Preston said. "Two different groups of individuals."

"Also, according to the witness, the shooter yelled out "*Incoming Call*" before firing." Eldon said. "You know anyone who's ever heard anyone yell that phrase out before?"

"I have." Preston said. "I have an idea who could've done this. The bank is another story."

Preston walked toward his car. Eldon looked at him and asked him where's he going. Preston told him that he's going to visit and old friend. Preston gets into his car and drove off. Emily and Cody walked toward Eldon and asked him where Preston's going. Eldon told them that's he going on break.

CHAPTER 9

Coover and Rusty drove to Billy's mobile home. They walked to the front door and knocked. The door opened and its Billy. He is surprised to see his two older brothers. He welcomed them inside. As they are inside, they notice that Hoyt is in there as well. Rusty turned to Billy.

"Billy, what's this dick doing in here?!" Rusty asked.

"I have a dick, but I'm not one." Hoyt said. "Rusty, you should ask yourself that same question. Before someone throws it back to you"

"Shut your damn mouth, Bennett." Coover said. "We already know about your deals with our brother here and we're here to tell him to turn a new leaf. Get him away from your crazy ass."

"Calling people names doesn't get you into any places anymore, Coover. So, how would the two of you have a way of taking Billy from my what I had offered him?" Hoyt asked. "You have something better in mind that what I'm offering at the moment?"

"We work for Ray Colby." Rusty said. "You remember him, don't you? The man that put you out of business after you were sent to DC."

"I surely do." Hoyt said. "The big, tall black son of a bitch that took over most of the work in this city."

"Well, how does it feel to have the knowledge of all your former employees working for him now?" Coover asked. "They left your ass high and dry and now they're working for the big man now in the big leagues."

"Overall, it feels quite refreshing, actually." Hoyt said. "Takes weight off of my shoulders from those lazy bums."

"Well, you'll have to release our brother here, since, he's coming with us to join Ray's alliance." Rusty said. "If you don't mind."

Hoyt stood up and looked in the eyes of both Coover and Rusty. Billy sat at the counter and just watched. Coover and Rusty stared a hole through Hoyt as he just gave them a grin.

"Billy, you're leaving with us." Rusty said. "So, get off your ass and come with us."

"You heard him, Billy." Hoyt said. "Go ahead and follow your worthless brothers out of the door and ruined your chance at a better life."

Billy's jaw dropped. He didn't make a move. Not even a flinch as he was stuck between a hard place at the wrong time.

"What! Are you serious, Hoyt?!"

"Indeed I am." Hoyt said. "Go on, now."

Billy stood up from behind the counter and started walking toward his brothers. But, Hoyt held him back and pulled out a magnum. Coover and Rusty begin to back off as they watch Hoyt's hand on the gun. Billy turned to Hoyt and back to his brothers.

"You really believed I would let your brother ruin his life for the sake of tagging along with his shitty brothers. I don't think so. Billy's got a bright future with me on his side."

"Billy, if you don't leave with us, you're on your own." Rusty said. "You hear me. You're on your own if you stay with this piece of trailer park shit."

"Are you coming with us, brother?" Coover asked. "Be with your family and live big."

Billy stayed quiet and finally spoke his answer., "I'm staying on Hoyt's side. We'll take over this city with or without your help."

"Goddamn it. Fine." Rusty yelled. "But, when mother finds out about your death in the paper, you'll realize what big of a mistake you've just made."

They leave the mobile home and Billy turned to Hoyt, who's still grinning, looked at Billy and said that this city will be theirs, but, they must get rid of Ray first.

Preston drove back to the hideout, continuing his constant search for Hoyt, a moment passed by that he realized Hoyt couldn't be inside. Once Preston pushed the door opened, Hoyt and Billy were nowhere in the hideout. Preston rubbed his head as he glanced around the front.

"Damn it." Preston said. "Where would you be right now, Hoyt?"

He gets into his car and headed for another location. One he believes Hoyt could surely be. Preston decided that it's getting late and he drove back toward his apartment. Preston's cell phone ringed. He answered it.

"Hello."

"It's Eldon. We just got something on our plate and I'll like you to do the job."

"What's the job if I may ask you?"

"We need to deliver around twenty-five thousand dollars to a man named Joel Green. He lives in the suburb area."

"I'll come over to the office after I pay a visit to Hoyt's apartment."

"Very well, Preston. Just make it quick."

"I will. No need to worry there."

Preston hanged up the phone and sat it down in the cup holder as he continued to drive.

Ray and his gang walked into a fancy nightclub, which Ray owns. They walked in and spot lots of women, barely wearing clothes, dancing around the club. Ray allowed his men to enjoy themselves as he walked toward the back office. He entered the office and sees Hoyt waiting for him inside.

"What the hell are you doing here?!" Ray yelled.

"Firstly, tone down your voice and I'll explain why I'm here." Hoyt said.

Hoyt asked Ray to sit and he does. They sit right in front of one another, staring each other down. Ray started balling his fist as Hoyt smirked at him.

"What are you doing here, Hoyt?" Ray asked. "You've playing a big risk standing in my presence right now."

"Be that as it may, Colby. I'm only here to speak to you about Billy, the youngest of the Bronson brothers. I'm sure you know of him."

"Yeah, I know of him. I've already spoken to his two older brothers to track him down for me and tell him to leave your sorry ass, so he could join my alliance and have a better chance of living."

"Well, that's why I'm here. His brothers had arrived at his home earlier and so I pushed them out. Told them that Billy is on my side and not yours. Figured it would grind your gears a little bit."

"I hope you realize the dangers you are putting that boy in with your narcissistic personality and you are most certainly bound to have him killed the second either of you make a mistake."

"Me narcissistic? Old Ray. Let's both face the facts here at this moment, we both know you're the only dickhead I see here who would be considered a narcissist. But, I am highly impressed that you're using big words. Truly a good job done there on your part."

Ray grinned. Staring into Hoyt's eyes. Piercing them with his anger. Hoyt stared back, showing a slight grin.

"I'll say this last word and you can get off your ass and leave my airspace."

Hoyt leaned in and smirked.

"Go ahead, friend. Say what you must speak so I can get out of your so-called airspace."

"The next time I see you, it doesn't matter where we are or who's around. When the day comes around, I will kill you on the spot. It might be tomorrow, it might be next week. But, it doesn't matter, because, soon you will be dead. Thanks to me."

Hoyt stood up and walked toward the door, he turned his head looking at Ray, Hoyt smiled.

"I can't wait for the day to arrive, friend. Because when it comes along, maybe the two of us will meet our end by our own hands."

Hoyt left the office as Ray sat at the desk, looking down at his pistol that was in his pocket to begin with. Ray thinks to himself that possibly, he could've just killed Hoyt right there on the spot. He later took his hand off his pistol and showed a slight smirk. To which he decided to wait for a better time and a better place to finally execute

Hoyt.

Following the day after, Eldon and Cody are at the office, discussing the wallet that was found at the bank scene. Eldon looked at all the information regarding the wallet's owner. Cody walked into the boardroom as Eldon turned toward him.

"Chief, the owner of the wallet has been found." Cody said.

"That's some great news. So, where is the fellowman?"

"He's here waiting downstairs."

"Good. Bring him in so we can get this all set and done."

"Sure thing, sir." Cody said as he leaves the office.

Eldon put down the information sheet onto the desk and sat in the corner, awaiting the presence of the wallet's owner. Preston and Emily arrived in the office and Eldon told them about the wallet as Cody walked back in.

"While I'm here, I also have the results of the strap cap from the bank scene."

"Well, any leads?" Preston asked.

"There were no traces of DNA on the strap or the cap. I take it that whoever was utilizing it had enough intelligence to know what they were doing and how to keep their fingerprints off it."

"That's a damn shame." Preston said.

Emily turned to Preston and he does the same. She gave him a smirk. He didn't appreciate it.

"What is it this time, Emily? What's the smirk for?"

"It's a damn shame, huh."

"What else could it possibly be. No trace at all. Very clever the shooter."

Emily turned to Eldon.

"What about the wallet? Have you found anything in there that could lead to some information?"

"The wallet belongs to a Richard Ward." Cody said. "He was one of the bankers who escaped the bank before it exploded. According to his documents, he is highly intelligent in physics."

"Wow. That's something." Preston said.

"So, he must've dropped the wallet as he was escaping the area." Emily said.

"Exactly." Cody said.

Eldon walked toward Cody and said, "Is he coming up here yet?"

"He's on his way, sir." Cody said. "He should actually be up here any minute now."

Preston turned to Emily and said, "Well done, Weston. Well done."

"I appreciate your answer, but, I don't really give a shit what you say." Emily said.

Eldon and Cody left the office and only Preston and Emily are inside. Preston turned to Emily and said, "Watch your mouth when you're speaking to me. You're still a rookie in this town."

"What's that supposed to mean?" Emily asked. "I'm been a US Marshal for over seven years now. So, the reality is that I'm not a rookie. No matter where I go."

Emily left the office as Preston stood at the table, watching her leave. He looked down at the information sheets and started grinning.

"She needs some work done." Preston said.

Eldon approached him with an envelope containing the twenty-five thousand dollars. Preston took it and placed it in his jacket pocket.

"You mind if I go ahead and deliver this now?"

"I suggest you do it after we have a chat with the banker. That way it's less on your plate."

"Figured you would say something of that nature."

At the warehouse, Ray is having another meeting with the crime lords of the city. He talked about how they should take out Hoyt and how many ways there are in controlling the city for their own purposes. As Ray continues speaking, one thug told him that a woman is here to see him. Ray told him to let her in and she walked in.

The room is quiet and astounded by the woman's appearance. The woman is Carla. She welcomed herself into the warehouse and Ray stood up and walked over to her.

"From your appearance, you must be Carla Garcia." Ray said. "The ex-girlfriend of the Instinct Marshal."

"You could say that." Carla said. "I'm only here to give you an offer."

"Which is?" Ray asked.

She took out a sheet and showed it to Ray. It is all of Preston's tricks and ideas regarding his position as a Marshal. Ray looked at it.

"How would this help me out?"

"Let me borrow one of your men and you'll see how it will help you in your plan." Carla said.

Ray nodded, "Very well."

He pointed toward one of his men and told him to go with Carla to work on the plans. He agreed and left the warehouse with Carla. One of the crime lords looked over at Ray, who sat back down at his seat.

"She's a fine woman, don't you think?" he asked.

"Indeed, she is." Ray said. "Hopefully, she won't let us down."

CHAPTER 10

Preston, Emily, Eldon, and Cody sit at a table inside the boardroom waiting for the banker to arrive. The banker, Richard Ward walked into the room. He sat at the table, in front of Eldon. Eldon shook his hand and began asking questions regarding the robbery incident at the bank.

"Mr. Ward, if I may ask, what did you see at the bank during the incident?" Eldon asked.

"Well, I saw what appeared to be a male, who was dressed in all black. Wearing a ski mask." Ward said. "He was also carrying a brown bag to put the money in and he also carried a gun also."

"What else did you witness?" Emily asked.

"Well, I also witnessed when he walked up to the counter and slammed the back onto it." Ward said. "He, later, began to point the gun towards the banker, while yelling at him to place the money inside the bag."

Eldon looked at him.

"Is that all you saw during the event?"

"Well, not exactly." Ward said.

Cody leaned in.

"Can you please give us more information on the case. If you can."

"Well, as the banker was filling up the bag, the guy made everyone crouched to the ground, threatening to shoot them on the spot." Ward said. "As he was doing that, another banker reached under another counter and pulled out a shotgun. He raised it up and started blasting it towards the guy. He ducked the shots and killed the banker by shooting him directly in the forehead."

"So, you're telling us that while all this was transpiring, the individual killed a banker inside?" Eldon asked.

"Well, yes. He did" Ward said.

Preston looked over to Eldon and to Cody. He later looked over at Emily, who's listening to Ward. Preston leaned in and looked at Ward.

"Excuse me, Mr. Ward." Preston said. "But, can you do all of us a favor and stop using the word, "well". You're toning it out."

"Well, I apologize, but that's the way I speak." Ward said calmly.

"Preston, don't worry about his vocabulary right now." Eldon said. "Focus on the important things here at the moment."

"It's not the mission at hand. Is that all the information you have for us, Mr. Ward?"

"Well, yes sir it is." Ward said.

"Thank you for your cooperation and you may now leave." Eldon said.

Ward stood up from the chair and Cody handed him his wallet. He thanked them and left the office. Preston looked over at Eldon.

"You can't tell me the guy wasn't annoying."

"He was annoying." Cody said. "Very much, so."

"True, he was annoying." Eldon said. "But, he did give us information that we can use to find out who exactly pulled this stunt off."

"Of course." Cody said. "But, I have to agree with Preston on one particular thing. I just don't understand why Mr. Ward kept saying "well" before every sentence."

Preston smiled, "Tell me about it. Sounds like it's his favorite word to begin every sentence with."

"Enough about Ward's way of speech." Eldon said.

Eldon looked over at his clock and saw it was noon. He told them that they can go on break. Preston said he'll go ahead and deliver the money and afterwards he's going to visit a bar to search for Hoyt. Emily decided to go with him. Eldon allowed it as Cody decided to stay at the office and continued finishing up some research.

Carla and Ray's henchman arrive at a small diner across town and they speak about the plan.

"First off, tell me your name." Carla said. "Since, Ray didn't tell me while we were at the warehouse."

"My name's John." He said. "John Elroy."

"Well, John, are you sure you're qualified to do this task for me and for your boss?" Carla asked.

"Lady, I'm Ray's most valuable asset in his alliance." John said. "Anything that he can do, I can do. So, show me the plan."

"Sure." Carla said.

She pulled out the sheet and showed it to John. He looked at the sheet. Glancing and plotting out the sheet's plan. He squinted his eyes and looked at Carla. Carla looked at him and noticed he was slightly confused by what he saw on the sheet.

"Correct me if I'm making a mistake here. These skills and techniques look like they belong to a United States Marshal or something?" John asked.

"Indeed, they do. That's because I took them from Preston Maddox. I'm sure you heard of him in different discussions."

"This sheet belongs to the Instinct Marshal? Wait a minute, you sure you want to bring him into this? I mean, come on, Carla. You've stolen a very important item from one of the most targeted marshals in all of Connecticut."

"No need to worry of him." Carla said. "Me and him have a long history."

"How long a history?" John asked.

"Our history is long enough that we've shared a bed for years." Carla said. "So, no worries when it comes to Maddox or any of his ways of persuasion. Neither should you worry about his marshal friends."

"Oh." John said. "I need not ask any more questions regarding your history with the Marshal."

Carla goes over the plans with John as they discuss the pros and cons of the situations and begin plotting points to start with.

Arriving at a car dealership, Karen visited her husband, Richard. She walked in and sees him speaking with a customer that is screaming about wanting a eight-powered Mustang. She walked over to him and tapped him on the shoulder. He turned and smiled as he saw her. They hugged, as he commanded one of his employees to handle to loud-mouth customer.

"What are you doing here, Karen?" Richard asked. "I thought you were at work at this time of the day."

"An early lunch break brought me here. I was just curious about what's been going on around here." Karen said. "I just wanted to see how things worked is all."

"Curious about what?" Richard asked. "What have you been hearing?"

"Nothing." Karen said. "I just wanted to see you, that's all."

Richard smiled and hugged Karen. He told her to go back to her workplace and everything is fine. She agreed and left the building. Richard continued his work at the dealership.

Preston and Emily arrived at the home of Joel Green. They approached the front door and Preston knocked. The door opened, and a young man stood on the other side.

"Hello. What do I offer this pleasure?"

"I'm Preston Maddox and this is Emily Weston. We're United States Marshals and homicide detectives. We're here to meet a Mr. Joel Green. Is he here at the moment?"

"Um. No sir, he isn't. I'm watching the house for him while he's out of state. Is there something you're supposed to deliver to him? I could take it off your hands until he comes back."

"That won't be necessary, sir." Emily said. "We'll just return when Mr. Green makes it back in town."

"Are you sure about that, ma'am. Please, I can do a good service here."

Preston turned to Emily and shook his head. Emily only stared.

"This man is not Joel Green."

"Exactly. So, we'll return when he gets back."

"Point taken."

Preston turned to the man at the door.

"We'll just take it back to the office and await Mr. Green's return."

"The hell you will."

The man pulled out a Glock and pointed it toward Preston. Emily went to reach for her Glock and the man spotted her hand inching down to her side.

"I hope you placing your hand on your side to make a pose instead of reaching for that weapon of yours."

Preston held his hands up as Emily slowly raised hers above her head. She glanced over at Preston. He shook his head in confusion.

"Now, the two of you, inside now."

"Excuse me." Preston said. "We don't know what's in there."

"Just get in the goddamn house Right now!"

Preston and Emily slowly walked into the home. Seeing its neatly designed features. Preston turned his head toward the man.

"I hope we don't have to destroy this fine place all for the sake of a delivery."

"Give me whatever it is that you've come over to deliver."

"I don't think that will be necessary, sir."

"Give me the goddamn delivery. Before I shoot one of you in the forehead and leave you here to rot."

Preston reached into his jacket pocket and pulled out the envelope. The man extended his hand for the envelope. Preston handed it to him as Emily turned toward Preston with a confused look on her face as if she's about to yell.

"Preston. What the hell are you doing?" Emily said.

"Just shut your damn mouth, whore. This is between the men in the house. Women aren't allowed to speak until they are given the proper say so."

"So, are we all on the same page or what?" Preston said. "Just being the curious fellow here."

"Yeah, we are. Turn around and face the front door while I check this out."

Preston and Emily turned and faced the front door as the man opened the envelope and seen the amount of dollars that were stacked inside. He pulled them out and held them. He sniffed them and rubbed them on his face.

"I forgot how great new dollar bills smelled. They smell like the new season of a new year. This is amazing to me and you guys just don't get it."

"That's great and all. But, can we go now?" Preston said.

"No, you can't. Not until I've counted all of this. Damn this is a lot of bills. So, how much was this supposed to be anyway, Marshals?"

"Twenty-five thousand." Emily said. "I believe."

"You're shitting me right now. Twenty-five thousand dollars this is? Wow, what a load."

As the man screamed and hollered about the money, Preston and Emily looked at each other. Both conjuring up a plan of their own.

"I can't deal with this." Preston said. "How about yourself?"

"Let's just get this over with so we can continue our previous work."

The man began to kiss the pack of dollar bills when Preston turned around and reached for his gun. He raised it up and fired a shot to the man's heart. The man paused and held his chest as he fell to the ground. Preston and Emily walked over toward him and looked down at him on the floor. He began coughing as he tried to catch his breath.

"The least you could've done is let me keep the cash."

"I don't believe the dead use cash I'm afraid." Preston said.

Preston gathered up the money and placed it back into the envelope. Placing it into his jacket pocket. He and Emily leave the house as the man laid on the floor bleeding to death.

CHAPTER 11

Preston and Emily arrive at the bar and they sit down at the bar itself. They both order a glass of water. They start having a conversation regarding New Haven and each other's lives. The bar was halfway full of customers going in and out.

"I have a quick question." Preston said. "Why did you want to come along with me? Thought, you didn't want to even speak with me. Let alone work alongside me."

Emily smiled and said, "I know I'm new to this town and that you're a pain in the ass. But, since Eldon paired us together. We are partners and we must work together on any case that comes along our way."

"You're right about that." Preston said. "Solving cases to save many lives as we possibly can."

"All of us at least try to accomplish that from time to time. Some succeed and some fail. Depends on how the job was done."

"If they were assigned the correct case to solve instead of picking and choosing what kind of case favored them."

"There's truth in that. I've worked with some who've done that before and it didn't turn out well for the victim nor the detective. But, not getting too much into your personal life. From the information that travels through the agency, I heard that you were once married."

Preston smirked and drank from his glass. He looked at Emily and then smiled.

"Eldon told you, didn't he?" Preston asked. "Can't keep that to himself."

"Yeah." Emily said smiling. "He told me that she filed for

divorce and left you. Because of your anger."

"My anger they say? I can believe that to a certain extent, since, everyone believes that I have anger issues. Which I don't. I try to be as nice and polite as I can with everyone. Some take it and some don't. That's one reason why I put my job first in my life. I would guess the anger comes from whatever case I may be on or what fugitive I'm chasing during the time frame."

"That makes sense to me." Emily said as she drank her glass of water. "I've had similar ways back in Newark."

"Similar ways as in being angry most of the time."

"You could say that. There was one time where I was pursuing a sexual abuser and it came to the point that we found him raping an innocent woman. The image drove me insane and I pummeled the guy."

"You pummeled a guy? With those soft bare hands?"

"I'm sure you know how much strength you can gain with you're in a complete rage."

Preston puts his glass down and asked, "Enough about our anger and rage. Back to what you brought up about my previous marriage. What about you? Your little life story?"

"Basically, I'm not the relationship-type of woman." Emily said. "I had one boyfriend while I was in college and that went straight to shit in a heartbeat."

"By your independent attitude, I take it was you." Preston said.

"Not really." Emily said. "I discovered that was cheating on me with my roommate. Something, huh."

"I've heard that kind of story numerous amounts in my day." Preston said. "I've had friends with the same issue and never understood what they did or what they caused."

"Haven't we all been friends with people like that." Emily said smiling. "So, what's this "Instinct" thing that people say about you. I've been hearing it a lot lately and every time someone mentions it, they get uncomfortable."

"I don't know what the hell it is myself." Preston said. "I'm guessing that they mean how I react to my instincts and I follow them.

Without hesitation. I just believe it's something the agency created to cause a stir in the field and to scare the fugitives and such."

"So, you just go in with your first instinct?" Emily asked.

"Pretty much." Preston said smiling. "The funny thing about it is my first instinct is always the right one. Never been wrong before and probably never will."

The sound of the bar door opening alarmed the entire establishment. Hoyt an Billy entered the bar and see Preston and Emily talking further down on the counter.

"Billy, look who's here."

"Shit. Why don't we go to another bar. There's one further down the street and it's probably not crowded."

"We're staying and we're sitting over there with them. Just for the sake of fun."

They're approaching both Preston and Emily. Preston had finally found Hoyt. Hoyt walked over to Preston and Billy has entered the bar.

"We meet again, eh' Preston." Hoyt said.

"I could say the same thing." Preston said. "Though, you've already said it. So, no point in saying it."

Hoyt smiled, "Funny. Still with the jokes I see."

"I have to add a little humor every now and then." Preston said. "I've been looking for you by the way."

"Really? You have? So, what is it that I have done this time to bring you onto my coat tails?"

"You heard about the jailhouse incident that took place. From what we received from the witness is that the shooter yelled out, "Incoming Call" and took the shot. Reason being, I only know one man in New Haven who would yell that phrase out before exploding something and the man I'm referring to is you."

"Alright. I'll come out with this one and I know Billy won't be too pleasured about this. It was me. Me and Billy to be exact. It was our first task in changing the foundation of this city. Something you don't have the balls to do."

Billy jumped up from the stool and his jaw dropped as he looked at Hoyt. Billy shrugged his shoulders and shook his head.

"What the hell is your problem, Hoyt. You're giving away plot information and details."

"You want to test it out?" Preston said. "Go ahead and try it."

Hoyt looked over Preston's shoulder and sees Emily. He walked toward her and leaned on the bar to the right, staring straight into her face.

"So, who is this beautiful young lady, Preston?" Hoyt asked. "Because, she surely isn't Karen or Carla. From my perspective, she looks better than the two of them combined. If that was possible, we would have ourselves a Old West-style stand-off."

"She is Emily Weston, my new partner on the job." Preston said. "I wouldn't take her too kindly."

"It's a pleasure to meet someone of your stature, Ms. Weston." Hoyt said. "I'm sure you've done your homework and now know who I am and what I've done in this city's history. Plus, what I'm capable of doing if I'm pushed to the proper stage of behavior."

"I know as much about you that I need to know. The infamous, Hoyt Bennett. The man who caused trouble across this city and throughout the state. The one who just got released from prison in D.C. Ready to go back in your little cell over there?"

"I'll tell you one thing, sweetheart. Hoyt Bennett will never go back to DC's super max prison. The reason is simple, I'm not doing anything that's against the law." Hoyt said.

"Number one, if we're going to be speaking with each other. Don't call me sweetheart." Emily said. "You shouldn't test your luck with me."

"Oh my. You don't want me to call you sweetheart? May I ask why you prefer not? Does it make you feel good or bad about yourself in a physical mindset? Not that I care anyways about your mindset."

Preston tapped Hoyt on the shoulder and he turned toward him. Preston wasn't playing around as his face became serious as it was when he shot Cartel. Hoyt knew Preston was serious and decided to play along with him. Testing his buttons, it would seem.

"Why are you here at this time?" Preston asked. "Specifically, I might add."

"Me and Billy would always come to this place for a drink. It relaxes and sooths our bodies of what the world has done to us. In simple terms, it places us from the world and the world from us."

"It's only twelve twenty-five. Past noon." Preston said. "I knew you were a crazy man, but I don't recall you drinking alcohol at this hour."

"The timeframe doesn't matter, Preston. Funny how you said that about me but left yourself out of the picture frame. Try to remember the way you used to drink, you know that more well than us. I look at it this way and see if you can understand where I'm coming from. As long as we can drink and be separate from the world, we're doing just fine."

Hoyt turned to Billy and asked him what drink would he like. Billy, in a problematic mood said he wanted a glass of water. Hoyt looked at him and told him to order a beer and Billy decided on doing so. Billy started to shiver because he's about to drink a beer in the presence of two marshals. Hoyt sat in the seat next to Emily. He glazed at her and smiled.

"Don't mind me of where I sit. So, since you're new to this city? How has it treated you? If you don't mind me getting into that part of your life."

"Just to shut you up, I'll tell you a slight of detail. The city has treated me well. Just came in a few days ago and no problems have I had to deal with that arose from this place. Until, you popped up of course."

"Well, let me ask you this since we're on your traveling and living subject. Where do you live previously before you arrived here?"

"Excuse me, well-established fugitive and pyrotechnic. I'm not telling you where I once stayed. If you want to talk, we'll focus on the here and now. Nothing to do with the past or what happened in the past."

Hoyt leaned in toward Emily's face, getting into her personal space, causing Emily to feel highly uncomfortable and to back away from him.

"You will." Hoyt said with a straight face.

Preston stepped behind Hoyt. He looked over his left shoulder, smiling.

"I see you're watching her back." Hoyt said.

"Of course. She's my partner. Though, she can handle herself." Preston said. "But, when it comes to someone I know, a man especially, they should have some respect for women. Hoyt, last time I checked, you were already heading into some trouble with a certain group of women. May I say, prostitutes, or do you prefer hoes. Your choice."

"Preston, why have only one when you can have them all." Hoyt said. "That's the grand prize."

Billy started laughing and Preston turned to him. Once, Billy saw Preston looking at him, he placed his head down and was quiet. Preston turned back to Hoyt.

"That sounds like me when I was twenty-two." Preston said. "I'll just say this right now, Hoyt. Originally, when the double homicide occurred, I thought you had a hand in it."

"How would I have had a hand in it when I was in D.C. at the time?" Hoyt said. "Answer that for me, Preston."

"Because the murders were so unusual and strange that, since, everything unusual in this town always has a track record that somehow reverts toward you." Preston said. "Though, you were in D.C. before the incident, I thought that some of your drug lords that stayed behind might have heard from your word to cause those two murders."

"Preston, I'm afraid that my men have all gone to work for Ray Colby." Hoyt said. "I would assume a man of your stature would've had the knowledge of knowing that."

"Ray Colby, the elite crime lord?" Emily asked. "I know of Colby. We go way back during my days in Jersey. He's here?"

"Yeah, he's been in town for a few months now." Preston said. "Planning and plotting as he comes. He hasn't started anything yet that we know of."

"Speaking of Colby, Billy and I have a master plan that will soon come to light." Hoyt said.

"What are you talking about?" Preston asked.

"Soon, you will begin hearing about certain events that are occurring around the city and when the time's right, you'll see the demise of Ray Colby." Hoyt said. "It's just around the horizon."

"Hoyt!" Billy said. "You have to stop telling people about the plans! It will only make the operations worse to go by!"

"You're not doing anything, Hoyt." Preston said. "Don't even try to do anything."

"Or what?" Hoyt said. "Or what, Preston? It seems that someone's lost in shadows as to what's about to happen. Before me and Billy leave, I'll give you this only warning."

"Go ahead." Preston said. "Warn me. Give me the warning."

Hoyt smiled, "If I catch you, your sexy partner, or any of your friends from the agency, I will kill them all and that's a promise."

Hoyt told Billy that they're leaving and they leave. Preston stared him down as he leaves. Emily turned to Preston.

"What are we going to do about him?"

"Nothing." Preston said. "He'll lead us to the events."

Preston and Emily left the bar, but, on the outside are Ray's two henchman.

They are waiting in their burgundy car on a street corner. They are watching them going to their cars. The Caucasian looked and pointed.

"That's him!" the Caucasian said. "That's the "Instinct" guy."

"I see." the African said. "I'll call Ray and see what he wants us to do."

The African pulled out his cell phone and called Ray. Ray's assistant answers on the other end.

"Hey, is Ray there? Put him on for me."

"That's the female Marshal too." the Caucasian said. "She looks good as they say."

"Yes, Ray." the African said on the phone. "Sorry to bother you, but, do you remember that "Instinct" Marshal? Well, he's here at the bar. I don't know, he must be tracking Hoyt too. That's exactly what I was thinking, sir. Alright."

He ended the call as the Caucasian looked over. Waiting for an answer.

"Well?" the Caucasian asked. "What did he say?"

"Once we take out Hoyt, we'll take out the Marshal as well."

"What about the cute female Marshal?" "We go ahead and kill her too? Just wanted to bring these things up before we had to do the tasks ourselves. Imagine what would happen if we killed them and we go back to the boss and he wanted them alive. We would be in deep trouble."

"Which is why you're not in charge nor in my position."

The African turned with an emotionless look on his face away from the Caucasian. The Caucasian kept his gaze on him.

"So, back to the previous question. Do we kill the female Marshal, or do we leave her alone?"

"What do you think. Of course, we'll kill her too."

CHAPTER 12

Carla and John returned to Ray's warehouse to speak with him, regarding the plans. Ray is already inside, sitting in the same seat. Carla sat in front of Ray as John stood behind her.

"So, how did the talk go about?" Ray asked.

"Your man, John here, will be a very good asset in this plan." Carla said. "So, when do you want to start?"

"We can start as soon as you see fit." Ray said. "It's all on you, Ms. Garcia."

Carla smiled, "Well, it's good to get this going and don't worry, everything will go as smoothly as possible."

She left the warehouse when Ray spoke with John concerning her.

"How was she during the conversations?" Ray asked. "What did she bring up?"

"She's highly intelligent, boss." John said. "She knows what she's doing. Exactly what she's doing."

"That's great." Ray said. "That's very great. At least we know she's on our side for this battle and not that piece of shit fuck head, Hoyt Bennett."

Coover and Rusty returned to Billy's mobile home to give him one more chance to join Ray's alliance. They knocked on the door and Billy opened. Rusty is upset as he tried to convince his younger brother to join the alliance. Billy declined and said he's sticking with Hoyt and that they will rule over the city. Rusty walked away as Coover tried to be the oldest and convince his brother to join. Billy declined again and Coover wished him luck on his choice and walked away with Rusty.

Billy closed the door and from behind, Hoyt is sitting on his couch.

"I see you declined both your brothers, Billy." Hoyt said. "Impressive skill. you're finally learning."

"I'm trying to stand on my own and make my own choices." Billy said. "I've always followed my brothers since we were kids. I never was granted attention or had any appreciation for the things I've done. Now, it seems with me on your team, I can make something of myself."

"You will make something of yourself on my side." Hoyt said. "If you were to join Ray, you'll only be his pawn. Just like your two older brothers. Apparently, they like to be sheep because they only follow, since they can't lead."

Preston and Emily come back to the office, where they told Eldon about Hoyt's upcoming events that will lead to a breath-shaking disaster across the city. Eldon decided to put the entire agency on high alert for any of these events.

"What took you two so long to return?" Eldon asked Preston and Emily.

"We had a long conversation." Preston said. "Nothing much really."

Cody walked over and said, "You guys were gone for quite a while. I was starting to wonder."

Preston turned to Eldon and said, "We saw Hoyt at the bar."

"What did he say?" Eldon asked. "Did he mention anything related to the murders or to the jailhouse attack?"

"He did say that the jailhouse attack was him." Preston said. "Him and Billy Bronson."

"Billy Bronson?" Eldon said. "Never would expect him to do something like that. His brothers though, you can definitely expect that from them."

Preston later said, "He also said that he has something planned for the city and I'm here to tell you that we must do something about it."

Afterwards, Darius arrived inside the area to speak with Eldon, regarding the double homicide. Eldon turned and walked toward him.

"Sorry to disturb you, Chief." Darius said. "But, we've finally found out who was the culprit in the double homicide."

"Who is it?" Eldon asked.

"From what we've covered up. The DNA matches both Coover and Rusty Bronson." Darius said. "We found both of their fingerprints on the kitchen stove and the dryer handle."

"Finally, we know who to look for." Eldon said. "I'll tell my two marshals to go on the search for them."

Eldon walked over to Preston and Emily and told them to search for Coover and Rusty. Preston said he knew exactly who they were, saying they all went to the same high school. Eldon told them that he and Cody are going on a search for Hoyt's plans as they look for the Bronson brothers.

"So, where do we find these Bronson brothers?" Emily asked.

"We'll head to their mother's home." Preston said. "She might know exactly where they'll be."

"You know her?" Emily asked.

"Just like her sons, we have a long history." Preston said.

Preston and Emily headed out to speak with the Bronson brothers' mother. Eldon and Cody left the office, going out to search for clues of Hoyt's plans. Eldon and Cody talked with each other about possible clues that they could find around the city.

"What are we looking for exactly?" Cody asked.

"Any areas that may have significant clues regarding Hoyt."

"So, where are we headed?"

"We'll head to the Westside. Search the areas around those spots." Eldon said. "It might give us some ideas."

Carla and John parked in front of the Marshal Agency, sitting inside a red corvette. John sits in the driver's seat as Carla sat in the passenger's seat. John is starting to become impatient for waiting and turned to Carla.

"May I ask why we're just waiting here, Carla?"

"Just be patient, John." Carla said. "This is only a part of the plan. Just relax. For my sake."

"Alright now." John said. "So, what are we doing here? You just saw the Marshal and his partner leave, so why are we here when we should be following them?"

"Because, eventually, he'll have to come back." Carla said. "Then, once he does, you'll take him out. For your alliance and for your own good."

Preston and Emily entered the New Haven County on the south-central side of Connecticut. They turned corners and Preston recognized a house on the right corner. He drove towards that direction. Emily looked around at the homes and noticed Preston heading towards a specific house.

"Do you see the house?" Emily asked.

"I do." Preston said. "It's right here. Still looks the same too."

Preston drove into the driveway and parked the car. They exit the car and walked towards the front door. Before, they get to the door, it opened and it's the Bronson brothers' mother. Barbette Bronson. She walked out and looked at both Preston and Emily.

"Oh my." Barbette said. "Is that who I think it is standing before me today."

"Yes, ma'am. It's me in the flesh."

"The well-known Preston Maddox." Barbette said. "It's been a long time since we've seen you in this neck of the woods. Around ten to fifteen years at least."

"You're correct, Ms. Bronson." Preston said. "It's been a long time indeed for most of us."

Emily walked over and shook Barbette's hand as she looked at her.

"Preston, who is this lovely young lady?" Barbette asked. "You never spread the word about you having a lady on your arm again."

"This is Emily Weston." Preston said. "She is my partner in the Marshal and Detective Service."

"Great." Barbette said. "It's nice to see there's a woman in a man's position and doing the job even better too."

"Don't start on that, please." Preston said.

"Thank you, ma'am." Emily said. "I do what I can to help."

Barbette allowed them inside the house and they walk in. Preston sees that the house hasn't changed a bit from when he was just a small child. The inside is still the same with an old couch and wooden walls.

"This place really hasn't changed." Preston said. "You must've loved the way it looked."

"I'm not going to change anything here, just to fit in with this new society we have." Barbette said. "I'm old school and I intend on staying that way."

"However you feel, Ms. Barbette." Preston said.

"You could just call me, Barb, Preston." Barbette said. "You've known me since you were a child. So, don't bother with calling me Ms. Barbette or Ms. Bronson."

Preston smiled.

"So, Barb. We're here on business to ask of your sons. The two older ones exactly, Coover and Rusty."

"What about Coover and Rusty?" Barbette said. "What kind of trouble have they caused this time?"

"They're the suspects of a double homicide." Preston said. "I'm sure you've seen it on the news. CNN had it on not too long ago. MSNBC on the other hand tried to make a joke out of it."

"I heard about the murders that transpired in that neighborhood." Barbette said. "It's very sad. Though, I wouldn't expect my sons to be the culprits. They wouldn't do such a thing."

"I believe The President made a speech about it not too long ago." Preston said. "Not really sure, but, I'll check and see once I get back to the office."

"Well, for one I didn't vote for him." Barbette said. "Do you know where they are right now?"

"No ma'am, we don't." Emily said. "That's why we're here in your presence to ask you if you've seen or heard from them since."

"Last I heard, Rusty said, that he and Coover were headed over to Billy's home to convince him of teaming with that Ray Colby fellow."

"So, your two older sons, they're working with Colby?" Emily asked.

"It would appear so I guess." Barbette said. "They wouldn't be speaking of him unless they were."

"We saw Billy earlier at the bar with Hoyt Bennett." Preston said.

"Hoyt?" Barbette said. "Hoyt Bennett you say? That no-good son of a bitch who nearly drove this county and the city into hell with his actions. Billy should know better. That's probably the reason why Coover and Rusty went to visit him. Though, he always wanted to go on his own, but, he would never listen to anyone."

"It seems he's listening to Hoyt." Preston said. "So, what do you want us to do about your boys?"

"Do what you will with Coover and Rusty." Barbette said. "I'll take care of Billy. Show him the right way of living his life. Instead of working with that no-good bastard."

"Do what you have to do Ms. Barb." Preston said. "Well, it's time that we leave and head back to the office."

Preston and Emily left the house, returning to the office. Barbette went back into the house. She looked toward the back of the home and the back door creaked open Coover and Rusty walked in from the back and notice their mother's expression on her face. Coover whispered to Rusty, saying their mother looked pissed. Rusty looked and shrugged his shoulders. They began staggering as she stared deeply at them.

"When the hell were you going to tell me that you murdered two people?" Barbette asked. "When were you two going to tell me?!"

"Mama, we were going to tell you about it." Coover said. "But, we didn't know the right time to tell you is all."

"When?! When the fuck were you were going to tell me about it?!" Barbette yelled. "I need an answer right this minute!"

"We were going to, but, we wanted to have Billy on our side before going along with it." Rusty said. "That's all, mama."

Barbette stared and said, "It seems that the two of you are being hunted down by the marshals and since I saved your asses this time, you better give me something in return."

"Like what?" Coover asked.

"Either you speak with Billy one more time or I will." Barbette said.

She walked toward the back of the house as Coover and Rusty leave through the front. She murmured to herself about his sons as they glanced back. Rusty tugged Coover's sleeve as the left the home.

Carla and John continue to wait outside. The two are still awaiting Preston's return to the office and now John is out of patience. He gets upset and leaves the car. Carla followed him and said to him that plans have changed. He looked at her as she tells him to go inside and wait for Preston to return on the upper floor and that she'll go in with him to distract the other officials. He agreed, and they walked in. As soon as they go inside, Eldon and Cody returned. They have no clues or information regarding Hoyt's upcoming plans.

"We couldn't find a damn thing." Eldon said. "Not one trace whatsoever at all."

"Something will come up eventually." Cody said. "I'm sure of it."

"Yeah." Eldon said. "Hopefully, Preston and Emily have something for us to follow."

They walked inside and have no idea what's about to happen in the office. Inside the office, Carla is distracting the officials as John headed to the elevator. He held the door opened as he signaled Carla to join him. She told him that she'll find her own way. He stayed inside as the door closed on the elevator, as he's heading toward the third floor. He arrived on the third floor and no one pays any attention toward him. He reached his side for his handgun, not pulling it out, but, his hand in position to do so.

Hoyt arrived at a location across town and walked into the small building nearby. He opened the door and turned on the lights. The building, he could tell it was used as a former pawn shop before it went out of business. The building is now for sale and Hoyt is highly looking into it. Someone else comes through the door and it's the owner of the building.

"Who in the hell are you and What the hell are you doing here?" The owner asked.

"I apologize for entering without calling, even though I don't have a number to this place. But, I'm here to discuss a business proposition with the owner the price on this building." Hoyt said. "You wouldn't happen to be the owner, would you?"

"That would be who you're currently eyeballing, boy. I am the owner of this place." He said. "So, what kind of interest do you have in a building like this and why should I even bother to listen to your offer?"

"Well, my good sir, my interest in your building is quite a simple answer." Hoyt said. "I need a small place for my stash of items."

"My I know what these items are?" The owner said. "If you want to have this building, I must know some details."

"The stash is really just my items that I have back at the house." Hoyt said. "It just some things that should be kept in storage."

"I don't know about that, Mr.?" The owner asked.

"Hoyt, Hoyt Bennett." Hoyt said smiling.

"Oh, so you're the guy who caused the whole mess of things a while back and went to prison for it." The owner said. "I knew I recognized you from somewhere."

"Yes, I am he." Hoyt said. "So, do we have an agreement on this building of yours? I can take it off your hands."

"I'll think it over and speak with you tomorrow about it." The owner said. "Do we have a deal?"

Hoyt shook the owner's hand and said, "Yes, we do have a deal."

CHAPTER 13

Hoyt left the building with the mindset of intending on having the building, by any means necessary. He drove down the streets and passed by a group that he noticed. He turned around and passed by the area again. He looked closely and noticed that the men standing in that spot used to work for him. He smirked as he drives away.

Preston and Emily returned to the office and walk in. But, they realize that everyone is armed and searching the building. Preston walked over to one official as Emily glanced around the entire location before approaching the officer.

"Officer, what's the hell is happening here?" Preston asked. "What is going on?"

"Some pissed off guy came in with a gun and started threatening everyone near him." The officer said. "They're saying he's up on the third floor. No one's gone up there so far. They're awaiting backup."

"No shit, pal, we're the backup." Preston said. "Emily, we have to go up there."

"I'm aware of that, smart guy. How do we get up there without being noticed by sound or anyone in general?"

"Just follow my lead and we'll get up there in a hurry."

Preston and Emily ran toward the stairs, heading to the third floor. On the third floor, the majority of everyone is either hiding or sneaking up on John, who's standing in the middle of the room, pointing the gun at all the locations around him. Carla is standing by his side, smiling and laughing at the officials.

"I'll ask again god damn it." John said. "Where's Preston Maddox?! Where's the Instinct Marshal?!"

No one responded to his question and he fired the gun to the ceiling. Sounds of harsh screaming are heard around the room as he repeated the question. But, this time Eldon stepped out of the office and Cody stood with him.

"You aren't Preston. Neither of you." John said. "So, who the fuck are you, then to stand up in front of a gun?"

"I'm Eldon Ross, the Chief Commander of this agency." Eldon said. "I'm also Preston's boss and you're trespassing on my territory and threatening my people."

Carla smiled and said, "Preston's boss. Wow, I wouldn't expect him to have a boss. I always assumed that he would go into work for himself. Not someone else."

"Listen here, woman. Either the two of you go ahead and leave this building or it's a slight possibility that the both of you might just have to die here and leave in a coroner van."

"Die here?" John said. "Really? Let me tell you something, old boy. The only motherfucker that might possibly die in this place today is either you and your little bitch standing next to you. How's that sound for a threat."

Eldon pulled out his gun and fired at John. He moved out of the way and started shooting the surroundings. Eldon and Cody hid behind the office walls as John continued to fire toward them. Preston and Emily arrived on the floor and crouched down by the entrance wall.

"Who is this guy?" Emily asked.

"Must be one of Ray's men." Preston said. 'They're probably here for us I assume."

"Didn't expect us to be on a hit list this soon."

John stopped firing the gun and looked at Carla.

"When is he coming, Carla?" John asked. "We can't wait this long for him to show up."

"Don't worry. He'll be here soon enough." Carla said. "He can't resist making a save for innocent people."

Preston and Emily ran into the room as John pointed the gun

toward them. Preston spotted Carla standing by John and he's confused, yet remembers his plans were stolen back at his apartment.

"We meet again, Preston." Carla said. "So, who's your friend, there?"

"Carla. What are you doing here?" Preston asked. "What are you doing with this man?"

"We're here on a mission assigned by Ray Colby." Carla said. "We're here to kill you basically."

Preston smirked and looked at John.

"So, you're one of Ray's men." Preston said. "I knew it would have to be. Neither the Bronson brothers or Hoyt would do something like this. They would just shoot everyone they see."

"I do this shit different, Marshal." John said. "Now, since people are always saying that you have the "Instinct". Whatever that's supposed to be. I was wondering, do you know exactly when I'll decide to shoot your head off."

"If you really want to know. Just try me." Preston said. "See, where we go from there."

John laughed and glanced toward Carla.

"You sound like you aren't afraid of being killed on the spot." John said. "A man without any fear of a gun."

"No one's ever had the chance of doing it." Preston said. "I've always been the one doing the shooting and putting people down. So, what makes it different if you're on the other side of the gun this time and I'm in the same position as always."

"Alright. Let's just see how good you really are." John said.

"Oh, I like the way this is going." Carla said. "Exciting stuff we're seeing here."

Emily looked at Carla and said, "Just keep your mouth closed, alright. Before, I become the one to put a bullet through your head."

Carla laughed and said, "You have a feisty partner, Preston. I wonder what else she can do beside talking."

"You'll probably find that out sooner than you think." Preston said. "She's not one you'll like to piss off. Believe me, I know for a fact."

Eldon and Cody peeped out of the office, seeing Preston and

Emily standing in front of John and Carla. Cody turned to Eldon.

"What should we do, boss?" Cody asked. "We need to help them in some way at least."

"We could create some form of a diversion for them." Eldon said. "Make it a little easier for them."

"Like shoot the guy in the leg?" Cody asked.

"We could try." Eldon said.

Just as Eldon pointed the gun, Darius snuck into the office and pointed his gun toward John. Eldon looked at him.

"How'd you get in here?" Eldon asked.

"I was already in here. Just was waiting for you, that's all." Darius said. "What should we do? Let Preston and Emily handle it, or shall we just cause a minor disturbance?"

"I have one suggestion. Why don't we just try shooting the guy in the leg." Eldon said. "Will open up some kind of chance."

"Alright, it makes sense to me." Darius said. "Let's do it."

Darius fired his gun and the bullet went through John's leg. He stumbled as Carla pulled out her pistol and pointed toward both Preston and Emily. They stood still as Carla smiled.

"Who the fuck did that?!" John said in tremendous pain. "Where the fuck did that come from?! Shit!"

"Just be lucky it wasn't aimed for your head." Preston said. "That wouldn't have been so pretty to see your brain splattered."

"You're making jokes, boy. You know something, I'm getting a little tired of being in this damn marshal joint place anyway, so I'll just put your ass down right now."

John had set up his gun stance and prepared to aim, before he can fire the gun, he is shot in the back of the head and fell to the ground. As John fell, Carla stood behind him, with the pistol up and smoke coming from the muzzle. Preston is appalled by Carla's decision and so is everyone else in the office.

"The hell just happen here?!" Eldon said.

"Why did you do that, Carla?" Preston asked. "I don't really understand what that was for?"

"You've never understood me, babe. I'm the only person that's allowed to kill you. The *ONLY* one."

Carla smiled and looked down at John's dead body. Blood slowly begins forming a puddle around his head.

"I'll explain the news to Ray." Carla said. "Just tell him it was a accident. He'll be fine with it."

"Speaking of him. Where is Ray?" Emily asked. "Since you know where he's located?"

"You really think I'll tell you? After the threat you gave me." Carla said, "You really have a lot to learn about New Haven, sweetheart."

Carla walked toward the front door, Preston stood in front of her.

Preston stared and said, "Either you tell us where Colby is or I'm personally taking you to prison for murder. We have eye witnesses to attest to it"

"Wow. I like your options. It turns me on." Carla said. "OK. He operates at a warehouse on the outskirts of town. It was a former trucking company building. Now, may I leave?"

Carla left the office as Emily turned to Preston.

"Let me ask a question here. Why did you let her leave?" Emily asked.

"Because she'll lead us to Colby himself." Preston said. "Simple solution right in front of us."

CHAPTER 14

Hoyt arrived at Billy's home. But, once he opened the door, he discovered that Billy isn't there. He walked in and searched the home.

"Billy, where the hell are you?" Hoyt said to himself.

As he prepared to leave, he turned around and was hit directly in the head with a wooden baseball bat. Hoyt fell to the ground. Being knocked out from the bat. He was completely unconscious and unaware of what had happened. The holder of the bat was Rusty. He laughed as he looked down at Hoyt. Coover walked in behind him and looked down.

"He went down quick, bro." Coover said. "The bastard couldn't take a beating. No shit, he couldn't take a swing of a bat."

"It was easy." Rusty said. "Easier than I expected it to be. Let's drag him to the truck and take him to Ray. See what he wants us to do with him."

Coover looked around the home. Searching around the area for someone or something. He walked back outside toward Rusty.

"Rusty, where's Billy?" Coover asked.

"Billy's over at mama's house." Rusty said. "She'll convince him to join us with Ray. You'll see. Mama has it all under control."

They drag Hoyt's unconscious body to their truck. They tossed him in the back and covered him up with some sheets that were lying in the back. They drove off the premises, returning to Ray's hideout.

Back at the office, officials are cleaning up the amount of blood left on the floor from John's head after being shot by Carla. Preston, Emily, Eldon, Cody, and Darius are inside the boardroom, talking about the recent event.

"Why did you let her leave, Preston?" Eldon asked. "You saw

what she did. She shot another human being right there. Right outside this room."

"I let her leave, so she could lead us to Colby." Preston said. "It's a very simple plan."

"How is it simple?" Darius asked. "She killed him, but, she could've easily killed you and Emily. As well as the rest of us on this floor if it had come to that."

"I see that I somehow placed everyone in danger." Preston said. "But, me and her have a long history with one another."

"Please, don't tell me that she's an old flame?" Eldon asked. "We don't need any more of your personal details falling into business again."

"She was." Preston said. "Kind of. We met when we were very young, and I also taught her some techniques. So, that could explain how she knew how to use the gun in the first place."

"So, her with the gun is really your fault." Emily said. "Should've seen that from the start."

"Everyone just relax." Cody said. "We must have a plan to go by in case she comes back with others."

"Ok, so what's the plan, guys?" Emily asked. "If any of you have one."

Preston looked around and said, "I say that we follow Carla's trail, so that we know for sure where Colby is and how to stop him."

Darius nodded.

"I'll have to go with Preston on this one. The plan sounds good. Good enough to start from."

"Alright then." Eldon said. "We'll track down your old flame and hopefully, that leads us to Ray Colby."

As they prepared to leave the room, Cody thought and brought up Hoyt's plans. Preston looked and decided that he'll go search for Hoyt as soon as he leaves. Emily agreed to join him in doing so. They leave the boardroom.

Carla went to another one of Ray's hideouts. This time a cabin in the woods. A cabin larger than the average cabins. She walked in and

Ray is sitting behind a desk. He looked up and saw Carla. But, he doesn't see John.

"Where's John?" Ray asked. "What happened out there, Carla?"

"John didn't survive the initials of the plan." Carla said. "He was shot."

Ray stood up, as he's angry about what happened with John. But, he's still concerned if the plan went the way it was supposed to go.

"Did the plan go as followed?" Ray asked.

"No." Carla said. "As soon as John was shot, I left the building and that brings me to you at this moment, standing before you and telling you this terrible news."

"You said you could get the job done." Ray said. "Apparently, you couldn't. I find out that a lost one of my soldiers and I also find out that Preston is still alive and that's gonna cause problems for me, my lady. Lots of problems. How am I supposed to explain this news to the head chief? How do I explain this?"

"I'm sure you'll find a way to do so." Carla said. "That is, if you want me to explain it to him. I could do that, if you like."

"Very well." Ray said. "Since all you seem to be used for is bringing news, go ahead and tell the chief this. I'm sure he'll love to hear it from you. Right from your mouth."

Carla left the cabin as Ray looked down at the table and slams his fists.

Preston and Emily traveled down the interstate in search of Hoyt. Emily asked him about his history with Carla and why he let her leave. He told her that because Carla looked innocent and nice, she isn't. He also told her that Carla is highly skilled with armed weapons, thanks to him training her during their past relationship. Emily wonders if Preston can stand up against her, instead of falling prey to her seductive ways.

"When was the last time you actually saw Carla in person?" Emily asked. "And I'm not talking about in the office."

"A few days ago, she was inside my apartment." Preston said.

"She must've picked the lock or something, because she doesn't have a key to it. I didn't even live here during our relationship."

"That must have been a surprise." Emily said.

"It was shocking to say the least." Preston said. "But, enough about me. What's the history between you and Ray Colby?"

"Ray was one of New Jersey's top crime lords." Emily said. "Him and I always had confrontations with one another. Later, I find out that he fled from the state and went somewhere else to hide. Now, I find out that this is the city of which he flocked to."

"It seems our past lives are coming back to us." Preston said.

"Looks that way." Emily said. "Strongly, too."

Emily then asked, "Also, at the bar, what was that phase Hoyt had said to you?"

"Which one?" Preston said. "Because, I can't fully remember what that jackass said to me. To make it even stranger, I was drinking water."

"He said something about being lost in the shadows. Something of that nature. Though, I believed it was like that or maybe it was lost shadows. Something around that I know."

"It was lost in shadows." Preston said. "It's basically a phrase used to tell people when they have no idea what's either going on around them or they have no knowledge of what's about to happen around them. To put it short, Hoyt is about to do something around this city and that's what he meant when he told me that I was lost in the shadows."

"I was just asking about it." Emily said. "In a sort of way, I kind of like it. Sounds interesting."

"I'll tell you what's interesting." Preston said. "The term *Pteronophobia*."

"*Pteronophobia*? Never heard of it. Why is it supposed to be interesting?"

"It means fear of feathers."

"That is interesting. Never knew something like that existed." Emily said.

Preston said, "I didn't either, until my cousin ran from some chickens on his parents' farm in Arkansas."

"You learn something new every day, don't you?" Emily said.

"Pretty much." Preston said smiling.

Right back at the cabin in the woods, Coover and Rusty arrived with Hoyt in the back of the truck, still unconscious, blood slowly flowing from a cut on the back of his head. They dragged his body to the front door and headed inside. Ray sat at the desk reading some files as he noticed Rusty and Coover entering and dragging Hoyt's body across the wooden floor.

"Boys, for the love of the Heavenly Father, just pick the son of a bitch up. I don't want any of his blood on my wooden floor. Especially, blood from a Bennett."

"We brought him here." Rusty said. "Just like you asked, boss."

"I should thank you, boys." Ray said. "You're doing a much better job than that slut I hired. What about your little brother? Has he decided to join my alliance?"

"We should be receiving an answer soon." Coover said. "Mama's currently speaking with him about it."

"I'm sure she'll convince him to join." Ray said. "She has that strong presence amongst us. Especially, among her sons."

They place Hoyt onto a metal table, a table that belongs to Quarles Funeral Home. Hoyt is completely unconscious.

"What do you need us to do with him?" Rusty asked.

"Leave him here and I'll send him to the funeral home." Ray said. "Since, I'm good friends with the owner, they'll know exactly what to do with Hoyt."

Preston and Emily arrived at Hoyt's hideout location and they realized that he isn't there, not seeing his truck parked at that spot. Preston decided to visit Billy's mobile home, believing that Hoyt could possibly be there.

"Are you sure he could be there?" Emily said.

"It's worth a shot to check out."

CHAPTER 15

Billy is at his mother's home as she continued to convince him to join Ray's alliance. Billy disagreed with his mother and said that he feels better being on Hoyt's side, saying that he has full control over himself and that he's not following. Barbette continued to try and get through her son, she knew she's not getting anywhere by speaking to him.

Billy jumped up from the couch and decided to leave the home. He turned around and looked at his mother. His mother could see the sadness in his eyes for disobeying her. So, could Billy see the sadness in his mother's eye for not joining Ray and herself.

"I'm truly sorry, mom. But, whatever happens to me in this line of work, it just happens."

As Billy leaves his mother's home, she walked out the front door and watched him drive off. As he drove off, she contacted Ray and told him to do what he must, since Billy didn't listen to her.

Funeral assistants from Quarles Funeral Home arrive at Ray's cabin and they take Hoyt's unconscious body and place it in the back of one of their white hearses. The assistants thank Ray and tell him that the owner is quite pleased. They left and Ray smiled as something finally was accomplished.

At the office, Darius told Eldon and Cody that there was a fugitive on the loose in town and that they've been assign the task of capturing him. Eldon had agreed and sent Darius and Cody on the job.

Cody became very excited to work on another mission as Darius turned toward him.

"Please tell me, you've done this before?" Darius asked.

"They've never sent me out to search for a fugitive." Cody said. "I've only visited case sightings, like the bank and the jailhouse."

"Hopefully, you do a great job on this one." Darius said. "Since the guy we're looking for is on the government's top ten list of fugitives."

"This is going to be fun." Cody said smiling.

Darius and Cody left the office, heading towards Darius' black Kia Forte. Cody liked the car and said, "This is a nice ride. Can I drive it once we head back?"

"You're not driving this car." Darius said. "The only thing you're driving is that head of yours on this mission. Got it?"

"Yeah." Cody said. "Sure, I do."

Preston and Emily made it to Billy's mobile home. They notice Hoyt's truck parked, but no sign of him. Preston gets out of the car and walked to the front door. He knocked. Receiving no response. He knocked again with no response. He decided to open the door and once his hand touched the doorknob, the door opened with no one inside. Preston walked back to the car.

"Find anything?" Emily asked.

"No sign of Hoyt or Billy." Preston said. "There must be a place."

Hoyt had awoken and regained a little consciousness as he saw himself lying on the table in an embalming room. He looked around and saw no one inside. He gets up from the table and walked to the back door. He opened the door as he bumped into one of the funeral assistants.

"What are you doing up?" The assistant asked.

"What am I doing here?" Hoyt asked. "That's the real question."

The funeral assistant begins to back up from Hoyt as he walked closer to him. Hoyt stared at the assistant and said, "I'll ask again. Why am I here? What is this place?"

"You're at Quarles Funeral Home." The assistant said. "You were brought here on Ray Colby's command."

"Ray Colby's command you say?" Hoyt said. "So, you're telling me that, Ray had someone to knock me out. Then, they brought me here. For what? I'm not dead."

"They probably brought you here to take your organs." The assistant said. "Possibly your kidneys or something else."

"My organs." Hoyt said. "You're telling me that this funeral home also takes organs from unsuspected people. This is a new thing."

Hoyt reached in towards his back for his gun, but, realized it isn't there. The assistant smiled and pulled out a gun from his back. Hoyt looked up and noticed that the gun the assistant was holding was his.

"Why do you have my gun?" Hoyt asked.

"I might be a dull kind of guy, but, I'm not stupid." The assistant said. "Start backing up, Bennett."

"You know my name as well, I see." Hoyt said. "Interesting. You know how to fool someone don't you. Just like how you're fooling yourself right now."

"What are you talking about?" The assistant asked.

Slowly slipping from Hoyt's right sleeve, appeared another gun. Hoyt clenched it and shot the assistant in the forehead, blowing his head and killing him. Hoyt walked over to his body and started smiling. He also took back his gun.

"I'll take that, thank you." Hoyt said, taking the gun back. "I surely appreciate you holding on to it for me."

Hoyt heard someone coming towards the front door and he exits out through the back. He sneaked around to the front and steals one of their hearses and drives off with it. As Hoyt drives away, he looks at the interior of the hearse and smiled.

"Never knew it looked so good in these things."

Hoyt reached in his pocket and found his cell phone. He contacted Billy and told him to meet up at a local Convenience store on the outskirts of town. Billy agreed with a stumble in his voice as he headed toward the location.

Darius and Cody arrive at a small loan office. They walk in and speak with the lady in the front. They speak to her about a fugitive named Douglas Greene. According to the information given to Darius and Cody, Douglas used to work at the loan office, before his quit and went into a life of crime.

"We're only here to ask if you have any information regarding Mr. Greene." Darius said.

"I'm sorry, gentlemen. But, we have no information on him around here." The lady said. "All we know is that he decided to quit. We never seen him again."

Cody leaned in and said, "Do you know anyone who was good friends with Mr. Greene? Someone that used to work here?"

"There is a guy named Richard Dillon." The lady said. "He goes by the name, RJ Dillon. He lives in Hartford. If you find him, he might have the information that you're searching for."

"Thank you, Ms." Darius said. "Have a good day."

Darius and Cody leave the loan office and walked toward the vehicle. Cody looked over to Darius with a small grin on his face

"So, looks like we're heading to Hartford." Cody said. "This is starting to become one great trip."

"Keep in mind that we're here on business, Cody." Darius said. "Nothing more and nothing else."

Preston and Emily returned to Barbette's home to find any information on Hoyt and to see of Billy is there with her. They knock on the door and she opens it with mid pull, blowing a small gust from the inside of her home toward Preston and Emily.

"You've returned I see." Barbette said. "Something I never would've expected in my short wilds."

"I am truly sorry to bother you again, Ms. Bronson." Preston said. "But, we are looking for your son, Billy. Have you seen him?"

"He was here about an hour ago." Barbette said. "He left to head back to his place. He should be there at this moment."

176

"We've just come from his home, ma'am." Emily said. "So, we thought that he would've came here."

"Well, he did." Barbette said. "He just left before you arrived."

"Did he mention where he was heading off to? Any particular place?" Preston said. "Just a question that I thought I could ask."

Barbette looked with a frown and said, "No. But, I believe that he was going out to meet with Hoyt Bennett someplace in town."

"That's a problem." Emily said. "Because we can't find Hoyt either."

"Hmm." Barbette said. "That's none of my concern. If you do find my Billy and that prick of a human being, you let them know for sure that Barb told you where they would be."

"We'll pass on that message. We sure will." Preston said. "Have a good day, Ms. Bronson."

Preston and Emily left Barbette's home. She watched them drive off and returned into her home and shut the door, murmuring to herself.

Hoyt is parked in a Convenience store parking lot, which is surrounded by cars and people. He's sitting in the hearse waiting for Billy to arrive. He looked to his right and saw Billy's truck. Billy pulled up next to him and Hoyt tells him about the events and this is the first place of where they will start. Billy walked slowly with a look of confusion.

"What the Sam hell are you doing driving a hearse?" Billy asked.
You're an undertaker now suddenly?"

"The hearse? It's a long story and I'll explain to you the details at another time." Hoyt said. "Though, I am undertaking this line of work for a short while."

"Speaking of time, what do you mean about the events starting here?" Billy said. "I'm not getting the big picture here."

"Just watch the shopping center, Billy." Hoyt said. "Just watch and watch very closely."

Billy looked and watched for about a couple of minutes. As nothing is happening. Billy turned to Hoyt with a midst of disbelief.

"Watch what, Hoyt?" Billy asked. "What's going on?"

"Billy, look inside your glove box." Hoyt said.

Billy looked inside the glove box and finds a detonator. He pulled it out and looked toward Hoyt. Billy, he starts to shiver in fear.

"Hoyt, what is this?" Billy asked in fear.

"That is a detonator, my friend." Hoyt said. "When you press the button, we will all witness an explosion that will be seen across the land and later, on the nightly news."

"I…. I can't do it, Hoyt." Billy said. "I'm sorry, but, I can't do something like this."

"Just hand it to me, my good friend." Hoyt said. "I'll take care of it."

Billy handed the detonator to Hoyt and he grabbed it. Hoyt flipped up the detonator's top and looked at Billy, smiling with intense energy running through his body. Billy shivered.

"Ladies and gentlemen. Also, you too, Billy. The events have officially begun." It's time to finally blow some shit up!"

"Oh my God!" Billy yelled. "HOYT!!!"

"*INCOMING CALL!!!!*" Hoyt yelled loudly.

Hoyt pressed the button, detonating the bomb and caused an explosion to the entire Convenience store store. Flames fly up into the air as they begin to engulf the entire building with people running from the doors on every corner, screaming in fear and terror. Billy is terrified completely as he looked over at Hoyt, smiling and laughing insanely.

"Let's go!" Billy yelled. "Hoyt, let's get the hell out of this place!"

"What's that, Billy?" Hoyt asked. "I can't hear you through the screams coming from the sheep running from the barn."

"Let's go!" Billy yelled again. "Right now! Let's go!"

"Right now?!" Hoyt asked. "Right now?! You mean right now?!"

"Come on, Hoyt! Damn it!"

Hoyt puts the hearse in drive and exited the parking lot, passing by people who are scattered across the lot. Hoyt stuck his head out of the window and started hollering toward them. Screaming various words and famous quotes. They drive off the lot and head back on the main street.

CHAPTER 16

At the office, Eldon tells Preston and Emily that a Convenience store has been blown to smithereens. Preston asked how it happened and Eldon has no answer to give him. Emily tells them they should head there to ask any questions about the incident. They leave the office, going to the Convenience store. Once in the jeep, Eldon calls Darius and Cody to tell them about the incident.

"Hello, Darius." Eldon said.

"Darius here." Darius said. "Eldon, what's the situation?"

"We just received a call that a Convenience store was blown up." Eldon said. "So, I, Preston, and Emily are heading there now to figure this all out."

"Ok. Do you need us to come along?" Darius asked.

"No, just continue what's your doing on your case and we'll deal with this one." Eldon said.

He hanged up the phone, while he drove down the street, heading to the decimated Convenience store building.

Ray learned of the Convenience store incident and he knows Hoyt is behind it. He commands his men to track down Hoyt and kill him. By any means of force. His men leave the warehouse, entering their SUVs and driving out of sight. Inside the warehouse is Barbette, who Ray didn't realize was inside with him. She sits in front of him.

"Ms. Bronson. I wasn't expecting to see you here." Ray said. "A place such as this of all the ones we have."

"I'm here to ask you about my sons. Mainly I'm here to ask about my Billy." Barbette said. "Do you have any information on him of where he is or anything in particular?"

"All I am aware of is your son being partners with Hoyt." Ray said. "I sent Coover and Rusty to speak with him, but they didn't receive an answer."

"So, you have any information on where Hoyt's whereabouts are right now?" Barbette asked. "Any information?"

"He was at Quarles Funeral Home." Ray said. "But, it seems that he escaped and blew up a Convenience store downtown."

"He blew up a Convenience store?" Barbette asked. "That's the best he's got to offer? I could give two shits on a paper plate about some goddamn Convenience store being blown to smithereens."

"You believe that you can do better?" Ray asked. "That's what your voice is telling me."

"Of course, I can do better!" Barbette said. "I can do a hell of a lot worse than what he's just done. I could cause panic across the entire city. Hell, I can cause panic across this entire state."

"I believe you there, Ms. Bronson." Ray said. "So, what's the plan concerning your baby boy?"

"Do what you will with him." Barbette said. "I tried speaking with him, he wouldn't listen. Coover and Rusty tried, so just do what you must to keep the alliance going."

"To keep the alliance going, we must kill Hoyt." Ray said. "I've already sent some of my men to take him out as we speak. They'll do a fine job."

"Let's hope they do." Barbette said. "Bring us a bundle of good joy and good fortune to our tables."

They shook hands and she left the warehouse. Ray gets up from the seat and leaves through the back door rubbing his head.

Hoyt and Billy are at the hideout and Hoyt is happier than a little boy during the holidays. Billy is still shaking with fear as Hoyt tried to calm him down.

"Billy, just relax, my friend. The first event is over. So, now we celebrate it."

"How can I celebrate when thousands of people were killed

right in front of my eyes. How can I live with that in my mind, just popping up continually?"

"You can get through it, friend. You just have to relax your mind and prepare for the second event."

"Ok. So, I'll ask this right now. What this second event you have planned?"

Hoyt turned and smiled.

"It's time that we take our skills to a bigger location." Hoyt said. "We'll head up to New Haven City Hall eventually and just blow that place up too. Blow it to complete shit."

"Wait and excuse me. But, City Hall." Billy said. "That's a pretty big spot to do this, Hoyt and you're going to need some heavy artillery and explosives to complete something of that status."

"That is why you call it an event. Because it's a huge location for our city and it's the only location where the entire city will actually pay attention to our needs. Once City Hall blows to shit, we will have complete control over New Haven."

"If that's how you feel, Hoyt. If you say so."

Hoyt picked up a glass of vodka and hit Billy's glass and drank it. Hoyt smiled as he believes his events are finally coming into play. Billy continues to join in, even though he's scared.

Preston, Emily, and Eldon arrive at the decimated Convenience store. Still with charcoal-like smoke arriving from the building. Fire trucks, ambulances, and police cars are surrounding the location. They walk toward one of the officials. He is checking each person that arrives at the scene with a clipboard.

"What's the clipboard for, officer?" Eldon asked. "Don't think we'll need one on this investigation."

"It's to check if anyone inside is either injured or dead." The officer replied. "So, I see you got the call."

"Yeah we did and while I have you in front of me. Maybe you could tell me if there are any witnesses that seen anything unusual before the explosion took place?"

"We only have one witness so far. He's over there at the

ambulance. He's being checked for injuries."

"Thanks." Eldon said.

They walk over to the ambulance and see the witness being searched for any signs of injury. He is not injured, and they release him. Before he walks away, Preston stands in front of him.

"I'm sorry, but, who the hell are you?" The witness asked.

"I'm Preston Maddox. United States Marshal and Homicide Detective. Me and my partners here just want to ask you some questions regarding the incident."

"All I saw was the explosion and nothing else after that but people running for their lives."

"What else did you see?" Eldon asked.

"Smoke, debris." The witness said. "What did you think I saw? UFOs beaming down at us?"

Preston and Eldon smiled. Emily walked toward the witness.

"Please, just tell us what else you saw and we'll be out of your way." Emily said.

"Since you put it that way, lady. There was one thing I did see."

"Well, by all means, please tell us, then." Eldon said. "For your sake I suppose."

The witness paused for a moment and uttered, "I saw these two guys, both white. They were both in trucks, parked next to each other. They stayed in there until the explosion and once that happened, they were the first ones gone."

"Did one of them yell out anything?" Preston asked. "Anything that may seem familiar to you or to this place?"

"One of them did yell out the words. Some of them I couldn't understand. But, I noticed he yelled out the phrase, *"Incoming Call"*. Don't know if that will help you or not."

"Shit!" Preston said. "It was Hoyt. It was him."

"How can you be so sure about that, Preston?" Eldon asked.

"He's the only son of a bitch that would yell out that phrase before an explosion would take place. I'll go ahead and look for him."

"We're coming with you." Eldon said. "You hear me, Preston."

Preston leaves the scene as Eldon and Emily get into the jeep and follow him. Preston stops at a red light and on the side of him arrives Eldon and Emily in the jeep. Eldon rolled down the window.

"Where are you headed?" Eldon asked.

"Going over to Hoyt's hideout in the outskirts. From my understanding, that's where he'll be currently."

CHAPTER 17

Darius and Cody arrive at a small home in the suburbs of Hartford. They find a large brick home with a mailbox on the front lawn. The initials on the mailbox are, "RJ" Cody looked at it and turned to the house.

"Appears to be his place, Mr. D." Cody said. "What do you think?"

"Looks like it could be." Darius said. "Also, don't call me, Mr. D. Wherever you thought up that name."

"Sure, no problem." Cody said.

They walked to the front door and Darius knocked. He knocked again, no response. Cody looked over at him, believing that he's not at the house. Darius knocked one more time and the door opens. An African American male is standing on the other side.

"Excuse us, sir." Darius said. "But, we're United States Marshals from New Haven on a case concerning a man named Richard Dillon. Also known to some people as, RJ Dillon."

"Never heard of the guy." The man said.

"What's with the RJ initials on the mailbox, sir?" Cody asked. "According to that and my knowledge, it makes you appear as the guy who we're looking for."

"What has this guy done to have some marshals on his trail?" The man asked. "If I am able to know."

"RJ Dillon is a fugitive of the United States government." Darius said. "To put it in a short sentence for you, the guy's a con artist."

"A con artist you say." The man said. "From what you're saying is the guy's been giving lots of people trouble in a lot of various ways."

"A little too much trouble." Cody said. "We were given information from a loan office and the information states that RJ lives in this very house. In the end, that's why we're here and the initials on the mailbox plainly give it away for us."

"Well, I'll say this and you two can be on your way off this property. I don't know any RJ Dillon." The man said. "So, if you please leave my home, we will have no trouble."

"We can't leave this property until we receive concrete information regarding RJ Dillon and this location." Cody said. "So, if you don't mind, we'll wait here until he arrives or comes back from wherever he's currently placed."

"You'll just wait for him? Ok. If you say so." The man said as he shut the door in their faces.

Cody turned to Darius, curious.

"Did he just slam the door in our faces?" Cody asked. "Because, its looks that way."

"Yeah." Darius replied. "By that means of action, he knows something we don't know."

Darius knocked on the door again. No answer as he knocked twice as hard on the door. The door opened, and RJ Dillon walked out, facing Darius and Cody. Wearing his expensive white suit with nice black shades.

"Didn't my assistant just tell you two dickheads to leave this property." RJ said. "So, why in the blue hell are the two of you still here?"

"So, you're RJ Dillon I see." Darius said. "If you're not aware, me and my partner here are on your property to take you into custody for your con artistry."

"My ass you aren't. I'm not going anywhere in any shape or form."

He reached behind him and pulled out an RPK machine gun. Darius and Cody backed up a couple of feet with their hands in the air. Their faces show a slight fear within them. Though, they stand their guard.

"Wow, an RPK. OK. That's a nice firearm you have there, RJ."

"Thank you, boy." RJ said. "I won it in a poker game a few

months back. Thanks to the great ace."

"Did you shoot the loser after the game was over?" Darius asked. "Just seems obvious that you would do something like that and since you're a con man, you've probably did more than just that with anyone."

"How about I just shoot the two of you, right here on the spot." RJ said. "That way I can be rid of you easily. Since you won't leave my property."

"You don't have to do that, Mr. RJ." Cody said. "We'll just leave right now if you like."

Darius and Cody start walking towards the car slowly as RJ has the machine gun pointed toward them. They get to their car and RJ commands them to get inside. They get inside and once RJ puts down the machine gun, Cody fires a gun at his knee. RJ yelled and dropped the RPK. His assistant runs out of the house, with an AK. Darius pulled out his pistol and shot the assistant in the chest. Cody runs out of the car and drags RJ with him. They place RJ in the back of the car and Darius looked at Cody.

"Didn't think you had it in you." Darius said. "Very good skill set."

"I might be a rookie Marshal in training, but I'm highly skilled in the presence of marksmanship." Cody said.

Handcuffing RJ's hands and legs, they left the area, heading to the interstate, returning to New Haven. Darius looked in the back toward RJ and glanced over to Cody, who's driving the vehicle.

"You're sure he'll be comfortable back there all cuffed up?" Darius said.

"Who gives a damn if he feels comfortable. I say he deserves it for what he's done to many innocent people."

Ray's men arrive at a small location, where they meet with Coover and Rusty about assassinating Hoyt. Coover tells the group that they must be silent on this mission and Rusty tells them that their primary target is Hoyt, but, by Ray's order and Barbette's answers, if Billy pops up on the scene, that they must shoot him as well. Rusty decides to also tell the group about the marshals. Rusty said that if any of the marshals arrive on the scene, they must take them out as well.

"We must do what we can to keep this all quiet." Rusty said. "If the marshals arrive on scene, we take them out. Completely."

"Every single one of them." Coover said. "Whether its Hoyt, our dear brother, Billy, or the marshals, we have to put them down."

"Basically, men." Rusty said. "No witnesses. No casualties. That way there won't be any traces that will lead to us, Ray, or mother."

"You're sure about all of this?"

"I'm damn sure about it."

They begin to march out with their guns and weapons. They head toward their vehicles and leave, driving to Hoyt's hideout.

Preston, Emily, and Eldon arrive at Hoyt's hideout. Eldon looked around the deserted area of grass. Emily looked around as well. Though, they spot both Hoyt's and Billy's trucks, confirming that the two of them are currently inside the hideout. Preston walked toward the front door. He knocked, and Billy opened it.

"Marshal!" Billy yelled. "Marshals!"

Preston shoved Billy out of the way, letting Eldon and Emily walk in. Hoyt arrives from the kitchen area, smiling. Preston doesn't smile, not an inch. Neither does Eldon and Emily. Preston delivered a right-hook punch to Hoyt, which knocked him to the ground. He picked him up and shoved him against the wall, knocking down one of the mounted deer heads.

"You no good son of a bitch!" Preston said. "You no good piece of shit!"

"Preston, what have I done to cause such anger from you?" Hoyt asked. "Killed someone you loved in the process or something worse than that?"

"I know, we know. Hell, everyone now knows." Preston said. "The Convenience store that exploded, that was you. It's all on you, Hoyt. The witness gave you out with your "Incoming Call" battle cry."

"Preston, just relax for a minute." Eldon said. "Let the man get a breather."

"No!" Preston yelled. "There is no relaxing right now, damn it. He's killed thousands of people today and I'm not going to stand by and let him kill a thousand more! To hell with his breather!"

Preston punched Hoyt again and threw him across the counter to the kitchen. Eldon tries to calm Preston down, but, it isn't working. Billy crouches in the corner to avoid Preston. Preston continues pummeling Hoyt and Emily stopped him from doing any more damage to Hoyt as he's bleeding from nose to mouth.

"Preston, enough is enough now." Emily said. "Just calm down, please. So, we can settle this like civilized people."

Preston responded to Emily and stopped attacking Hoyt.

"I'm starting to like her even more so now." Hoyt said.

"Don't push your luck." Emily said. "Or I'll just let him continue to beat your ass to a pulp."

"Come on, Emily. There's no need for that right now." Eldon said.

Preston looked over at the corner, where Billy is and he pointed toward him, saying he's next if he tries anything that Hoyt has done. As they prepare to take Hoyt to their car, they notice headlights coming towards the house. They ducked down to avoid being seen.

"Who's that outside?" Emily asked.

"Probably someone that's come to kill Hoyt." Preston said. "For all the shit he's caused so far.'

Eldon took a peep outside the window and saw what appeared to be seven cars, all having dozens of men walk out, with weapons in their hands. Eldon ducked down and told the rest of them what's going on outside.

On the outside, Coover and Rusty are leading the pack of Ray's men toward the hideout. Coover recognizes Billy's truck and points it out to Rusty. Rusty looked at the hideout.

"Billy!" Rusty yelled. "Billy, we know you're in there, little brother. We know your good buddy, Hoyt is in there too. So, why don't the two of you do use a favor and just walk on out here nice and calm, so we can finish our business here."

"Come on little brother." Coover said. 'We're only here to talk with you. But, Hoyt, we're here to kill that no-good bastard."

Inside the house, everyone is crouched down, preparing their firearms. Hoyt looked over at Preston, still in pain from Preston's attack.

"You have to help me, just this once." Hoyt said. "Please."

"Why?" Preston said. "So, you can kill more innocent people. You've done enough. I should just let you die here."

"But, you won't." Hoyt said. "Because, we were once friends."

"We were friends a long time ago, Hoyt." Preston said. "That time has come and gone and its over for you."

The pack of men are closer to the house as they start banging on the windows and the front door. One man decides to kick the door down. But, he couldn't do it, since he hurt himself in the process. Coover and Rusty pull out their handguns and fire at the windows, knocking them out. Preston looked over to Hoyt and asked him of a back door. Hoyt pointed toward the kitchen and they all head out the back. Just as they left, Coover knocked down the door and they entered the hideout. They didn't find anyone around the area.

Just as they searched the hideout, they heard engines sound. Coover and Rusty looked at one another and walked to the outside. To which, they see Preston, Emily, Eldon, Billy, and Hoyt leaving in their vehicles. Rusty now upset, turned toward his brother. Pointing at them running off in the distance.

"Shit! They're running away, fellas!" Rusty yelled. "Grab your gear and get in your vehicles!"

They jumped into their vehicles and proceed to chase them all down. Now, on the highway, there's a chase between the two groups. Coover drives behind Hoyt's truck and Rusty begins firing at him. Hoyt ducked down as the shots came in inches closer toward his head.

"Did you hit him, bro?" Coover asked. "Did you hit him?"

"What's it look like to you, no I didn't." Rusty said. "Just keep your eyes on the damn road and just drive."

Now, Emily started to fire a couple of shots toward the pack around them. She popped out the tires on some of the men's vehicles, stopping them from the chase. She fired more shots toward Coover and

Rusty, knocking out their back window. Coover started to yell as he's in a fury.

"She just knocked out our damn window, bro!" Coover said. "That isn't going by easy with me, man."

"Don't worry, mama doesn't like the bitch anyway." Rusty said. "So, we'll kill her for mama's sake."

Rusty begins firing toward the jeep as Eldon and Emily both ducked. Eldon covers his head, while continuing to drive.

"I didn't think it would be like this down here." Emily said. "I thought it would be more subtle and a little quieter."

"This is New Haven, Ms. Weston.' Eldon said. 'Not your kind of New Jersey feel of the day.'

Emily continued to fire at the pack. The intersection turns into a two-way street. Now, Coover and Rusty are driving on the side of Hoyt. Rusty fires toward Hoyt, he ducked his head and reached for his gun.

Once Rusty stopped firing, Hoyt rose up from the door and shot Rusty in the chest and also shot Coover in the right arm. Coover screams in pain, losing control of the truck. The truck drives off the interstate and dives down into a ditch on the side. The truck started flipping over around three times. Hoyt cheerfully yelled out the window.

"That's right my people!" Hoyt yelled. "That's how you handle these bastards around here!"

Coover and Rusty dragged themselves from the damaged truck. Coover helped Rusty walk his way up toward the road. Staggering and stumbling in pain, the two of them try to gain more strength as they inch closer to the road.

"Come on bro." Coover said. "I got you, don't worry."

Another one of Ray's men drive on the left lane, directly next to Preston. He looked over at them as they threat him by screaming out words. He pulled out his gun and shot their tire, causing them to turn and flip across the interstate.

"These assholes never learn." Preston said.

Emily looked over at Preston's car and he's pointing in front of them, telling them to go forward. They pass him and so does Billy and

Hoyt. But, Hoyt slows down a bit next to Preston. Hoyt looked over at Preston.

"Preston." Hoyt yelled. "The next time you come into my place of business and proceed to beat me down, you won't be so lucky."

"I'll take my chances." Preston yelled. "You best be careful on this road."

"I'll be just fine and dandy. See you next time, Preston." Hoyt yelled as he drove away.

"That son of a bitch." Preston said. "He'll never get it straight through his head."

Ray, Barbette, and Carla meet at his nightclub, inside his office. Ray is pleased to see Barbette there, but he isn't pleased at all, seeing Carla.

"I have to thank you, Ms. Bronson." Ray said. "I never would expect to see you in this type of place."

"Wherever business must be settled, Colby, I'll be there." Barbette said. "So, what's the reason for us being here at such time?"

"I received a call from the chief and he's not too pleased with what's going on." Ray said. "He heard about the Convenience store incident and has told me take out Hoyt."

"We're all trying to take out Hoyt, Mr. Colby." Barbette said. 'The real question is how are we supposed to do that with the marshals on his trail?"

"You can leave the marshals to me." Carla said. "I can deal with them easily. Instead of killing them, I'll just use my persuasion on them."

"How can you convince me to trust you this time, Carla?" Ray asked. "You've already had one of my most allied men killed at the agency."

Barbette looked over at Carla. She took another glance before keeping her glaze locked on Carla. He raised her finger and pointed toward her.

"Wait a god damn minute now. You're the lady who lead John into that building?" Barbette asked. "You lead him in there, armed and not in the state of mind to do so?"

"He seemed like he was ready to me, Ms. Bronson." Carla said. "I just didn't know he had it in him to proceed with the mission at hand. He was a strong-minded guy."

"What happened to John isn't our main priority of the matter now." Ray said. "What currently matters to all of us is we find a way of taking out Hoyt, getting rid of these marshals, and ruling over this city."

"May that be done in a hurry." Barbette said. "Very quickly, before more shit comes into play and ruins what we already have here ongoing."

She shook Ray's hand and left the office. Ray leaned over to Carla and told her that she cannot fail him one more time or he might have to put her down himself. She laughed as she left the office.

CHAPTER 18

Darius and Cody returned to the office. They've taken RJ to the downtown jailhouse and left him there, until the morning. They walk into the office and placed all of their equipment back into their locations. Cody leaves the office, heading home. Darius is doing the same. As they both head downstairs, Cody turned to Darius.

"We did a good job today." Cody said.

"I could say, yeah we did do a good job." Darius said. "A great job, really."

They walk towards their cars and they leave, heading to their homes.

Preston returns to his apartment and realizes that its unlocked again. He decides not to pull out his gun and walked in. Once he was inside, he turned on the switch and he's standing toe-to-toe with Ray Colby. Preston grunted as he saw Ray standing in front of him with a pistol pointed directly towards him.

"It seems that everyone has a key to my place." Preston said. "So, Carla gave you the heads up on my resting spot or did you just bully the owner into giving you an extra key?"

"It's the best thing Carla's done for me so far in her line of work." Ray said. "You have no need to worry if I try to kill you here. I'm only here to tell you about Hoyt's current situation and how it concerns me and my elite group."

"I could give a shit about your elite group. What's this situation have to do with Hoyt and your pals?" Preston said. "Is it about his patterned explosion attacks over the past few days or is it something that he's done to you in a way that I have no knowledge of? I assume its something more personal going on here?"

"I'm going to say this once and only once in a way that you can understand, Marshal. Either you leave Hoyt to me and I'll spare your entire agency from a total disaster. You and your marshals are invading my business. My property, you guys even ran some of my men off the road during that chase you guys had."

"Well, I'll say this, Ray." Preston said. "I'm not going to leave Hoyt alone because he is my task to accomplish. As of right now, I'm going to give you a ten-second count to leave this place, before I put a bullet through you and tell your elite friends that another one has been brought down."

Ray smiled. He nodded as he stared at Preston.

"Ten seconds, you say?" Ray said. "Sounds like a threat towards me. How should I take it from you when your weapon isn't even in your hand and mine is? Explain that to me? I can put a, what you say, bullet through you, before you even pull out your weapon."

"You'll pay to find that out." Preston said. "Just like your old buddy Cartel did. He played this game as well and you know how it ended for him don't you."

"Smooth. Ray said. "So, before I go I would want to say."

"Ten." Preston said. "And counting."

Ray laughed. He shook his finger toward Preston, who continued to stand still. Ray nodded his head.

"Funny and clever." Ray said. "You really know how to intimidate your enemies, Marshal. In ways that other marshals or detectives wouldn't even give a mere thought towards."

"Nine." Preston said. "The countdown is still on going, Colby."

Preston slowly moved his right hand to his side, almost ready to pull out his weapon. Ray doesn't even notice it. Ray placed his gun back into his back and slowly moved inches closer to the door.

"Ok." Ray said. "Alright. I'll leave. But, take my advice under serious conditions, Marshal or there will be consequences on your head."

Ray left the apartment and Preston turned around and made sure that Ray left the area.

The next morning, Coover and Rusty are visiting the hospital to search for any injuries on their bodies due to the crazed speeding chase. They find bruised ribs on Coover, but a broken rib and a dislocated shoulder on Rusty. Barbette arrived and seen her sons in the hospital room.

"What happened?" Barbette asked. "What happened to my two babies?"

"Mama, we were ran off the road by those marshals." Coover said. "We were just trying to do the job."

"Don't talk about it in here, Coover." Rusty said with pain in his voice. "We don't need anyone hearing about our business. They might try to pull something against us, so we would have to pay more."

Leaving the hospital, walking towards their mother's partially clean brown Durango. They helped Rusty walk to the car and help him into the passenger's seat.

Coover inched closer to Barbette so he could whisper the information to her. In order to avoid confrontation with people in the hospital.

"Mama, we tried to take out Hoyt." Coover said. "But, those marshals invaded the plans. If they didn't we would've had him."

"Was Billy there as well?" Barbette asked. "Was he with Hoyt when this was taking place?"

"Yes ma'am." Coover said. "We tried to have spoken conversations with him, but, he didn't respond to us. Nor, did he come to visit us here."

"It's alright, my sons." Barbette said. "Billy has decided to leave the family that raised him. There's nothing we can do to save him now. He's on his own at this point."

At the office, Eldon speaks with Darius and Cody about their case in Hartford. Darius tells Eldon that the case when nice and they've placed RJ in custody. Eldon is impressed and thanks them both for their help in finding RJ. Preston and Emily walk into the office and

Preston told Eldon that Ray was inside his apartment last night, giving him a warning not to have any marshal or law enforcement officers involved with Hoyt. Eldon tells Preston that he should take Ray's words and shove them up Ray's ass. Preston laughed.

"So, if I may ask you of this. Your anger craze, yesterday." Eldon said. "What the hell was that all about?"

"Throughout most of his adult life, Hoyt has killed thousands of people across this city and state, Eldon." Preston said. "It's about time that someone gave him a beat down and to be honest, I wasn't even quite finished with him."

"He deserved a lot more, I believe." Eldon said. "Though, you can't let your anger take control over yourself. It could cost you dearly."

"He deserved a lot more." Preston said. "A thousand times more. Since, he's killed that number of people, some innocent and some not. He deserves it."

"If Emily didn't calm you down, you've would have possibly killed the guy." Eldon said. "Imagine how that would look upon you."

"Me and Hoyt were once good friends, long ago." Preston said. "Times have changed and so have the friendships and trust."

Eldon later told Preston to head out toward the courthouse, so they can discuss RJ's case. Preston looked over at Eldon, asking if Darius and Cody should be there, since they picked the guy up in the first place. Eldon said that they will be there and so should him and Preston.

At the courthouse, the judge is sentencing RJ to four years in prison for his previous crimes such as being a con artist, he's also convicted of burglary, kidnapping, and a case of three homicides. The security handcuffed RJ and took him out of the courtroom through the back doors and towards a police car, that's parked in the front of the building.

They open the front doors and it is crowded with reporters and journalists, asking RJ questions concerning what he's done over the years. He gives them no responses as he gets into the back of the police car and it drives off. Eldon and Preston walk over to Darius and Cody and congratulate them on solving RJ's case.

"You guys did great." Eldon said. "I should tell the head office to give you guys some higher power of authority."

"I don't think you should do that, Eldon." Preston said. "Might cause their egos to take over and when the ball drops their careers would be over in a nutshell."

"I don't have that much of an ego, Preston." Darius said. "Though, I think we all know that Cody does to a certain extent."

"Not really, guys." Cody said. "When it comes to egos, you won't have to look toward him for being some kind of a narcissist.

At the warehouse, Ray finds out about what happened with the chase and that he lost a few of his men during the event. Coover and Rusty walk in with Barbette on their side.

"Coover, Rusty. Are you alright?" Ray asked.

"We're fine, boss." Rusty said. "Just some minor injuries, that's all."

"Hoyt and those damn marshal folks hurt my two sons, Colby." Barbette said. "They ran them off the road and into that foul ditch. Now their means of transportation is completely damaged."

"You shouldn't have to worry, Ms. Bronson. I'll go ahead and purchase your boys another truck. Though, we seriously need to consider the process of finding Hoyt and your youngest son." Ray said.

"It would be best if you could lead both Hoyt and that Instinct Marshal into some kind of a trap." Coover said. "You know, lead them both there, simultaneously, so that way, we can kill them both at the same time. Good plan, huh."

"The two birds and one stone play. It could work. But, how would we lead them to the same location?" Ray said.

"You let me handle that large obstacle, Ray." A female voice said from the front.

Ray looked and its Carla once again. Ray's had enough of her and commands his security to take her out. She tells Ray that she knows exactly how to lure both Preston and Hoyt into the same location to be killed. Ray asked her how and she said that she'll handle it, since she doesn't want them involved with it. Ray stood up and decided to allow Carla to go forward with the plan and that he has to leave for a trip to Newark, New Jersey.

Barbette stood up and thanks Ray for her son's new vehicle and said that they must take them all out soon. They leave and Carla leaves behind them, telling Ray not to worry. One of Ray's men walked up to him with a photo from the Caucasian and African-American men who were waiting inside the car.

"Sir, the two watchers told me to bring this picture to you." The thug said. "They suspected it would be highly useful to you."

Ray looked at the photo and it's a picture of Emily. Ray thought back to his New Jersey days and remembered who Emily was and knew she's also from Newark. He only focused on the picture as he decided to place a hit on her by hiring one hit man. He even exceeded the plan as to let the marshals know where he's headed, saying to his group that it would just to fool them and lure them into the trap.

"By doing this, they will never know what's going to hit them." Ray said. "Won't even have a clue what will be coming up on their front steps."

"You got it boss." The thug said.

The thug left the warehouse as Ray continued to read some unknown documents that were stacked on his desk.

At the office, Eldon contacts Preston and Emily to tell them that Ray has made an announcement that Ray is traveling to Newark for a business trip. Emily suggested that she'll go ahead and search around the city for Colby, since she's a native of the area. She left the office. Preston looked and turned to Eldon.

"So, as of now, I'm on my own?" Preston asked. "Due to Emily running off on her own merry goose chase."

"That appears to be the case." Eldon said. "Also, since Cody is currently partnered up with Darius, that does leave you on your own."

"Alright." Preston said. "I'll take only small portions of this to savor in."

"I almost forgot about this because of your savoring. Something did come up that I personally believe you'll be happy to solve on your own." Eldon said.

"Which is what?" Preston asked. "Picking up lunch for the agency. Or the fugitives in questioning."

Eldon leaned over his desk and pulled out a document from underneath a small pile of paper notes. He handed the document over to Preston, in which he opened it and found it containing a picture of Carla meeting with Ray at the warehouse in the outskirts of New Haven

"You have got to me shitting me. This is what you wanted to give me to do. Go around town to search for an ex and an elite crime thug."

"I figured it would do you some good. Get some of that steam off your chest at least."

"I'll manage my stream progress. So, who exactly am I searching for on this case? Can't be Colby because Emily's already on the chase."

"There have been reports of seeing your old flame circling around town. Talking and making deals with a many of people that seem to be getting paid under the radar by Colby and his elite crime friends. So, you're on this case. Since you know her very well."

"I'll go ahead and do it. But, once I am finished with this one, I'm going ahead to look for Hoyt. Some of those events haven't happened yet and we need to stop them."

"Go ahead and do that. I won't stop you there."

In the outskirts of New Haven, just around a small field near a steep hill, Hoyt and Billy are sitting in a truck, over viewing Ray's warehouse. Billy looked around at the area, searching for any of Colby's henchmen around the location.

"So, far I don't see any of Ray's guys out here." Billy said. "What are we going to do when everything is in complete order, Hoyt?"

"Good of you to ask. The last plan will involve his warehouse in a huge way. It will be an epic event for us. But, so far two of the events have happened and we can't look too far into the near future."

"Wait, I thought only one of the events had took place." Billy asked. "The two have actually happened?"

"Listen very closely. The jailhouse was the first event in the long process. The Convenience store explosion was only the second one and that went somewhat how I expected it to go. As of this moment, we have just two more events to go before the main course, being the warehouse here, takes its place atop the other four."

"If I may ask you, what are the next two events? I take it you're going to blow up Target next or a mall? Because, personally I don't like Target, Hoyt. They're just cheapskates over there. Don't do shit about their customers."

"Convenience store didn't either. I would expect you to hate nearly all of the retail stores."

"That was a good point. I never thought of it in that way."

"One thing's for sure, Billy. I'm not blowing up another shopping place. That already took its course. This time, it has to be something quieter than the last two places. Something to get people off their asses when it culminates."

"Could you give me some kind of a hint as to what place would be like that? Because, I don't know any quiet, quiet places that you could actually blow up without causing a problem."

"Believe me when I say, there's a place, Billy. There's a place around this land that's point-blank right up our noses and around the corner. But, I'm starting to think that we need more members, just to have a full overview of the entire city."

It's nightfall in New Jersey as Ray arrived in Newark. After exiting his private plane, he's escorted out of the airport approaching his vehicle. He's heavily guarded with security as they lead him towards his black SUV waiting for him out front. They walk out of the airport as Ray entered the SUV and it pulled away with three of his henchmen already inside the back of the SUV. Ray nodded at them as he reached into his jacket and pulled out his phone and started dialing a number.

"Hello, chief. This is Colby. Yeah, I'm in Newark. Everything will go as planned as we discussed. The female Marshal? She shouldn't be too far gone behind us. We'll have her in place as soon as she's in our sights. Don't worry, chief, it's all in good hands."

Ray hung up the phone and started smiling to himself.

CHAPTER 19

Carla sat in a room as she was having a meeting with six of Ray's thugs and she discusses the plan to lure both Preston and Hoyt into the same location, only for them to be killed by the six thugs. As the thugs sat at a round table, looking at Carla standing up in front of them. One of the thugs stood up. He gained the attention of the other five thugs and Carla herself as he began questioning Carla's proposed plan of attack in the woods.

"So, what's your position in this plan, sweetheart?" One thug asked. "If you don't mind a man like me asking such a question."

"My plan is to be the backup." Carla said.

"Backup?" The thug said. "What kind of backup are you talking about? More guys like us or some highly trained folks that are in this for the sake of execution and a little extra profit."

"You'll just have to wait and see who they are." Carla said. "The backup will do us some good in this task."

Another thug stood up and said that she's responsible for John's death and why should they trust her on this mission. Carla said that she can be trusted, since what happened with John wasn't her fault. The six thugs look at one another and turned to Carla.

"We'll help you out on this one, Carla." The thug said. "But, don't think for a second to turn on us. By any means."

"You won't have to worry about that." Carla said. "You're all in good hands being with me."

The thugs nod as Carla left the room. Though, the first two thugs are a little uncertain about Carla's motives in the process.

Eldon contacts Darius and Cody to come to his office. They enter his office and sit at the desk. Eldon turned to them with documents in his hand.

"What's going on now, chief?" Darius asked.

"We've just received a new case that concerns a hit man." Eldon said.

"Hit man? Cool." Cody said. "Sounds like it should be great case to work on."

"Who's this hit man and what's his case of being the cause?" Darius asked.

"The hit man's name is currently unknown at this moment." Eldon said. "But, for some odd reason, his only targets are female prostitutes."

"Prostitutes? He has some obsession with prostitutes." Darius said. "I wonder why he would have that type of agenda. For whatever reason, sure doesn't sound like fun."

"That's what I'm trying to figure out." Eldon said. "Since Preston is busy with a case and Emily's out of state, I'm going to join the two of you on this one. Just to have some time out of the office."

"Where's the first place that we should look?" Darius asked.

"We'll head to a local street in the low side of town." Eldon said. "That's where most of the prostitution business takes place. If its crowded with women by tonight, we should find out hit man."

"Hopefully." Darius said.

Hoyt and Billy enter small building. Inside is a group of people playing poker. Hoyt looked at the guys and yelled to get their attention. They turned in fear and started walking towards him, pulling out their guns and knives.

"From my perspective it sure looks like a nice game of poker is being played here in the centerfolds." Hoyt said. "Mind if me and my friend here join in on the game and try to win some prizes of our own."

"Who the hell are you two boys?" One man said. "What the hell you're doing here in our place?"

"Gentlemen, gentlemen, please. No trouble has entered into

your doorstep." Hoyt said. "Now just calm down and relax yourselves. I'm only here to present you fellow gentlemen an offer that you cannot possibly refuse according to how you're behaving as of this moment."

"Oh yeah. What type of offer?" The man said.

"An offer that will bring in a lot of money." Hoyt said. "As well as some control over the city."

The man looked over at his friends as they start to nod their heads in acceptance. The man turned his attention back to Hoyt. Staring him into his eyes.

"Money and control, you say? Alright." The man said. "I'll say we're all in. What do you need us to do?"

"If you and your group just follow me to my new safe haven and everything will be explained there." Hoyt said. "Please follow quickly and quietly, so we don't cause a disturbance."

Emily arrives through the interstate, entering Newark, New Jersey. Once inside the city she's already determined and going on the hunt for Ray. She drives down and travels through the downtown area to search for any evidence that will lead to him. Though, she doesn't find anything, she drives past an office building, she notices a man who looked similar to Ray physically. She slowly entered the parking lot to have a closer look. The man she was looking at wasn't Ray.

"Damn it." Emily said. "No sign of Ray here. Where could he have gone? I could check the agency. They should remember who I am."

Preston is visiting a small diner. The diner is quiet, as there aren't many people inside. He walked toward the counter, where he speaks with one of the waitresses about Carla, since that's the diner where she was located.

"Excuse me, Ms." Preston said. "I'm here to asks some questions regarding a woman who was in here a few days ago."

"Sir, you are?" The waitress asked.

"Oh, I'm Preston Maddox." Preston said smiling. "United States Marshal and Homicide Detective. I'm here to ask about a woman that was seen in this very place not too long ago."

"Marshal, huh. You can ask me anything you want, baby." The waitress said. "And I mean anything that's on your mind."

"Ok. I'm just here to ask about this certain particular woman." Preston said. "That's all there is."

"Well, do you have a picture of the woman?" The waitress said. "That way it would be easier for me to help you out, sir."

"As a matter of fact, I do." Preston said. "Here it is right here."

He showed her a picture and she looked at the photo and glanced toward Preston and back to the photo. She recognized Carla in the photo.

"I remember her and the guy she's with." The waitress said. "They sat right over in that corner, towards the window."

"Ok. You're getting somewhere now. While they were here, did you over hear their conversation or anything related?" Preston asked.

"They were talking about a plan that they were trying to do." The waitress said. "It involved something with officials and such. But, I didn't hear anything else."

"Did they mention a location of any kind?" Preston asked. "Or anything related to that matter?"

"They spoke about a warehouse across town." The waitress said. "They were saying that after they finish their plan, they'll head back there. But, they didn't mention any other locations, sir. But, you can visit an antique store across town. There's a gentleman there named Tanner. They spoke about him, so he could possibly give you some information."

"If that's the case and it seems that it is. I thank you for your honesty, sweetheart." Preston said. "I really appreciate all of the help you've given me on this task."

"You're welcome and here's my phone number." The waitress said. "You can call me if you want to know more. Whether it involves your case or just a personal call."

Preston smiled, "I'll keep the personal call in mind. Have a good day, ma'am."

Preston left the diner drove away as he continued to search around other possible locations for more information.

CHAPTER 20

Hoyt and Billy arrived at the old pawn shop building along with the group of poker guys. They walk in and see all of the weapons that are laid out through the building. The place is also painted white and it's all clean. Billy turned to Hoyt.

"Whoa, whoa! Wait a second now?" Billy said. "Please tell me that you bought the place before you start talking with these fellows?"

"I sure did." Hoyt said. "It wasn't much. Just negotiating, really."

"Nice place, Hoyt." The man said. "We agreed to your offer. So, what you need us to do?"

"I need you and a few of your guys to head out towards the downtown area and cause a scene." Hoyt said. "A big scene."

"A big scene? What kind of big scene? A riot? A shootout? Rob drivers and steal their cars kind of big?"

"A shootout will do just fine." Hoyt said. "Though, I like the riot idea a lot, that can wait another time and you never told us your name?"

"Sorry about that, my newly found friend." The man said. "My name is Russell. Although, my guys call me Leader."

"They call you Leader, huh." Hoyt said. "Sounds good. But, you know that I'm the leader of this organization and you're the leader of your groups. So, they'll call you Leader and I'll just call you Russell. Alright."

"You got it, Hoyt." Russell said. "Whatever you say from this point on end."

Hoyt smiled and shook Russell's hand. After shaking his hand, Hoyt and Billy leave the pawn shop, letting Russell sit with his men.

Thinking about Hoyt's offer.

Coover and Rusty are at a car lot with Barbette as they pick out their new vehicle. They are looking at the trucks. Coover spotted one and pointed it out.

"How about this one, Rusty." Coover said. "This one could help us out at least."

"It could work." Rusty said. "But, I don't like green. Green doesn't suit me well. As long as it's an F-250 and not a bright color, I'll be fine with it."

"How about the silver one over there?" Coover said. "That one suits you well enough. Come on, brother. It's only a vehicle we need to use."

Rusty walked over to the truck and looked at the interior. He started smiling and turned toward his mother slowly.

"Rusty, do you like this one?" Barbette asked. "You look like you do."

"Yes ma'am, I do." Rusty said. "Brother, how about you? You like this one, here?"

"I do." Coover said. "I really do."

"Let's go inside and speak with the dealer." Barbette said. "After this, the both of you should thank Mr. Colby for doing this. This is his money we're dealing with after all."

Preston had arrived at the antique store across town. He walks in and sees tons of priceless antique glasses and statues. Preston looks around toward the counter for the cashier or any employees.

"Excuse me! Anybody here?!" Preston yelled. "Hello?!"

The clerk walks from the back and looks at Preston. Preston stood still as he stared at the clerk. Who walked slowly toward the counter near Preston. The clerk took a big swallow before speaking to Preston.

"What do you want?" The clerk said. "Sir. Good sir."

The clerk had noticed Preston's badge and gun on each side of his belt. He becomes startled as he took one step back from the counter."

"Oh. A badge and a gun." The clerk said. "I take it you're a policeman, huh."

"What? No. I'm not a cop, I'm a Deputy United States Marshal and Homicide Detective." Preston said. "Since you know what I am, what's your name, slick?"

"My name's Tanner." The clerk said. "Tanner Powell."

"Well, Tanner Powell. I was told by a waitress at the diner across the block from here that you could have some possible information regarding this woman and this man."

Preston showed Tanner the photo of Carla and the thug. Tanner looked at the photo and turned back to Preston.

"No, man." Tanner said. "I have no idea who those two are. Sorry, I can't help you there, sir."

"You said your name was Tanner, huh?" Preston said. "Almost forgot after hearing you speak like that in such manner. By the look of you, I would've though your name would've been something like Troy or Steven. Hell, maybe even Freddy."

"I have some relatives named Troy and Steven." Tanner said. "Cousins on my father's side. No Freddy in my family, though I believe not to be. I really don't know everyone in my family, so I couldn't really tell you exactly."

"Yeah, great. I'm sure you'll find out sooner or later." Preston said. "And what's going on with both of your eyes? You've been smoking dope or something?"

"It's a rare form of pink eye, sir." Tanner said. "It very, very contagious, so, I would recommend that you don't touch me, sir. If you do touch me, you could get infected too and wake up the next morning with one of these or maybe something worse."

"I don't think I'll end up turning into a Dead of any sort. Though, you have no need to worry. I'm not going to touch you by any means." Preston said. "No worries there. I'm just looking for the woman on the photo. Her name is Carla Garcia by the way. The waitress told me that they spoke about you. Saying that they came by this location."

"Never heard of her in my entire life." Tanner said. "Don't

recall seeing her in this place."

"From what I understand, according to my knowledge is she operates at a warehouse not far from here." Preston said. "With that warehouse nearby this area, you're sure you didn't see her?"

"Sorry, I can't help you." Tanner said. "Truly can't."

"Ok, then." Preston said. "If that's the way you want to go on this day."

Preston walked over to the shelf and tampered with the antique glasses on the shelf. He started saying a rhyme before he tapped on one and knocked down one of the antique glasses. The glass smashed on the floor in pieces. Tanner freaked out and Preston looked at him.

"Oh shit." Preston said. "I thought it was plastic. My bad."

"Come on, man." Tanner said. "Please don't do this. Don't break anything else. I'll get in trouble over this."

Preston knocked down another glass as Tanner continues freaking out, rubbing his head and grinding his teeth. Preston picked up one of the statues from the bottom shelf. He walked toward the counter with it.

"Oh, goddamn it, man!" Tanner said. "Please!"

"Listen, Tanner Boy. All I'm trying to do is incarcerate a very bad man and the woman on the photo, Carla Garcia, may help me in completing this task. So, unless you want me to continue being a clumsy asshole in your store, why don't you tell me if she came in here. And if so, where was she headed?"

"Alright. She came in here one day with the guy on the picture. She was buying an antique to take to Quarles Funeral Home." Tanner said. "She also spoke of a hair salon. That's all I know."

"A hair salon." Preston said. "You're sure about that?"

"Yes sir."

"You're positive about it?"

"Yes sir."

Preston placed down the statue and took out of his jacket pocket a one-hundred-dollar bill and laid it on the counter. Tanner looked at it while glancing at Preston.

"There you go, Tanner. I broke it, I bought it. Make sure you take care of those eyes will you."

Hoyt, Billy, Russell, and his group of men arrive in the downtown area during rush hour. Hoyt pulled Russell aside as he commanded him to bring him men towards the eastern side of the area as he and Billy decide to watch over the western side. Russell commands his men to stand still by the wall on the building next to them, which is New Haven City Hall. Billy pointed it out to Hoyt that they're standing right in front of City Hall. Hoyt's eyes lit up as he smiled.

"Oh my. This plan is proceeding excellently."

"How do you figure that, Hoyt?"

"Just watch, my good friend. Prepare to see something truly amazing in this area. City Hall is just icing on the cake for us."

Hoyt pointed toward Russell, who later commands his men to set up their gear and prepare themselves. His men reached toward the pair of duffle bags that sat in front of them, pulling out their assault weapons such as RPKs and AKs. A few of Russell's men appeared to have carried shotguns on their shoulders. The traffic later stopped, as to the light turned red. Hoyt turned to Russell and gave him the signal. Russell signaled to his men as they run out in the middle of the open road and start firing shots all around the street. Hoyt and Billy ducked behind a wall, as Hoyt laughs while watching Russell's men. Billy stared at Hoyt as he laughed.

"This isn't funny, Hoyt! What the hell is this?!" Billy said. "What have you placed them under?!"

"All of this was only a test for Russell and his men, my friend." Hoyt said. "I just wanted to see if they had the loyalty to go along with it. Besides, it was Russell's idea for this shootout. They also picked this spot and Russell gave them the signal to fire."

"Why couldn't you have just chosen the riot. It would've been so much safer compared to what we're watching. We wouldn't have to duck our heads for Christ's sake if they were just hijacking people from their cars and beating them down on the street. We could've stood by and just watched as it was happening."

"True point you have there. Though, he did mention having a

riot here instead of gunfire." Hoyt said. "But face it Billy, this is more fun!"

Russell's men continued firing all around the area. They've knocked out windows on the nearby building, even blowing out the windshields of the cars. the stoplight turned green and the cars suddenly started to move without any hesitation. They're drove quickly to avoid the gunshots.

Russell screamed at his men to move, in which only a few had done. The drivers within the cars appear to be pissed and start to run over the remaining men on the road. Hoyt looked up and saw what was happening. Billy turned and looked as well with fear in his eyes.

"Holy fucking shit! They're being ran over! Goddamn it, those people are running them over nonstop!"

"I didn't think today's society would have this sense of mind in them. Shit, Billy, we could recruit more people like these drivers here. A lot more of people like this."

Russell's men are jumping out of the roadway and one turned to Russell.

"Leader, what do we do?" The thug asked.

"Let me ask Hoyt." Russell said. "He'll tell us what we should do."

Russell ran across the road to the other side of the street. He looked over at Hoyt, who's still crouched down beside the stained walls.

"What in the hell shall we do, Hoyt?!"

"Head back to your cars and return to the site. Me and Billy will meet you and your remaining men up there and then we'll regroup there and begin the process."

"Got ya, boss." Russell said. "Let's go men."

He commanded his remaining men to head back to the cars. They get in their vehicles and drive off, heading back to the site. Hoyt and Billy do the same.

"What are we going to do about him and his men?" Billy said. "Are you going to promote them in some kind of way or just get rid of them when the time is right?"

"I won't do anything to Russell or his men. They've done a great job here and have proved their loyalty to us."

Emily had arrived at the Marshal agency in Newark. The building is a five-story structure facility. Its taller and larger than the agency building in New Haven. She walked inside, and she runs into an old partner, an African American woman. She spots Emily and walked over towards her. They both hugged and greeted each other.

"My, my, Emily. What brings you back to Newark?"

"Some serious issues, Gloria. I'm here on a case that concerns Ray Colby. I'm sure you remember him, don't you?"

"Wait, he's back in town? Where the hell has he been all this time because we haven't seen a trace of him or heard about it?"

"He's been in New Haven for quite some time now. He appeared to have moved his occupation of doing some of his dirty work up there. Though, I have yet to run into him yet. I've only had recent encounters with a few of his thugs."

"Are they like any of the guys here would be?"

"Not exactly. They're worse. Much worse. Appeared to have been trained for this particular job."

They head to the fifth floor by use of the elevator. Emily recommended the stairs, but Gloria denied her entry due to the stairs repaired for some damage that occurred prior to Emily's arrival.

Once on the fifth floor, Gloria walked into her office, walking behind her desk, she pulled out a document from the drawer that contained the files of all Ray's previous and reported locations and hideouts throughout the state of New Jersey. Emily looked at the map and took a photo of it with her Samsung phone. She turned to Gloria.

"I have to say I should truly thank you for helping me with this."

"Don't mention it, Emily. Remember when you were stationed here. We were once partners. Whenever you need help, I'll always be there for you anytime you need it. So, who's your partner over at New Haven?"

"Preston Maddox. I'm sure you've heard about the guy."

"The Instinct Marshal!" Gloria said. "The guy who shot Jonny Cartel is your partner!"

"Yeah, the guy who shot Cartel and is known for using his

supposed instincts to solve his cases. For those who don't know, the guy is also a huge pain in the ass. A complete narcissist."

"I thought he would be a nice one." Gloria said. "Since, he's a handsome gentleman."

"He is a nice guy." Emily said. "Only whenever he decides he wants to be."

Emily thanked Gloria again as she leaves the facility. As she enters her car, she took out her phone and looked at the photo of the map. After reading through the map's targeted locations, she decides to go for the first location, which is a construction site. As Emily leaves and drives off, there's a small black corolla sitting across the street not too far from the facility. Inside is a man, wearing a brown fedora. He watches as Emily leaves and proceeds to follow her.

CHAPTER 21

Russell and his men return to Hoyt's site as Hoyt and Billy are already there waiting for them. Russell exited out of his truck and walked toward Hoyt, furious look on his face as he approached him.

"May I ask what in the hell just happened out there?!" Russell asked. "We were nearly hit by those damn cars, Hoyt!"

"I didn't expect that, Russell." Hoyt said. "But, you only lost about what, two, three of your men. They can be replaced very quickly. No hard feelings."

"That's not the case. They were good men." Russell said. "They put their lives on the line doing this kind of shit."

"I still say that you should've gone with the riot plan." Billy said. "Otherwise, your men would still be here."

"You have a point there." Russell said. "But, that's not the case here at the moment."

"The case is over." Hoyt said. "We now focus on what's in the next case. In which, the next one won't be so terrible as the one that's just transpired."

"Why won't it be so terrible, Hoyt?" Russell asked. "Why, is it located in a safer location?"

"Because we're going into the woods for this one." Hoyt said. "Think of it as trying out your stealth movements."

"Great. Great. Right up my alley." Russell said. "Going into the woods for what?"

"You'll find out when I tell you." Hoyt said. "You and your men may return to your homes now. You're done for the day."

Russell and his men left the site. Billy turned to Hoyt, asking him about the woods and why they're heading that direction. Hoyt decided to tell him that there is a secret cabin hidden in the woods and when the time is right, that they will have to blow that cabin into entire pieces.

Eldon, Cody, and Darius are on a street at the lower town. Cody looks around the area and tells Eldon that this is the location where the prostitution takes place. Eldon says that they'll come back later and patrol the area in search of the hit man. Eldon tells Cody to have his sniper ready for use, because he might need it. Darius asks Eldon how they're going to patrol the area. Eldon pointed across the street.

"We'll have to set up a secret location across the street there." Eldon said.

"At that abandoned building?" Darius asked. "It looks like it could help us out."

"Yeah. It could work." Eldon said. "Me and you will be on the inside, as Cody will be on the roof."

"Why the roof?" Cody asked. "I can shoot from the windows, you know."

"The roof is best for your sniper." Eldon said. "Unless it rains, then you can shoot from the windows."

"Well, hopefully it pours." Cody said.

Preston arrives at a hair salon. He walked inside, seeing all the women getting their hair done and the smell of washed hair surrounding the salon. He walked toward the counter, where the cashier was standing.

"I'm sorry to bother you." Preston said. "But, I'm Preston Maddox, United States Marshal and Homicide Detective. I'm here on business and I'll like to ask you something."

"Ok." The cashier said. "And your point?"

"I'm looking for a woman." Preston said. "Carla Garcia. Have you heard of her?"

"Do you have a picture of this Carla?" The cashier said.

"Right here, Ms." Preston said. "I just came from an antique store down the street and the clerk said that she's was headed here. So, I'm just here for some information."

He took out the photo and the cashier quickly denied seeing

her. Which through Preston off for a second before he was able to gather himself.

"Well, Ms., according to some documented information, she came in here a few days ago." Preston said. "Are you sure you didn't see her. She had to be wearing red, that's all she wears."

"Listen, in this line of work, someone like me sees a lot of different women that come into these places who wear different styles of red, sir. I'm afraid that you have the wrong location or maybe you were fooled."

"According to you, it seems I have." Preston said. "Have a good day, ma'am."

Preston leaves the salon and gets into the car. He pulled out the folder containing the documents. On the document, it mentions that Carla might have visited Quarles Funeral Home. Preston reads it and heads over to the location.

Ray sat inside a meeting at a Newark office. The meeting concerned the crime lords with their deals involving the drug shipments. One crime lord gets the attention and started asking about their shipments. Another one asked the exact same thing.

"My question is simple, gentlemen." One crime lord said. "How do we move our shipments around the country and deal with these officials and their marshal service?"

"We must create a strategy that will confuse the officials and certainly those marshals." Ray said. "I've already had to deal with two and I don't need anymore."

"How do we create this strategy?" The crime lord said. "There has to be some form of way that we could create something of that category."

"Gather your men for a meeting and hire yourself a strategist." Ray said. "That's what I've done."

"You hired a strategist?" Another crime lord said. "Never would expect you to do something like that, Mr. Colby. Thought, you plotted out your plans on your own and didn't take hardly anyone's advice. Unless it was handed to you."

"The strategist I've hired for my alliance is a former lover of a marshal." Ray said. "The Marshal that shot one of our associates, Jonny Cartel."

"The Instinct Marshal?!" The crime lord said. "You have him on your case? If he's watching you, he could possibly find the rest of us. That guy never makes a mistake. He uses his instincts for crying out loud."

"Everything will be fine." Ray said. "You won't have to worry about the Instinct Marshal. My strategist has already designed a plan that will take the marshal off the face of the earth."

"I hope so, Mr. Colby. I hope she does." The crime lord said. "If not, we'll have to tell the chief to let you go or better yet. He'll probably have us kill you if the plan doesn't go as followed."

Ray stared at the other crime lord. He grinned toward him before clearing his face of the grin.

"Anything else you'll like to say, Mr. Colby." The crime lord said. "Since, you won't join in on our little part in this situation."

"No one can get rid of me." Ray said. "I'm the best crime lord around these parts. I make things happen and I also end things. The chief will never get rid of someone who's highly intelligent and skilled as I. You can say what you want, but get this straight. You cross a line with me, I'll take the marshal's job and put you down myself."

Emily arrived at the construction site. Seeing that they're in the middle of building a new office building. She walked toward a few of the constructors to ask them about Colby. Some of the constructors look at Emily and check her out.

"Pardon me, gentlemen." Emily said. "Do any of you know the whereabouts of Ray Colby?"

"He's not here at the time." One constructor said. "Though, he frequently visits. Since this is his office that we're building at the moment."

"This is his office?" Emily said.

"Yes ma'am." The constructor said. "We don't know what it's for, but, this is commanded by him. He's paying for it. He usually comes by on Tuesdays and Thursdays just to see how it's all going. Sometimes, he'll pay some surprise visits. We all hate those."

Emily looked around as she thanked the constructors for their help and left the construction site. She looked at the photo again to search for another location. The location that she's looking at now is a shooting gallery.

From behind her is the man in the corolla. He picks up his cell phone and contacts Ray.

"Ray, sorry to bother you right now. This is Desmond. I'm on the female Marshal's trail at this moment." Desmond said. "What do you want me to do once I have her?"

"Do what I'm paying you to do." Ray said. "Kill the bitch and you'll receive your reward."

"Very well, then." Desmond said.

Desmond hung up and drove off down the street, making a left turn into the small traffic.

Eldon, Cody, and Darius returned to the street where the prostitution line takes place. Eldon decided to set up camp inside the abandoned building. The moon shines down on them during the night sky. Thunder started to rumble and the rain proceeded to pour down. Cody looked at Eldon, smiling.

"Fine, you get the window." Eldon said.

"It makes it easier for me." Cody said.

Cody reaches into the back of the SUV and pulled out a Barrett M82. Darius looked over at him, nodding his head.

"That's a nice one, Cody." Darius said.

"It's my favorite one." Cody said. "I've tried a bunch, but, this one stands out the most for me. Plus, its easy for me to handle. The other ones were just bulky and slow on reload in my opinion."

Eldon pulled out an array of weapons from handguns to pistols to rifles. Darius walked over to the table as Eldon set up the gear. He looked through the weapons.

"We're going to need all of these?" Darius said. "Chief, he's just one man, not an entire army."

"We're dealing with a hit man, Darius." Eldon said. "We're going to need as much as we can possibly get our hands on. Besides, we don't know where his location will be. So, just grab whichever weapon you like and mark your place."

Darius grabbed an AK and stood guard at the metallic garage door. Cody went to the upper floor, placing and pointing the sniper rifle out of the window at a minimum. Eldon stood by the windows on the first floor, looking out. On the other side of the street, a limo pulled up slowly. Eldon looked outside and sees the chauffer open the back doors. Coming out are six prostitutes, all carrying umbrellas.

"They look hot don't they, chief?" Darius said.

"They seem to be alright." Eldon said. "But I'm disease-free and I'll like to keep it that way."

The prostitutes stood on the sidewalk as an array of vehicles went back and forth on the road. Few of the cars parked over near the sidewalk, the prostitutes walk toward the cars and some leave. As Cody was looking out the window, he noticed an unusual occurrence to the left side of the building. He pulled out his communicator and contacted Eldon.

"Cody, what's the situation from your point of view?" Eldon said. "Do you have anything in your sights?"

"Something's going on to the left of the building. Appeared to have looked like a man sneaking across. Looked to me as if he was carrying a weapon of some sort."

"Me and Darius will keep watch down here and search the area. Just keep your position and stand your ground until you have a full visual of what's moving around."

Eldon and Darius noticed a few of the prostitutes were already taken by buyers as they see only three are remaining on the sidewalk. Darius shrugged shoulders as Eldon shook his head.

"It looks like they're going fast." Darius said. "They must be good or something. I mean, to go that fast, that's incredible for prostitutes. Especially in today's age."

"I don't know how this business goes and works, Darius. Though, from the way you're talking about it in such a high manner, it seems to me that you know some stuff about this line of work. But, as for me. I'm a married man with three children, so I have no idea how the prostitution business works nor, will I ever get in line at the academy of whoredom."

"I'm currently in a relationship as well." Darius said. "Though, my brother is a pimp. So, that's where I learned a lot about the prostitution business. Growing up with someone like that shows you a lot in your youth years."

Cody looked out of the left window and seen another individual, who's standing on top of the building to the left. Cody spotted a man, wearing a black fedora, black leather jacket and some black jeans, aiming at the prostitutes with a sniper rifle. Cody contacted Eldon and warned him of the hit man being on the roof of the left building. Eldon ran up the stairs and stood by Cody, looking out the window toward the hit man.

"That's him." Cody said. "The appearance, the sniper, and the stance. He's the guy we're looking for."

"Make sure you have a clear go around just in case he decides to move over an inch."

They continued to look out the window at the hit man. Cody turned his rifle and aimed the weapon out the window through a small crack. Pointing it toward the hit man, Cody goes into deep focus as he slowly prepared to fire the immediate shot. Eldon reached to his side and raised his gun, aiming out the window to the hit man.

"Do you have a clear view to gain a clean shot?" Eldon said.

"Yes I do, chief." Cody said. "Ready for the commanding order."

As Cody prepared and placed his finger on the trigger to fire, the hit man turned to the right direction and started firing toward them. Eldon and Cody ducked down as glass began to shatter all around them from the broken windows. The gunfire caused the remaining prostitutes to run away from the sidewalk. Meanwhile, downstairs, Darius began to hear the gunshots coming from the upper floor. He stood up and ran upstairs. The hit man continued firing shots from his rifle as they're still crouched on the ground.

"We now know it's him." Eldon said. "And he knows it's us that's followed him."

"What are we going to do? Are we just going to wait till he runs out of ammo and take the shot?"

"Just wait for the moment where he assumes we're dead and then you take the shot."

Darius burst through the upstairs door and crouched down on the ground to avoid being shot by the hit man. He slid over to where Eldon and Cody were hunkered down.

"Looks like whatever you did gave him some knowledge of our whereabouts. So, you found him and he found you." Darius said.

"Yeah." Eldon said. "Could you see him from downstairs? A clear view at least."

"If he were to move closer to the edge, I could get a shot at him from downstairs. we should be able to see him."

"Alright, I'll go downstairs and attempt to take the shot." Cody said. "I will need you two to cover my back by firing shots toward him for a distraction."

Cody swiftly sprinted downstairs and ran to the left side of the building, looking outside the small pair of broken windows. Once he looked out of the window, seeing only half of the hit man close to the edge of the building.

Cody aimed the rifle out the window toward the hit man and used the scope to have a closer view. He knew from then on that he had a clear shot.

"I have a clear shot, chief. What should I do now?"

"Take the damn shot."

"Yes sir."

Cody stood still and fired the shot. The round went through the hole of the window and flew through the air, inching near the hit man, who continued firing at the upstairs floor. Eldon and Darius were stilled ducked underneath the windows. The round went pass the brick wall and hit the hit man in the chest. Holding his chest, the hit man crouched down as he fell to the ground. Not hearing anymore gun fire, Eldon and Darius took a small look out the window and saw the hit man down on the ground, slowly moving.

"So, we're going to the roof to check if he's still breathing?" Darius said.

"Something like that." Eldon said. "Let's get up there."

Upon reaching the other building and making it to the rooftop, other police officers with many officials had arrived at the scene as well. They make the discovery that the hit man survived the sniper shot from Cody as the officer slowly placed the hit man in the back of the police car. Shutting the back door, they thanked Eldon and his marshals for helping out with the cause and drive off. Eldon turned and told Cody that he was good at keeping his eyes open at his surroundings, otherwise, they probably wouldn't have caught the hit man. Eldon walked over to another officer.

"Did you find the name of the hit man, officer?" Eldon said. "Because, we didn't have any sort of information on the fellow."

"We don't have any knowledge of his real name, sir." The officer said. "From what we've gathered, the name he goes by is The Jackal. Something within that category."

"What's all on his record?" Eldon said."

"According to his criminal records, The Jackal was one of the country's most primary hit men. He primarily completed jobs and tasks for certain companies who were involved with the prostitution business. He also did some small duty in the marijuana business and the crystal meth business."

"So, he was basically killing off prostitutes because he was paid by a competitor to do so." Eldon said. "Never knew a job like that ever existed."

"Though, we hope to question him as soon as he recovers. We should have more information tomorrow at noon, hopefully. We'll contact you when we've gathered enough information."

"Thank you, officer." Eldon said.

Eldon walked over to Darius and Cody, who were discussing the type of rifle The Jackal used for his assassinations. They turned toward Eldon as he approached them in a slow manner.

"What's next on the agenda now, chief?" Darius said. "Any more places we should probably be looking out for."

"I'm going to get a drink." Eldon said. "I would assume that the two of you would be coming along with me? Just to celebrate what we've just accomplished here."

"Sure." Cody said. "I'm up for it."

CHAPTER 22

Inside his hideout, Hoyt and Billy discussed the cabin location with Russell and his men. Hoyt tells them how the cabin is hidden deep within the woods and he discovered there were a trail of tire tracks that lead to the location.

"So, how are we going to be able to head over there on foot?" Russell said. "We're going stealth mode on them or something?"

Hoyt told him that they will have to drive at a closer location, then they'll walk to the cabin on foot. Russell agreed to the decision and they start preparing themselves for the plan. Billy looked at Hoyt and leaned over toward him across the covered table.

"Now, this cabin that we're going to hit, Hoyt. Is there any chance that Colby and my brothers could be inside at the very moment we drop ship?"

"I wouldn't assume they would be, Billy. According to a reliable source of mine, Ray's currently out of state and your two brothers are currently going car shopping for a new truck. So, from adding all of that up, I doubt that they'll be inside the night we invade the place. Don't concern yourself with possible outcomes. I'll take care of those situations."

"I'm just checking, because my mama might cross paths with us and you know how she feels about you." Billy said. "I don't want anything to go down between my mother and you, Hoyt. Things could turn very ugly if that were to happen."

Hoyt smiled and patted Billy on the back.

"I'm sure your mother and I will be just fine if we were to cross paths on this task. I'm well aware that she doesn't like me at all and I'm fine and dandy about her opinion for someone such as myself. But, for right now, let's just concentrate on the plan ahead, alright."

Emily entered a small convenience store and when she glanced around the area, she noticed the same black corolla that's been following her. She walked into the store when Desmond gets out of the corolla and followed her inside. She walked down the small aisle and Desmond continued to follow her. She looked back as Desmond pulled out a magnum and started firing. She ducked and the cashier crouched behind the counter.

"Take the money! Take it!" The cashier yelled. "Please don't kill me!"

"I don't want your money and I'm not here to kill you, fool." Desmond said. "I'm only here for the female Marshal."

Emily peeked around the aisles as she began loading up her gun. She stayed quiet as Desmond walked slowly through the aisles one at a time.

"Emily." Desmond said. "Emily Weston. I know you're in here, baby girl. I suggest you just come on out and take this bullet from your good friend, Colby."

"So, Ray sent you to do his dirty work?" Emily asked. "Not a surprise there? He's always had pawns to do the work, he was afraid to do."

"He sure did." Desmond said. "He's also paying me to do it for him. Since, he's on business at the moment."

"Business, huh?" Emily said. "You sure its business and not murder?"

"I don't give a shit what Ray does with his time." Desmond said. "All that matters to me, is killing you and getting paid. So, just come on out, so we can end this."

"Sure, no problem." Emily said.

Emily slowly took a peek toward her right and saw Desmond walking through the aisle. She turned and fired at Desmond's leg. He fell to the ground as Emily ran over toward him and immediately, she kicked the magnum out of his hand and kicked him in the gut two times.

"You're good aren't you?" Desmond said. "Surprised me there for a bit."

"Better than you think." Emily said. "I'm not your average officer."

Eldon, Cody, and Darius sat inside a bar, having a share of beers. The door opened and Preston walked in. From his slouchy appearance, it appeared he also had a rough day in searching for Carla. He sat next to Eldon and glanced over toward Cody and Darius.

"Look who else decided to join us." Eldon said. "How's your day of investigating been?"

"It went as fair as it could possibly go." Preston said. "It's been a busy day overall."

"Don't assume that its just you that's had a rough day doing your job." Eldon said. "The three of us just dealt with a hit man who only targets prostitutes and nearly took us out with a sniper."

Preston turned, "Say that again. A hit man whose only occupation was to target prostitutes and you're saying that he nearly had all three of you in his range?"

"Not exactly." Cody said.

"Me, Cody, and Darius just captured the son of a bitch who was targeting prostitutes, while we were there searching for him. Though, apparently from the brief information we had, he was hired by a competitor to take out those prostitutes. Seems like he had an easy job to live by."

"It would seem so." Preston said. "Though, killing prostitutes isn't one on my list of things to do. Nor would I ever assume that there would be such a occupation for one man to take upon himself."

"Maybe he needed to money for some major crisis."

"That is possible."

Darius looked over at Preston.

"Just imagine how that job would be like." Darius said. "Hunting down women and assassinating them."

"Just sounds like a pervert with a sniper to me." Cody said. "Though, I'm not a pervert, by any means."

Eldon took a gulp of his beer and looked at Preston.

"So, how did your search go for Carla?" Eldon said. "Did you find any information on her?"

"Not exactly as I thought it would." Preston said. "I went to the diner and the waitress told me that she was indeed there but didn't know any other information. The next location was an antique store. Freaked out the clerk and he told me to head to a hair salon. The cashier there, acted like a complete bitch, but she didn't give me any information. So, tomorrow, I'll head out to Quarles Funeral Home. Hopefully, I'll find some information there."

"You might." Eldon said. "Because, according to some sources, Ray and the owner of the funeral home are good friends. So, Carla might've visited the place and gave the funeral assistants some information regarding her plans."

"I hope so." Preston said. "Otherwise, I might just have to visit Ray's warehouse myself."

"As long as you have backup when you decide to do that." Eldon said. "We'll have your back on that one, no worries about it."

Preston smiled, "I appreciate that. A lot."

CHAPTER 23

The next morning, Preston headed for Quarles Funeral Home. He arrived at the funeral home, seeing their white limousines and hearses parked in front, each with a license plate saying, "Quarles". Preston walked towards the front door. He opened it and went inside. Preston looked at the interior of the funeral home. Seeing the nice brown colored walls and its burgundy carpet. One of the assistants walked toward Preston.

"Nice place, it really is." Preston said. "They must be having some good business here."

"Welcome to Quarles Funeral Home, sir." The assistant said. "How may I help you here on this particular day?"

"Yes, please. Though, I'm not here to make any arrangements. But, I'm looking for a woman named Carla Garcia." Preston said. "And to be fair I'll show you a picture of her. Maybe it can refresh your memory."

The assistant looked at the picture.

"Do you recognize her?" Preston said. "Because if you do, you can say so."

"No. No sir." The assistant said. "I don't recognize this woman. Perhaps, you have this place mistaken."

"No." Preston said. "There's no mistaken identity here. I have documented proof that she was inside this building. She had spoken with someone inside this building. Whether it's you or one of your other co-workers, she spoke with someone here. Would the owner happen to be here? If he is I would love to speak with him on this matter. So, is he here?"

"He's not here, sir." The assistant said. "But, if you'll like to leave a message, I could tell him."

"I'm not going to leave any kind of message." Preston said. "Look, I'm a United States Marshal. So, you better give me some type of information now or I'll search this entire funeral home, room by room. Hell, I'll even pay a visit to the embalming room if that's what I'll have to do."

"I'm terribly sorry, sir." The assistant said. "But, there's no information here regarding who you're looking for. I can help you out with something else."

Preston squinted his face and pulled out his gun and shot it in the air. The assistant ducked down on the ground in fear, covering his head. Preston leaned down toward the assistant, holding the gun in his hand and smiling.

"I didn't want to do this." Preston said. "But, if doing this completes this case, then I'll do whatever's necessary to get the job done. Now, I'll give you one more chance to tell me what you know. Starting right now. Go."

"There's a cabin." The assistant said. "A cabin in the woods not too far from here. Its right around the interstate, sir. She came in one day and spoke with one of our directors about it. She told the director that the location is one of Ray's hideouts from you people."

"Wait, I'm sorry. Did you just say, you people?" Preston said. "You going racist here, pal? I'm very sure your family raised you to have just a little respect for people and their racial backgrounds. Didn't they?"

"No sir. I didn't mean it in a racial sense." The assistant said. "By you people, I meant the law. That's all I know. The cabin in the woods. That's it. Nothing else."

"Ok then. Thank you for cooperating with me today." Preston said. "Really, you should've told me earlier, otherwise you would've pissed your pants in front of me like a coward."

Preston leaves through the front door as the assistant realizes that he just pissed his pants. He shook his head in shame as he walked down the hall toward the restroom. Outside, Preston gets into the car and contacted Eldon on the phone.

"Eldon, its Preston." Preston said. "I found a location. A cabin in the woods on the outskirts of town. I'm heading there now. I'll contact you if I need backup of any kind."

Preston leaves the funeral home and drives toward the interstate. He passed through the vehicles on the road as he's heading to the New Haven forest.

During the moment in which Preston headed to the forest, Emily arrived at the shooting gallery place. She gets out of her car, but, noticed the place was surrounded by thugs. She believed those men to be associates of Ray. She decided to walk in, but, the men won't allow her.

"Look honey, no one inside without an appointment with Mr. Colby." One thug said. "Not even someone who's sexy as hell such as yourself."

"Well, go inside and tell your boss that Emily Weston is out here waiting to see him." Emily said. "He knows exactly who I am. The supposedly sexy as hell woman."

"Alright." The thug said. "Wait right here, baby. Guys, please watch her."

The thug walked inside approaching Ray. He tells him that Emily is waiting for him. The thug walked back out and allowed Emily entrance to the shooting gallery. She walked in and looked to her left and she finally sees Colby. She walked toward him as he was sitting down in a chair, with a silver revolver in his hand.

"You don't want to try anything stupid, do you Watson?" Ray said. "Seems after a long search, you've come across this way and have finally found me. Though, I am impressed that you did in such short time and not your new partner."

"Preston doesn't fully understand what you're capable of." Emily said. "But, I do. I know what you've done and how you've done them. I've chased you down for years and you're still doing the same damn shit as you were once before."

"So are you, Watson." Ray said. "You're still a marshal. Going around solving cases and capturing fugitives across the country. Sometimes even going across the world to find your criminals to save countless people from trouble. So, don't come to me and tell me that I'm doing the same shit. Because you're doing it as well."

"At least all the shit I do, isn't illegal." Emily said. "Think about that for a change and maybe you'll just realize it for once that you're on the opposite side of the law."

"I realize it very well, indeed I do." Ray said. "You and I have a long history with one another. Right here in this city for exact. Though, tell me something, Watson. How come you were moved over to New Haven in the first place and left New Jersey? You seemed to be well at home over here."

"I'm not here to talk about my business life, Colby." Emily said. "I'm here to tell you that I'm taking you straight to prison. Also, I know about John Elroy, you thug. The thug that was shot by Carla."

"What do you mean, shot by Carla?" Ray said. "Not from what she's told me. She told me he was shot by one of your marshal buddies."

"He was shot in the leg by one of my partners." Emily said. "She's the one who killed him. She shot him in the back of his skull and I'm kind of surprised that you put your trust in her to use a few of your men. Seemly enough that she might kill them as well behind your back and tell you another complete lie. The woman's only trouble, Ray and since you like trouble, you just planted yourself into a lot of trouble."

"I'll tell you this, Watson." Ray said. "You let me go for only this time and this time only, just let me deal with Carla and once that's done, then I'll take my place behind the prison walls. Do we have an agreement on that?"

"No, we don't have an agreement on that." Emily said. "You leave Carla to Preston and I'll deal with you. This is our battle. Carla is Preston's problem to handle, not yours or mine. Now, you're coming with me right now. Let's get moving."

"Very well, then." Ray said. "If that's what you want. You've made your decision and so have I."

Ray looked down and smiled. He then raised up the revolver, Emily looked toward it and Ray fired it. Emily moved out of the way, quickly as she pulled out her handgun and fired a shot at Ray, hitting him in the shoulder.

"Nice try, asshole." Emily said. "You forgot I'm highly skilled in marksmanship. You know that knowledge full well."

The thugs outside could hear the shooting taking place and without hesitation, they ran inside. Emily finds a back-exit door to her left and escapes using it. Once she's outside she headed out and ran toward the front. She got into her car and drove away. The thugs ran back out and start firing at Emily in the car. The thugs helped Ray into his SUV. Where he sat with rage.

"Are you alright, sir?" A thug said.

"I'll be fine." Ray said. "Just track her down quickly."

"Yes sir." Another thug said.

CHAPTER 24

Coover and Rusty test out their new truck, by driving it across town and they're loving it. They even try to impress some women they pass by during a red light. The women aren't impressed by their lack of seriousness. They drive the truck back to their location. They walked towards the house, but, Rusty smelled something that's similar to gasoline.

"What is it, Rusty?" Coover said.

"You don't smell that, Coover?" Rusty said. "It's coming from the house."

"I smell something." Coover said. "You sure it isn't mama cooking us a nice hot meal."

"Hell no it isn't mama's cooking. We need to move from the location." Rusty said. "As soon as we can. Get in the truck and let's get out of here."

They ran back towards the truck and as soon as they pull off, the house exploded and is now engulfed in flames. Coover looked back and is enraged.

"What the hell!" Coover said. "What the hell is going on! Someone just blew our home up, Rusty!"

"I think I know who done it." Rusty said. "Let's go tell mama what just happened and after that, we'll go visit Hoyt and Billy."

After they left, from the other side of the house, rises both Hoyt and Billy. Hoyt is laughing as Billy turned to Hoyt.

"You could've killed them." Billy said. "They're my brothers. My two older brothers."

"They'll be fine, Billy." Hoyt said. "You see they escaped the area. Besides, they were already going to hand your over to Ray, so you could be killed. I'm basically doing you a favor by causing them to leave. As soon as they track you down and find you, the first thing they'll do is hand you over to Colby. Now, do you want that to happen?"

"No." Billy said. "I don't want that to happen. They wouldn't do that to me. I'm their brother."

"Yes, you are. But, they take the commands and orders from Ray and your mother." Hoyt said. "Whatever your mother commands, they will do it and so will Ray."

"What's the plan now?" Billy asked. "We gather up with Russell and his group and head to the cabin? Or do we wait on something else to happen?"

"We'll gather up with Russell and head straight for that cabin." Hoyt said. "They won't know what will hit them."

Eldon received a call from Emily, stating that she's on her way coming back to New Haven and her job in Newark was done. Cody walked in the office and Eldon tells him that Emily is coming back soon. Cody nodded while implying that the judge wants them both at the courthouse to discuss The Jackal case.

"Why do they need us at the courthouse?" Eldon said.

"We're the guys who brought him into custody." Cody said. "In that sense, they would need to speak with you, me, and Darius about the case. They just want to know what went down that night."

"Oh Goodness." Eldon said. "Let me contact Darius and we'll meet up at the courthouse."

"Sure thing, sir."

Cody walked out of the office as Eldon picked up his cell phone and contacted Darius. Darius answered, Eldon tells him that they must meet up at the courthouse, commanded by the judge to discuss the case of The Jackal. Darius agreed and told Eldon that he'll show up at the courthouse.

Ray is inside of a hospital in Newark as he is being bandaged up on his shoulder. Two of his henchmen are inside the room with him. Ray looked at one and asked him if they found Emily. The thug tells him no, but, they could contact Carla and see if she knows if Emily's returned to New Haven. Ray agreed and sent his henchmen out of the room.

The doctor finished up the bandages and he leaves the room. He walked outside and turned to the left, The SUV was sitting outside, waiting for Ray. Ray gets into the SUV. Inside the SUV, one of his henchmen looked and told him the news that Emily was headed back to New Haven. Ray smiled and said that he must do something that will bring Emily to her knees.

On the outskirts, Russell showed up in the front of the woods, along with his men behind him. One of his men walked over and asked Russell if Hoyt and Billy are nearby the forest. Russell tells the guy that they should be coming soon, since Hoyt's hideout is close to the forest. Russell pulled out a set of binoculars and looked around the interstate for Hoyt and Billy's trucks. As Russell uses binoculars to look around the woods, he sees two trucks coming near them.

"I see something over there." Russell said. "It should be them I would suspect."

The trucks pull up in front of them and stopped on the side of the road. Hoyt and Billy jumped out of them. Hoyt walked in front of Russell and his men. Hoyt stopped and smiled.

"See, my men." Russell said to his men. "They wouldn't let us down."

Russell looked at Hoyt and Billy. Smiling.

"Great to see you. So, what the plan, boss?" Russell said.

"Russell, I know the shootout didn't go correctly as planned, so, I'm apologize to you and your gentlemen, regarding that incident." Hoyt said. "But, this mission right here, will go as planned. No need to worry there. First, we will head out into these woods, find that cabin and once we've done that, blow it to shit."

"Hoyt, what about bears?" Billy said. "You know that bears live in these woods. What should we do if we run into one?"

"I'm sure you've been told what to do when you encounter a bear in the woods." Hoyt said. "Make sure if you encounter a bear. Just llie down and play dead. That whole crock of shit."

"I'm not too sure about that." Billy said. "Not too long ago, some guy said that doesn't work. They can still kill you. you're still breathing."

"Don't worry about the goddamn bears, Billy." Hoyt said. "Fellers, let's head out toward the cabin. We should at least reach the location by nightfall."

"Alright, guys." Russell said to his men. "You heard Hoyt, let's get a moving on."

They start walking through the woods, heading towards the cabin.

Eldon, Darius, and Cody are at the courthouse, where they're sitting inside the courtroom, observing The Jackal case. The judge is demanding that The Jackal be sentenced to eight years in prison. Right after the case is over, the judge calls Eldon, Cody, and Darius over to his office in the back of the courtroom. They walk in and the judge tells them to sit down in the chairs, in front of his desk. They sit in the chairs as the judge sits behind his desk, drinking a cup of coffee.

"You needed to speak with us, your honor." Eldon said. "That's the reason why we came. We didn't come to see the hit man get handcuffed."

"I called you guys here, on this wonderful day, to just ask you about your encounters with The Jackal." The judge said. "So, how was the whole thing? How did it play out?"

"It was all as well, judge." Eldon said. "We were just doing our jobs as officials of the law. That's all and nothing else."

"The whole thing was crazy at the time as well." Cody said. "Though, we got the job done. No worries."

"No worries, huh." The judge said. "Let me ask you gentlemen something. How did those prostitutes look? Were they delicious? Did they look smoking hot? Would any of you try them out just for the sake of pleasure and desire of your own hearts?"

"They looked hot, alright. I can tell you that." Darius said. "But, I wouldn't put money down to see if they're delicious in any way."

"You have a point there, Marshal." The judge said. "They might have some of those STDs out there. Just spreading their sickness across lives and ruining families. Nothing but filthy whores they are."

"You could say that again, judge." Eldon said. "But, all things go to Cody here. He's the one marksman who put the hit man down for the count."

The judge stood up and placed his cup of coffee on his desk. He walked over to Cody and extended and shook his hand.

"You don't know how you've made so many people happy by doing what you did." The judge said smiling. "Congratulations, Marshal on your fine job."

"Oh, I'm not a marshal yet, sir." Cody said. "I'm still in training for that spot. Right now, I'm only considered a Contemporary Marshal."

"Very well. Good job anyway."

The judge turned to Eldon with a smile on his face.

"The Jackal fellow is in the other room. I'm just telling you because if you want to get more information out of him. He's all yours."

"Well, thank you, Your Honor."

Eldon told Cody and Darius about The Jackal. He walked out of The Judge's office and into the room next door. Inside the room were concrete walls and only two windows on the front and back. Two chairs and one table. Sitting in one chair was The Jackal sitting at a table with his hands cuffed. Eldon looked at him through the window.

"He seems calm right now. Thought, he would be highly pissed off."

"He might be pissed when we walk in and have a chat with him." Darius said. "So, shall we piss him off."

They entered the room and The Jackal raised his head up toward them. Giving all three of them a demeaning glare of intent rage. His eyes pierced them and later they subdued. Eldon sat at the table while Cody and Darius stood behind him, on both sides of the table.

"So, we hear you'll be in federal prison for a total of eight years. How do you feel about that?"

"How do I feel about that? It's simple to be honest. Funny, you law enforcement types never understand the truth about people like me."

"Well, explain to the three of us how you're so different about you than the rest of the rotten criminals and fugitives that we've come across in this line of work?"

"I'm one of the best there is in my field and my boss knows that. So, he won't let me stay in a room with three walls and a cot with a pot to piss in. He knows he'll need me when a situation occurs."

"You're saying your boss will bail you out or something? Or will he just find a way for you to escape the cell."

"My boss is a man who has enough Federal Reserve notes to bail me out and to buy me a mansion that I could live in for the rest of my days on this Earth."

Cody leaned in, gaining Eldon's attention as the Jackal looked at him from the chair.

"Chief, you mind if I have a word with Jackal here?"

"By all means. Have a word with him. He's done me wonders today. Your turn, Cody."

Eldon stood up from the chair, allowing Cody to sit down in front of The Jackal. They have a ten second stare down before Cody smiled.

"So, tell us, what is your job exactly? Besides just going around killing innocent women for the sake of money."

"I am a hit man. Which you're already aware of. I hunt down and kill whoever I'm ordered to buy the ones who pay me the greenbacks to do it."

"So, you don't just hunt down prostitutes for the sake of paper. You're telling us that you take operations to hit anyone you're order to by the one who's paying you."

"You're smarter than you look, young one. You sure you're in the right type of fieldwork, pal?"

"I'm nowhere in comparison with you or anyone that's in your line of duty. That's all I needed to know. Thank you for your time, Jackal."

Cody leaned up from the chair. They looked over to Darius,

seeing if he wanted to have a word with Jackal. Darius declined as Jackal laughed. They leave the room as Jackal continued to laugh. Eldon was last to leave as he looked back.

"Chief, I just want you to know. When I'm bailed out, I'm sure my boss will have me come for you and your two Marshal boys. Believe you me."

"If and when that day decides to take its course along our lives, me and my Marshal boys will be ready to take your sorry ass down once more, Jackal."

Eldon shut the door as Jackal smirked and looked at his handcuffs.

CHAPTER 25

Preston reached the entrance to the forest. He gets out of his car and he looked to the right and saw a pack of F-150 trucks sitting on the side of the road by the trees. He walked over to the trucks and looked inside. He recognized two of the trucks. Preston showed a faint grin.

"I see Hoyt and Billy's trucks." Preston said. "I wonder what's their business here?"

He walked into the forest as the sun is slowly setting. The forest becomes darker as he goes deeper, he pulled out a flashlight to watch his surroundings. He looked down and noticed some tree branches, scattered across the ground. All of which were broken and smashed, as if something passed through this area. He notices human footprints within the dirt and proceeded to follow them.

While Preston headed deeper into the forest, across the street is Carla and her pack of thugs. The thugs are all armed with automatic weapons. Carla commanded them to cross the interstate to reach the forest. They crossed the interstate by running, neither of them walked across. Carla is the last to cross. She reached the other end as one thug took out a flashlight and they proceed into the forest. Carla pointed out the trail that goes straight to the cabin, which the thugs followed her.

"We should follow this trail, my men." Carla said. "This trail was made by Ray, so it will lead us straight to the cabin."

Hoyt, Billy, and Russell, and his men are now in the middle of the forest as they hear howls from coyotes and wolves. Billy, shaken in fear of being attacked by a bear of some sort of animal, turned to Hoyt.

"How far are we from the cabin, Hoyt?" Billy said. "It's getting very freaky out here."

"We're not too far from the cabin." Hoyt said. "You should see the reflections from the windows. Once you see those, you know we've made it there."

"So, once we've reached the cabin, Hoyt." Russell said. "What do we do at that point? Just blow the place straight to Shit-Ville?"

"Now that's some smart thinking there, Russell." Hoyt said. "But, I would prefer we looked around at the interior, see what we can take and then, we'll blow the place to Shit-Ville. As you like to call it."

Russell turned and saw what Hoyt was carrying over his right shoulder, which was a black metallic box. Russell, now curious, decided to ask Hoyt what's inside the black box. Hoyt stopped in his tracks and turned to Russell, showing his grin toward him.

"You'll find out once we've reached the cabin." Hoyt continues walking as Russell catches up with Billy.

"He sure is secretive about his work isn't he." Russell said.

"Don't say it to him, Russell." Billy said. "You'll only put yourself in much greater danger. Hoyt doesn't like it when people talk about him behind his back. Believe me when I tell you that."

"Why is that?" Russell said. "Something happened to the last guy he was partners with?"

"The last guy who talked about Hoyt behind his back ended up six feet under." Billy said. "That should clear your thought of mind I would assume."

Billy continued walking with Hoyt as Russell showed a worried grin upon his face.

Preston continues walking through the forest and he hears the howls of coyotes and wolves around the area. He heard something moving through the trees toward his right. He reached down for his gun and pulled it out, holding it in his hand, he slowly continued walking and he heard the sounds coming closer. Preston looked to his right and saw a average sized brown fox run past him in a pace.

"Nothing, but a fox." Preston said. "Lucky bastard has me a little freaked out."

Preston later hears something behind him, he turns and its one of Carla's thugs. He grabbed Preston by the neck, choking him. Preston delivered several elbow shots to the thug's head and punched him. The thug fell to the ground as Preston began kicking the thug and afterwards tossing a pile of leaves onto him.

"Useless asshole." Preston said. "You should never attack a marshal from behind. Doesn't do you any good."

Preston leaned down and snatched the thug by his shirt. The thug bled from his nose and mouth. Preston stared at him, grinning.

"What the hell you are doing out here at the brink of night?" Preston said. "Tell me. Tell me now before I put a bullet through you."

"I was with Carla, until I took a wrong turn and lost the group." The thug said. "That's it. I haven't done nothing else I swear."

"That's not all I'm looking for, shit kicker." Preston said. "Why is she out here, and why is she leading a pack of Ray's thugs from his pack?"

"I'm not telling you anything else." The thug said. "You no good motherfucker!"

Preston put the gun directly on the thug's head, with his finger inches away from pulling the trigger. The thug began to panic.

"Ok. Ok!" The thug said. "We're here to kill you. That's why she brought us out here. To kill you. That's our purpose."

"Kill me?" Preston said. "Why would you want to do that? I'm only after your boss and that witch from my past. So, I would really like to know something right now and that is who assigned this operation to you?"

"It was all Carla's idea." The thug said. "She told Ray about it and he accepted it and granted her the use of his men. That's all I know, honestly."

"Well, I have to thank you for telling me the truth." Preston said. "While, you're at it, get a real job for Christ's sake. And make sure it's a legal one."

Preston leaves the thug, laying on the ground in a pile of leaves as he continued walking through the forest as he places his gun back into its holster. As he walks, he notices a reflection, coming from in front of him. He started moving faster and he saw that he reached the cabin. Preston walked around the entire cabin with his gun in his hand. He walked toward the front door, grabbing on the knob, he opens the door. He looked around and sees Ray's desk and some of his equipment scattered across the cabin. He notices that the cabin is a two-story house. As he proceeds to walk upstairs, the lights turn on. Preston stops in his tracks and hears people coming in. He turned and saw Hoyt, along with Billy, Russell and his men.

"Hoyt. Billy." Preston said. "Who's your new group of buddies here?"

"Preston, this is Russell." Hoyt said. "Known to his men as Leader."

Preston stared at Russell and smirked before turning toward Hoyt.

"I now can see why they call him 'Leader'." Preston said. "Because they're just like you. Followers. Can't lead for shit, so you decide to just follow whoever you see around you."

Hoyt smiled and said, "You know Preston. What the hell are you doing here? Would you care to tell us that?"

"Unlike you and your pack of shit, I'm here on business." Preston said. "Now, I just ran into one of Ray's thugs and he told me that his men are heading this way to assassinate me."

"Assassinate you?" Hoyt said. "This is a great day after all. I get to see a longtime friend die and I get to see something blow up. This is indeed a great day for Hoyt Bennett."

"No, it isn't, Hoyt." Preston said. "This isn't awesome. What will be awesome though, is throwing you, Billy, and your pack of followers here into prison. Where you can rot."

Russell pulled out his AK and points it at Preston. Preston doesn't move an inch and smirked at Russell.

"You really think you can put one through me?" Preston said. "Be honest here. You think you can, before I put one through you? Just give me your honest answer, *Leader.*"

"You are one funny son of a bitch, Marshal." Russell said. "I should do those guys a favor and take you out myself."

Hoyt turned to Russell. Telling him to put down his AK. Russell nodded and lowers the weapon. Preston turned to Hoyt.

"See what I mean." Preston said smiling. "Followers only follow. Can't make any decisions for themselves. Tell me, Hoyt. Where do you go to find people like this, because I'll never figure that out myself."

A bullet rams through one of the front windows, hitting one of Russell's men. Everyone inside the cabin ducks down behind the walls, the desk, and even the chairs. Hoyt turned to Preston, who's crouched on the ground, reloading his handgun. Hoyt takes out his pistol. Preston looked over at Hoyt and the pistol.

"Nice firearm, Hoyt." Preston said. "Where'd you get it? Or should I say, where'd you steal it from?"

"It was a gift from my dad." Hoyt said. "You remember him, don't you? He and your father were business partners back in the day."

"Yeah, they were." Preston said. "Right now, we need to focus on the guys out in the front and not on our past."

"Let me ask you something, Preston." Hoyt said. "They say you use your instincts to solve your cases. So, tell me, what do your profound instincts tell you about the outcome of this cabin shootout event?"

Preston nodded and smirked.

"My instincts are telling me that we'll live." Preston said. "Though, you'll be heading back to prison. Not so good for you, huh."

Carla and her thugs surround the entire area of the cabin. She walked toward the front door, with two thugs behind her. She looked inside the windows, seeing all the guys inside, all of whom are still scattered and crouched down. She looked to her right and saw Preston. She smiled.

"I'll go through the back door." Carla said. "You gentlemen find a way to get those men out of the cabin. Leave the Marshal for me to handle."

Carla heads toward the back door as he thugs begin shooting out the windows of the cabin. Preston, Hoyt, Billy, Russell, and his men are still crouched behind the walls and desks. One of Russell's men comes up from behind a chair and fires his machine gun out the windows. He kills a few of the thugs, but, one thug comes across and shoots him in the chest, right over the heart, instantly killing him.

More of Russell's men begin to fire, but the thugs begin to take them all out instantly. Russell watches as he sees his men falling dead on the ground.

"No!" Russell yelled. "Goddamn it! Hoyt, we need to try

another tactic, now!"

Hoyt raised up his pistol, looking at Russell.

"As you command, Russell." Hoyt said. "As you command."

Hoyt leaned up out the window and started firing at the thugs. He began taking most of them down. The other thugs begin shooting toward him. Hoyt ducked back down behind the wall and moved over toward the desk. Billy is shaking with fear and has no clue or idea of what to do.

"Hoyt!" Billy yelled. "What in the hell do I do!"

"What the hell you think, Billy." Preston said. "Shoot back at the assholes!"

Billy raises up and fires his machine gun out the windows. He ducks as the thugs continue to fire back.

"It's not working!" Billy yelled. "There's too many of them out there!"

"Just keep shooting!" Hoyt yelled. "Just keep firing! You'll take some out. It shouldn't be that many left standing!"

Preston looked out the windows and starts firing. He's taking out the thugs one by one. He ducks as they fire back. Preston moves across the cabin to the left and continues firing out the window as he moves across. The thugs fire back and continue firing. All of the windows are all knocked out. The thugs stop shooting. Preston takes a peek out of the windows. He sees only four thugs remaining, as the others are all dead. Preston looked at Hoyt.

"Hoyt, just take a shot for Christ's sake." Preston said. "There's four of us and there's four of them. Russell, Billy, I suggest you two take some shots, now."

"You heard, Preston, boys." Hoyt said. "Aim and take your shots."

They start taking shots out the windows at the four thugs. Billy shoots one thug in the head and starts jumping up and down in excitement. Another thug fires towards Billy and he crouches down, back against the wall. Hoyt looked down at Billy.

"What the Sam hell are you doing, Billy?!" Hoyt said. "Shoot the worthless pieces of shit kicking assholes, goddamn it! Shoot!"

Preston and Russell are firing at the remaining thugs. Preston kills one and now there's only one more thug remaining. Preston looked at Hoyt.

"You want to take this one or shall I go ahead?" Preston said. "I'm going to need an answer now."

"Let me take the shot, Marshal." Russell said. "I got this motherfucker in a clean spot."

Russell fired a shot and killed the last remaining thug. They lower their weapons and look at one another. Billy stood up from the wall, Hoyt only stares at him. Hoyt turned to Russell.

"I'm truly sorry about your men, Russell." Hoyt said. "I truly am. They served their purpose for you and this group and have done a great service."

"They sacrificed themselves to protect their leaders." Russell said. "They knew what they were going into."

Preston looked and placed his gun back into its holster and looked at Hoyt. Seeing him with the pistol in hand.

"You're not too bad with that pistol." Preston said. "Must've been training for some time."

"Same to you with that Glock of yours." Hoyt said. "You know how to use that weapon."

"I was a former marksman instructor." Preston said. "It helped out a lot."

As they prepare to leave, they hear the back-door opening. Hoyt walked over to the door and sees Carla walk inside with two thugs. They backed up against the windows as Carla stared at them. She turned her attention toward Preston, who's not pleased at all to see her.

"Why are you doing this, Carla?" Preston said.

Hoyt looked and started smiling.

"Carla." Hoyt said. "So, this is Carla? Wow, I didn't recognize you there. How's life been so far?"

"Life's been truly great to me, Hoyt." Carla said. "You didn't think that I would forget about you, huh?"

"There was some doubt in my mind that you would." Hoyt said. "You should've called me. We could've hung out together. Just like we did in the old times."

Preston turned to Hoyt. Showing a faint grin.

"This isn't a social visit, Hoyt." Preston said. "She's here to kill me on Ray's behalf."

"Wait. She's working with Ray?" Hoyt said. "How interesting indeed. More sheep scurrying in the field for me to slaughter."

"Why do you think she's here?" Preston said. "Didn't you see those thugs walking behind her?"

"You shouldn't have to worry, Hoyt." Carla said. "Ray can take care of you. I'm only here for Preston."

Russell raised up his AK and shoots one of the thugs, the other thug pulled out his weapon and Billy shot him in the head. Hoyt and Preston turned toward Billy.

"SHIT! Goddamn it! He shot at me!" Billy yelled.

Carla pulled out a revolver and aimed it toward Preston. He looked at the revolver and stared her in the eyes before scouting the surroundings of the cabin. Looking out for any of Carla's men.

"Meanwhile, I'm only here to kill you, honey." Carla said. "The rest of these guys are Ray's problem, not mime. So, babe, are you ready to go to heaven?"

"Depends on the time their open. Speaking of time, do you have a watch on you? Because, if you do you could tell me the exact time. Because, correct me if I'm wrong. But, I believe that the gates are closed around this time of a day."

"So funny all the time. Yet, you're only as funny as the ones who laugh at your joking and smartass remarks. Now, I suggest you close your eyes, babe. I don't want you to look at what I'm about to do to your pretty face."

"But, I want to see your face before you take the shot. Last sight of my time in the world would be looking upon you. So, I'll just keep my eyes opened if you don't mind me doing so."

"Your choice."

Hoyt ran over and backslapped Carla with his right hand. She fell to the ground as he escaped along with Billy and Russell. Preston knelt down at Carla, as she held her face.

"You shouldn't trust Hoyt. Never" Preston said. "Even in your contorted and disfigured mind, you shouldn't trust a man like him."

"I shouldn't trust anyone, Preston." Carla said. "Not even you."

"I agree with that as well." Preston said smiling. "Only to an extent."

On the outside, Billy and Russell are backing up as Hoyt opens the black box and pulls out a grenade launcher. He aims toward the building as Preston and Carla look toward him. Preston and Carla run toward the back door as Hoyt aims the launcher toward the front room. He gets to the aiming in its position and starts smiling. Hoyt turned to Russell and Billy.

"Billy, Russell, grab your pairs of socks and hold your balls in your vices. For this is it, my friends!" Hoyt yelled. "INCOMING CALL!!!"

Hoyt fires the launcher, blowing up the entire cabin. Russell and Billy duck down to avoid being hit by debris. Hoyt stood and watched at the cabin as it was engulfed into flames. Russell looked at the cabin, so does Billy. Hoyt turned to them.

"That's what I'm talking about, guys!" Hoyt yelled. "That's what we came to see! This is what we want! Now, only one more place remains, and we will have started a new era across New Haven."

They ran off the area, going into the darkness of the forest. From the right side, Preston and Carla walk out of the forest. Preston looked at Carla, both are covered in ash from the explosion and smell like burned wood

"The next time you want to try something with Hoyt being involved in the location, don't try it." Preston said.

Preston leaves the area as Carla walked toward the left of the forest. The cabin is completely engulfed in flames. The cabin now, is falling toward the ground, as its now decimated from top to bottom. The cabin is now just a pile of ashes as the smoke reaches above the trees in the forest, alarming some of the nearby residents of the area.

CHAPTER 26

Emily returned to New Haven and arrived at the airport. She walked outside and sees Preston waiting for her inside his car. She walked over to the car and gets in. She looked at Preston.

"Didn't know you were picking me up." Emily said. "Should've called someone to do it instead."

"You don't worry about me." Preston said. "It's only for Eldon that's all."

"So, how's New Haven been since I was out?" Emily said. "The standard way I presume."

"Extremely crazy as usual." Preston said. "How was New Jersey? Interesting?"

"It was crazy." Emily said. "Not crazy as here. But, just crazy."

"Well, it seems you're heading back to the office." Preston said. "Since, your car is parked there for some reason. You should've parked it here, that way you could've drove yourself to the office without anyone, such as myself picking you up."

"Just drive, Preston." Emily said. "The faster you go, the quicker we'll be on the same page."

"If that's what you really want."

Preston drove off, leaves the airport.

At the office, Eldon and Cody are talking about the stock market as Darius walked inside, telling them that Emily's back in town. Eldon said he's happy and asked where she was. Darius told him that Preston and Emily are heading to the office as they speak.

"It's a good thing she's back in New Haven." Eldon said. "Some great news there. Hopefully, she solved that case of hers, so she can continue her work with us."

"Looking at the time, Chief. Emily and Preston should be here any minute now it appears." Darius said.

From the front door, Preston and Emily arrived. They approached Eldon's office Eldon walked out of his office with a smile on his face as he greeted Emily back from her visit to New Jersey. Preston walked into the office behind her with his arms crossed.

"Good to have you back here in New Haven." Eldon said.

"Just doing my job, chief." Emily said. "That's all. So, what's been going on since my absence?"

"A few things, really. Me, Cody, and Darius had to settle a case involving a hit man who only targets prostitutes." Eldon said. "Cody took the guy down with one shot."

"Wow." Emily said.

"Just doing what I've been taught." Cody said.

"Wish I was on that case." Emily said.

Emily looked at Preston.

"So, I'm sure you had something to do, Preston." Emily said. "What did you go out and do for yourself?"

Preston stared and later smiled toward them.

"Nothing much, really." Preston said. "Just went to certain places to track down Carla and her devious plans."

"Speaking of her, did you find Carla?" Eldon said. "I've been meaning to ask you that? So, from what you've just said, you found her?"

"I did find her." Preston said. "Though, Hoyt and his group of followers intervened. As did some of Ray's men and afterwards, everything went to hell."

"What happened?" Emily said.

"I went into the cabin, at that moment is when I ran into Hoyt and his men." Preston said. "Afterwards, the shooting started and once I and Carla escaped, Hoyt blew the place to shit."

"He blew the cabin to shit?" Eldon said. "He's always blowing things up."

"That's what Hoyt does. That's what he always does. When he and I were kids, during the Fourth of July, Hoyt would take all the fireworks and place them in a certain location and light them up.

Causing a massive explosion wherever he was. I can say he's destroyed at least ten to twenty buildings in his lifetime. It's what he's good at so he continues to do it. That's what he does."

Eldon turned to Emily.

"Did you find Colby?" Eldon said.

"I did." Emily said. "After a long search, I found him at a shooting gallery and managed to shoot him in the shoulder."

"You shot him in the shoulder?" Eldon said. "Did he survive?"

"Yeah, he survived barely." Emily said. "He's probably somewhere plotting his revenge against me."

"If that's the case, Emily. He'll be at the warehouse." Preston said. "Since his cabin has been destroyed."

Hoyt and Billy speak with Russell at his newly designed hideout location, sitting at a round wooden table, speaking about the final event. Russell says that they need more men to back them up on this final event. Hoyt tells him that the three of them will do just fine, since this one will require a bigger weapon, rather than the typical grenade launcher. Billy looked at Hoyt with a questioning look.

"Now, what do you mean when you say a bigger weapon?" Billy said. "How big are we talking here? Because, the grenade launchers will do just fine."

"Of course they do, Billy." Hoyt said. "But, since this is the final event that will change all of New Haven and its people. The event must require an even bigger weapon to do the job and the weapon will be in our hands the day that event comes."

"So, I take it specifically, you already have this weapon in your possession, boss?" Russell said.

"I already have it." Hoyt said. "I'm always prepared before the time is upon us. Keeps me on the complete balance."

Coover and Rusty are at the warehouse, seeing Ray with his shoulder bandaged up under his coat. Rusty's face showed a slight concern for his boss as Coover had no words to conjure up from his mouth.

"What happened to you, boss?" Rusty said. "Was it Hoyt? If so, me and Coover can go now and take him out."

"It wasn't Hoyt, gentlemen." Ray said. "He had nothing to do with it. That I know of at this time. It was Weston."

"I'm sorry, boss. But, who in the blue fuck is Weston?" Rusty said. "If, you could tell us."

"The blonde female Marshal." Ray said. "She came to me and shot me in the shoulder, when I was in Jersey. I had her, but, it seemed that she knew exactly when I was going to shoot her. Like she saw it before."

"You think she also has the "Instinct"?" Coover asked. "Because it's been said it's possible she has it."

"I'm not too sure." Ray said. "During her time in Jersey, the officials, as well as the crime lords would always say that she had some sort of technique, similar to Maddox's Instinct."

"Well, boss, is there anything you need us to do for you?" Rusty said. "Since, we're not busy at the moment."

"No, I'll be just fine." Ray said. "Just contact your mother for me. We're going to have a plan for this task very quickly."

"You got it, boss." Rusty said.

They walk out of the warehouse and in comes Carla, Ray looked up at her and noticed the bruise on the right side of her face.

"What the hell happened to you?" Ray said. "One of my men didn't do it? Did they?"

"No, none of your men are responsible for the bruise on my face." Carla said. "Hoyt. He hit me in the face."

"Hmm. I see" Ray said. "Don't think that I didn't hear about my cabin in the woods. How you allowed it to be destroyed."

Carla's face showed a faint grin as Ray looked up at her with dire disappointment in his face.

"Carla, I give you one primary task to take and looked where your actions have done to my secret location." Ray said. "I know that Hoyt was there, along with his new group of vigilante buddies and the Bronson brothers' youngest blood. I suppose that's how you received that bruise upon your face. When Hoyt bitch slapped you and left you for dead."

"I had them where you wanted." Carla said. "I would've killed them if I saw what Hoyt was about to do."

Ray smirked and said, "From my point of view, you deserved that slap to the face. You were too highly focused on Maddox that you forgot the task at hand, which was to kill him without any hesitation. Only if you didn't let your emotions get in the way, he would be dead, and I would be thanking you right now. But, he's not dead and neither is that bastard, Hoyt Bennett."

"I understand that my emotions got caught in the task." Carla said. "But, I was close to finishing it completely."

"Being close enough doesn't mean shit to me, Carla." Ray said. "You had a job to do and you didn't get the job done. So, how am I supposed to feel about that? Knowing that the men I let you use for the job are now dead, because of your selfish emotional needs. The cabin, my only known secret location is now destroyed because of you. Speaking of which, I don't know what else I can use you for, Carla. I don't know anything else."

"Just give me another chance, Ray." Carla said. "Please, just give me another chance. I know I can do it this time. I can promise you that on this one."

"I have no need of you or your false promises, Carla." Ray said. "Just leave my warehouse at this moment. Leave yourself or I'll have one of my men here make you leave. Leave this earth that is. So, I suggest you make your choice right now."

Carla walked out of the warehouse as Ray's facial expression showed he's highly upset about what happened to his men and his cabin. He slammed his fist to his desk and tossed the sheets of paper to the ground.

CHAPTER 27

Hoyt and Billy head out toward the warehouse. Russell is behind them inside his truck. They stop and get out of their vehicles and Hoyt uses the binoculars, looking in front of him. He sees the warehouse.

"There it is, my wonderful congregation. There's the warehouse, my boys." Hoyt said. "That's where Ray does most of his dirty work. Now, we've got him where we want him."

"You want to go in there right now and take him out?" Russell said. "You know we could do that for you."

"Russell, I appreciate your bravery. But, we'll save the chaos for a later time." Hoyt said. "Right now, we're only scouting the location just to make sure where we'll be once the time comes along."

Billy looked around the area, scouting out the entire area. He turned to Hoyt, thinking.

"So, when the time is accurate, Hoyt." Billy said. "How do we complete the job here? We're going be in this spot or are we going to be a little closer to the place? What if someone catches us while we're out here on this. We're going to be screwed."

"Billy, Billy. I'll say this once and only once directly to you, my friend." Hoyt said. "You focus on the plan and I'll focus on the ones that you're speaking of. Things will come into plan, I'm highly sure of it."

Coover and Rusty walked into their mother's home. She walked out across from the kitchen. She looked at them as Coover smiled. Rusty walked toward his mother.

"What in the hell are you boys doing here?" Barbette said. "You should be helping Ray out right now with his problems. You know that his cabin was destroyed last night. And we all know who did it."

"We know about the cabin, mama, but, he told us that he didn't need anything, mama." Rusty said. "He only wanted us to speak with you."

"Well, what did he say?" Barbette asked. "Not something terrible I hope."

"He said something about planning something fast." Rusty said. "He also wants to speak with you in person. About the situations concerning Hoyt and the marshal people."

"Very well, I see." Barbette said. "I'll pay a visit to Ray and see what he wants to talk about. But, I want to make sure that the both of you stay by his side. As of this moment, he'll need all the help that he can get."

Preston, Emily, and Eldon are sitting at a diner, at noon, eating lunch. Eldon speaks with Emily about her trip in Jersey. Preston turned and looked at Eldon.

"I'm highly surprised that you survived the trip, Emily." Eldon said. "I was a little worried that you wouldn't return. But, you proved me wrong."

"She can take care of herself, Eldon." Preston said. "You heard what she said about Colby. She shot the guy in the shoulder. Not too far from the chest. Good job, Emily."

"I was only doing my job." Emily said. "Though, I don't let my emotions get in the way, like Preston when he's facing Carla."

"It's not that my emotions get in the way of business." Preston said. "Just that I knew her for so long that I wouldn't think that she would be able to do something like this of this caliber."

"Preston, you should know that everyone you've either dated or slept with over the years, will eventually come back into your life one way or another." Eldon said. "You of all people should have that in mind."

"Eldon, I don't know how you conjure up all this kind of shit."

Preston said. "Exactly, where do you find all of this information?"

"The library, Preston." Eldon said. "It's the sort of place that carries all kinds of books. Fiction and non-fiction. They also have books on nature and politics."

"I know what a library is, Eldon." Preston said. "I've been to one before."

"I'm sure you have." Eldon said. "Probably when you were in high school. Was that the last time you saw a library? Or you didn't even attempt to walk in a check out a book."

"Very funny, Eldon." Preston said. "Hilarious."

Emily looked at Eldon and asked him about the plan to take down Ray. Eldon said that they will have to come up with something clever to pull off, so Ray and his alliance don't figure out the marshals have in store for them. Preston said that they need to watch their surroundings. Emily asked why would they, because of Ray's crime partners? Preston nodded and told them that they need to watch out for Hoyt, Billy, and Russell. Since, Hoyt has been trying to kill Ray and take back his place as crime boss of New Haven.

"Well, no shit." Eldon said. "We'll have eyes across the entire location. Ray and his friends won't even see us on the outside"

"How is that, Eldon?" Preston said. "You're going to spread all of us out across the warehouse or have you brought in a group of interns to do the scouting."

"Not exactly, though I decided to contact the CIA and I also called in some SWAT groups to cover our backs." Eldon said. "No big deal about it."

"Did you make sure that they bring grenade launchers?" Preston said. "Because, they could come quite in handy for this one."

"Why do we need grenade launchers, Preston?" Eldon said. "We're not like Hoyt and his group of *let's blow shit up* buddies."

"I'm just saying that we should have some with us." Preston said. "Only to have an even match against them. Who knows what they'll bring with them."

"I see your point on that." Eldon said. "I'll think it over with the CIA. See what answer they'll give me, if I choose to do so."

"Very well." Preston said.

Barbette arrives at Ray's warehouse, where Ray is looking at a map of the entire city. He looked up and asks Barbette to sit. She sits in front of him and he moves the map to the side of the table.

"I'm pleased you could make it, Ms. Bronson." Ray said. "I'm sure you know our times are starting to get rough around here. Mainly on me."

"I can tell." Barbette said. "My boys came to me and told me that you wanted to discuss something you have in mind. Some sort of plan that will change the state of this city."

"I have a plan and I'm asking you to be a part of it." Ray said. "Just to see how you feel about it."

"I would like to hear it, Mr. Colby." Barbette said.

"This plan concerns all of the crime lords that surround this city." Ray said. "I'm going to have a meeting at this warehouse in a few days to speak with them about it publicly. But, I'll tell you about it right now. The plan involves taking out Hoyt and his group of explosive buddies."

"What about my son?" Barbette asked. "Specifically, Billy. What do you have in mind for him?"

"I figured that you would deal with him yourself." Ray said. "I don't want to be the cause of you losing one of your boys, even if it's one that didn't listen to his brothers or his mother's warnings."

"I see your point there. So, tell me how soon will this plan come into play?" Barbette asked. "Sooner than we hope or not to soon?"

"Once I have settled it with the other guys, the plan should begin to unfold." Ray said. "But, once the plan begins, we must take out Hoyt and afterwards, we'll deal with those marshals."

"I've heard the history between you and the blonde one." Barbette said. "I also heard that she's the one who shot you in the shoulder a few days ago. So, I figure that you'll handle her and leave the Instinct Marshal for me. My two boys will deal with those other marshals they have backing them up."

"I'm up for that." Ray said. "So, do we have a deal?"

Ray extended his hand and Barbette looked at it. She shook his hand in agreement. Ray smiled.

"Let the process begin." Barbette said smiling.

In downtown, a meeting is being held at City Hall, concerning the economy and how they should increase jobs across the city. The room is entirely full, from left to right of over a dozen citizens. Every seat is taken as some extras stand in the back because of it. As one of the lead gentlemen stand in front of them, behind a podium, he talks about the cause and says that they should increase jobs across the city, therefore there won't be any problems to cause someone to turn to a life of crime.

As he continued saying his speech, the doors opened up and everyone looked toward them. The gentlemen behind the podium looks straight and in comes Hoyt, Billy, and Russell. Hoyt, holding his arms out and hands open, smiling as he looked down at the gentlemen.

"My, my. It's been a very long time, since I've stepped foot inside of a crowded location such as this." Hoyt said. "Usually, I'm the one who brings in the big crowd. For parties of the rightful ones of course."

"Sir." The gentleman said. "Who are you and what concerns you about the economy? If you may ask?"

"If I may, I'm the guy that will change the foundation of this city's economy for years to come." Hoyt said. "Ladies and gentlemen of New Haven, Connecticut. We are all trying our hardest to find jobs and to work. Some of us have families to take care of, while some of us are only in it for ourselves just to make a buck or a name for ourselves. I am here to say that there's something new coming to New Haven and it will bring happiness across the entire landscape of this city. Once the dark cloud that's currently above us, passes along. A new and brighter cloud will emerge, and the sun will shine down upon us and we will have succeeded against this broken economy and its vile operators."

The audience began to clap as they started to agree with Hoyt. He walked up to the gentleman at the podium. The gentleman stared at him as Hoyt smirked toward him and extended his hand toward the podium.

"May I?" Hoyt said to the gentleman.

The gentleman moved away from the podium, letting Hoyt take his spot. Billy and Russell stood behind him, watching the gentleman and his associates.

"Don't try anything funny." Russell said. "I mean it."

"He won't." Billy said. "He's too afraid to do anything. He could barely speak when we walked in here. So, don't expect anything from him."

Hoyt grabbed the microphone and looks out toward the audience.

"Now, since I have a microphone, I don't have to raise my voice to speak the truth." Hoyt said. "Now, when the time comes when we all have jobs and this city is out of the economy's path, that will be the start of a new era for New Haven. Now, the rich folks and the crime lords that surround this city will also learn of that new era. An era that will bring them down to our level. A level that will show them that there no better than the rest of us. A level that will stand the test of time against crime in the city. Once, they feel that era upon them, they will look at us all and fully understand the true ways of life."

The audience continues to clap, as some of the civilians start to yell in joy. Hoyt smiles and looks back at Billy and Russell.

"This is going better than I hoped." Hoyt said. "Just keep your eyes on these guys right over here. I got the crowd in my hands."

Russell and Billy turn around and stare at the gentleman and his associates. They sit back and just look on at the audience, seeing how they're accepting Hoyt when he just walked into the building. Hoyt continues his speech.

"Now, I know some of you are asking yourselves, how is this man, who just walked in here a few minutes ago, knows so much about the economy and how to fix it. Well, for those of you that don't know who I am, my name is Hoyt Randall Bennett. The younger son of Ory and Loretta Bennett and the younger brother of Darren Bennett, who's currently in Hartford, obtaining his psychology doctrine. I was born and raised in this city and so, I'm currently stating that this city, with my profound help, along with my two partners, who are currently standing behind me, Billy Bronson and Russell, also known as Leader, will stand together to wipe out this depression upon our city and will restore the good inside of it and inside of us all New Haven citizens."

The audience began to clap louder. More cheers of joy began to pour out of the civilians. Russell looked out towards the audience and looked at Billy.

"Looks like he's got them." Russell said.

"Hoyt sure loves to talk." Billy said. "You can clearly see that."

Hoyt smiled and looked back at Billy and Russell. They smile as well.

Hoyt nodded toward the crowd of people and continued smiling at them.

"We got them on our side now. They won't accept or take anyone else's word except for mine."

CHAPTER 28

Preston walked into Eldon's office, as Eldon reads some documents. Preston sits down in the chair. Eldon looks up at him. Preston just stays quiet.

"Something on your mind, Preston?" Eldon asked.

"May I have a word, Eldon?" Preston asked.

"Sure." Eldon said. "As long as it doesn't involve anything to do with your personal life, I'm all ears."

"Nothing to do with my personal life." Preston said. "I heard that Hoyt was present at a City Hall meeting today. Thought, you knew about that."

"I didn't know, Preston." Eldon said. "Though, if you look on the bright side of things, it seems that nothing's been blown to shit, so, what's the problem?"

"I'm only wondering what he's told the people." Preston said. "He could've said anything to them and they probably fell for it. Not knowing that they're being used as his pawns. It just aches me to see that."

Eldon gets up from the chair and walks toward Preston.

"We'll just have to see what comes up next, Preston." Eldon said. "That's the only way we'll know for sure what Hoyt and his boy band are up to with the city."

"Yeah." Preston said. "As long as he's not recruiting them just to blow their shit up, I'll have no problems. Well, its Hoyt. He's known for doing this kind of shit and later doing even worse shit."

Meanwhile, Coover and Rusty sat inside their rental house,

sitting on the couch watching the Outdoor Channel. They hear a knock on the door, they look at each other.

"Well, go answer the door, Coover." Rusty said. "I'm busy at the moment."

"Fine." Coover said. "But, if its Hoyt, Billy, or one of those marshals, you're dealing with them. Not I."

Coover opened the door and its Barbette. She walks inside and Coover closes the door. Barbette grabbed the TV remote from Rusty and turned off the television. Rusty looked at his mother, questioning.

"What was that for, mama?" Rusty asked. "I was watching that."

"There's something more important than watching animals get hunted down." Barbette said. "I've spoken with Ray and I'm going to tell you what he told me."

"What did he say, mama?" Coover asked. "Is it a raise? Is it about Hoyt and Billy?"

"Let me talk and I'll tell you what it's about." Barbette said sitting down in a chair. "Me and Ray have come up with a plan that will bring Hoyt and the marshals down."

"Really?" Rusty asked. "This already sounds great."

Later during the day, Karen and Richard sit in a living room, watching the TV. The doorbell rings and Richard takes a look back at the door and turns to Karen.

"Should I answer it?" Richard said.

"Yeah." Karen said. "Why wouldn't you."

Richard gets up from the couch and walks toward the front door. He opens the door and sees Preston, who's leaning against the wall, staring a hole through Richard.

"Detective." Richard said nervously. "Marshal. Detective Marshal."

"Richard." Preston said. "Richard Rogers."

Karen sees Preston standing in the doorway. She gets up and walks toward him and Richard. Preston looks behind Richard's shoulder and sees Karen approaching him.

"Preston." Karen said. "What are you doing here?"

"I'm here to speak with you." Preston said. "If you don't mind."

"Oh, I mind, Detective Marshal." Richard said.

"I was talking to Karen." Preston said.

Richard walks off to the kitchen as Karen allows Preston to enter their home. Preston walks to the living room and sits on the couch. Karen walks in and sits in the chair in the corner.

"Why are you looking at me like that?" Preston said.

"Because I find it quite strange to see you here." Karen said. "I spoke to you at the restaurant the last time we crossed paths. What more do you want?"

"I don't want anything." Preston said. "I just came by to see how you were doing with Richard."

"Why do you care?" Karen said.

"I don't care about Richard." Preston said. "I care about you and your safety."

"Don't see why you do." Karen said. "We're not together anymore. So, no feeling should be attached."

"You're telling me that you don't have feelings for me anymore?" Preston said. "Is that it?"

Karen gets up from the chair and walks toward the front door. Preston does the same, following her to the door. She opens the door, but Preston presses his hand against the door, closing it. Karen looks up at him, while Richard peeps through the kitchen.

"It's a yes or no answer." Preston said. "You seem not to tell me."

"Because it doesn't matter, Preston." Karen said. "If it did, I would not be married to Richard, nor would I be speaking to you about this matter."

Preston paused and stayed quiet for a quick second.

"Fair enough." Preston said.

He opened the door and walked out toward his car as Karen watches him. Once, Preston leaves, she shuts the door and turns back to Richard.

"Everything alright, honey?" Richard said.

"Everything's fine." Karen said. "Just something to get off his chest, that's all."

CHAPTER 29

Hoyt, Billy, and Russell are all waiting in their trucks, looking dead ahead at the warehouse. Hoyt looked at his watch and turned toward Billy.

"It's time." Hoyt said. "Let's get this party started."

"Are you sure about this, Hoyt?" Billy said. "I'm positive that there's another way we can do this. My brothers are in there for Christ's sake!"

"Then, it's their fault." Hoyt said. "Besides, I've been waiting for this moment for a long time now."

They get out of the truck and mark their positions. Russell has his AK ready for use as Billy carries his machine gun. Hoyt goes to the back of the truck and pulls out a rocket launcher. Billy and Russell look toward Hoyt.

"Holy shit, Hoyt!" Russell said. "A rocket launcher! That will do the trick perfectly."

"That's the reason why I chose it." Hoyt said. "A grenade launcher was alright. But, a rocket launcher is even better. Gives you a greater aim as well."

Preston, Emily, Eldon, Cody, and Darius arrive at the warehouse location. Preston and Darius head toward the western side of the trees as Eldon and Emily stay at the eastern side of the trees. Cody walks up a nearby hill and sets his sniper up there. Cody looked down and was able to see the entire location. Preston looked to his right and saw two trucks, he knew for certain that those were Hoyt's and Billy's. He also knew that Russell was along with them.

"What do you see, Preston?" Darius said. "Colby and his pals?"

"No, I see Hoyt and Billy's trucks over there to the right." Preston said. "Looks like this will turn into a show for us."

Preston pulled out his communicator and contacted Eldon.

"I see Hoyt and Billy's trucks, Eldon. You want us to take them out right now or wait? Because, from the way this is all being set up and placed, we're in for a major shootout."

"I hear you clear. Just wait for now. I called the SWAT team for a little assistance. They'll give us all the help we can get on this one once they arrive on the scene."

Emily looked at the surroundings of the warehouse with all types of vehicles parked in front. From Corvettes to Chargers to even Lamborghinis. The area looked as if a party was going on. Emily turned to Eldon.

"So, what do we do once the SWAT teams arrive?" Emily said. "Go straight in and take them out?"

"That's a good plan." Eldon said. "But, let's see how Colby and his gangbanging friends handle it first. Don't want them to get too startled by our arrival."

Eldon contacts Cody through the communicator.

"Hey, Cody. How's the view from up there" Eldon said. "Is it looking great or what?"

"The view's just great up here, chief." Cody said. "I can see the entire location from this point of view. If I wasn't here for this moment, I could come out here on a good and have me some good hunting."

"I'm sure you would. Just keep us posted on anything you see that's unusual, alright." Eldon said.

"Sure thing, sir." Cody said.

Inside the warehouse, Ray is continuing a meeting with the crime lords that he spoke to while he was in Jersey. They continue speaking about their drug shipments and how they can transport them across the state and country.

"By doing the transporting on that trail, we will have no problems moving our shipments across the state and across the country." Ray said.

"If that's the case, Mr. Colby." One crime lord said. "How do we make sure that we don't get caught in the process?"

"You getting caught by the officials is not on me." Ray said. "It's on you."

"I agree with Colby on that one." Another crime lord said. "He has a point with that. If you get caught, it's your fault. You let yourself slip out for them to find and capture you."

Coover and Rusty lean forward towards Ray and the crime lords.

"That's good thinking, sir." Rusty said.

"Yeah, that's a great thought." Coover said. "But, none of us, should get caught. Unless we're either drunk or high."

"The chief has demanded that we take more and charge directly into the promise land." Ray said. "It's what he wants us all to do."

"I don't take orders from the chief, Colby." One crime lord said. "I do what is best for my alliance. Most of the chief's orders are inexplicably erratic."

"Which is why he gave me the choice of taking you gentlemen out." Ray said. "So, what will you do? Will you obey the chief's commands and live? Or will you follow your own path and die? Make a choice, pal?"

On the outside, Hoyt is slowly moving closer toward the warehouse with the rocket launcher on his right shoulder. Billy and Russell watched Hoyt as he continues getting closer.

"What are you trying to do, Hoyt?" Billy said. "You trying to get yourself caught or killed?"

"I'm only getting a closer shot, Billy." Hoyt said. "Gives me an adrenaline rush and makes for more entertainment."

"Does he know exactly what he's doing?" Russell said. "He could be seen, captured, or even killed by Colby and his gun thugs."

"I have no idea." Billy said. "He's trying to get us captured by Colby. Because, I don't want to deal with my mama at this point. She'll kill me."

"She'll kill us before she'll get to you, Billy." Hoyt said. "Just relax and prepare to enjoy the show."

Preston looked over and sees Hoyt with the launcher. He looked at Darius, who's keen on the warehouse.

"Darius, you continue your watch on the warehouse." Preston said. "I'll be right back."

"Where are you going?" Darius asked. "Though, Eldon wanted us here?"

"I've got something to finish here." Preston said. "Won't be too long."

Preston crouched down behind the bushes as he slowly walked over toward Hoyt, Billy, and Russell.

Hoyt continued to aim the launcher and moves his hand toward the trigger. He starts to smile as Billy and Russell started backing up behind the trucks nearby. Hoyt's eyes light up.

"INCOMING CALL!!!"

"Don't think so, Hoyt." Preston said across from Hoyt.

Hoyt looked at Preston, but also fired the launcher. The rocket flies across the ground and hits one of the crime lords' vehicle. A blue and white Charger. The Charger exploded and flies into the air, covered in flames. Debris starts to fall and inside the warehouse, Ray and the others hear the explosion. They walked toward the front door and debris falls in front of them, a few of them back away from the door as others run out the door, heading toward their cars.

Hoyt looked at Preston with an angry glare. Preston stared at Hoyt, with his right hand to his side.

"What the hell have you done, Preston?" Hoyt yelled. "I had them right where I wanted them. You've just destroyed the entire event! I even gave you a warning that you should not come here, but you didn't listen to that either!"

"I lied, Hoyt." Preston said. "You, of all people, besides Eldon, should know I do that for a reason. The right reasons actually."

Billy looked up from behind the truck and seen Preston. Preston turned and saw Billy's head peeking out from the back of the truck.

"Aw shit!" Billy said. "He caught us! We're all caught! We're going to jail! We're going to jail!"

"Yeah. Aw shit is right, Billy." Preston said. "You're all headed to prison and Hoyt, you just got out of the cell. Looks like you're going back for another vacation."

"Preston, I'm not going anywhere, until those men inside that warehouse come with me and the price of their consequences." Hoyt said. "If not, I'll have to pull some drastic measures to make sure of that. Either they come to prison with me or they die here on the spot. Your call, Instinct."

Preston grinned.

"I'm sure they'll be headed to prison, along with you, Hoyt." Preston said. "You and your boys here. You'll all fit just fine, behind bars."

As they stand completely in the open, a gunshot is sounded as Preston and Hoyt duck down around the trucks. Billy decided to dive into the front of the truck, laying under the windshield. Russell laid under his truck, looking around the area. Preston pulled out his communicator and contacted Eldon.

"Eldon, what the hell's going out?!" Preston asked. "Who's doing the shooting at us?"

"It seems that the crime lords have taken matters into their own hands." Eldon said. "I suspect that they're trying to kill us."

"You think?" Preston said.

The crime lords and their thugs continue to fire at Preston and the rest of the group. Eldon and Emily are hiding under the bushes as Preston and Hoyt hide behind the trucks. Billy is still laying down inside the front of the truck, so does Russell under his truck.

"Hoyt, what the hell do we do, man?!" Russell asked.

"We'll have to fire back." Hoyt said. "Just like the cabin. But, this time, we fire until we fall."

Preston continues speaking with Eldon through the communicator.

"Eldon, what should we do?" Preston asked.

"It looks like we're going to have to fire back." Eldon said. "Straight shots, no misses."

"Now you're talking." Preston said.

Preston stood up and began shooting toward the warehouse and its front door. Hoyt does the same and fires as well. To the left of them, Darius is also firing at the warehouse, so do both Eldon and Emily. Atop of the hill, Cody is firing down and aiming with his sniper rifle. Through his aim position, he sees one thug with an AK. He fires the sniper and the bullet goes clean through the thug's chest and out through his back. The thug falls dead.

"That was very sweet." Cody said.

The warehouse door slammed open, pouring out dozens of thugs, all carrying AKs, shotguns, machine guns, and even handguns. They run out through the door and start firing back at them. Most of them shoot towards the trucks. Billy hears the bullets hitting the truck and he screams in fear. Hoyt looked at Billy inside the truck.

"Billy, get out here and shut the fuck up!" Hoyt yelled. "You're part of this too."

"I'm staying in here, Hoyt!" Billy yelled. "I'm not going out there and getting my head blown off!"

Preston and Hoyt moved from the trucks and crouch behind the metallic fence close by. They hear the bullets bouncing off the fence. Eldon, Emily, and Darius are continuing their share of firing back.

"I haven't done something like this before!" Emily said.

"As I've told you before, Emily." Eldon said. "Its New Haven. I suggest you get used to it."

They continue to shoot and duck from the incoming shots. Cody is still firing his sniper from atop the hill. He pulls out his communicator and its Eldon on the other end.

"Eldon." Cody said.

"How are things on your end?" Eldon said. "Or should I say, below you."

"Very good, actually." Cody said. "I guess they don't even know that I'm up here. You can still see me, though?"

Eldon looked up towards his left and he could still see Cody, atop the hill, firing down at the thugs.

"I can see you clearly, Cody." Eldon said.

"Appears that the thugs and their bosses aren't minding their surroundings." Cody said. "Shows their intelligence."

"Yeah." Eldon said. "Shows it alright."

Preston continued firing back and so does Hoyt. They notice that the two of them haven't missed a single shot at all. They looked at one another, impressed.

"I've always known that you were good with a weapon." Hoyt said.

"Yeah. I proved that at the cabin." Preston said. "You're not so bad yourself."

"I do what I must to survive." Hoyt said. "That's what my father always told me."

The gunshots continue to sound as the thugs continue to fire. Ray and his men leave out of the back door of the warehouse, leaving the other crime lords and their thugs to defend for themselves. As soon as they reach the outside, they hear sounds in the sky, as if something's is coming. They look up and see a SWAT helicopter flying over the area. Preston looked up and sees the helicopter. From the left, arrives a SWAT van and over six police cars. The thugs stop firing and run toward their vehicles.

SWAT members pour out of the van and tackle the thugs by the cars, knocking them to the ground. Some of the thugs run into the woods, not able to track down. One thug gets into a car and drives toward the exit, but a police car drives in the way and the thug rams into the police car, knocking himself unconscious.

Cody looked at the SWAT surrounding the scene.

"Finally, they've arrived." Cody said smiling.

Eldon looked at the scene as SWAT members run past him. Eldon smiles.

"It's about time they showed up." Eldon said. "Business has now been picked up."

Russell and Billy noticed the SWAT officers. His men run off into the woods, Russell looked back at Billy.

"If you see Hoyt, tell him we went for cover." Russell said, as he ran off into the woods with his men.

"He did not just leave me here with a SWAT team." Billy said. "Oh, the days that will come."

They walk over to the warehouse and see that the SWAT

members have handcuffed all the thugs around. Preston walked over and looked to his right, seeing Ray running into the woods.

He proceeds to chase him, Hoyt looked over as well and followed Preston into the woods. Ray runs through the woods and as he dodges the trees, he runs into Hoyt, holding his pistol. Ray began slowly to back up as Hoyt walked closer.

"Now, Hoyt. Let's just talk this over." Ray said. "We can make a deal here."

"No, Colby." Hoyt said. "There's no need for talking, because I've already made my decision to take you out. You've taken my men, you've destroying the city with your corruption. So, I believe it's time for you to go, my friend."

"Not that way, Hoyt." Preston said from behind Hoyt. "Now, move away from Ray before I have to put one in your back."

Hoyt moved to the left. Smiled as he turned over toward Preston.

"You really going to shoot me, Preston?" Hoyt asked. "Because, if that's the case, I would love to see you try."

Ray stood still with his hands over his head. Quiet and not even moving an inch.

"Looks like the two of you are busy." Ray said. "So, I'll just leave you guys alone to speak among yourselves."

"You're not going anywhere." Preston and Hoyt both said.

"Don't mock me." Preston said to Hoyt.

"Mock you?" Hoyt said. "Don't mock me is what you mean."

"My point exactly." said Ray.

Ray looked to run but was stopped by Preston, who jumped in front of him. Ray slowly turned back around as Hoyt aimed directly at his head.

"Preston, I think you should just leave please." Hoyt said. "We have so much business to discuss."

"I'm not leaving him here only for you to murder." Preston said. "He's coming back with me to the agency."

"Well, I believe we should let Colby, here decide his own fate" Hoyt said. "What will it be, Colby?"

"Would it be alright if I were to make up my own option?" Ray said. "It would be a much fair deal."

"No." Hoyt said. "Either option one, you go along with Preston to prison or option two, where he leaves you here for me to finish the job that needs finishing."

"My god, this isn't happening." Preston said.

Preston moved over quickly to Hoyt and smacked him in the head with his gun. Hoyt fell to the ground, knocked out from the collision. Preston looked down at him and turned around, where Ray is nowhere in sight.

"Shit." Preston said. "Damn it!"

CHAPTER 30

Back at the warehouse site, most of Colby's crime thugs were arrested and taken to jail by the SWAT team. Preston walked back to the site from out of the woods with Hoyt in tow, handcuffed. Eldon thanked one of the SWAT officials and turned, seeing Preston with Hoyt.

"I see you have him." Eldon said. "Great news there."

"Yeah I do." Preston said. "Wasn't an easy task, you know. Had to deal with him constantly talking on the way over here"

"You keep telling your fairy tales, Preston. We'll see who's living in reality, who's waiting for his chariot to arrive."

"Could you please take him over to the SWAT van. That way we can't hear him speaking."

"I CAN TALK LOUDER IF YOU WANT, CHIEF! HOW DOES THIS SOUND TO YOU?!"

Eldon fanned his arm as the SWAT members walked over and grabbed Hoyt, dragging him to the van. Preston smiled as he turned and focused on Eldon. Eldon shook his head as he watched Hoyt being dragged off.

"From what just transpired, I'm sure it wasn't easy for you to deal with."

"I manage as much as I possibly can."

Emily walked over to Preston and Eldon. They turned toward her as she looked around to see who was being arrested and placed in police cars and SWAT vans. Her face began to change as didn't see Colby being placed or sitting in any of them. She looked at Preston with a slight concern.

"Something wrong, Weston?" Preston said.

"Have you seen Colby anywhere?" Emily said. "You can't tell me the bastard got away."

"Last saw him, he was in the woods. I caught up with him and Hoyt came in right after. It was between him or Hoyt. I couldn't risk Hoyt of escaping, so I went for him first and as I turned around, Colby was gone. He ran off as I was apprehending Hoyt. Hoyt was very close to killing him."

"So, what you're saying is Ray's still out there. Free and at large? No one to chase after him."

"Afraid so. I would believe he shouldn't be too far along from this location it would seem. I mean, the forest where he was is right behind me. Probably if you take some steps, you could find his tracks and follow them to the finish line."

"Thanks for information." Emily said. "I'll go ahead and do that."

Emily went to walk into the forest as Eldon raised his arm in front of her. She glanced over and faced him as Preston held his head down for a second before raising it up and facing Emily himself.

"Fine. I'll wait until when we have an appropriate time of doing the task. Contact me when its settled."

She walked off as Eldon looked at Preston, uneasy.

"You do realize that the emotion she's currently in that she's going to go on a hunting spree now." Eldon said.

"Yeah." Preston said. "Wasn't much I could do except to shoot him."

"Good thing you didn't. Otherwise, we would all be looking at another "Jonny Cartel event" with you killing another elite crime boss in New Haven."

"It would've given us some media attention time. That would've helped us in some way of having an advantage."

"I prefer we don't have any of those kinds of people running over to the agency, asking for a god damn interview about our jobs. When they can't even do their own damn jobs."

"I feel your pain, Eldon and it's a cold one indeed."

"You'll be feeling something of that caliber if you continue to piss me off in such a manner."

277

Nearby Preston and Eldon, Coover, Rusty, and Billy were all being arrested and taken to jail. As Eldon went to answer his cell phone, Preston walked over to them and placed Hoyt inside the truck. Coover and Rusty stared at Hoyt, which he does the same to them.

"You have something to say to me?" Hoyt said. "If so, I would like to hear it please."

"I've got a lot to say to your ass. You and Billy. The two of you don't know who you're dealing with here by causing all of this."

"It doesn't matter who we're dealing with. What matters is showing Colby and his group of lapdogs that Hoyt Bennett is in town and is here to stay. You understood all of that, Rusty."

"Don't play smart with me, Hoyt." Coover said. "Because, I'll show you what I can really do and it doesn't involve me using my mouth."

"Is that right. I assumed you used your mouths for countess things. Who's to tell exactly what for when you walk around with stains across your face."

Coover lunged at Hoyt, ramming his shoulders into Hoyt. Rusty and Billy tried pulling Coover off as Hoyt kicked him in the knee. Coover yelled in pain as Hoyt laughed at him. Preston walked over to the van, gaining the attention of the four men.

"I suggest to the four of you. No fighting in here guys." Preston said. "One mistake could put an extra charge on your timeslot."

"You've made a big mistake, Preston." Hoyt said. "I could've taken them all out and would have done a great service to my city."

"I have to say, you were doing a good thing." Preston said. "You just went about it the wrong way."

SWAT officer walked by and closed the back door of the truck, as Hoyt smiled at Preston when the last door was shut. Preston watched as the SWAT truck drove off from the site. Emily walked back to Preston, looking at the truck.

"It's a shame really." Preston said.

"How is that?" Emily said.

"Because Hoyt just came out of prison and now it looks like he's going back in."

"He made his choice to do what he does." Emily said. "Nothing could've changed that."

Eldon walked toward them, placing his cell phone back into his pocket.

"I just received a phone call from the coroner's office that contained information regarding the double homicide in that neighborhood." Eldon said. "Appears they were also responsible for blowing up the bank as well."

"May we know who you're talking about here?" Preston said. "At least on a job extent."

"The DNA and witnesses' descriptions added up and lead to Coover and Rusty Bronson. The two older Bronson Brothers."

"No wonder they were the first suspects that many were expecting. It was obvious to a certain degree."

"At least they were in that truck and are heading to prison. Where they can settle their losses and find a way to move on with their lives or better yet, just rot in prison"

"You couldn't have said it any better." Preston said. "Job well done I say."

"We'll deal with the rest of this in the morning." Eldon said. "Because I'm tired and I need some sleep."

"Same here, Eldon." Preston said. "See you tomorrow then."

"I'll see you at the office tomorrow. Good and sound."

Eldon walked away as Preston approached Emily.

Preston turned to Emily.

"I figured we'll search for Colby right away, first thing in the morning." Preston said. "That way, we'll have enough energy in our systems to track him down long term."

"I very well could use the energy." Emily said. "I'm up for the task."

Late in the night, Richard and Karen are sleeping in their bed as the front door's bell ringed. Richard raised his head from his pillow, believing that the TV was still on. From his point of view, he knew for certain that the TV wasn't on. The doorbell ranged again as he got up from the bed and walked downstairs toward the door. He took a slight peek through the blinds next to the door. Seeing no one as the bell continued to ring. He opened the door and Preston stood before him.

"Jesus Christ." Richard said. "I couldn't see you through the blinds."

"You're that paranoid that someone would come over to your house and try to do what exactly."

"Never mind, Mr. Maddox. May I ask what you're doing here?"

"I need to speak with Karen. It'll be a quick word and I'll be out of your hair's reach."

"I don't know if she's awake."

"Well can you go ahead and check. Just to make sure. If she's asleep, I'll go ahead and leave. If not, I just need a word."

Richard nodded as he let Preston enter into his home. Preston looked around at the interior of the home. Glancing at his museum-like qualities and the fireplace that sat in the living room near a large flat-screen TV.

"If I may ask, how many TVs are in this home?"

"What's it to you?"

"Just curious is all. I've seen one of those TV's before. Though, it was inside a store weeks before the Black Friday fiasco took place. I decide I shouldn't get one because I would have to worry about the possibility of someone coming over to my place and trying to kill me over a damn flat screen."

"I'll tell you. I was lucky to get one of those."

"Really. When did you get it?"

"Black Friday. Last year. Had to fight through an entire mob just to put my hands on it. Luckily, I checked out before the police arrived and nearly electrocuted everyone inside the store with their taser guns"

"Sounds like a crazy morning that was."

"It was around eight or nine in the evening."

"Holy shit. Stores are opening on the day of the supposed thanks."

"Yeah. These are some crazy times when you have people nearly killing each other over TVs."

"Can you imagine how'll they react when there's no food or water available for them to purchase. They'll turn into pure savages."

"When that day comes, I will be ready for certain."

"Same goes here, Richard."

Preston glanced up and saw Karen coming down the stairs. She looked at him as if he stole something from the house and returned to take even more of the items. Preston smirked a bit before Karen approached him up close.

"You can leave us here, Richard." Karen said. "I'll be just fine."

"Are you sure, sweetheart? I mean, I could join in on the little conversation you two are having."

"No need, Richard. It'll be quick and savvy."

"If I may ask you, why are you here at my house after midnight?"

"I just needed to have a word with you and like I told Richard, I'll be out of your hair. Just a word is all I need from you."

Uncertain of Preston's motives, Karen agreed to speak with him as they entered the kitchen. Preston pulled up one of the wooden stools from the counter and sat down as Karen stood on the other side of the counter. She opened the refrigerator.

"You want anything to drink while you're here?"

"No thanks. I don't want to take any of your water or soda or alcoholic beverages."

Karen closed the refrigerator as she walked over to the counter and faced Preston.

"So, what did you want to talk about? Especially at this time of night. Just unusual to me that you would do this. Well, not too unusual."

"I just came from a massive shootout in the outskirts of town and I just need some word comforting is all."

"Word comforting?"

"Yeah. That sounds about right I believe. Shouldn't be so difficult I suppose. You used to give me a lot of word comforting back when we were together."

"I did that because that was the only way to get you to relax about anything and afterwards you wanted physical comforting."

"I didn't come here for anything physical. Just some small words of advice and that would be all."

"Ok then. How about these words of advice? You just came from a shootout in which you could've been killed and currently lying down on the table in a morgue. But, you didn't die and you're not lying down on the morgue table. So, the words of advice are you're still alive and you're able to correct any mistakes you've made in your life to move forward. You know, continue saving people's lives and giving them hope for a better world or at least a better city.

"Same sort of frame I get it. I understand what you're saying"

Preston looked at his watch and his eyes grew as he stood up from the stool and tucked it beneath the counter. He walked over to Karen and hugged her. He kissed her on the cheek.

"It was nice speaking with you, Karen. It really was. The word helped in their own way."

"Glad I could help out in some sort of way."

Preston walked to the front door as Karen walked behind him. He opened the door and took a step out before turning toward her.

"Oh. Richard seems like a good man. Just try to keep him home on Black Fridays can you."

Karen laughed as Preston smiled.

"I'll manage my best on that one. it's a big task."

"I'm sure it is. Well, nice speaking with you and I'm out of your hair now."

Preston exited the home and walked toward his car. Karen watched him leave the area as she went back upstairs to bed. Richard waited for her in the bedroom, guessing to himself if she would return to bed.

Preston drove back to his apartment, he opened the door and walked in. As he laid down on his bed, placing his hands onto his chest and slowly closing his eyes, prepared to go to sleep, his cell phone began to ring. He grabbed it and answered the call.

"Hello." Preston said. "Who's this?"

The voice on the other side was mumbled. Preston couldn't

understand what they were saying.

"Who is this?" Preston said. "Hello? Is anybody there?"

He hung up the phone and began thinking. He noticed that the caller sounded like a woman.

Around close to midnight, Emily arrived at her apartment. She placed her bag and other gear onto the desk nearby the counter. As she took off her leather jacket, her cell phone began to ring. She glanced over and looked at the number. Knowing it from her past, she knew it was from New Jersey, so she answered it quickly.

"Emily Weston speaking." Emily said.

"This is the Newark Marshal and Detective Agency." The caller said. "We wanted to make sure we contacted you straight ahead. Detective Gloria gave us your number, so we could speak with you on this urgent matter?"

"Yes, ma'am." Emily said. "What is it that you would need to speak with me and why is it such an urgent situation?"

"We contacted you because your father was found dead." The caller said. "We figured you were the first to call on this matter."

Emily paused as she cannot even continue to talk. She shakes a bit before placing the phone toward her ear. She tried to catch her breath and she started breathing calmly before she spoke on the phone.

"My father's dead?" Emily said. "May I ask what the cause of death was?"

"From what we understand here at this moment, it appeared he was murdered."

Three weeks total have passed since the incident that occurred at the warehouse between Ray Colby and Hoyt Bennett. Preston stayed calm and to himself as he's seemly sat in a courtroom, reviewing a case involving his old friend. The Judge is recommending that Hoyt stay in prison for a total of six months. Preston agreed with the judge to a certain extent, but insisted on visiting Hoyt at the prison.

Within a couple of days, Preston traveled to Washington D.C. to visit Hoyt and arrived at the prison to speak with him in person. Preston awaited Hoyt's presence in the calling room as took a glance to the side and spouted Hoyt, wearing an orange prison suit coming towards him being guarded by security officers of the prison. Hoyt sits in front of Preston, smiling.

"What a sight to see for myself. I am highly surprised to see you here in my presence, Preston."

"Just came to visit." Preston said. "To see how you were, really. Being back behind bars to where no harm can come from your hand."

"So, if I may ask, what's been going on in New Haven so far? What have my allies been doing in this spare time they possess? Have the people forgotten who I am or do they still remember the actions that I've taken?"

"They still remember what you've done to the city and its innocent residents." Preston said. "But, they don't want to remember you or see you, for that matter. Your line of guys are not really in the limelight these days. Seeing how they beloved and devoted leader is currently behind bars and won't be able to speak with them until his six months of jail time is officially off."

"Funny, how you speak about me directly toward myself. Good stuff you're pulling here. Though, overall, I don't blame them at all one bit for staying out of the spotlight. In time, they will return under that light with me by their side and we will continue what we started. Only this time we won't have any interferences from either side of the law."

"From the sound of your voice and how your body reacted along with it, I can tell you're being completely serious about what you just said. Least they won't have to worry anymore about you or what you've got conjuring up in that head of yours that could put the rest of them behind steel bars. I figured that your time here would give you enough hours to clear your head of that ruckus that goes around. Try thinking of happy thoughts. While you're here, you could write a book of your own or some music lyrics like other inmates have done."

"Funny. Hoyt Bennett writing a book or even a song in prison. Crazy shit and even I would say no to that kind of offer. No matter how much money were thrown in my face for such garbage that was created. While I have you here, let me ask you a question, Preston. Have you ever heard of the theory? A theory that involves someone like myself to corrupt someone such as yourself to do unspeakable things to his co-workers and loved ones."

"Can't say that I haven't." Preston said. "Does this supposed theory have a name exactly? Something that I can keep my attention toward if it ever comes across."

"Well, I'll just say this. Preston, you need to always remember flat out that I'm your equal. The Yin to your Yang." Hoyt said. "Take it how you want. But, believe it or not, I am."

"We'll see about that when or if you're released from prison once again, Hoyt."

Preston left the booth as Hoyt watched on and continued to speak. He raised his voice so Preston could hear him. Preston turned around, he stared at Hoyt, who smiled. Preston shook his head in shame for Hoyt.

"I am your equal in pure magic, Preston Maddox! Remember that phrase and keep it in your head for a long time to come. I am your equal in pure magic!"

"Maybe in pure madness."

"That one was great, Preston. Really good job on that one."

Preston turned back around toward the front entrance and walked out. Hoyt smiled as the police grabbed him by his arms and returned him to his prison cell.

"I'm his equal. It's funny." Hoyt said.

Hoyt sits inside the prison cell laughing hysterically as Preston left the premises and headed toward the airport, returning to New Haven.

MARK PORTER OF ARGORON

CHAPTER 1: THE INCIDENT

United States Army Lieutenant, Mark Porter is currently on a mission to Roswell, New Mexico. His focus is keen as he traveled alone, listening to musical instrumentals. As he drove, his cell phone rings and he answers it.

"Lieutenant Porter." he said.

"Porter, this is General Dunlap." the caller said. "How far are you from the site?"

"I'm looking at it as we speak." Porter said.

Porter drove to the entrance gate, where two soldiers stood. They opened the gate , permitting him entry. Porter recognized the location, while still speaking with the General on the phone.

"General, I must ask, what is this place?"

"This is Area 51."

"Area 51." Porter intrigued. "I never thought I would be here."

"See you inside, Porter."

Porter hung up the phone, entering into the front entrance of the buildings. Area 51 had the appearance of a small city, with dozens of soldiers and officials moving throughout. Most of which are military soldiers and scientists. Porter stepped out of the car, heading towards the front doors layered with bulletproof glass. He entered, being greeted by soldiers. Porter took a left turn toward the elevator. Inside the elevator were two scientists.

"Excuse me, but are you Mark Porter?" one scientist asked.

"Yes I am."

"Its an honor to meet such a well-known Lieutenant." the other scientist said.

"Thank you."

The elevator had reached its destination floor. Porter is the first one to walk out, only to avoid the two scientists. Porter walked down a hallway and in the distance, he saw General Dunlap. Porter begins walking toward him. General Dunlap saw Porter coming down the hall near him.

"Porter, right on schedule."

"Yes sir, General."

Porter and General Dunlap entered another room. As they walked, Dunlap began telling Porter a few details to the secret operations being held within the facility. Porter took a guess to what it may be with only Dunlap smirking without saying a word.

"Porter, there are some rules that you must obey, since you're here."

"Ok, General. What are they?"

"You must not tell a single soul what you're about to see in this next room." Dunlap said. "If you do, we will have no choice but to rid you of the world."

"I see. Must be something very important."

"Important?" Dunlap said. "Try highly secretive. If anyone found out about this, the world will turn for the worst."

They reached the room and the metal door slowly slides open. The room was surrounded with military security. Little light was emitted into the room as the rest was covered in darkness. Porter gazed around, seeing scientists doing autopsies on unknown beings.

"General, what is going on here?" Porter asked.

"I'll tell you once we've reached our location."

Passing through the security, walking into yet another room. This room was lit up with plenty of light and wasn't nearly as shrouded in darkness like the other. Inside the room is a long table with a device sitting in the middle. Porter and Dunlap approached the table, looking at the device.

"Porter, this device you see here is able to transfer beings, human or not, to other worlds."

"Other worlds? Like planets?"

"Yes. Perhaps even dimensions are a possibility. Testing will only reveal how soon."

"How is that possible?" Porter asked. "Has it been tested?"

"Not yet. We're still awaiting an answer from the President."

They walked around the table, looking from all angles. The device was shiny, projecting a blue light which directed into the air. Porter slowly held his hand over the device before Dunlap snatched it from getting closer.

"You don't want to do something that you'll regret."

"Sorry, sir."

As they stood looking at the device, an alarm goes off. Porter and Dunlap look around. Dunlap ran toward the doors, questioning the security as to what triggered the alarm.

"What the hell's going on?!" Dunlap yelled.

"The base, sir, its under attack!" a soldier yelled.

"Porter, stay where you are!"

He pulled out his pistol, looking outside the door. From the outside, he saw soldiers and scientists being attacked by an unknown force. The opposing force appeared to have tentacles, while wearing peculiar white robes with long white hair extending to their lower back. Dunlap glared out of the glass window of the door, staring at them, watching them kill the soldiers and scientists. Gunshots are heard from the outside, but they're dying left and right.

Porter approached toward the door, but is stopped by Dunlap, who commanded Porter to stay by the table.

"General, what's going on?!"

"Sit tight, Lieutenant!" Dunlap said. "We're in for a show."

Dunlap backed from the door as it bursts open. He began shooting at the beings, but the gunshots have no effect. Porter takes out his revolver and shoots one of the beings in the head, which kills it. Dunlap looks at Porter, astounded.

"Try that, General."

"I surely will."

They both begin shooting the beings that are coming into the room through the damaged door. They aim for the head and shoot them directly there. They've killed the beings and look at each other. Both astounded and calm.

"Good job, Lieutenant."

"Same to you, General."

They shook hands, but from the ceiling a bright light shines down on them and Porter pushes Dunlap out of the way and a loud bang is heard with a large flash of light, nearly blinding Dunlap. The light fades away and Dunlap looks around for Porter.

"Porter?" Dunlap spoke. "Porter?!"

Dunlap looks around and realizes that Porter is nowhere in sight, but he also realized that the device's light is now dim, which before it was bright. He now knows that someone has happened to Porter.

Porter, who's opening his eyes, realizes that he's in a desert. He looks and stands up, brushing the dirt off of his uniform. He walks around the area, looking around at it surroundings.

"Where the hell am I?"

CHAPTER 2: CAPTIVE FOREIGNER

He continued walking, although realizing that he can move faster and jump higher than usual. Knowing now something isn't quite right. He continued to move ahead, but in front of him, he sees something running towards him. He tries to get a closer look and he sees that they looked human. He begins running the other direction, but is shot down by a bow and arrow. Porter lays on the ground as the beings get closer to him. He now hears silence, but the beings are surrounding him.

The beings appeared to be humans, yet there was a difference to them. Their skin was darker and their bodies were toned. They stared down Porter as he glared at them. They spoke to each other in an unknown language that Porter couldn't understand. He stood up, staggering from the arrow wound, stepping back from the beings and points to the one wearing white fur over his shoulders. His stature gave Porter to belief to be the general.

"You, where am I? Tell me where the hell I am?!"

The humanoids looked at Porter, their thoughts ponder if he's not from their world. One approached Porter and looks at him from all angles and stands back with his group. Porter stares at the group, reaching for his revolver, but he doesn't have it. He looks at what he perceived to be the humanoids' general and saw he had his revolver.

"How did you get that?!" Porter asked with rage. "Where am I?!"

Porter walked over to the beings, but he's knocked unconscious by one of their punches. They dragged him back to their location, locking him up. Hours later, Porter awakens and is now chained to a rock with no way out. He sees the beings from before, but this time, there's more. Porter begins thinking that he may not be on Earth anymore. He know believes that he's somewhere else, somewhere unknown.

Porter tried to break himself out of the chains, but he's too tired and weary to do so. He looks around as he's surrounded by dirt and feces. He continues to look around to find an object that could break him out of the chains. He doesn't find any tools that he could use, so he sits in the dungeon through the entire night. The next day, he awakens and sees himself surrounded by the tall, green beings. One in particular, releases him of the chains and helps him up, Porter stares at the being and looks into its eyes.

"What are you?" Porter asked.

"We are the Micrans." The being said. "Warriors of Argoron."

"What…? Argoron? Where am I?"

"You are on Argoron, stranger."

"Argoron?' Porter said. 'Where is that? I've never heard of Argoron.'

"If you're not from here, then, where do you come from?.' The being said. "What is your origin?"

"I'm not understanding what you mean? Where exactly am I?"

"You're on Argoron. A planet in the vastness of the stars."

"Argoron?" Porter questioned. "No. I was just in New Mexico."

"Where do you come from? Truly?"

"My name is Mark Porter." Porter said. "."

From the entrance came the leader of this particular warrior clan, Saban Jai. Saban walked toward and stood in front of Porter. Porter stared, not knowing what to expect.

"Mark Porter." Saban said. "How can you be from Jagoron?"

"What? No, I'm from Earth, not Jagoron? What is a Jagoron?"

"That is what I said, Mark Porter of Jagoron The world you come from is called Jagoron in this land. To your species, the earth-walkers, Jagoron is called Earth."

Porter sat confused. The Micrans didn't know what to make of his reaction. Saban didn't bother with him, rallying the others to bring him to the carriage. The carriage seemed to be made of a reddish wood as were the wheels, decorated with spears and red flags with no markings. Two of the Micrans carried Porter into the carriage, which was pulled by two eight-legged creatures. Which Porter saw them, he immediately thought them to be horses. However, he spotted they each had two tails and two sets of eyes on both sides. Speaking the word, Saban chuckled.

"Moreks." Saban said. "That's what they are. The fastest beasts in all of Argoron."

Saban jumped into the front of the carriage, gaining control over the horses as they rode off from the vast desert toward the massive metropolitan city as they approached the gates of the city of *Taranopolis*, as the inhabitants called it. Porter took a look outside of the carriage, seeing the massive city with its pointed skyscrapers and layered structures. The vehicles which moved throughout the city were a mix of the carriage and anti-gravity ships. The ships appeared to have four sets of transparent wings in the colors of rubies. The sky above the city was orange with a hint of red. The city was surrounded by red flags, flowing calmly with the wind throughout the city as the temperature was warm enough to have the people dressed in light clothing. Some even glanced at Porter, seeing his attire. From there, Porter knew he was out of place, especially when glancing upward toward the ships.

"Where am I?" Porter asked himself.

The carriage stopped in front of the city's palace. The Micrans stood by the carriage door, dragging Porter to the outside as they entered the palace. Porter stood on his feet, being held by two Micran soldiers, walking toward what he guessed was the throne room. In the room, Porter saw three chairs. Two were empty and the center one was full as there was a man sitting, speaking with another man. The man standing up had the wings of a dragon folded on his back and claws for fingers. Dressed in armored leather. The man sitting down was decked in armor, linen, and fur. On his head sat a crown made of what appeared to be gold or bronze. Porter couldn't make out any of it, yet, he knew they were royalty in their own way.

"You know why I've come and visited you, my lord."

"Yes, I am aware of your need for warriors. As of right now, there aren't many who are at my disposal for combat."

"What of your prisoners? What use will you have for them other than wasting away behind cell doors?"

The one in the chair nodded, rubbing his chin.

"You have a point."

They looked toward the entrance, seeing the Micrans carrying Porter. The man standing pointed and his yellow eyes widen. The man in the seat stood up, glaring toward the Micran warriors and the prisoner they held.

"A new prisoner?"

"My lord." Saban said, kneeling. "We have another prisoner in need of interrogation."

The man stared at Porter, seeing his clothing and his tone. He was uncertain of Porter's ethnicity to his own and the others around him. He turned back to Saban, raising his hand, giving him the order to stand.

"And what has this man done and what is he wearing?"

"We're not sure, sire. He was dressed in this manner when we found him."

"And where did you find him?"

"Out in the wilderness. He appeared dazed. Confused you might say. He was speaking strangely, so we brought him here. To get more answers. If you request it, my king."

The King nodded.

"Very well. Take him to the room. Ivo will be there to get any answers we may need."

"And what of him after you received your answers?" The other man said.

"When the time comes, I will call to you, Wyvern King. Right now, best you return to your domain. Prepare your warriors for the entertainment of the masses."

"I will keep my eyes and ears open."

The Wyvern King's wings buckled as he nodded his head, walking toward the exit. The King looked back, seeing Saban and the warriors leading Porter into the interrogation room. He sighed as he sat down and from the entrance arrived a young woman, dressed in a silver dress and long reddish-orange hair. She bowed before the king and he smiled.

"My daughter. I see you've returned from your journey."

"I have, father. I also have some news regarding the people of the city."

"News? What kind of news?"

"The people are aware of the coming war with the Celedians."

"And how do they know this?"

"Some have described a strange man coming into the city, warning them of the war and giving them the choice to choose which side they're on."

"A speaker of war in my city." The King said. "I see I must find him. Or, perhaps Saban has already brought him in."

The Princess wasn't sure what her father had meant. He chuckled and stood up, walking toward his daughter.

"Let me handle the matters of war. You must prepare for a wedding. Saban is a good man and a future leader."

"I... I understand."

The King looked at his daughter as she let out a small smile.

"I have other matters to attend to. Make sure you keep yourself protected when you're out in the city."

"The guardsmen will stand by me."

"Good, my Arribel."

CHAPTER 3: WHO ARE YOU?

Porter struggled against the strength of the two Micrans as they chained his wrists to the wall before exiting. Porter stared quietly, hearing footsteps approaching the cell. The door had opened for Porter to glance at two other warriors and a peculiar following the middle. He stood about the height of Porter, but he was much older as his white hair could attest.

"Who are you?"

"What?" Porter said slowly.

"Who are you? What is your name?"

"My name is Mark Porter."

"Mark Porter." Ivo said. "Strange name. never heard of such a one. Tell me, Mark Porter, where are you from?"

"I'm not from here. So, that's a start."

"Your name tells me all I need to know. Why have you come here, Mark Porter? Are you a spy for the Celedians? The Ceruleanians? Orgons, perhaps?"

"What are you talking about? I'm not from this place. "

"Your physical tells the tale. You're a warrior."

"I'm a soldier. A lieutenant."

"Convenient." Ivo chuckled. "And you've come here for what purpose other than being a spy or an invader?"

"I am not an invader nor am I some kind of spy. I didn't come here on my own accord. It's hard to explain. Even for myself. The place I come from is Earth. Earth is my home."

"Earth? You speak of Jagoron, the blue world where the waters move across the grounds."

"I guess you can detail it as much."

"Who sent you here?"

"I don't know."

"Then, start with something for me to go along. To understand your plight."

Porter sighed, waving his hands slight in a non-caring manner, yet, Porter began to tell Ivo of the encounter in Area 51, the ambush, and the instant transportation. Ivo listened closely to every word Porter had spoken. Once Porter had come to the conclusion of his sudden appearance in the desert, Ivo ceased him.

"You were brought here."

"Yes. But, I'm not sure by what or how."

"What is it you truly desire at this moment?"

"To be out of these chains and to be sent back home."

Ivo chuckled.

"There will be a time for that. Getting you back home however, is a tricky obstacle. For if you do not know how you came to Argoron, how does it make sense for you to find your way back."

"I saw the ships you people have. They're far beyond what I've seen. Now, I can take one of them and fly it back to Earth. A safe passage to get home."

"Enough." Ivo said, silencing Porter. "Our customs are far different than your kind. For one to achieve the freedom which one craves, they must earn it and win it."

"Win it? I'm not understanding."

"Combat. A trial to test your strength. To learn your endurance. Mentally. Physically. Spiritually. Only then will we and yourself see the conclusion to the whole matter."

"Are you telling me I must fight to get home?"

"Yes."

Porter sighed. Hanging his head low. He thought for a moment if this was only a dream. A hallucination, yet, with the small pain he felt in his legs, he knew it was real. All of it.

"I'm sorry. But, I am not going to be treated as some sort of amusement to you and your people here. I demand to be sent home."

Ivo turned back and walked toward the cell door. He opened it before taking a look back at Porter. Measuring him with a gaze.

"Your freedom demands on your fighting spirit. I hope you have one."

Ivo exited the cell, calling over a Micran guard. Ivo signaled the guard to keep watch of Porter's cell for the remainder of the day and throughout the night. Several hours later, nightfall fell over Taranopolis and the city was sleep. The sky which as glowing red had become as dark with glares and glistens of a peculiar bluish hue. Porter sat inside his cell. Barely ate the food they delivered to him. He looked over toward the guard sitting at the door. With the faint light shining from the window above him, Porter caught the glimpse of a key. Believing the key to be the only way out of his cell. Porter made a move, but remembered his wrists were attached to chains embedded into the concrete wall.

"Hey." Porter whispered. "Hey."

The guard jolted a bit, no movement afterwards. Porter sighed as he looked around the cell for something. Anything to get the guard's attention. Porter thought and glanced over to his left, seeing the tray of food. His eyes moved from the tray to the guard. Porter swiped his foot, kicking the tray against the cell doors, rattling up the guard as he jumped up with a sword in hand. Porter saw the blade.

"What's going on in there?" The guard asked.

"Water." Porter said. " I need water."

"Water? Where do you see any water?"

"To drink. I need something to drink."

The guard sighed and walked off, leaving Porter waiting. Unsure of what he could've waited for, the guard had returned, holding a small flask in his hand. He opened the cell door and entered, putting the flask on the ground as he unlocked the cuff from Porter's right wrist from the chain. Porter sighed and paused, quickly snatching he flask and smashing it into the guard's face before kicking the guard in the throat and stomping on his head. The helmet which the guard had word was cracked on the side. Porter looked to the guard's hand, seeing the key. He grabbed it and unruffled his left wrist. Being free from the wall, Porter grabbed the chest plate and helmet of the guard. Taking the sword last as he made his escape from the cell. Porter moved through the corridors quietly, avoiding other guards and even those who were playing a game of *L'agh*. In the distance, Porter saw the moonlight peaking from a doorway. Porter reached the door and found himself staring at the outside toward the vast desert. He sighed, knowing if he wanted to escape, going back into the desert was his only option. Porter made his move and ran out into the desert with only Argoron's moon as his source of direction.

CHAPTER 4: THE FLYING MEN

Porter had went afar out into the desert, he even glanced back and could only see the tips from the skyscrapers which stood in Taranopolis. Gasping for breath and of thirst, Porter continued walking. Even in the chilling cold. The air was almost below freezing to Porter's understanding. As he walked, he took a gaze up into the sky, seeing the peaking sun hovering behind a set of clouds. The heat began o rise throughout the desert sands as Porter continues trekking along the dunes around him. No sign of life. No animals. No plants. Porter walked alone in the desert.

From there, he came to a stop at what he believed to be a entry into some kind of cavern. Exhaling from the long walk, Porter approached the entry point, discovering the entrance into a small cave. He stepped forward to the cave and let out a faint shout. Nothing responded. He took the time to sit down and relax himself. He closed his eyes and calmly breathed. Afterwards, he heard what he believed to be something running within the cavern. Using his remaining strength to stand, Porter entered the cavern deeper and found a small pond which was set by a waterfall within the cavern. Pleased, Porter ran over into the pond, soaking himself in the water. He went and drank from the waterfall. In a strangeness to him, the water was cool. Near icy.

"Where does this water come from in a place such as this?" Porter thought to himself.

Taking several minutes to relax himself within the pond. He stepped from it and returned to the entry point. Once he saw the sand in the distance, he caught three shadows in the sand. Hearing the wind above him. Porter ran out to see what was in the air and what he had seen were the wyvern men. Half-man and half-wyvern. Their bodies from their head to their waist were similar to a man. Yet, their legs and wings were of wyverns. Porter went and hid in the cavern, but one of the wyvern men caught him as he sat back against the rock wall. The wyvern man flew down to the cavern as Porter remained silent.

"Whatever you are," The wyvern man said. "Come out and face us."

Porter sighed in regret and slowly took his steps out of the cavern for the wyvern man to see. Unknown to Porter of the wyvern man's height. He stood over Porter by nine-feet and a half. The second wyvern man flew down, standing besides his partner as they stared at Porter. Seeing his garb. They were dumfounded.

"You're a strange one."

"I'm strange?" Porter said. "Look at the two of you. Hybrid beasts."

"What do they call you?" The wyvern man asked.

"My name?"

"Do you have one?"

"Mark Porter."

"Very well, Mark Porter. Myself and my colleague are elite soldiers for the Wyvern King. This cavern and the water within belong to him and him alone."

Porter chuckled.

"You're saying this king of yours owns this?"

"Precisely. As of this moment, you are trespassing."

"Listen, this is the best place I've come to so far on this planet or wherever the hell I am. Now, I am going to give the two of you to the count of three to leave me alone. Go fly up and bother someone else."

"You are not authorized to give us orders."

"I just did. What are you going to do with them?"

The second wyvern man looked over to his partner. Pointing at Porter's body. Noticing his demeanor and attitude. The first wyvern man took notice and nodded before turning his gaze toward Porter.

"If you won't leave our king's cave, then we must take you to him."

Porter balled his fists and clashed them. Standing tall before the wyvern men. They looked to one another and only came to a silent agreement. Before Porter to throw a punch, the wyvern men tackled him, stomping him into the sand. Porter tried to block the stomps with his arms, but one of the stomps collided with his head and chest, knocking him inconspicuous. Once the wyvern men knew of Porter's current status, they agreed to take him and they did. Carrying him in the air as they flew back to their place of origin.

CHAPTER 5: FINDING THE WARRIOR

Within Taranopolis the same day and hour, the guards searched the city searching for Porter under the orders of King R'akl. The guards returned to him, informing him of Porter's disappearance and lack of trace in the city region. King R'akl wondered how Porter made his escape in the night and several guards approached the king, detailing in of the discovery of a dead guard in the cell where Porter was kept. With murder being the case, R'akl called for a manhunt on Porter to be searched out and arrested on sight. The guards took in the king's command and headed out to find Porter even outside the city region. Princess Lola approached her father with caution, asking for alternative ways to find Porter. But, the king did not want to hear a word from his daughter regarding the foreign prisoner.

"What if he comes across the others? Like The Wyvern King?"

"If he does come across the Wyvern King, then the Wyvern King will bring him back to us. He knows our ways and if he doesn't want Micran warriors on his doorstep, then, he will return what is ours without haste."

"You know the Wyvern kind just as much as the rest of us. They will take whatever they can and use it for their own cause. If they come across him, they will use him against your kingdom. Against all of us under your command.

"Enough, my daughter." R'akl yelled. "Leave such matters to me. Right now, you should be concerning yourself with your upcoming marriage to Saban Jai. Focus on that and leave the duties of warfare to me. For these will become such matters for Saban when he is king."

"Yes, father." Lola replied, bowing before her father as she took her leave.

Leaving the palace, Lola commanded two guards to bring her one of the traveller-chariots. She instructed them to leave outside of the city gates. Unknown to her reasoning, they did not bother to question her, for she is the king's daughter and future wife to Saban Jai. Obeying her word, Lola arrived outside the gates, seeing the chariots. She stepped onto the chariot as one of her handmaidens approached. Getting on the chariot as well.

"What are you doing?" Lola asked.

"I'm coming with you. No need for you to travel out there alone."

"If we're caught, you'll be in serious trouble. Possibly banishment or death."

"I will do what I must for the future queen."

Lola nodded with uncertainty as they rode off into the desert. While riding in the desert, the handmaiden, who's name was Serai asked Lola where they were heading. Lola informed Serai she was heading to the landmass of the Hibarian Forest. Serai questioned why would Lola seek help inside the deep forest, Lola only responded by detailing they will need to speak to the dwellers who live within and without the forest.

After some time had passed, Lola looked ahead, seeing the palm-like trees in the distance. The Hibarian Forest was near. A land parallel to the desert. Lush with grass, flowing water and many, many trees. Trees standing nearly the height of Taranopolis' skyscrapers. Nearing the entrance to the forest, they are stopped by two figures. Standing over ten-feet tall. Their skin was as green as the grass and their eyes were as golden as the sand. Brute physiques and rough demeanors. Lola knew what they were as she raised her hands in the midst of them aiming their weapons toward her.

"I come not to bring trouble. I am looking for someone. Perhaps you might have seen him."

"We do not understand what you speak of."

"There was a prison who escaped Taranopolis. I have come to ask if you've seen the man."

"We've seen no Micran."

"This man is not a Micran. He is something else. Beyond Argoron."

From the trees behind the guards came forward another one of their kind, yet covered in fur and jewelry. The two guards knelt down before him.

"Princess Arribel. Why have you come to our domain?"

"Lord Tartarus Kai. I have come to speak to you and your kind on an urgent request."

"How urgent is this request you have brought?"

"There was a man who was taken captive by my father. He escaped and fled. Most likely out in the desert. I have come to ask if you have seen this man."

Tartarus nodded, rubbing his chin. He shrugged shoulders without question. Just calm.

"I have not come across a Micran. Nor would one of them step foot near this forest by any means."

"As I told your guardsmen, this man is not a Micran. He's not from Argoron. He's from someplace else."

"Then, where did this prisoner originate from? The stars above? A planet far from our own?"

"Those are a possibility." Lola said. "I just need to find him before-"

"Before the Wyvern King has him, right?"

"Yes."

"Well, for all that it's worth, the Wyvern King probably has the prisoner by now. We have not seen this man anywhere near the forest."

Lola sighed with worry as Serai went to calm her. Tartarus stepped forward, looking down at the princess. He saw she had concern for the prisoner, which he deemed strange considering she didn't not fully know the origins or personality of the prisoner. However, he saw that she could see what would come to pass if Porter had been taken by the Wyvern King and what he could be used for. Being the Wyvern King is an adversary to his own ruler ship, Tartarus laid his hand on Lola's shoulder.

"I have an offer for you."

"Which is?"

"Sense the prisoner did not come across this region and it is more than likely the Wyvern King has taken him to Alderan, I will lend you two of my warriors to accompany you in your search."

"Um, I'm not sure what to say to that."

"No need. The better the Wyvern King doesn't have an upper hand the better."

"And what will you do if my father discovers you helped me?"

"Then, I will have a share of words with your father. Respectfully. No need for Micrans to fight against Celedians while the Wyvern kind continue to roam above our heads like *turuls*."

Lola agreed as the two Celedians stepped onto her chariot and they rode off with Tartarus watching as he turned back and entered the forest.

Elsewhere, the Wyvern Men flew down over a city. The city was complete made of mud bricks, detailed in the sand of the desert. The wyvern men carried Porter as they entered into a huge kingdom, the kingdom of Alderan. Overseen by the Wyvern King. The city was surrounded by full-grown wyverns hovering and flying across the sky. Inside the kingdom, the others who dwelled there appeared to be part-human and part-wyvern themselves with only a slight few being completely humanlike or wyvern-like. They took Porter into the rock-layered palace. Inside, they set Porter on the ground and stood beside him. Porter remained unconsciousness as he was overseen by other wyvern men. Dressed in armor from their heads to their feet..

"Is this the man you saw, my king?" one of the wyvern men asked.

"Why yes." said the Wyvern King as he entered the palace. "This is the one who caught my eyes."

Porter's body jolted as he began to regain consciousness. Raising his head slowly, finding himself surrounded by wyvern men and standing before him, the Wyvern King. Porter raised up quickly, attempting to stand on his feet as the wyvern men rushed over, holding him down on his knees with their hands pressing against his shoulders.

"No need to worry, strange man." The Wyvern King said. "You'll soon get the answers you seek."

Porter stared at the Wyvern King as he sat down in his throne seat, sitting with one leg stretched out and a sinister grin on his face. His eyes piercing like a dragon and his claws sharp both on his hands and feet. His skin was rough and darker than the sands.. Porter staggered as he continued to try and stand up.

"Who are you?" Porter asked.

"I am your new lord and master, I am the Wyvern King."

"The Wyvern King. Where the hell am I?"

"You're in the city of Alderan. My domain of ruler-ship. Where else could you be?"

"I demand my exit. I demand to return home."

"Oh, you wish to return to Taranopolis?"

"Taranopolis? I'm not from this place. This planet. I want to return to Earth."

The Wyvern King paused, standing up from his seat, steeping down the stairs toward Porter. The King inched closer to get a better look at Porter. Seeing his skin, his hair, and his eyes. The wyvern King scoffed.

"You're telling me you're from the world beyond?"

"the world beyond? I'm from the planet called Earth."

"My lord," a wyvern men said. "I believe he speaks of the world of Jagoron."

"Jagoron. Ah, the place where the waters outnumber the land. You come from such a place?"

"I do and I wish to return there."

"Well, I'm not sure how you ended up here. But, I am most definitely unsure how you'll return there."

"You cannot keep me here." Porter said. "I am not some prisoner."

"I beg to differ. The Wyvern King rebutted. "You see, when I saw you back in Taranopolis, the Micrans were bringing you in as their prisoner. In between then and now, you somehow made your escape and now, you're here in my city. In my kingdom. Therefore, you and now my prisoner and the only way those who are granted their leave from my kingdom is through combat."

"Combat?"

"If you can survive the Pit, you can have your freedom."

"I'm not a gladiator." Porter said. "I do not fight for sport!"

"You are one now. Survive my Pit. Entertain my guests and freedom will be yours."

The Wyvern King commanded his soldiers to take Porter to the dungeons. They stand Porter on his feet and Porter lunged toward the King with his fists, the King, using his own weight, pushed himself back as his wings emerged, taking up much of the space surrounding the throne. Terror had slithered into Porter as he eyes widen from the wingspan. The Wyvern King rushed toward Porter, punching him in the face. Porter fell to his knees from the sharpening blow.

"Take this specimen to the dungeons, now." the Wyvern King said.

"Yes, my king."

CHAPTER 6: TO WIN BATTLES IS TO WIN WARS

They drug Porter to the dungeons, throwing him in and shutting the doors. Porter rushed to his feet, taking a gander around the dungeon, seeing no one else inside with him. He approached the steel doors and gazed out, seeing a group of wyvern men standing and talking with one another. Unable to make out their conversation, he heard a thud against the wall on the opposite side of the dungeon. From there came muffled sounds of screams and beatings. The wyvern men turned back, looking toward the opposite dungeon and rushed over, opening the door. Porter could hear the wyvern men yelling and their wings flapping. Afterwards was only silence as the wyvern men stepped out from the dungeon, carrying a prisoner dressed in golden armor. Porter looked, seeing the prisoner appeared to be a human.

"What have you done to him?" Porter questioned.

"Quiet, slave. We do not answer to you."

"He's a human. You're keeping humans as slaves for what?"

"You ask why you're here? Because the audience needs entertainment. Today, is your attempt at giving it to them. By the orders of our king."

A loud horn roared across the sky. Porter gazed up and so did the two wyvern men. They looked to each other before turning toward Porter. One of them approached the door, unlocking it as the other entered the dungeon, fighting off Porter as they dragged him out and into another room. This room was full of other soldiers. Warriors from other lands outside of Alderan. Porter looked at them. Seeing the appeared to be human to his understanding. However, they only stared at him with confusion and strangeness. One of the gladiators stepped forward. A rugged-looking man. He stood over Porter by three feet. His stern demeanor proved he had been in Alderan for quite some time. Staring Porter in the eyes.

"The hell are you supposed to be?" He said, measuring Porter. "You're no Azurian."

"Get out of my face." Porter replied. "Before you end up on the ground."

"Or what? You'll kill me?" The gladiator chuckled. "Seeing as how we're all here to die anyway."

One of the wyvern men pointed toward Porter, demanding he remove his clothing. Porter disagreed, declaring he will keep on his uniform. The wyvern men rushed to him, stripping away his clothing. They left him naked as he looked around for something to cover himself with. One of the gladiators tossed him a tunic, which was detailed in its blood-red appearance with a golden sash. Porter put on the tunic as the wyvern men presented to him two golden leather gauntlets for his forearms. One of the gladiators tossed him a pair of boots with a leather-like appearance. However, when Porter touched them, the leather seemed unusual.

"What's this made of?"

"Enfield hide." the gladiator replied.

"Enfield?"

"They're very rare around these regions. Strong, brute creatures. You'll run in terror if you ever see them."

Porter nodded.

"I understand your concern."

Porter put on the boots when a wyvern man stood before him, holding a chest piece. He tossed it to Porter, commanding he put on he chest piece. Porter looked at the armor, feeling its ruggedness and its smoothness. Porter had asked if the armor had been previously used, only to receive the answer the armor belonged to a gladiator who was killed in battle several days prior. Porter looked at the center of the chest piece, noticing an insignia.

"What does this mean?"

"It means a stranger across worlds." The gladiator told him.

"Must mean the one who wore this came from another world." Porter said.

"He did. The place called Vanagon."

"Vanagon?"

"The second world from the distance of the Great Sun."

"Venus." Porter said quietly to himself.

Standing by the entry point of the armory and preparation room were two larger wyvern men. Both carried spears. They rallied the gladiators and Porter to prepare themselves for the fight ahead. Each of them formed an orderly line. Porter only looked on as they were searched and measured by the wyvern men. Seeing only their nods as the they were led toward the coliseum doors. The doors were over twenty-feet in height and the cheer of the crowd began to echo through them. Porter saw the gladiators were ready for the battle. Others were crying in fear. Porter kept himself calm as the gladiator he talked with stood beside him. Each of them were handed swords. Porter looked at the sword, seeing its sharpness and its light-weight.

"Strange material."

"Only found in the deepest parts of the Hibarian Forest."

"What's it made of?"

"Fallen star I was told. Possibly not."

"I see."

"Whatever you see out there, make sure not to give in to fear."

"What are you saying?" Porter questioned.

"What we're up against may seem terrifying to you. If you're like the others. For there are many beings and creatures which appear in these fights. All for the glory of sport."

"I'm not afraid. I just want to get out of here."

"Very well then. Survive the coliseum and you'll have it."

"I'm aware. Thanks for the tip. What is your name by the way?"

"Nakir. Yours?"

"Mark Porter."

One of the larger wyvern men stood by the door, glaring at the gladiators. He slammed the spear into the ground as the roar of the crowd soared behind him.

"Gladiators! Warriors of Alderan. This day, you will enter these gates and fight your way through a collage of beasts. A sea of soldiers from distant lands. I do not expect many of you to survive. For our king has gathered himself quite the nice spectacle for each of you to see. This fight will be one of the biggest ones Alderan has yet to put on and you all should be lucky to have participated within it. Now, I ask you. Do any of you seek your freedom? Then, if you do, you know what must be done. Survive and you'll have your freedom. Die and you'll have your freedom. If the gods permit it, of course."

The doors opened as the gladiators rushed out into the open field with only the sand of the grounds surrounding them. Porter and Nakir stood close as the other gladiators looked around at the crowd. Seeing the audience of a mixed-multitude. Porter was astonished by their presence.

"Didn't realize there were this many people living out here."

"Alderan is only a place for entertainment." Nakir said. "These people come from other lands. Distant from Taranopolis among others."

Porter looked straight ahead, seeing three other doors with wyvern men standing beside them. Porter pointed toward them as Nakir took notice.

"What's behind the doors?"

"The terror and dread which shall soon wash over the gladiators."

The Wyvern King walked out in the midst of the crowd, overseeing the grounds. Porter looked up, spotting him as he showered himself in the cheers. The Wyvern King sat down in a seat of his own. Similar to his throne. He raised his right hand toward the wyvern men at the first door. Signaling for it to open. They obeyed and the first door opened with all the gladiators prepared.

"Here we go." Nakir said.

Busting from the first door were tall, thin, and green looking creatures. Ten of them. They walked upright similar to humans, but they were not as they had shades of grass growing on their arms and legs and mushrooms on their shoulders, covered up by the armor around their torsos. No hair, long arms, legs, and their eyes were as white as snow. They roared together as they rushed toward the gladiators.

"The hell are they?" Porter wondered.

"Plant Men." Nakir answered. "Dwellers from the Hibarian Forest in the secluded lands."

"Noted."

The Plant Men collided with the gladiators. All fighting with swords. Some had shields which were scattered throughout the coliseum grounds. Porter saw one shield and ran over to grab it. Once he had it, a Plant Man dove over him with a sword and Porter blocked the attack with the shield and found an opening as he swiped the shield across the Plant Man's face and impaled him with the sword. Nakir battled a Plant Man, killing him by cutting off the legs and head. Porter looked round at the other gladiators, seeing them being overrun by the Plant Men. Porter couldn't take the sight as he intervened, crashing against the Plant Men with sword and shield. Nakir joined in and fought alongside him. So far, eight of the twenty prisoners were killed by the Plant Men. Porter and Nakir continued to fight as did the remaining prisoners. Inspired by Porter's relentlessness. Porter led the remaining gladiators against the last four Plant Men and they quickly decimated them with their swords. The Wyvern King stood up in awe and anger. His sight focused on Porter. He knew there was something to him and signaled for the second door to open, which came out were six-legged beasts. Two were hairless aside from the large manes around their necks. Four of them roaring and snarling. Porter stared as he saw hem walking out and the gladiators began to show signs of fear.

"Are those lions?" Porter asked.

"No." Nakir answered slowly. "Those are Beoths."

The Beoths roared in fury toward the gladiators. Mixing their ferocity with the cheers of the crowd. The gladiators banded together as the beoths charged toward them with their fangs and claws. One beoth leaped, lunging atop the gladiators as they held their shields overhead. Porter looked for an opening and slicked the back leg of the beoth as they shoved the large beast off the shields. A second beoth snatched one of the gladiators by his leg, dragging him and tossing him in the air as the others scattered around the area in sight of the beoths.

"Move with me!" Porter screamed.

The gladiators did not take heed to Porter's command as two beoths circled them. In front of Porter and Nikar jumped another beoth. Snarling as it stared into their eyes. Porter swiped the sword across the beast's face before kicking it in the nose. The beoth swiped with its pawed claws, scratching Porter in the leg. The beoth swiped again, knocking the shield to the ground. Nikar grabbed the shield as the beoth jumped over him. Nikar pressed against the beast's strength as it went for his head with its jaws. Porter saw Nikar on the ground and the beoth over him. He pressed on in pain from the scratch and leaped atop the beoth like a bull. The beast jumped around, trying to toss Porter from its back. Porter held his ground, raising the sword with one hand and impaling the beoth in its neck. One down as Porter helped Nikar to his feet.

"Thanks."

"No problem."

They looked on, seeing the gladiators stood no chance against the two circling them. They went to aid them before the other beoth jumped in front of them. This one more hairy than the last as Porter swiped the sword against it, but the hide and hair of the beoth was took thick for a strike. The beoth charged, slamming Porter into the arena walls as it chased Nikar. Porter stood up, rubbing his right shoulder, seeing the blood. He sighed as he made a run toward Nikar. Nikar dodged a paw swipe as Porter jumped on top of the beoth in similar fashion. The crowd savored all they were witnessing as did the Wyvern King. Porter held the sword, impaling the beoth in its neck, but the hair and hide were too durable.

"Dammit!" Porter shouted. "What are we going to do now?!"

Nikar stood, thinking. He looked over to the walls, seeing on the ground a long chain. Running over, he grabbed the chain and smelled it. Recognizing what material it was made of and he tossed it toward Porter. Porter caught the chain with his left hand as his right was occupied by the sword. The beoth leaped, tossing Porter from its back. Nikar ran toward Porter as the beoth charged at them both. Porter held the chain and told Nikar to stand back. Nikar moved as Porter stood up and wrapped the chain around the beoth's neck and pulled it back from the charge. The beoth's neck had snapped from the sudden strength of Porter, which startled Nikar and the crowd. Even the Wyvern King was intrigued. The beoth's body lumped into the sand as Porter looked at his hands and the chain.

"Where did that come from?"

"The other two!" Nikar yelled. "We need to finish them off!"

"Leave it to me." Porter answered. "Toss me the shield!"

Nikar grabbed the shield, tossing it toward Porter. He exhaled and ran toward the gladiators as they fought off the two beoths to a less result. Porter yelled for them to spread out and they followed his order. While the spread, they split up the two beasts, separating them from a distance. One was hairy and the other was hairless. Porter targeted the hairless one first by using the chain and pull its leg as he leaped over, stabbing it in the neck. Moving without haste, Porter used the chain to pull the final beoth, wrapping the chain around its neck and tossing it on its back. Porter looked,realizing the abdomen was not covered with hair nor was the skin thick. Porter jumped over the beoth and impaled the beast in its chest with the sword. The audience cheered as Porter whipped the chain back from the beoth's neck and stood in the middle of the area, looking at the audience. They began to applaud him. The other gladiators took notice and Nikar nodded.

"Ugh!" The Wyvern King said, standing up from his seat. "Give it up for Mark Porter!"

The audience cheered louder and chanted Porter's name. the Wyvern King grabbed a spear and threw it directly in front of Porter. Crashing into the sand within two feet of him. The Wyvern King pointed toward him and the other remaining gladiators.

"You have won this day. But, on the morrow, oh, it will be the day you shall die."

The Wyvern King swiped his hands as the wyvern men escorted Porter and the gladiators back to the dungeons. The night had settled and this time, Porter was kept in the dungeon with Nikar and the two spoke about their past before the arena. Nikar told Porter he had come from a place in the southern region of Argoron. A place he hoped to see again. Opening up, Porter began to tell Nikar of his home world of Earth. Nikar paused.

"You come from Jagoron?"

"I do. I guess Jagoron is your language for Earth."

"How did you get here?"

"I don't know. That's what I'm trying to find out."

"Once you achieve your freedom, I'm sure the answers will come."

"I hope so."

Elsewhere, Lola, Serai, and the Celedians took a stop at one of the Celedian camps several miles near Alderan. Lola looked ahead, seeing the city lights as the cold air blew over them. Serai handed Lola a cloak, one decorated in the royal redness of Argoron.

"We were informed of an event which happened in the city early this day."

"What did they say?" Lola asked.

"They said the audience was intrigued by a man. A strange one. He defeated beoths with ease. They said his strength was beyond comprehension."

Lola paused. Nodding to her own thoughts.

"It's him. It has to be."

"We'll find out in the morning. Right now, it is best you rest as shall we."

In the dungeon, Porter looked on, seeing Nikar was asleep. The area was silent. More silent than any place he's been since he had been on Argoron. He smirked, dreaming of his return to Earth and what he will tell those of his current adventure. He closed his eyes and fell into a deep sleep.

CHAPTER 7: FREEDOM OR SLAVERY

The next morning, the wyvern men bolted into the dungeons, awakening Porter, Nikar, and the gladiators. They prepared themselves and gathered their weapons which sat at the entry point of the arena. Porter listened as he heard the roaring crowd once again. The doors had opened and they went out. The Wyvern King stepped forward, commanding with a shouting voice that they open all three doors. The wyvern men obeyed as the doors opened. What Porter and the gladiators saw terrified them. From the first door entered a pack of wyverns. They flew toward the gladiators and they were prepared. Their hands gripped the hilts of their swords. Porter whipped his chain as he held the sword in his right hand. From the second door had arrived gladiators, however these were different. They were more brute in size and their skin glistened with the sunlight. Even their height towered Porter and the others.

"Those are the warriors from the faraway land." Nikar said.

"What's their stats?" Porter questioned.

"They kill whatever pleases them. Killing is only a sport for them."

"Noted." Porter nodded.

The brute gladiators ran toward them with force. While they were making their way near them, Porter looked ahead at the third door and he could feel the trembling in the ground. Looking at the sand, seeing it rise up and fall. Nikar could feel the tremors as well and he stepped back, leaving Porter in confusion.

"He has them." Nikar said. "He caught them."

"Has who?" Porter questioned. "Caught what?"

From the third door walked out two great and powerful creatures. Standing over thirty-five feet in height and incredibly hairy. One was as white as snow. The other was as dark as coal. The creatures smashed their arms in the ground, roaring to the cheer of the crowd. Porter stared at them. Impressed by their height and size.

"Are those gorillas?" Porter said.

"No." Nikar answered. "They are the Beasts of the wilderness. The white one is the Hoary Beast. While the black one is the Ruin Beast. Both are creatures of great destruction."

"We have to survive this."

"How?"

"Leave it to me." Porter said. "We're getting out of here this day."

The Beasts charged into the battle as the gladiators fought the brutes. The wyverns flew overhead, striking whenever they found an opening in the crowded swordfight. Porter gazed up toward a wyvern, using the chain to snatch the creature from the air to the ground. Once the wyvern had fell, Porter rushed over and impaled the creatures. He continued the same tactics to the other wyverns, only for one of the brute gladiators to tackle him to the ground. Porter rolled out of the path from the gladiator's large mace. Nikar ran into the fight, slashing his sword across the gladiator's arm, cutting it off with the mace in hand. Porter nodded to Nikar as he decapitated the brute. The wyverns continued with their snapping jaws, grabbing gladiators from the ground and throwing them across the arena, only for them to be stomped on by the Beasts. Porter took on two of the brutes with Nikar at his side. The gladiators who remained were quickly killed by the wyverns and Beasts. Leaving only Porter and Nikar to fight for themselves. Seeing themselves outnumbered. Porter focused his movement, striking the last two brutes with the chain and slashing the wyverns in the air as he jumped. Showing his impressive skill. Skills he didn't know he had before. Surprising the audience as Nikar stabbed the brutes after they were struck by Porter's chain. Several of the wyverns landed on the ground, seeking to lung on Porter. The wyverns went to pounce and the Beasts behind them trampled them without notice. Staring at Porter and Nikar as their prize.

"This is the day they die." The Wyvern King uttered.

Porter and the Hoary Beast come face-to-face. Porter jumped across the Beast to get a better shot with the sword, however the Beast took notice of the chain and snatched it, jerking Porter from the air, swinging him around until he is slammed into the sand as the Ruin Beast chases Nikar through the arena. Porter stood up, grabbing the chain with both hands, jerking it back towards him from the Hoary Beast. The Beast glared at Porter, huffing. The Hoary Beast slammed its fists into the sand, running toward Porter. Porter followed suit, charging toward the Hoary Beast himself with the sword in hand. Mark leaped into the air over the Beast's head, slashing the large creature down its back while landing a kick to the back of its head. The Beast stumbled from the slash and the kick fo only a few seconds as Porter landed on the ground. He turned around to face the Beast, twirling the chain. The Beast turned, staring at Porter. Porter grinned as he swung the chain with such force, it slapped the Beast in its head. The force of the chain whip caused the massive creature to fall and it laid in the sand with the audience in silence. Nikar looked over as he hid from the Ruin Beast in a corner, seeing the downed Hoary Beast. He smiled.

"He killed it!"

The Ruin Beast looked back, seeing the Hoary one dead. It roared with anger, preparing to charge toward Porter. Porter twirled the chain again, smirking. The Hoary Beast began to move slowly, attempting to raise itself up to its feet. Seeing the creature moving, Porter jumped on top of the creature's body and dug the sword through the throat, officially killing the creature. The Wyvern King glared with anger, yet signaled an applause for Porter's achievement. He began to clap and the audience followed suit. Porter turned to face the Wyvern King.

"I've taken down one of your Beast, Wyvern King." Porter yelled. "What more must I do to prove my freedom?!"

The Wyvern King raises his right arm as the wyvern men signaled the Ruin Beast's attention. Directing it toward Porter. The Beast roared and charged toward him. Porter paused for a moment, showing a faint sign of tiredness. Nikar stood up against the arena wall, cheering Porter on. He took notice and stood firm in the sand. Standing still in a fighting stance. Sword and chain both in his hands.

"Slaughter him!" The Wyvern King yelled.

The Ruin Beast looked down, seeing Nikar and proceeded to grab him from the wall. Porter ran over, pointing the sword toward the creature.

"Come at me!" Porter yelled toward the Ruin Beast. "Leave him alone!"

The Beast charged and once it reached closer, Porter jumped in the air, moving over the beast's head. He turned himself around in midair and raised the sword. The chain swiped against the creature's back and the sword itself was shoved through the back of its head, immediately killing it. The Wyvern King starts clapping and the audience begins clapping. Porter turns, facing the Wyvern King.

"I've taken down both your beasts, Wyvern King." Porter yelled. "What more must I do to prove my freedom is granted?!"

At the entrance to Alderan, Lola, Serai, and the Celedians arrive. Hearing the cheers of the crowd at the coliseum, they made haste toward it. Meanwhile, inside the arena, the Wyvern King stood up from his seat, walking down to the arena grounds to confront Porter. The audience was intrigued by their king's motives. Two wyvern men accompanied their king as he stepped foot on the sands drenched in the blood of his gladiators and creatures. The Wyvern King stood before Porter. Nikar sat back against one of the podiums attached to the arena walls.

"You seek your freedom." The Wyvern King asked.

"Yes. However, not only my own. But, his as well." Porter said, pointing toward Nikar.

The Wyvern King chuckled.

"I see. Very well. You have achieved your freedom. You are a free man. But, you have sought to gain the freedom of another. Therefore, there is one more fight you must endure."

Within the crowd, Lola, Serai, and the Celedians entered. Looking ahead as they saw Porter standing face-to-face with the Wyvern King. Lola wanted to go down and save him, but the Celedians resisted. Demanding she wait and watch what might come. Unsure of their ideas, she hesitated her own hastiness and sat down to watch.

"And what must I endure?"

"A final battle."

"Against what?" Porter asked. "More gladiators? More beasts?"

"No. Against me"

The wyvern men handed their king a spear. He stretched forth his wings, showing them to the audience, only to hear their cheers as they screamed his name. he grinned at the sound as Porter stepped back, gripping the chain and sword. The wyvern men on the ground flew away. Leaving their king and Porter on the field. Nikar stepped forward, only for Porter to raise his hand toward him. Nikar stepped back, nodding.

"Are you ready to die?" The Wyvern King asked.

"I won't die today." Porter answered.

The Wyvern King quickly attacked with the spear and his long tail covered in spikes. Porter deflected the spear and tail with the sword. Porter swiped the chain across the Wyvern King's chest, only to hit the armor. The Wyvern King laughed as he used the spear to trip Porter. He stood over him, holding the spear and Porter moved himself out of the weapon's path and wrapped the chain around the Wyvern King's leg, pulling him to the ground. He went to impale the Wyvern King to the ground, but the wings pulled him back and the tail of the King swiped Porter across his chest, knocking him to the ground. The audience was back and forth in reactions to the two dueling.

"You won't win this." The Wyvern King said.

"Keep fighting and we'll see."

The spear was raised, only for Porter to slash the sword across it, snapping it in half. He grabbed the end of the spear and shoved it in the side of the Wyvern King, causing him to stumble in his steps. Through the pain, he continued to fight, pulling the spear from his ribs and throwing it to the sand. He punched Porter across his face several times before grabbing him by his throat and slamming him. He set his foot over Porter's chest, raising his spiked tail above him.

"Give up."

"I will never."

Porter swiped the sword, cutting the ankle of the King. He kicked him back and stood up, using the chain to swipe against eh armor as it began to break from the constant blows. Porter had the Wyvern King down on his knees as he ripped the chest piece from him and impaled the sword. Gasps filled the air as Porter stared into the Wyvern King reptilian eyes.

"I am… not dead yet."

"Don't be sure of yourself."

Porter removed the sword and decapitated the Wyvern King. His body collapsed to the ground and the wyvern men around the arena let out a screeching yell. A yell in pain and agony. It was there, the Celedians busted into the arena, killing any wyvern men that did not fly away. At the entrance entered Tartarus Kai. He looked out at the audience and glanced down at the dead body of the Wyvern King.

"Citizens of Alderan! The tyrant is now dead! From this day forward, Alderan belongs to the Celedians!"

Porter approached Tartarus and nodded, holding the chain and sword.

"I think I'll be keeping these."

"Suit yourself. But, you have visitors who are expecting you."

Tartarus pointed toward the arena gates, seeing Lola standing. Porter looked at her and was unsure, yet, her beauty caught his gaze. Something he was not familiar with on this planet. Otherwise, Porter nodded to Nikar. Their freedoms were won as they exited the arena with the crowd cheering around them. In front, Lola approached them both, but her eyes were set on Porter.

CHAPTER 8: A HERO?

"I am Princess Lola Arribel of Taranopolis and I've been searching for you." Lola said.

"Ok, Princess." Porter replied. "Why, madam have you been searching for me?"

"Because you're needed. I saw you fight. Your skills. Your strength. You have what it takes to save us. To possibly save us all."

"I'm needed? Needed for what?"

"To help us stop what's coming."

"And what is coming?" Porter questioned.

"Her father, King R'akl has been betrayed by Saban Jai." Tartarus said.

Lola looked toward him, questioning how he would know of such information. Tartarus informed her that he set spies throughout Taranopolis and many of them received information of Saban's betrayal after making an alliance with the Wyvern King. Tartarus described the plans of Saban's intentions to have been revealed after he married Lola. Striking them at a most vulnerable position.

"Mr. Porter." Lola said, standing in front of him. "I need your help in this matter. Please, help my father and his people from Saban's betrayal."

"Porter looked down, nodded and gazed the surroundings. He shook his head in decline.

"I'm sorry. I just want to go home."

"Home?"

"Yes. Home. I'm not from this planet. Your political matters do not concern me."

"But, you're here on Argoron. Yet, there is something strange about you. You don't have the complexion to be an Argoronian."

"Of course not. I'm from Earth."

"Jagoron? Wait, how can you be from a world beyond ours?"

"I'm not sure myself. I seek to return there. I need to know how."

"I know of a way." Tartarus said.

"What is it?" Porter questioned. "Whatever it is you are."

"I am a Celedian. King of my kind. The name is Tartarus Kai."

"Mark Porter. Of Earth. Now, tell me what you know? How can I return home?"

"There is a portal caught in the rift of a pillar. A strong one."

"Where is this pillar?"

"Between the borders of Taranopolis and Alderan. If you take one of the travellers, you can make it there before nightfall."

"And if I go on foot?"

"Then, you'll be trekking in the dune sands for several days. Two at most."

Porter agreed to the offer as one of the Celedian warriors had presented him a traveller. Porter scoffed as he saw the vehicle. He walked around it, measuring it out.

"No tires?" Porter said.

"Tires?" Tartarus asked. "What is that?"

"They go on the bottom. Four on each side."

"This traveller needs no bottom compartments. Once you're inside, the controls will tell you what you must do."

"And how does it travel?"

"Anti-gravity."

"Interesting."

Porter entered the traveller as it powered up. The gear was in place and Porter was prepared to leave. Tartarus asked if Porter wanted a test run of the vehicle, yet Porter denied the request, preferring to learn as he goes. Tartarus understood and stepped back. Lola rushed toward the traveller, placing her hands on the door.

"You cannot just go along and leave us to a possible destruction."

"Look, madam. I'm sorry for what is happening in your home. But, I'm not from here. I'm just a foreigner and I want to return home."

"And will your conscience be content with your decision?"

Porter sighed. He gave Lola a stare.

"We'll see."

The traveller roared as it levitated over the ground. Porter jerked the wheel as he glared down at the ground, seeing the sand blow around the vehicle. Porter nodded to Tartarus and Lola as he rode away. Lola sighed in slight anger as Tartarus approached her.

"Don't worry yourself. There is a reason why myself and my warriors are here."

"What do you mean?"

"We cannot allow you and Serai to return to Taranopolis only to fall in Saban's hands. We'll accompany you and protect you and your father from Saban's army."

"And I guess you'll want my father to grant you something in return?"

"We'll talk about that after Saban is dealt with."

Lola agreed to Tartarus' assistance as he rallied all the Celedian warriors and they rode off toward Taranopolis.

CHAPTER 9: THE EARTHMAN'S CHOICE

Mark Porter rode out into the desert, gazing up toward the sun as he took note of its slow descending. He continued to ride and far out in the distance, Porter saw something standing in the middle of the sands. Coming up onto the object closer, Porter knew it was the pillar. Standing over twenty feet and carved out of what may have been a small mountain in the area. Porter reached the pillar and exited the traveller.

"What kind of structure is this?"

Porter looked around the pillar, finding a small pond and several small trees growing around it. From the pillar itself fell a waterfall. Porter wasn't sure how such an object or environment operate in the middle of the desert. Porter approached the waterfall and began hearing faint sounds of voices. The voices were familiar to him. Familiar to the point the began to call out names.

"General?"

Back at Taranopolis, Lola and Serai had made their return with Tartarus and the Celedian warriors behind them. Entering the city and startling the people, Lola made haste toward the palace and she entered just as her father was speaking with Saban. She stooped herself in her steps with Serai by her side as they turned to see her. R'akl stood up from his throne and approached her as she knelt down. Saban was confused by her sudden appearance.

"We've been searching for you, my daughter."

"I'm sorry, father. But, I had to go out and find the prisoner."

"And did you?"

"Yes. He was in Alderan."

"Alderan." R'akl replied. "I knew it. I knew the Wyvern King would've taken him. He disobeyed my orders to keep him here. When I speak with him again, I will have much words for him."

"Father, the Wyvern King is dead."

Saban jolted and stepped forward with concern. R'akl only shook his head in hearing the words of the Wyvern Kong's death.

"What do you mean dead?" Saban questioned. "How do you know of this?"

"My daughter, who slew the Wyvern King of Alderan?"

"The prisoner. He called himself Mark Porter of Earth."

"Him." Saban said. "So, an earthman chooses to thwart Argoronian laws."

"You cannot blame him, Saban. He doesn't know our rules. How else could he have abided by them."

"We need to find this prisoner, my king. Before he comes here and tries to do the same to you. To me. To your daughter even."

"He had no intensions on killing me." Lola said.

"As of this moment." Saban replied. "My king, allow me and my warriors to go out into the dunes and find him. Bring him back and then, we can be rid of him."

Lola sighed, gathering their attention.

"There is something else, father. Something you must know."

"Speak it."

"The Celedians are here in he city."

"Celedians?!" Saban yelled. "Those savages!"

"Why are they here? And under who's orders did they receive permission?"

"They came to accompany me."

"Accompany you for what?"

"To protect you, father."

"Protect me?" R'akl replied with confusion. "Protect me from what?"

"Him." Lola said, pointing toward Saban.

R'akl turned toward Saban and they both gave looks of uncertainty.

Layered with confusion. R'akl turned back to his daughter as Saban stood still, his eyes looking around the throne room.

"What proof do you have of this?"

Lola turned around as Tartarus Kai entered the throne room, ducking his head as he entered. Saban raised up his sword as he eyes widen toward the tall king. R'akl stood his ground, with his hand gently on the hilt of his blade. Tartarus stood before them both, yet, bowed his head before R'akl.

"King of Taranopolis. I did not come to make war."

"Why are you here, savage king?" Saban asked.

R'akl raised his hand, silencing Saban.

"Why have you accompanied my daughter back to her home?"

"I've placed several Celedian spies across your city for several months, king. I also had spies centered around Alderan and what they have informed me of, you must truly know. For it concerns the life of your daughter, your own, and your people."

"And what is this information?"

"Saban Jai is a traitor and a deceiver. He's been making plans alongside the Wyvern King to bring forth your demise. I told you daughter of this news and she has agreed to return here to tell you herself."

R'akl turned toward Saban. His eyes already speaking the truth.

"Why?" R'akl asked. "Why would you betray me? Betray all of us?"

Saban sighed, sheathing his sword and shrugging his shoulders.

"Because, it is time for all of Argoron to enter a new ruler-ship of power and might. In truth, my king, your rule has become weak. You grafted peace with this savage king and from there, you have only grown weaker. I knew it was the truth when the earthman appeared in the sands. There is other life out there. Other worlds in need of us. We have enough power to invade those planets and conquer them. Make them bow under Argoron laws and to worship our gods. Yet, you refuse. You want peace and nothing else."

"So, you sought to marry my daughter only to bring forth your plans of conquest?"

"I did. I have no reason to lie."

"It was never about love?"

"My king, it never was. Besides, you daughter is a beautiful woman. But, her hastiness and attitude can make even the best of men fall to their demise. I would not become one of them."

"Father, you know what must be done."

R'akl nodded.

"Saban Jai, I hereby place you under arrest."

Two Micran guards entered the room and stood beside Saban. R'akl commanded them to take Saban to the cell, but they refuse. Removing their helmets and presenting themselves as Warriors to Saban's cause. They raised up their swords and wetn to strike R'akl. Tartarus intervened and deflected the blows with two swords of his own. Saban ran out of the throne room as Serai moved beside Lola as they went and stood by her father as Tartarus commanded them both to leave and find safety.

Outside, the city is quickly placed under lockdown by Saban's warriors. In the streets stood Celedians and Micrans. Both on opposite sides as the Taranopolis civilians ran into their homes and evacuated themselves from the streets and open roads. Lola, Serai, and her father ran into one of the king's studies and locked the doors. At the palace, Saban stood at the balcony, overlooking the city and seeing his armies on the streets confronting the Celedians with their swords and spears. He grinned at the sight of it. Change appeared imminent.

"This day will prove that I am the new king of Argoron. The conquest is nigh."

In the desert, Porter continued to hear the voices coming through the waterfall. He slowly placed his hand in the water, feeling its coolness. Behind the waterfall seemed to be a cavern. From there, Porter placed his head through the waterfall and what he saw inside the cavern was a bright, spherical light.

"A wormhole."

He stepped into the cavern and approached the wormhole. Gazing inside, Porter began to make out an image. Looking closer as the seconds passed. Porter saw within the wormhole was a facility. Still looking, he recognized several vehicles parked. Porter's eyes widen.

"Area 51. Earth."

Seeing he was standing at the door, Porter took one step forth and-

CHAPTER 10: THIS IS ARGORON

Taranopolis is set between two forces as its civilians have fled into their homes and other nearby buildings. All in the fear of what's before their eyes. In the streets of the city, the Micrans and Celedians stood facing one another. Each of them wielding swords, spears, staves, and maces. Micrans even held shields as they stepped in the front of the face-off. Saban remained on the balcony, overseeing the two armies.

"This day, my warriors will overcome these savages and the city will thank me. Everyone will thank me."

Saban grabbed a bow and arrow from the table and set the arrow into one of the firepots on the balcony. He aimed smoothly and fired a shot into the middle of the armies. They saw the arrow pierce into the sand. The Micrans gazed up to the balcony, seeing Saban. From there, they yelled and charged toward the Celedians with force. Seeing the Micrans coming, the Celedians rallied themselves and ran into the fight with both forces colliding with weapons and shields.

Meanwhile as the battle commenced, R'akl remained inside the study with Lola and Serai. He hung his head, sulking in the shame of having such favor in Saban, only to have been betrayed. Lola informed her father that all will be well and once Saban is gone, they can continue on in life. R'akl took note of his daughters' words and yet, he continued to say that a king must rule Argoron. It is the natural law of the planet and the balance of their faith. Lola did not argue. She understood everything well. From the doors bolted in Tartarus, calming them down from his sudden appearance.

"Where is Saban?" R'akl asked.

"I do not know." Tartarus answered. "He fled from the throne room as soon as the fighting began."

"He's still here." Lola said. "He wouldn't have fled the city. He wants to look like the victor once the fighting has ceased."

"Then we must find him." Tartarus said.

"Go." R;akl said. "find Saban and bring him to me. He will face a swift justice."

"And what if he refuses to come alive?" Lola asked.

R'akl sighed and waved his hand. Lola nodded, looking back to Tartarus. The Celedian king understood the king's answer without a word and left the study.

On the streets, the Micrans and Celedians are slaughtering each other. Spears impaling, swords slashing, and shields deflecting. Some Micran warriors jointed into units of two and ambushed several Celedians who's heights exceeded even the average ones. Saban continued to watch as Tartarus searched for him throughout the palace. Lola sat with Serai and whispered something in her ear as she stood up and went for the door.

"Where are you going?" R;akl asked.

"To find Saban."

"Without someone to accompany you?"

"Tartarus is out there. I'm sure he'll be with me."

"Watch yourself out there."

Lola nodded with a smile as she headed out for Saban.

Saban grabbed a chair and sat down, overseeing on the ongoing slaughter. He smirked, eating fruit and drinking wine. Standing behind him were two servants. Servants he rallied from within the city and stand with him as they watch the battle. Saban promised them greater positions under his rule. Bolting into the balcony behind was Tartarus with his sword drawn. Saban jumped up in a surprise fashion.

"Who let a savage into the upper floors?!"

"Only a fool would seem to find you on the streets in battle. Yet, you choose to watch like a worthless king."

"I am a king! Look down there! Your warriors are falling to mine.

This day, you shall bow before me!"

"Oh no, betrayer. My warriors are known to overcome any amount of forces that appear before them. Your warriors will disobey your commands. For you are not their king."

Saban paused himself, his eyes glanced down toward the edge of the balcony where his sword rested. He jumped for the sword as Tartarus slammed his sword down, breaking the furniture as Saban slid on the marbled floor, grabbing his sword. He raised it up just as Tartarus' own clashed with it. The servants left the balcony and Saban grinned.

"A fight you want?"

"How else can your warriors see you for the false king you truly are."

Saban yelled, jumping on his feet and swinging his sword. He and Tartarus fought on the balcony as the fighting in the streets continued. Lola walked through the palace in search for Saban. She arrived outside, seeing the fighting in front of her. Blood spilling from the dead warriors. One of the Micrans ran toward her, beaten and bloodied. The warrior begged to hear word from her father. She had no reply as he warrior returned into battle. Hearing the clashing of weapons. She noticed the sound of clashing coming form above. Stepping out on the steps, Lola glared up to see Tartarus and Saban fighting.

"Oh no."

She moved with speed to reach the balcony as they continued fighting. Saban gained the upper hand on Tartarus by tripping him and he hanged on the edge. Saban grinned.

"Let's see if a Celedian can survive such a fall."

Tartarus went for a swipe, only to be kicked by Saban off the balcony, breaking the edge. The armies paused as Tartarus fell to the ground. Saban looked down at Tartarus' body. He smiled and made his way down, using a rope attached to his waist armor. Tartarus was still breathing, only in pain. Saban cocked his head, placing his foot over the Celedian King's body and looking out at both armies.

"I am your king now!"

The Micrans paused themselves in confusion. Seeing Saban wielding the sword in the air. The Celedians were more concern with their king's condition. Lola had made it to the balcony, only to see the broken edge and both Tartarus and Saban on the ground. Saban commanded both armies to bow before him and neither obeyed. Sensing their opposition, he yelled again, commanding them to bow. They did not bow.

"I am your king! King of Taranopolis! King of Argoron. My marriage to Princess Lola Arribel makes me your king!"

"Yet, we are not married yet." Lola said from above.

Saban turned around, gazing up. He grinned.

"Ah. The feat I have accomplish this day grants us our marriage and my ruler-ship as king. Who else could have taken out the Celedian king. The king of savages!"

"Did you kill him?" Lola asked.

"He's barely dead. Little close I'm afraid."

"You'll pay for this."

"By who's hand? Your father's?"

"No." A voice replied from the streets.

Saban looked out as did the armies. Lola saw who was standing and a large smile formed upon her face. Tartarus' eyes looked up to see and he was pleased. Saban stepped off of Tartarus' body to confront him. Porter had returned.

"You come here uninvited?'

"I am." Porter said.

Saban chuckled, stepping down the stairs to face Porter. He looked him in the eyes and scoffed, backing up in his steps and raising up his sword.

"You think you can defeat me?"

"I know I can."

"That right?"

"Yes."

Porter raised up his sword and whipped the chain. Saban saw the chain and rubbed his chin. Impressed with Porter's choice of weaponry.

"Must be a Jagoron skill."

"You'll find out."

Saban screamed as he charged toward Porter with his sword. Porter deflected the attack and whipped the chain across Saban's back, cracking the armor. Saban paused, trying to look back at the armor.

Porter nodded as Saban ripped the armor from his torso.

"I do not need the armor to defeat you."

Saban swung the sword several times, hitting Porter's own with Porter kicking Saban in the knee and tripping him on the sand. Porter yelled for Saban to stand up and continue fighting. Saban flipped himself up and ran after Porter. From there, Porter used the chain and grab Saban's sword. Snatching it from his hand and slicing his chest. Saban fell back as Porter stood over him with the sword in front.

"Do you yield?"

Saban chuckled, wiping the blood from his face.

"I'm not finished here. I am king."

"You are NOT King!" said R'akl standing behind him.

The Micrans saw him and instantly bowed before him. The Celedians had already went over and aided their king. Lola turned to her father before looking out at Porter and Saban.

"Stand back." R'akl said.

Porter nodded, stepping back from Saban as he stood up and turned to face R'akl.

"You have betrayed me, Saban Jai and I will not tolerate it."

"King R'akl, I was to marry your daughter. I was to be king."

"No. You are not king and you will no longer marry my daughter."

"This is not how Micrans do business!" Saban yelled. "You're disobeyed ancient Argoronian laws by this decision."

"I am king. Seems you have forgotten."

Saban looked out at the Micrans, seeing them bowed before R'akl. He looked around at everyone as anger brewed within him. Turning back to R'akl in anger. He had enough.

"I will not tolerate this any-"

R'akl took the staff he carried and swung it across Saban's head, breaking his neck. Saban's body fell into the sand and R'akl stood tall.

"A swift justice is done."

Lola approached Porter, amazed by his return.

"You thought I was leaving?"

"I did and how come you chose not to?"

"There's something here. Something calling to me. I'm not sure as to what it is. But, this planet, it needs my help. My world will heal itself. This one needs help now."

R;akl approached Porter, measuring him and looking at his daughter. He nodded with a smile.

"The decision is done." R'akl said.

"What decision?" Porter asked, looking over to Lola, who's smiling.

"For the protection of this kingdom and this planet, you will marry my daughter."

Porter nodded. Looking over to Lola. R'akl held out the staff and Porter placed both hands upon it. Lola had done the same. It was at that moment the two were married. The Micrans stood up and applauded them as the civilians came out of their homes to see the two. The bodies on the streets were cleared out and a ceremony was set the following day for Porter and Lola. He two had married just as Tartarus and R'akl came to an understanding. Tartarus left with the Celedians as Porter and Lola spent their honeymoon together.

During the night of the honeymoon while Lola slept, Porter was awake and walked out onto the rebuilt balcony, overseeing the city of Taranopolis. He smiled. Turning back to go inside, a voice called to Porter from the balcony. A strange one. Porter turned back to find himself facing an entity. Made of complete light. A bright white light. The light even had arms, legs, and a head.

"What are you?" Porter asked.

"I've been watching you since you arrived."

"Watching me? For what purpose?"

"A greater kind of purpose."

"And you are?"

"I… am a God of Argoron."

RAIDERS OF VANOK

CHAPTER 1: VANCE HARLAN

As astrologists and astronomers continued their research pertaining to other living beings throughout the universe, Vance Harlan, a man specialized in the scientific community of interstellar space proposed a plan. His plans to travel into the stars through a wormhole, hoping to come out into another galaxy filled with life. Vance pleaded his plans and works to many other scientists. All of whom rejected. Vance even went as far as to proceed with funding from his own ship to travel into space. Backers were not impressed. Stating Vance was living in a fantasyland hoping to collude with alien beings.

During one meeting with the Department of Defense, Vance entered the room, brushing his blonde hair before seeing it was cornered by guards. He nodded with cockiness as he was unimpressed by their sheer attempt of intimidation. Vance stepped forward, sitting down at the desk with four members of the Department.

"I see you have my files." Vance said, seeing an open folder. "Well, did you read it? Or glance through it?'

"Mr. Harlan, we went over your works. Every bit of it."

"Every bit. Including the footnotes regarding the amount of energy needed to supply such a travel?"

The Officials sat still, and Vance nodded slowly.

"I guess you did. Now I'm impressed."

"What we decided is that we cannot give you the funding for such a proposal."

"Why not? You read the file. You saw the details of this kind of mission. You know it's possible."

"Yes. We do." The second official said. "However, events prior to this mission have reverted our attentions elsewhere."

"Elsewhere? Like what the oceans?"

"This talk of alien life has gotten the public too far into our affairs and we, don't like that fact."

"But, come on. It's aliens. An opportunity to speak with intelligent life outside of our own planet."

"We hear you."

"But?' Vance said with a quick sigh of breath.

"We're invested in or current public affairs. The funding must go there."

"I don't agree with this."

"Doesn't matter if you do or do not." The third official said. "The decision has been made regardless of your work."

Vance wiped his face and slanted his head. He clapped his hands, startling the officials and jolting the guards. Vance looked around at he guards, seeing their firearms slightly raised. He waved them off with a laugh.

"Even they get startled."

"Thank you for your time with us, Mr. Harlan. You may go."

"I do however have one question to ask you. Just one."

"What is it?" The first official said.

"What is the true reason you have denied me funding for this project?"

The first official sighed before gazing over to the other three. The second official shook his head, staying silent. The third official fanned his hands in the air and didn't give an answer. The fourth official stared at Vance and turned to the first official. Giving him a nod. Vance's eyes moved back and forth between the for officials.

"So, is he going to tell me or are you? I'm confused right now with all this staring and waving."

"I will speak it for you." The fourth official said.

"Good." Vance replied. "That's good. Now, what is it?"

"There was an incident that occurred over a month ago in Nevada."

"Nevada. Ok. I'm still not getting at what you're trying to tell me."

"An incident of forceful attacks took place at Area 51. One of our lieutenants went missing in the light of fire after the base was ambushed. He was unable to be found and is still missing."

"I see. But, with all due respect, what does a missing lieutenant have to do with my project's funding?"

"The cause of the attack were those intelligent beings you're so amazed by. They ambushed the base and attacked our men. Killed many and one of our best lieutenants is nowhere to be found. Now, do you understand why we cannot permit this project to go forward? Because those things you desire to meet, they want us all dead and this world theirs."

"Well, maybe they were antagonistic aliens. I mean all aliens cannot be enemies, sir. That's just not possible."

"Either way. This project is not going forward. You may leave us now, Mr. Harlan. Return to your other work. It's proven useful for our country and your life."

Vance stood up from the desk, grabbing his file. He still continued speaking with the officials, pleading they give him the funding. The officials continued to refuse until the guards stepped down from their post and surrounded Vance. Fully realizing his current predicament, Vance nodded and chuckled before taking his leave. Vance had returned to his home and from here, he set for to find a way to get his project going without the funding from the Department. Working nonstop for months while living in the outskirts of Phoenix, Arizona looking for an opportunity, Vance had come into communication with a much-wealthy foreign billionaire. The billionaire did not give Vance his name or location, only that he was interested in Vance's work and handed him the funding he needed. The billionaire's only request was for Vance to return to Earth once he had come into contact with extraterrestrials and that he should bring back with him physical evidence of their existence. Vance agreed to the commands and went ahead with the project. From there, a starship was built under the eyes of his colleagues and associates. Vance kept the project's workings to himself to avoid scrutiny and possible arrest from the government.

"Ah." Vance said, gazing at the starship. "She is finished."

The starship sat inside one of the hangars Vance had acquired from the military due to his previous works. Everything was in place for the travel and Vance had decided to wait until one clear night had come to make his launch. A week had passed and there was no clear sky due to the amount of clouds and precipitations of rainfall. Vance was annoyed by the weather's behavior. As if it was acting aggressive toward him, trying to get him to quit his project. Vance didn't quit and after a long day of rain, the night had come and the sky was clear. Vance had gathered all his gear and placed it inside the starship. The hangar had opened and the starship had launched into the sky. Vance was astonished at the speed of the ship and the stars around him. Several minutes had passed before Vance found himself in space, glancing out of the window looking down at Earth. Using a map he had placed inside the ship to navigate his goings. He went ahead and traveled. Passing through a stream of asteroids, a flash of light peaked through them, gaining Vance's attention. He moved toward through the meters toward the moving light. Once he came closer, the light flashed with such brightness that it caused the ship to jolt and from there, Vance could feel himself being pulled into the light and the ship with him. Vance kept his eyes shut from the blinding white-then-blue-then-red light. In a short spot of chance, Vance took a peek and saw the light was in fact a wormhole. A smile had formed on his face as he and the ship were sucked in and the light was gone. As if it was nowhere to be found. Like it was never in the stream of asteroids.

Within seconds, the ship was forced out of the wormhole with such speed, the ship had crashed onto a planet. Vance was calm, yet angry of his ship's damage. Exiting the damaged ship. Vance looked around, realizing he could breathe in the air. He looked down, seeing soil and grass. He grabbed the dirt and looked closer. It appeared to be no different than the soil on Earth.

"Shit!" Vance said. "Crashed back down to Earth."

While sighing in anger, the sound of a rushing wave crashed behind him. Vance had turned, looking at what he cold tell was a shoreline and the waves were crashing in with such force the ground had not flooded. Confused, he took a glance up to the sky and noticed it was a strange color. Not like the blue sky of Earth, but a very light greenish sky mixed with a layer of blue.

"What the hell?"

Vance had turned around to find himself quickly surrounded by beings that appeared to be hybrids. They had the upper bodies of animals and lower bodies of humans. They held what Vance could perceived to be guns toward him as he held his arms up. Somewhat shaking in fear. Not from the guns. One of the hybrids that appeared to be a Leopard-Man stepped forward, measuring Vance. He nodded.

"Take him back to the ship!"

"Ship?!" Vance said. "What ship?!"

CHAPTER 2: WELCOME ABOARD

Tossed onto a ship decorated with skulls of various creatures. Creatures unknown to Vance's knowledge, the ship took off across the waters as the crew passed him by, operating the ship's movement. Vance sat confused. Mainly confused by the living hybrids passing him by. Standing up, he wandered around the ship, attempting to ask questions concerning where he is. Turning around as the sea's waters rush against the ship, tilting it back and forth, Vance approached an somewhat middle-aged man dressed in Captain's garbs.

"Pardon me, but, where am I?"

"Where are you? My good sir, you aren't aware of your current circumstances?"

"What circumstances must I be aware of?"

"We found you on that small island. Looked to me, you must've crashed from the sea above us. We found you stranded out here. Brought you onboard to keep you alive. You do want to remain alive, don't you?"

"Well, yes I do. But, I'm not understanding. Where am I?"

"Where were you going?"

"I was going through a wormhole and I fell back down. I must be somewhere around the Pacific Islands. I have to be."

"Pacific Islands? What is that?"

Vance paused, looking at the Captain with uncertainty. He nodded while waving his hands, taking a gaze out toward the ocean.

"I'm still not understanding." The Captain said.

"We're on the Pacific Ocean, aren't we?"

"You're on the Sea of Aphro. The land around you is the Land of Aphro."

"Aphro?" Vance said. "What is Aphro?"

The Captain led Vance toward his study within the ship, passing by more hybrid creatures working. They enter the study with the first thing Vance noticed were the amount of scrolls laying on the shelves and the desk. The Captain approached his desk and opened a drawer, searching through, he grabbed a scroll and signaled Vance to approach the desk. Vance stepped forward as the Captain opened the scroll.

"What is this?" Vance asked.

"A map of this planet. Where we are right now is in the District of Aphro. Riding over the Seas of course."

"Planet? You said planet?"

"I did. Yes."

"Hold on. So, you're telling me, we're not on Earth?"

"Earth?" The Captain said confusingly. "What is Earth?"

"Earth. You know the third planet from the sun."

"Third planet? Third planet... Oh, you speak about Jarok. You're from Jarok?"

"Jarok? No. I'm from Earth."

"But, you said third from the sun."

"That is Earth."

"It is where you're from. Here, it's pronounced Jarok. Other words have been thrown out before. Depending on what planet you land on."

"So, if this is not Earth, then where am I?'

"Vanok."

"What is Vanok?"

"The second planet from the sun. second before Jarok and second after Firoh."

"Firoh? Jarok? I'm not understanding these terms completely. You mean Earth and Mercury?"

"If that's what they're called wherever you're from?" The Captain replied. "So, you are from Jarok. Tell me, how are things there? We never receive news regarding that planet. Only the other ones around it."

Vance took a moment to catch his breath. Taking all of the information in slowly. If possible. He glanced down at the map, seeing the landmarks. What Vance noticed quickly was the amount of water upon Vanok and the mid-to-small sized islands surrounding two larger continents. He pointed at the continents with questions. What were they and who dwelled upon them. Asking the Captain concerning the two continents. The Captain chuckled, using a cane to point toward the continents.

"The one we're nearby, Aphro. Of course. The other is Vetor. Now, there is a difference between the two."

"What kind of difference?"

"Well, for starters, Aphro is a continent filled with rugged structures and a plethora of diverse creatures. That's where my hybrid pirates come in."

"A whole continent filled with beasts."

"Yes. Now, Vetor. It's a much different place. Surrounded by beautiful landmarks and cathedrals. From tall skyscrapers to temples to the Vanokian gods. Vetor is the home of the Kingdom of Vetoria."

"And have you ever been there? To this kingdom?"

The Captain laughed, taking a breath before walking over toward his shelf, where a bottle of rum sat. Grabbing the bottle and taking a drink.

"Never. My kind, meaning my line of work isn't seen as acceptable in such a place. The people of the kingdom perceive myself and those like me as subservient. Lesser living beings. The kingdom believes they're above all life on Vanok. Even their own children to an extent."

Vance remained quiet as the Captain took a moment of silence. He sighed and returned to drinking the rum as the ship rocked. Strangely enough, Vance felt the movement of the ship a bit strange. The ship rocked once more with the sound of a bang following. He stood up from his seat, looking around.

"Did you hear that?"

"Hear what?" The Captain asked.

"The explosion. Something's happening."

"Let's find out."

The two run out to the front, seeing the pirates clashing against another set of pirates as the opposing ship crashed into their own. From the other ship jumped over pirates of a different kind. Wearing worn-and-torn clothing with a particular circular insignia layered on their chest. Vance kept his distance as the Captain yelled for his pirates to assemble and fight against the others. Vance watched on as the swords clashed and the gunfire rung. In the distance on the other ship, Vance spotted a figure making themselves known. Looking closer, he saw the figure in full form.

"A woman?"

The woman stepped onboard the Captain's ship and fought against several of his hybrid pirates with a cutlass of her own. She took them down in seconds as she made her way toward the Captain. Vance sought to help, grabbing a sword on the floor and rushing toward the woman. Seeing him from the corner of her eye, she turned with speed clashing her cutlass against Vance's sword. She glared into his eyes and showed a slight grin.

"You're different." She uttered. "This is the ship."

The woman signaled her pirates to grab Vance and they tossed him onto the other ship as the Captain looked on fighting against the invaders. Making the move to assist Vance, he was slashed in the back by one of the pirates before the woman rallied her own to return to their ship. They moved with motion, returning to the ship and they escaped the area. The Captain stood up, sighing in pain went around to check on his pirates. Seeing some of them dead on the deck, he sighed bitterly.

"Her." He whispered to himself.

CHAPTER 3: CALYPSO

Vance had sat on the deck of the opposing ship, surrounded by the invading pirates. Their eyes eluded him. Glowing in many glares of color. From black, brown, green, blue, and red. The pirates snarled at Vance, attempting to terrify him. Yet, Vance kept his composure and faced them. The pirates from that point had paused themselves and moved over to the edges of the ship, making way for their captain to step forward. She walked with a vigorous stature as her eyes were set only on Vance. She approached him and looked down onto him. A grin had formed on her face.

"What's going on?" Vance asked. "Why did you take me?"

"Poor one. You aren't aware of the workings here. I can sense you're not from this world."

"Of course not. I come from Earth. As I was telling the Captain on the ship."

"You mean the Captain of those degenerate pirates?! Ha! Such company will poison you. Eventually killing you."

"Then, why take me from them? I was seeming to be doing just fine. Doing well for the most part since I crashed on this planet. What is all of this and where are you taking me?"

"Hold your temper and follow me."

The pirates escorted Vance behind the woman into her study. Looking similar to the Captain's own, yet detailed with colorful marbled walls and a stone-layered floor. Vance saw the floor and took a look back out to the deck, looking at its wooden bottom. He had questions and the woman only replied with the notion of her ship's design was possible due to her line of work. Vance wondered what work she spoke of as she sat down at her desk, covered with books and maps.

Even a small emerald sat on the desk in the right corner. Like a pedestal of her achievements.

"Leave us." She told her pirates.

Exiting the study, Vance stood in the center of the room with the woman signaling him to sit down. He went and faced her. Sitting down and staring while admiring her exquisite interior design work. Vance gave a nod. Impressed by her choice of style. She waved it off like a small gesture of good fortune.

"You may be wondering why I took you from those hybrids and why you're here."

"I am wondering? What was the reason. How come you're different than your crew?"

"Because they've learned to respect me."

"I guess you were just a woman looking to do something others refused?"

"Refused is a slight word to use in my line of work. No, they did not refuse, yet, they didn't survive the pathways."

"Survive?"

"Most of the people on this planet strive to live. It is a necessary evil one must do in order to obtain food, water, and supplies to maintain their lives. The majority on this planet have even scraps to survive. To make amends to their gods and to keep their families safe. The some, they only seek to acquire whatever it is they need and they're content. So they shall be. But, the few. Oh, the few. The few do what they must to survive. Even if they have to slaughter, make war, or enter conflict with the others. In the end, the few have always won. Vanok is their world and not the other way around."

Vance nodded slowly, taking in her words.

"And you happened to be one of the few?"

"I am now. Before I was one of the majority. My mother and father did what they could to give me a proper childhood. However, war had fallen and my father went into battle. He survived the conflict, of course. But, his health declined due to the weapons used in the war. Chemicals that have transferred the sky above into the warping it appears today. Afterwards, my mother took care of me until I was able to take care of myself. I learned as I traveled the two continents.

Searching for new ways of work and opportunity. The majority had always preached to me that marriage was in my future. That I would find a man who I would be suitable to match. Funny, after all the men I've encountered, none of them saw me as wife potential."

"I'm sorry to hear that." Vance said slowly.

"Don't be. It taught me something important. As I learned the true nature of this world, I became one of the Some. Learning new things and new ways to make things work. I tried to tell those I knew in my past abut these things and they refused. Saying, 'You can't live like that. It's too difficult to make such a path. The carving would be detrimental to one's own health.'. Crazy stuff they believe. Yet, that's what holds them down. Holds them back from increasing themselves. Elevating one's self is a sure way to make a move in this world."

"And what kind of carving did you make for yourself in this world?"

"First off, was military duty. I served in the Navy of the Kingdom of Vetoria. Fought countless battles on and off the seas. Most of my conflict was with the hybrids. We are taught in the forces the hybrids are responsible for more of the planet's dire circumstances. The increasing of the seas and the warping sky. All caused by their existence. The Navy's task was to eliminate any hybrids we encountered. And so we did."

"So, now you lead a group of pirates to do what exactly? Hold on. Is that why you ambushed the ship and took me?"

"Yes and no. Yes as in I ambushed the ship because they were hybrids. It's in my nature now. And no. I did not attack them simply to take you. Well, I didn't know you were onboard to start with. My intentions were simply elsewhere. That is until I saw you myself. From that point I had to take you."

"But why?"

"You're not a Vanokian. That much is true. Your essence oozes off your body. Your spirit's scent emits from you like a foreign soul."

"You know I'm not from this planet then."

"Certainly. What I want to know is why did you come here? What attracted you to Vanok in the first place?"

"First off, I didn't even know there was a Vanok to begin with. I was simply traveling through a wormhole and I ended up here. That is what happened."

"Truly?"

"Yes. Otherwise I would've had directions to go. I had no directions other than a wormhole."

"You said you're from Earth." The woman said, leaning in her chair. "Tell me, what is this Earth you speak of?"

"As I told the Captain of the Hybrids, Earth is the third planet from the sun. Second to Venus and first to Mars."

"I've never heard of Earth or Venus or Mars. They sound interesting though. That I'll give to you."

"I must be in a whole different solar system."

The woman reached down and picked up a map, she laid it out on the desk and slid it closer to Vance. He leaned over and looked. It was a map of a solar system. Yet not the one he is knowledgeable of. The planets on the map were bigger and the stars were brighter. Even it's sun was more of a darker fireball than the sun he knew.

"From what you're telling me, you most certainly are. Listen, this is what this system offers you. The first planet from the sun is what we like to call Firoh, a fiery planet. Its air will consume anything it touches. Second is Vanok, where we sit this day. A planet covered in much water and less land. Third is Jarok. A mysterious planet. We often wonder if there is life on it at all. Besides that, the tech capable of interstellar flight is kept in the secret chambers of the King of Vetoria. Fourth is what we call Arton, a planet covered in red dust. We speculate no life has been on that planet for millenniums. Fifth is Zutah, the planet of the Eye. Not sure what that means. Scholars here are still speculating. Sixth is Tharnog, surrounded with debris it gives off a bright light the father you're from it. You can slightly see it during the nights. Seven is Ocenia. Called that because it is known to be a planet of only water. No land."

"But, how are you certain of this? Of all of this?"

"Because of the scholars. They keep the records of the history of the system. The books have been around for ages."

Vance nodded, wiping the sweat from his forehead.

"This is a lot to take in."

"It has that affect on newcomers. But, don't you fret, there's still a lot more to learn."

"I see."

"Now, back to what I was saying. Oh, yeah. Now. The eighth planet is called Poston, somewhat similar to Oceania in appearance. However, instead of roaring waters, suffocating mists."

"I'm not certain as to how that works."

"You breath it in, you die. Simple as that."

Vance looked at the map again, seeing two remaining planets. The one after Poston was smaller and white as snow. The planet after was as dark as coal. the two planets seemed to mirror each other, according to Vance's understanding. The woman noticed his interest in the two planets as she smiled and tossing back her long wavy hair.

"Those two are enigmas of their own."

"And why is that?"

"The one before is called Hailon, a planet covered in dense snow. Often times, the scholars believe its pouring snow every second of a day. Can you imagine, nonstop snowfall for the rest of your days?"

"No I cannot. Where I live, snow is a rare occasion. Often appearances. But, rare."

"You're saying it doesn't snow on Earth?"

"No. It snows. Yes. But, not everywhere gets it. Only portions receive it. If you understand what I'm trying to say."

"I hear you."

"Does it snow here? In these waters?"

"Several times during the Sapphire Cycle. But, that's a whole 'nother tale."

"And what of the last planet? It looks a bit eerie."

"Because it is. We call that one simply Abyssian."

"Abyssian?" Vance said. "Like the abyss?"

"Why else name it after."

The woman sighed as she glanced over to a clock which sat against the ship walls. Seeing the time, she stood up and called for her pirates to return. Entering the study, they surround Vance and hold him up as he begins asking more questions concerning his fate. The woman laughed as she approached him closely.

"At least tell me what you want from me?"

"Oh. I want nothing from you. But, I know someone who will."

"I'm not understanding."

"We're on our way to the Kingdom of Vetoria. The King will like to have a word with you."

"The King?" Vance asked. "Why me?"

"Because you're the first being to come from another planet in ages. Such an event is one the King would not like to miss."

"Hold on. How does he know I'm here?"

"We have our ways of contact. Remember me saying something about tech earlier. It works in many ways. Ways the Majority will never come to understand and the Some refuse to use in order to advance themselves."

The woman commanded the pirates to take Vance to the guest room on the ship. Dragging him down the hallway, they opened the door and tossed Vance inside. Shutting the door before he could make a turn-around. Vance looked at the room, seeing a bed, a dining table, and a shelf of books. He looked over toward the shelf, looking at the books' spines, reading the titles. They were a mystery to him. All spoke about constellations and mysticism. Something Vance is not of interest in. While he were searching through, a knock came from the door, startling him. He stood up from his knees and called out tot eh visitor. The door had opened and it was the woman. Closing the door behind her as Vance stood confused.

"Why are you putting me in here?"

"To give you some comfort before you meet the King."

"None of this is making sense."

"I can't treat you like a slave and bring you to the King. He'll see the way you were treated and make a conclusion from that point. He has ways which are peculiar to foreigners."

Vance nodded while sitting down at the dining table. The woman looked and nodded. Something came to her attention. She called her hands, startling Vance as she laughed. He shook his head, trying to keep his composure and mental state. This is a day he never expected to live. But, here he is.

"Very well. I'll have some food brought to you and you can take a moment to rest before you meet the King."

"Well, thank you for your sudden hospitality. Could've doe this earlier and I may have taken you differently."

"The day is not over and I am not easy to comprehend. Nor are my motives."

The woman turned to exit the room, but Vance called out to her. Catching himself before even thinking of what to say next. She stood still, waiting for Vance to speak. He nodded and had a thought. A simple one.

"You never told me your name? That is if you have one."

"My name." she said. "You want to know my name?"

"I would like to. Otherwise, I would have to refer to you as the woman who took me from the ship or the Invader."

"As much as I would prefer those two, I'll tell you my name. although, I must warn you. Not even my crew knows of my name and for your sake, I would like to keep it that way."

"Wait, how do they not your name? so, they simply call you Captain?"

"Captain is enough for them to know who I am and my worth."

Vance nodded in agreement. He understood her intentions for once. The woman took a breath before uttering another word. Something which took Vance off his guard. Seeing a slightly vulnerable state from the woman who invaded another's ship and fought off the hybrids before taking him.

"Calypso is my name."

"Calypso." Vance said. "Sounds, a little frightening."

"As it should be."

Calypso turned and left the room, leaving Vance in a frozen state of worry and insight. Vance sighed as he could hear the waves moving across the seas.

CHAPTER 4: THE KINGDOM OF VETORIA

Vance woke up to the waves and the running sounds of the pirates heading toward the deck. Getting himself up, he rushed outside the room and followed the pirates, leading him to the deck where Calypso stood. She looked out to her crew and saw Vance in the distance. She smirked with a nod. Turning around, she faced the direction and toward them was the Kingdom of Vetoria. She held up her hands, shouting a war cry in Vanokian dialect to which all the pirates rallied with her while Vance stood confused. Calypso approached Vance as he began ask her of the war cry.

"I said, Hail Vetoria. Hail to the gods."

"Oh." Vance replied. "I thought it was something of the likes of taking over the city."

"I couldn't do that to the King. However, I could if I chose to."

The ship made its way toward the landing deck as the pirates tossed over the anchor. Jumping off the ship, Calypso kept Vance close to her in avoiding the Vetorians who saw them arrive, staring at them like guard dogs protecting their home. Vance stared at them, even to the degree of Calypso warning him not to cause a scene. The Vetorian people were dressed modestly. The men wore slacks and long-sleeve robes in which reminded Vance of the Ancient Greek imagery. The women were fully dressed from head to toe decked in dresses and head coverings. Even to Vance's surprise, he happened to notice the women did not wear any makeup. He rubbed his eyes looking closer as he passed them by. Calypso noticed his interest and tugged him.

"What are you doing?"

"They're not wearing makeup."

"Makeup?" Calypso said. "What is makeup?"

"The women I knew, they would design their faces. Making them look more appealing."

Calypso scoffed.

"Is that what they do on Jarok? They paint their faces like the jesters of the court?"

"When you put it that way, maybe." Vance shrugged.

The overall landscape of Vetoria was one of a beautifully appearance. Attractive to the yes were its polished grounds and structures. Merchants passed them by on marble-like wagons and carriages. Even the animals passing by were of a different breed. Vance thought them to be cows, but given a much closer examination he spotted black dots across the back of the animals. From the carved designs of their gods scattered around and nearby the palace to the monuments inscribed concerning Vetorian laws and guidelines.

They approached the entry point to the Vetorian Palace. The monumental structure detailed in much sapphire and built with a light blue stone. The paint covered across the palace was nearly transparent to the waters which roared nearby. Vance also realized the air was different than the island of Aphro, much smoother and the sky was much clearer. Clear to the point, Vance could see the stars peeking through the thin clouds. The palace doors opened with two guards standing by. Wielding tridents in their right hands. The guards nodded toward Calypso and her two close pirate guards as they gave Vance a stare. A look of uncertainty as Vance nodded to them. They did not respond. Entering the throne room, Calypso looked ahead, seeing the King sitting. She stopped herself and turned to Vance as he noticed the King. The King himself wore the diverse garb of land and sea. From the hides of the beasts of the land to the teeth and scales from the creatures of the seas. However, his crown was made of pure sapphire and his staff was made of pure emerald. Yet, there was gold layered upon his throne. Vance saw it and only shook his head. He has never seen so much sapphire, emerald, or even gold in his life. It was all just a dream to him.

"Before we enter, do what I say."

"Like what? Bow before him and don't give eye contact?"

"Exactly. You're smarter than you look, Jarokian."

Walking into the throne room, a room decorated with sapphire floors and ceilings. Painting layered across the walls detail a history of the planet. Vance stared at them. Seeing everything from pirates at war with royal navies, marriages, and even monsters from the seas clashing with enlightened beings coming down from the sky. The King saw them and smiled. waving toward Calypso as he stood up and hugged her. He greeted the two pirate guards and paused, looking at Vance. His eyes slanted over toward calypso with question. She nodded with a smile.

"I can explain this man's unknown arrival."

"Do explain."

The King sat down as Calypso began to explain Vance's reasoning for standing in his throne room. Calypso introduced Vance to the King, King Kharan. Vance waved to no reply from Kharan. Calypso told the king of Vance's possible value to his kingdom and what he can do in order to achieve a place in the Vetorian landscape. Calypso even pointed out the details of Vance's arrival from another planet. Kharan asked what planet did Vance originate from and Vance held his hand up to their surprise.

"Earth. I come from Earth."

"What is Earth?" Kharan asked Calypso. "I've never heard of this Earth before?"

"He speaks of Jarok, my King." Calypso answered. "This man is a native to Jarok. He came here by ship."

"Jarok. You came from the planet after us?"

"I did, King Kharan. Where I'm from, we call it Earth. It's simple."

"So it may be. Tell me, why come here? Why not traverse the stars and reach a planet filled with a much greater life than exists here? A planet with much land and sea for everyone to share?"

"To be honest, I wasn't even sure where I was headed. I traveled and discovered a wormhole and from there I arrived here. Or crashed here. However you perceive the arrival."

"And what do you intend to do from this point forward?"

"I would like to return home eventually. To tell everyone I know about this place."

"And tell them why? To entice some to war. If you could travel here through a one-way tunnel, then so could they. War is not what we need in this day and hour. We already have enough conflicts with the hybrids that roam the lands and scavenge the seas. From what I can sense, you had a confrontation with them."

"Not as much as a confrontation. More like a meeting without knowing."

"Calypso, my dear. Where did you find this man?"

"I found him on the ship of the Captain of the Hybrids."

"He was with them?" Kharan said, standing up from his seat. "And you brought him here?"

"It's not like that, my King."

"Then how is it?"

"I attacked their ship as you commanded all of us to do. While ambushing, I discovered Vance on the ship. To me, he appeared to be a slave to the Captain. He wasn't around the others nor did he act like them. His countenance told me he was of potential and that is why he's standing here before you."

Kharan sat back down and scratched his beard. Giving both Vance and Calypso eyes of questioning. Calypso hung her head while Vance looked around at the throne room's design. Taking another look at the paintings and smiled.

"Who designed those?"

"An artist who spent much time in Vetoria. He still does paintings for us this day."

"That's cool. Can I meet him?"

"No."

"Fair enough."

Kharan sighed, looking toward Calypso and Vance.

"I have a proposition for you. The both of you actually."

"I'm all ears." Vance said.

"What is it, my King?"

"I will see what this Jarokian can do. I will test his might, his skill, his mentality, and lastly, his spirit. I want to see if the people of Jarok are as, stable as the legends tell them to be."

"Wait. You said legends."

"I did."

"You mean you're aware on life on Earth. I mean Jarok?"

"I do. Many of the scrolls kept in the achieves chamber by my scholar have indicated the people of Jarok are somewhat above us. In skill, technology, and spirituality."

"I wouldn't put us up to that kind of stature. But, I see your concerns."

"But, since you're from Jarok. Are the people as the legends say or are they less?"

"It's complicated to say the least. Some are and some aren't."

"Depends on where one goes, doesn't it?" Kharan asked.

"It does."

"Hmm. Well then, time will reveal all things. This man seems to have some potential indeed, Calypso."

"He will not prove you wrong, my King. I am positive he has the skills capable of cleansing this planet of the hybrids just as you desire."

"We shall see once the tests are complete. Maybe your words prove right about this man, Calypso. However, maybe you're wrong. But in the end, it is this man who will provide us all with the answer."

While they spoke, the sound of a door opening creaked behind Kharan. He stood up and looked back, seeing a young woman entering the throne room. Kharan smiled as Calypso bowed and Vance stood still. Staring at the young woman. Dressed in red apparel from her neck down. She wore golden rings on her fingers and layered gold laced within her dress. She even had a golden tiara and necklace to match.

"Vance Harlan of Jarok, allow me to introduce to you my daughter, Serilda. She has been praying for a warrior to arrive to aid her father in his conquest of ridding this planet of the hybrids. Perhaps, you are that warrior. Perhaps, my daughter's prayers have been answered by the gods."

Vance nodded to Serilda and she nodded back. Yet, their eyes had locked with one another and immediately Vance was pulled into a void. A void unseen by anyone else in the throne room. Vance moved throughout the void, leaning he was outside of his body as he turned around seeing himself, Calypso, Serilda, and Kharan standing in the throne room.

"What is going on?"

"I have prayed for you to come." A voice said within the void.

"Prayed for me? I'm not understanding what you ask of me."

"You can be the light to Vanok. The pathway to a new world. A world where Vetorians and hybrids can live as one. As one people."

"Listen, I'm just a man. I don't fight wars for conquest that are beyond my comprehension. This isn't even my home."

"But, you are here for a reason. A reason which has been chosen well by the gods."

"I don't know these gods."

"In time, you will come to know. Everyone on Vanok does eventually. Now wake up."

Within seconds, Vance awoke to find himself standing in the same place and his eyes were still locked on Serilda. However, when Vance came to the understanding of the sudden void, Serilda gave him a smirk before she took her leave. Kharan stepped forward toward Vance, placing his hand on his shoulders. Kharan turned to Calypso.

"Calypso, I will take him from here. I'm sure there are a plenty things you have to attend to."

"Yes, my king. I do have one question. If I may ask."

"Speak."

"The Captain of the Hybrids will soon be coming for Vance Harlan. The sense in the air tells me he'll be making his way here to find him."

"And you want me to grant you permission to face him head-on?"

"If you would like him out of your hairs, then yes."

Kharan nodded with a grin.

"Good. Good. Go and cleanse our waters of the hybrid filth. Return to me when the task is complete. A reward will be waiting for you when you arrive."

"I will do as you command."

"Vance Harlan of Jarok. My guards will bring you to one of our luxurious rooms. You will stay here for the night as your tests will begin on the morrow. Best to rest yourself before the trails of your life begin."

Calypso bowed before she made her leave as the Vetorian guards escorted Vance to one of the guest rooms of the palace. Arriving at the room, Vance immediately noticed the layout of the room. Reminding him of the wealthy places to stay on Earth. From a nice balcony overlooking the city and the sea to the decorated furniture. Even the air was cleaner than the outside. The guards left Vance as he sat down gazing out toward the city, hearing the voices of the people mixed with the rushing waters of the sea.

Elsewhere on the seas, the Captain of the Hybrids sat down in his study, overlooking the map with a marking directed onto the Kingdom of Vetoria. From the study doors entered one of the hybrids. A being which looked to be a leopard mixed with a human. The leopard portion on the upper body and the human portion on the lower.

"Boss, we've received word from the others."

"What is this word?"

"They've said to have seen the foreigner. The one who fell from the sky."

"Have they? And where did they see him?"

"Vetorian sir. He was escorted by Calypso toward the palace."

The Captain raised his head from the map. Rolling up the map and setting it aside. He laid back in his chair as he thought to himself. He raised himself up back to the desk and opened the map again, this time staring at the red markings over Vetoria.

"So, she means to make him a tool of war for Kharan, huh. Well then, I guess they won't be expecting us when we arrive. They want war. Let's give them a war."

CHAPTER 5: A TEST OF FORTITUDE AND KNOWLEDGE

Vance arose to the sound of the waters as he gazed outside, seeing the Vetorian people going about their day as they did before. Taking in the scenery, a knock thundered from the door. Vance turned around, speaking for the visitor to enter. The door opened as Kharan himself entered the room. Vance saw him and nodded his head in reverence.

"I take it you received a well night's rest?"

"I did. One I haven't had in a long time."

"Very well. That is good to hear. Because you will require all the energy you can muster this day. For it will be a challenging one."

"What kind of trials are set for me today?"

"A variety of sorts. First, prepare yourself. Eat well and my guards will bring you to the arena for the first trial."

"Arena?" Vance paused. "Like a fighting arena?"

"Are there any others?"

"I see."

"You will once you arrive. Take this time, Vance Harlan of Jarok. Take it well."

Kharan exited the room, leaving Vance to take the moment to prepare himself. Vance had sighed, gazing back out to the open area of the city. From there, Vance knelt down near the bed and began to pray. He prayed for protection against any adversary which may be awaiting him at the arena. Afterwards, Vance ate the breakfast which was delivered to him immediately after his prayer. Once he was finished, a knock came from the door. Vance went and opened it, seeing two guards. He nodded and exited the room. Walking with them down the hall and followed them toward the arena. The arena itself was over thirty stories and there was no audience sitting in attendance, just yet. Standing in the middle of the arena was Kharan as he applauded Vance's arrival.

"You have come. Good. Good. Now, are you ready to hear what is being presented to you?"

"Ready as I'll ever be."

"Then let us begin!"

The arena doors shut and around Vance were several men dressed in light blue robes. Their faces shrouded by their hoods. In their hands were scrolls, worn and torn. The men opened the scrolls and laid them on the table which sat before Vance. Eight scrolls in total. Kharan commanded for Vance to approach the table and read the first one. Vance went and read it. Strangely to him, the scrolls were written in Vanokian, but he was able to read them as if they were English.

"What is this?"

"The first test of knowledge." Kharan answered. "To test your mind and your history."

Vance read the scroll in detail. Gaining the understanding he needed to comprehend this first test. Kharan kept his sights on Vance, seeing his mannerisms and facial changes.

"What does it say?" Kharan asked.

"It asks me to describe the difference between your world and mine."

"Then, describe it."

"What is there to describe. From what I've seen since my time on this planet, their behaviors and the appearances of the people are no different than the ones back on Earth. In a creepy way, they're both very similar."

Kharan nodded. He waved his hand toward the hooded one, who rolled up the first scroll and stood aside. Vance turned toward the second scroll and read it. Kharan asked Vance to speak what it says.

"This one asks of me to detail the differences between the skies between your world and mine."

"Tell us, what are those differences?"

"For starters, Earth's sky is not contaminated by the celestial storms

I see above us."

"Then what is it contaminated by?"

"A variety of things. Matters to discuss in a greater detail which would take up my time on this test."

"I see." Kharan noted.

The second hooded one rolled up the scroll and stood aside as Vance approached the third scroll.

"This one speaks of the difference between the arts of war."

"Arts of war." Kharan said. "This will prove useful. Tell us, what are the differences?"

"The difference is there are no differences." Vance answered. "War is the same wherever you go. No matter the species which dwells upon the planet."

"By such words, you confirm that war is eternal?"

"War is eternal. The struggle keeps civilizations going until the end of all things."

"Noted."

The scroll was rolled up and Vance approached the fourth. The fourth one detailed the similarities between the animals on Earth compared to Vanok. Kharan asked Vance to give the answer and Vance only sighed.

"So far, I've never encountered any hybrids until I came here."

"Interesting." Kharan replied. "You mean to tell me you've never seen any hybrids back on your planet?"

"None. I'm not saying they don't exist there. But, I've never encountered one."

"Good to hear. At least your world doesn't have to deal with the suffrage of those savage creatures. Seeking to destroy all you hold dear. Pillaging wherever they go. Such filth."

The fifth scroll was read and Vance took in the words. The words enticed him slightly as they pertained to the government rulings between both worlds. Kharan asked Vance to answer once more and Vance only replied by stating the governments between the two planets are not hat different. Pertaining to which country one visits to the individual in charge. Kharan nodded with intrigue. The sixth scroll was next to be read and upon the sixth scroll were two drawings. One of a man. Another of a woman. Kharan asked for Vance to give an answer to the question of the drawings. Vance looked at the drawings carefully.

"Without them both, the planet would be without those of dominion. It is the nature of the balance."

"Nature of the balance." Kharan said. "Interesting choice of wordplay. Next."

The seventh scroll was approached by Vance and detailed the societal order of both worlds. Vance quickly answered by saying the roles of man, woman, and child must remain in constant flow unless they deem the civilization itself to collapse and eventually end all that remains. Kharan took this words carefully, as it reminded him of how he became king. Through a much similar circumstance. The last scroll was approached and Vance stood still, taking in the question. Kharan stood boldly against the wall as Vance read the scroll.

"What does it say?" Kharan asked.

"It asks the question of honor between the two worlds. Honor is a must in all worlds. Without it, one will never see the days ahead. Only a quick and painful death awaits those who dishonor for a sport cause."

"Good words. Good words."

Kharan waved for the scrolls and the table to be removed from the arena floor. The scholars disappeared into the shadows circling them. Vance stood still as he began to hear the sound of doors opening and he gazed up to the seats, beginning to see the civilians enter the arena. Vance turned to Kharan, asking him what was about to happen. Kharan chuckled.

"Your next test. Combat."

"Combat?" Vance said. "Like right now?"

"Good place as any. Besides, you seem like a capable warrior who would defend himself if the cause came about. Now, the cause has arrived."

The guards entered the arena, tossing a rapier to Vance. He caught it and stared at the blade. Kharan walked toward him and handed him a firearm. Vance looked at the firearm and noticed there was something different.

"What kind of gun is this?"

"One you can only find within the walls of this palace. It will be of good use in your fights."

"But, how does it work?"

"You mean to tell me your kind don't have such weapons back on Jarok?"

"Oh no. we do. We have a lot of them. All different shapes and sizes. But, I'm just curious as to how this one works."

'You see the trigger?"

"Yes."

"Then you know how it works."

The crowds gathered within the arena and cheered as Vance looked up toward them. The doors in front of Vance on the other end of the arena had opened and out of them walked out three men. Two were guards of the palace while the third one appeared to be a pirate. One of Calypso's Vance had thought to himself. Kharan commanded the battle to begin and the three opponents rushed toward Vance. Hesitant to make an attack, Vance deflected the swords of the guards and the pirate. The guards moved with such speed that Vance had to double his efforts to keep up with their attacks. The pirate stood back and scoffed at Vance's defensive skills while making an attack in between the guards' own. Vance swiped the blade, knocking one of the javelins out of the guard's hand before shoving him to the ground to the audience's excitement. Te second Guard went to make a strike, Vance dodged the attack and used the gun to blast a hole through the guard's chest. Vance caught himself as he looked at the firearm, recognizing it was an energy gun as it fired a bright blue beam through the guard's chest as if it was nothing. The pirate stood still, looking down at the guard's body and made a run for it. Vance sighed as he waved to the audience and their cheers calmed him. Kharan nodded and approached Vance from his seat.

"Excellent work. You have done well."

"I hope this is over with. I'm not sure I can kill another. That was an accident."

"An accident or a gesture of self-defense? If you had not fired the shot, they would've killed you."

Vance knew this and took it well. Kharan nodded and waved toward the door. The doors had opened and this time only one figure emerged from the shadows. Vance saw the figure, seeing it was a warrior clothed in greenish armor made from the scales of the sea creatures and in his hands he held a trident made of horns.

"You do however have one more battle." Kharan said. "Defeat him and you will enter the third and final portion of this test."

The audience roared as the gladiator entered the arena. Vance stood firm as his right hand was gripped onto the hilt of the rapier and his left hand was steady with the energy gun. The gladiator screamed to the audience's cheer as he ran toward Vance with the trident head-on. Vance moved out of the trident's path, slashing the blade across the gladiator's back. The blade impacted the armor, shattering small fragments of the scales. The gladiator paused and stared.

"It's a fight." Vance said. "What else am I supposed to do?"

The gladiator screamed, slamming the trident to the ground in front of Vance. He stepped back as the gladiator went for a punch, hitting Vance across his jaw as he pushed him to the ground. Vance looked around and fired a shot from the energy gun to the gladiator's chest. The armor shattered, but the beam did not pass through. Vance was surprised.

"You thought a beam could take me out?!" The gladiator yelled. "Do you know who I am?!"

"I'm afraid I don't." Vance replied. "Who are you supposed to be?"

"You fool! I am Batrion the Destroyer! This day, you will learn why I've earned it."

"I'm not so sure I will."

Batrion went for another strike with the trident and Vance fired a shot at Batrion's hand. Dropping the trident from the blast, he looked at his hand. Seeing the shredded scales and feeling the burning over his skin. Vance grinned.

"I'm learning."

Batrion went for a punch and Vance dodged the attack, instead swiping the blade atop Batrion's hand, cutting it off. Batrion yelled as he fell to his knees, holding his severed wrist as hi hand laid on the floor to the audience's surprise. Vance sighed.

"Please yield."

Batrion glared into Vance's eyes, going for another attack with

Vance only hitting him in the head with the energy gun. Batrion collapsed to the ground as the audience cheered Vance's victory. Kharan applauded as he stood up and granted Vance the winner of the day's battle. The audience began to leave as Kharan stood still with the hooded figures making their return into the arena. Batrion himself was carried out by the guards and his hand was taken as well. The hooded figures surrounded both Kharan and Vance as Kharan began to lay out the final portion of the test. The third and final portion pertaining to spirituality.

"Spirituality?" Vance asked. "Like what about it?"

"We want to know. I want to know. What do you believe in? Are there any gods back on your world the people worship? How many do they worship?"

"Well, it all depends on where one travels."

"I see. So, in your area of living, how many gods to they serve?"

"Depends on who you ask. It's a mixed-multitude in the country I live in."

"So, you mean to tell me, there can be one who worships one god while the other can worship a plethora of gods and they live on the same field?"

"Yes. That's what it's like. Unless you buy out the land for yourself and those of your like-mindedness."

Kharan nodded.

"Interesting. Now, I must ask you this question and this one will ensure your future upon this planet and within my kingdom."

"I'm listening."

"How many gods do you serve?"

"Honestly. I serve one."

"One. You serve one god?"

"Yes I do."

"And those you've met on your travels back on your world? Others you've shared conversations with? How many gods have they claimed to serve?"

"Some several. Many a lot. Few only serve one god."

"Such an enigma back on your world. Do you not know that where there's more gods, the better?"

"I'm not sure that confirms the clarification of worship."

"And why do you say that?"

"Because, where I'm from and how I was raised. There was only one god. He created everything and everyone."

"Everything and everyone on your world?"

"No, your Majesty. He created all things. Even this world we stand on today. He created even you."

The scholars lifted up their heads, staring at Vance with hatred searing in their eyes. Vance caught them by the feeling of an unsettling energy moving around the arena. Kharan stood still, calmly taking in Vance's words.

"He is a destroyer." One scholar spoke.

"He will destroy all you have built!" A second scholar spoke.

"Dispose of him, my King." The third scholar spoke.

"He is a blasphemer to the gods!" The fourth scholar spoke.

"Death and fire will rain down over all of Vanok if he remains!" The fifth scholar spoke.

The following three scholar spoke their own minds as the first five continued to repeat their statements. Kharan shook his head and grabbed his staff, slamming it into the floor, causing a crack to form as the sound of a shockwave echoed through the arena field.

"Silence yourselves!" Kharan yelled. "I will deal with him in matters of my own making."

The scholars hung their heads and stepped back three steps. Kharan approached Vance, looking him in the eyes. He nodded.

"Very well. I see you stand by your belief. That is something I highly respect in any individual. For one who stands for their beliefs is one I would align myself with for any cause."

Vance nodded in respect to Kharan's honor. Kharan allowed Vance to return to his room as the test were complete. Vance had passed. The guards entered and brought Vance back to his room while the scholars continued to speak against him. Kharan heeded their words and commanded for them to remain silent. One scholar refused and proclaimed that the gods of Vanok would strike down Kharan if he not rid the kingdom of Vance. Kharan took his staff and smashed it across the scholar's head and beat him to death in front of the others. The remaining seven stood silent as Kharan commanded for his guards to take the scholar's body and toss it into the seas.

"What happens to Vance will be of my choice. My decision. Not the gods." Kharan proclaimed as he left the arena.

CHAPTER 6: PIRATES OF VANOK

The Captain of the Hybrids and his crew rode across the roaring seas, following the trail on the map. The Captain kept his gaze on the surroundings. Seeing nothing but water in his sights. Up ahead, one of the hybrids ran forward with binoculars, handing them to the Captain.

"Ahead, sir!"

The Captain looked on and saw Calypso's ship up ahead. He knew she was coming for him and he grinned. Looking further behind her, he could see land. He screamed toward his crew they have arrived on the continent of Vetor. The crew cheered as they prepared themselves for battle. Over on the other ship, Calypso looked out toward them with her crew ready as their swords were drawn.

"He continues to act as if he will survive the journey." Calypso said. "Well, he will realize his end is nigh by the sharpness of my blade."

The two ships reached one another as the battle began with the hybrids clashing with the pirates. This time, the hybrids allowed thee animalistic urges to consume them, in so much as slaughtering Calypso's pirates with a certain ease. Calypso herself was not bothered by their animal rages as she sliced her way through them to get to the Captain. She walked on the deck, killing hybrids as she saw the Captain waiting for her with his sword drawn and a smile on his face.

"You think this is funny?!"

"I do. I have a dark sense of humor."

Calypso and the Captain's blades clashed with the sound of thunder above them. They locked eyes as the ongoing battles continued around them.

"Where did you take the foreigner?"

"None of your concern."

"It is of my concern. I was the one who found him first!"

"You would've wasted his potential! His skill!"

"I would've?! You took him to your king, didn't you?!"

The Captain swiped the sword as Calypso deflected the blade with her own. The two circled one another while taking out one from the other's crew. Their eyes still locked onto each other as rain began to pour down upon them. The Captain laughed, taking in the scenery.

"The Jarokian will prove a useful ally to the King in ridding this planet of your crew's kind. Such nature cannot allow to continue."

"Who gave you the right to determine who lives and who dies?! Your King?!"

Calypso nodded.

"It's my job."

"Kill me and my crew here and now, and maybe we'll see if it's your job."

Calypso screamed as she rushed against the Captain with her sword. The two battled on the deck in the midst of their crews. The Captain laughed continually as Calypso screamed like a siren. The blades clashed and clashed as sparks flew from them. Calypso twirled the blade and kicked the Captain in the abdomen as he fell. Rushing over to impale him, one of the hybrids jumped onto Calypso's back, biting her in the shoulder. She screamed as she plunged the blade into the hybrid's chest. The Captain arose and fought back against Calypso. More hybrids went to intervene, only to be killed by Calypso's blade. The captain kept fighting as several of Calypso's pirates moved in to attack him. Only for his hybrids ambush them by biting their necks or impaling them with their tails.

"You cannot win." Calypso said. "You have no right."

"Again, who gave you the right to determine who wins and who loses? Oh, that's right. Your job."

Calypso went to strike the Captain again, yet, a large lightning bolt crashed into the waters. Startling everyone, even the Captain as he made his move toward the wheel of the ship. Calypso looked around, seeing everyone returning to their own ships. Even her crew was afraid.

"Where are you going?!" This battle is not over!"

"We must go, my lady!" One of her pirates said. "The gods, they're angry at us all. We're in danger if we stay out here!"

"You'll be in danger if you allow those savages to live!"

She stood over the edge of the hybrid's ship against her own. Calypso turned around as the Captain dropkicked her back onto her ship as his ship made their escape. Standing up in haste, she looked out seeing the hybrids' ship heading towards Vetor. Screaming in anger, she turned her attention toward her crew. Yelling for them to fight back against the hybrids. However, some refused stating the lightning bolt was a sign of a truce between the two forces. Believing the gods have called off the ongoing war. Calypso scoffed as she dug her blade into several of their chests. She looked at the remaining members of her crew.

"If you are not with me, then you are not with your King!"

The crew stared at her with fear. Uncertain for their lives as they saw her take out several of their own crew members. She walked in front of them, wielding the blood-soaked sword in their faces. The blood brought forth another essence of fear upon them. For they were more afraid of Calypso now than before.

"Make your choice now. Are you with me? Are you with the King? Or are you with those savages?"

The crew yelled they were with her and the king. Calypso nodded as she commanded them to toss the dead bodies over into the seas. Obeying her word, once the bodies fell into the waters, a massive sea creature arose, covered in dark emerald-like scales and its eyes were as bright as the sun. The beast gazed around the waters, seeing the bodies and took them deep into the seas with its mouth. The crew saw it and fell for fear as Calypso grinned, seeing it as a sign of their coming victory.

CHAPTER 7: A WAY HOME?

Vance walked through the palace after being given permission by Kharan. He was astounded by the architecture. By walking through the corridors, he was able to see more of the interior. Along his walk, he discovered more paintings across the walls. Only these walls depicted a great war between the hybrids and the royals. One of the figures in the painting was Kharan himself wielding a glowing trident made of sapphire. The trident was struck by lightning as he was clashing against a hybrid beast of man, lion, and serpent. Continuing his walk, Vance ran into Serilda, startling her and himself.

"Wasn't expecting to see you here." Vance said. "Especially during this time of night."

"I am the Princess. Therefore, I have permission to gad abroad."

"So I can see."

"It appears you have completed my father's tests."

"I did. And not to my liking. Although, his tests were a bit strange for me. Not that I am a fighter by any means. The knowledge tests with the scrolls was easy for me to overcome. The combat however, that was a challenge."

"And the spiritual test? Was that as challenging as well?"

"It was easy. Tough but easy."

"Explain to me how it was tough? And why?"

"Because, I don't speak much on my beliefs. Personality, I would prefer to keep them t myself. To avoid conflict."

"That's funny."

"How so?"

"Because we're taught to speak highly of our beliefs. It is those in which make us who we are. The things we do and the words we speak rely solely on the beliefs we share. If it were not for them, we would be vagabonds in the end. Heretics to a fallen cause."

Vance held his composure. He was amazed by the speech of a princess. Much less one who appeared physically to be so intelligent. Vance applauded her words of wisdom.

"You speak well. For someone like yourself."

"And they don't have women like me back on your world?"

"Women like you are a dying breed where I'm from. Although, there are a few every now and then. Scattered like the sands of the sea."

"Touching."

"It can't be all that bad." Vance said. "Seeing as how you're who you are. Your father must've done something well."

"He takes care of me and his people. It is his duty as king and as a father."

"Where is your mother?"

"She went off on some diplomatic duties to the west. The Kingdom of Nabel needed her guidance toward their concern regarding their women. My mother is skilled in setting places straight. To keep the balance in play."

"That's something worth knowing."

"I could tell you sense my father's rulings a bit harsh."

"In a sense. The ways he views the hybrids is something unnecessary. The hybrids only want to live in peace. They do not seek to fight."

"And how do you know this? Last I heard, you were aboard their ship. Possibly taken captive."

"No. I wasn't taken captive. They saved me."

"Saved you? From what?"

"My ship crashed. I was stranded on an island, and they arrived. Brought me in and treated me well. As best they could before they were attacked by Calypso and her crew."

"Ah, Calypso." Serilda said. "I'm surprised she still is seen in good spirits toward my father."

"Calypso told me she does well for your father's kingdom. She despises the hybrids just as much as he does."

"That much is certain. However, Calypso sees much more in this field of war than slaughtering any hybrids she comes across. She wants a place to rule."

"How are you aware of this?"

"Because I've been in council meetings before. Where she would be welcomed. Her words always spoke of some kind of rule. Whether it was an island to call her own or a kingdom to dwell. Ruler-ship is something is craves deeply and the killing of hybrids will not cease that desire."

"I see why she's the way she is."

"Anyhow, why are you walking through the halls of the palace?"

"Just taking a gander of things. I saw the painting in the throne room when I first arrived. Didn't know there were many more scattered throughout the place."

"You should check the library. There's much in there to grab your attention."

"There's a library here?"

"Of course. I will take you to it."

From there, Vance followed Serilda through several sets of corridors, passing by the guards who stood like statues. Entering the western portion of the palace, Serilda opened the large double-doors which appeared to be made of wood layered with coral. Within the room was the library. Nearly three floors filled with scrolls and maps. Scattered in the library were small statuettes of ships pertaining to Kharan's Navy and the Navy before his rule. Vance stood at the entrance, shaking his head in wonder.

"Endless amounts of scrolls."

"Indeed." Serilda chuckled. "Besides, only those permitted to the palace can step foot in this place."

"You mean the people outside have no entry into this library? For what cause?"

"It's a royal decree. The people have the Library of Vetoria to themselves within the city."

"But, what's the difference between them? One gets standard information while the other gains a little extra note."

"Some matters of this continent's history must be protected by the royals. It is the decree of the ancients. Their rule and my father continues it to this day."

Vance walked through the library, seeing the shelves of scrolls. Each shelf was detailed with a description. Some were focused on architecture. Others weaponry, history, technology, societal science, oceanography, cosmology, artistry, and spirituality. Serilda watched as Vance gazed at the shelves.

"If you're behavior like this over some scrolls, I can only imagine your reaction to the Science Hall."

"Science Hall?"

"Follow me."

He followed Serilda down another set of corridors, taking them to the northwest portion of the palace where the Science Hall remained. The doors were opened as Vance saw the technology without haste. The walls were layered with the energy guns. All in the shapes of handguns, rifles, machine guns, and even Gatling guns. Also on the wall were hung swords, staves, javelins, axes, maces, and three tridents. Each one a different design than the other. Serilda began to describe to him the purpose of the hall and how the technologists each operate within the hall unaware of those in or out of the palace. While she showed Vance around, a guard stepped forward at the entrance, calling for Serilda.

"Yes?"

"Your father requires your presence at the throne room."

"I'm on my way."

The guard made his leave as Serilda told Vance to continue looking around. He wouldn't have to worry about a thing with Serilda speaking for him. Serilda had left and Vance walked through the hall. Seeing the weapons and further through the hall, he saw the structure which he knew would be used to layer out the ships for the Navy. Further down, he caught the glimpse of something larger. Entering the hall, spotting the ceiling inching higher than before. Vance looked and saw his ship sitting in the larger room.

"How did they find this?"

Vance ran toward the ship and looked at it. The ship was polished. No cracks. No broken glass. The ship was restored. Vance stepped up the ladder and pressed the ignition and the ship activated. The ship was fully repaired. Vance took the moment to think. Now he can return to Earth. Vance looked ahead in the ship's targeted direction, seeing a pathway which led to the outside of the palace. The ship could take off and make the escape from there. Vance took the second to conjure a plan. While he planned his next move, the Captain of the Hybrids arrived in the city with his hybrids and they quickly made haste toward the palace. Clashing against the guards at every turn. Kharan is warned of their arrival as he spoke with Serilda. Kharan stood up from his throne and snatched his staff from the side of the seat.

"Remain in here until it is clear."

"Yes, Father."

Kharan's Navy battled the Captain and his hybrids during the nightfall as the people of the city slept. That is until they heard the bells gong and they awoke to the sound of battle cries and clashing swords. The people began to evacuate from the city and head into the country land, which was set outside of the city's jurisdiction. Some chose to evacuate by jumping into boats of their own. While they did, they were caught in a stumble as Calypso and her crew made their return. Jumping from their ship into the battle. Calypso moved with fierce as she searched the surroundings for the Captain. Unable to find him on the outside, she turned her focus toward the palace and made her steps there. Inside the science hall, Vance could hear the sounds of the battle taking place as he looked back and forth between his ship and the sounds of the swords.

CHAPTER 8: THE VANOKIAN PATH

The battles continued outside between the hybrids, Calypso's pirates, and Kharan's Navy Guards. Meanwhile, inside the palace. Kharan waited in the gardens as the Captain of the Hybrids arrived. Moving with speed as he stopped himself, seeing the King. The Captain stepped forward into the garden. Seeing the plants growing across the walls, as if they were hung there from the start. The Captain pointed and scoffed.

"Must be some work to get this done."

"Why are you here?"

"Why am I here? Because I'm looking. Looking for a friend of mine. The Jarokian."

"The Jarokian is here under my authority. What do you seek with him?"

"Um, what do I seek? Uh, a chance to speak with him. Tell him to choose his path."

"What path?"

"Simple. He can either come with me and help the hybrids reclaim their territory or he can remain with you and eventually die under your rule."

"The Jarokian can handle himself. I've seen it firsthand."

"So, he can fight!" The Captain yelled. "That's even better. I knew he had it in him!"

Kharan slammed his staff into the ground and quickly before the Captain's sights, the staff transformed into a trident. The trident sparked with lightning as thunder roared from above.

"Such legends are true I see."

"Leave my palace!" Kharan yelled. "Take your hybrids with you before I have them all killed."

"Good sir, they are well prepared to die. Just as I."

The Captain's rapier clashed against Kharan's trident as the lightning traveled across weapons, shocking the Captain's hand. Kharan grinned as he twirled the trident and struck it into the ground, causing the lightning to move with speed and strike at the Captain's feet. He jumped over the bolts before they turned back toward him. He grabbed his rapier and scrapped the ground, taking the lightning onto his blade and holding it out toward Kharan.

"I know a few tricks as well."

The two faced off as Calypso rushed into the garden, seeing them staring down with both weapons pointed. She screamed for the Captain as she ran toward him with sword in hand. The Captain moved out of her path as Kharan threw his trident toward the Captain. He looked back and ducked own as the trident struck into the marble wall. He laughed.

"Two against one?! That's not fair. You need help."

The three of them looked at each other. The trident bolted back as the Captain ducked quickly, seeing the trident return to Kharan's hand. The Captain never seen a weapon do such a thing and took his leave. Calypso ran after him. While she chased him, Vance entered the battle, clashing against the guards and aiding the hybrids. Calypso saw him and anger fueled her as she ran toward him.

"You help them?!"

"I have to. It must be done."

"You choose the path of the Majority! For what cause have you grown such a hatred for yourself?!"

"It's not hatred. It's honesty."

"Then you know I have to kill you."

"I know you'll try. But, this night will not e the time."

Calypso glared toward Vance as the sound of an explosion shook the city. Calypso turned back, seeing how the explosion erupted from the palace as she ran inside. The guards followed as the hybrids made their escape. Vance escorted them back to their ship as he saw the Captain retreating from the palace. He rushed toward him.

"The Jarokian still lives!"

"What just happened?"

"I set off something that might get their attention. I see you are helping my crew."

"I am."

"Then you are with us?"

"I am."

"Then get onboard! Before the guards return."

Vance jumped onto the ship as they made their escape. The following morning, the city streets were filed with dead guards, pirates, and hybrids. Kharan called for a search for Vance, believing him to have been taken by the Captain. Although, Calypso's words urged him to find Vance and kill him since she believes he was the cause for the explosion. Serilda stood back and watched the conversation between her father and Calypso. While they spoke, the guards entered.

"My King. You have visitors."

"Visitors?" Kharan said with confusion. "Bring them in."

At the entrance to the throne room came three men. Dressed in fine robes of silver. Their eyes were as pale as the moon and their demeanor was one of a foreign stature. They bowed before Kharan, showing him reverence.

"Who are you?"

"We come from a place afar. We seek someone who is here unwillingly and uninvited."

"Who do you speak of?" Calypso asked.

"We know of the Jarokian. Of how he came on this planet and the actins he's done. We even know of his blasphemous believes toward the gods."

"Just why are you searching fro him?" Kharan wondered.

"Because he is a disruption to the balance. He must be found before the dark forces of Vanok arise and consume you all."

"How do the three of you know all of this?" Calypso questioned. "Where are you from?"

"Again, we're from a place afar. Find the Jarokian before the dark forces begin to return."

The three robed ones left the throne room, leaving Kharan and Calypso lost for words. Meanwhile, Vance stood out on the deck of the ship as they headed out into the open seas. The Captain walked over toward him, holding a map.

"Where are we headed?" Vance asked.

"A little place south of Aphro. There's some things there that must be done."

"I understand."

Vance looked out toward the sea and nodded. He knew he would be on Vanok for a while. A new life. A new adventure awaited.

PRAXUS OF LITHONIA

CHAPTER I

In the early years, there was a kingdom.

A kingdom known as Bandoria.

Bandoria was a kingdom of great wealth and power as was its ruler, King Bantos. Many who had lived in Bandoria were truly successful in their lives, both personally and financially. Even though the rich had lived in Bandoria, there was another kingdom on the outskirts. A kingdom much smaller than the glory of Bandoria's towers and high walls. A kingdom which held a great many people. This kingdom is Lithonia. Lithonia was the sister kingdom to Bandoria, but did not share the rich and powerful delicacies of Bandoria's stature. Majority of the poor had dwelled in the walls of Lithonia, only due to the fact of not being allowed through the walls and onto the grounds of Bandoria.

One day, King Bantos had stepped out and gazed over the balcony of his palace. Looking out toward all the kingdom in its glory. As far out as his eye could wander. Glaring ahead, Bantos caught the glimmering light outside of the kingdom walls. He knew the light had sparked from Lithonia and his anger was quenched.

"This is my kingdom and these lands will belong to me." Bantos said toward his Vizier who stood beside him.

"My lord, what are your plans in overtaking the Lithonians from their kingdom? What of their king? What of their warriors?"

"We have hundreds of warriors prepped for battle, do we not?"

"Yes, my lord. Yes we do."

"Then we need not worry. That dirt-filled place they call a kingdom will be ours soon enough."

During these early years of the war between Bandoria and Lithonia, there was a great falling of many warriors on both sides. In another place within the boundaries of Lithonia, there was a woman who was known as Arinia who had given birth to a son. Her husband, Krotax, a warrior in the clan of Lithonians proclaimed his son's name as Praxus. A Lithonian name and in the Lithonian tongue meant *"ruler and conqueror"*. through the wars, they lived a happy life, even in the times of hardship and trouble from the Bandorian forces. They watched their son grow older through the conflicts.

Praxus himself in his youth became helpful to those in need as he watched Bandorian warriors invade their homes and slaughter the innocent. In one altercation, Praxus took it upon himself and slew two Bandorian warriors with his bare hands, proving to those who witnessed and his mother and father he possessed near superhuman strength. Once he became an adult, he volunteered in the battle against Bantos' forces and witnessed the death of his mother and father by Bantos' own hand. That day was the defeat of Lithnoia and it had fully become under the control of Bandoria.

Ever since their deaths, Praxus went into hiding in the undergrounds of Lithonia. Places Bantos and his advisors had possessed no knowledge of their existence. Gathering other mighty men and women of valor who saw Praxus' strength in times past. They came together and sought to overthrow Bantos and take by Lithonia for the people and to free the bonds of Bandoria from any other lands they may have conquered. Praxus made a vow to avenge the deaths of his people and his mother and father by killing Bantos himself and conquering Bandoria for the taking.

It all begins this day.

CHAPTER II

Now, Praxus and his small army of warriors had made their journey eastward, toward the Kingdom of Brithrow. A providence of Bandoria.

"What are we looking for, Praxus?" a soldier asked.

"Anything that could lead us to King Bantos." Praxus said.

"Then, why are we heading towards the Kingdom of Brithrow? I'm not sure on what you have planned."

"When we enter the gates of Brithrow, you'll see what my plans comes into being."

Riding along through the valleys, they come to a stop and find themselves facing the gates of the Kingdom of Brithrow. Standing by the gates are the Brithrowian Knights, dressed in their iron-clad armor and helmets. Their stained swords held in their hands and pressed against their chests. Their eyes are solely focused on Praxus and those of the Lithionian army. One knight made his way toward Praxus. Walking calmly, yet nervous.

"Might I ask why you have decided to come?"

"I've come to speak with your king." Praxus answered. "He and I are on good terms with one another and I would be pleased to speak to him."

The knight nodded and waved his right hand, signaling the knights to open the gates of the kingdom. The knights slowly open the gates as Praxus and his army enter into the kingdom. The residents of the kingdom look and see Praxus and his army coming through the kingdom, their horses moving with pace as they approached the castle of Brithrow's king, King Brithon. From the castle doors, walked out Brithon. His gaze looked around as he could hear the sounds of the horses and immediately turned to see Praxus and his army coming toward him.

"My, my. We have visitors." Brithon said.

Praxus' horse stopped in front of the castle. He looked at Brithon, whose standing at the doorway. Praxus gets off his horse and walked up the stony steps to approach Brithon. Brithon made his way to greet Praxus and they greet one another. As if they are close friends.

"Praxus of Lithonia has come to visit me."

"It is for an urgent matter."

"Come inside. We can talk there."

Praxus and Brithon enter into the castle walls as the Brithrow servants take Praxus' horse and his army's horses to their staples to rest up. The army followed the servants to the inside of the castle where they would be fed. Inside the castle, Praxus and Brithon talked about the current situations across the lands. Brithon already knows of the reasons for Praxus' rise in appearances ad why he's come to his kingdom on a short notice.

"I know why you've come here."

"Then you are aware that this is no time for any games to be played."

"I know you want to see King Bantos and his reign come to an end."

"I want his head impaled onto the tip of my sword."

"I figured as much. Which is why I have an offer for you concerning these dire matters."

"What is the offer you proposed?"

"That you aid me in your assistance against Bantos and his army. Granted, you know this Battle of Kings cannot last much longer."

Praxus thought to himself, detailing the proposal and what it would allow him to do, to get into Bandor and kill Bantos himself to avenge his parents' deaths. He nodded, facing Brithon. Praxus extended his arm in agreement.

"I shall assist you in this battle."

"Wonderful! When they see the two of us on the battlefield facing them, only fear will grab them by their throats and feed them to us."

"I do have one condition regarding this agreement of ours."

"Tell me."

"When we find Bantos, leave him to me."

Brithon nodded with a smile on face. He enjoys seeing the savagery coming through Praxus' words. He knew that he would be the right man to tag along with when it comes to war. Brithon extended his arm and the two came to an agreement. The deal was finalized.

"Agreed."

Praxus and his army remained within the Kingdom of Brithrow for the remainder of the day and spend the night within the kingdom. During those hours, Praxus and Brithon spoke to each other concerning the art of war and the use of weapons in the warfare. Praxus' army feasted and even laid with women that night. Praxus, on the other hand continue to have conversations with Brithon and they later went their separate ways to rest for the mission ahead.

CHAPTER III

The sun had risen and from the castle doors walked out Praxus and his army. They were prepared for the battle ahead. Brithon had approached Praxus from behind and patted him on his back. The two armies were easily to be told apart. Praxus' army dressed in simple garb. Loincloths of leather and fur with armbands and leather-padded boots. Some carried swords as the others wielded bows and arrows. Brithon's army were like a pack of wolves moving in a single-file line. Horned helmets and glistening armor. Swords bulging from their sides and arrows sharp on their backs.

"I surely hope that we can finish Bandor's army off before we come into conflict with him."

"Trust me, we will get through his army. They won't stand a chance."

Praxus and his army get atop their horses and gallop with Brithon and his army following them as they exit his kingdom. While they rode off, Praxus knew that Bantos was in his sights and he wouldn't let anyone or anything get in his way. Brithon's horse managed to catch up to Praxus.

"When we reach Bantos and his army, Praxus, I want you to know that whatever happens, happens."

"That's fair."

"I know for a fact that Bantos will indeed be present on the battlefield. But, he may have brought himself some form of assistance."

"What kind of assistance would he have?"

"We'll know once we get there."

"I understand."

Riding closer toward the field, in the distance one of Praxus' solders managed to catch a glimpse at the soaring army of Bantos. Pointing ahead, they each stare toward the field and see the soldiers moving in succession with the faint sound of chanting echoing through the air across the mountains of the valley. Praxus stopped and rallied his army to cease their movements. Brithon seeing this had done the same.

"What are they saying?" Praxus asked.

"I can't make it out. I know it's a war cry."

"Hmm. They know we're here. I can see that. Where's Bantos? Can you see him through the mess that is his army?"

Brithon took a gander toward the field in which was before them. The field itself laid near the Bandorian Jungle. A place filled with dwelling creatures of immense size. Although, no sign of the ravenous beasts were seen, Brithon believed Bantos had managed to keep them at bay for the battle ahead. Still looking, Brithon spotted one horsemen suited in armor from his head to his feet. An armor unlike the leather and metal pads which the other soldiers wore. With a single nod, Praxus knew the answer and rode down the valley toward the field as his army followed.

The armies moved with haste to reach the field as Bantos himself saw their arrival. His soldiers chanting had went still. Their hands attached to their swords and spears as Bantos rode forward to meet the opposing armies. Their numbers did not bother the Bandorian king, only amused him for a day of slaughter. Praxus and Brithon reached the field, stopping mere feet in front of Bantos and his army. Praxus' eyes seared with anger and Brithon knew it, waving his hands for Praxus to control himself.

"I am amused and yet surprised you managed to accept this battle." Bantos chuckled. "You even brought yourself some reinforcements. Only goes to show you knew this day would be your last."

"I don't think this day is my end." Brithon replied. "You see, my backup came to me to confront you themselves. Their leader, Praxus seeks to bring a better world for his people."

"His people? And who are his people?"

"Lithonians." Praxus answered boldly. "You massacred many of them during your conflicts of conquest."

"I did what a king would have done. I simply conquered lands suited for the better."

"And killing innocent men, women, and children was part of your conquest? The soldiers weren't enough? The warriors weren't proven enough?"

"Praxus, control yourself." Brithon whispered.

Bantos took a look toward Praxus. His eyes keen as he rubbed his chin.

"Have I done something to you in the past, boy?"

"You've done enough."

"Afraid I haven't. I won't be finished until all kingdoms belong to me. Your friend, Brithon's kingdom is just the next one on my list. Damn Brithrowians nor a pair of savage Lithonians will stop me from my conquest."

Praxus took out his sword, holding it high as his army follows. Dozens of swords for Bantos and his army to see. A grin grew on the face of the Bandorian king as he shouted for his soldiers to attack. The armies went and clashed their blades one o another. Bantos did not flee the battleground as some leaders in times past. This king was deep into the fight, slaughtering Brithrowians and Lithonians with ease. Even for someone of his older age. Praxus moved swiftly through the battlefield, taking out Bandorian soldiers like practice. Their heads slicing off their bodies and falling into the bloody grass. Praxus huffed as he moved with haste toward Bantos.

Over next to where Praxus walked, Brithon fought alongside his soldiers and the Lithonian warriors. The fight became bloodier as the minutes had passed. Praxus sliced his way closer to Bantos as he saw him take out three Lithonians with one blow. An impressive feat even in Praxus' eyes. With the three bodies falling to the ground, Bantos looked up and saw Praxus standing before him. Fire in his eyes. Anger boiling beyond its point.

"I did something to you, didn't I?" Bantos asked.

"You took my mother and father from this life. Robbed me of my heritage."

"Did I? Well, get in line with the others who have said the same and die for their honor."

"The only one dying today is you and your rule!"

"Make it so, savage!'

Praxus with anger in his forefront rushed toward Bantos, swiping his sword against Bantos' own. The two stepped back in the midst of the dying screams and flying sprays of blood across the field. Bantos relished in the moment while Praxus continued to let his anger control him. Stepping with speed and haste, Praxus slammed his sword against Bantos as the Bandorian king deflected the blows and kicked the knee of Praxus, knocking him back before Bantos delivered an elbow swipe to the Lithonian's forehead.

"Your anger. It's getting the better of you. Better get it in place, boy, before you end up killing yourself."

"Enough of your damn talking! Fight me!"

Praxus immediately rose to his feet, his sword in hand facing forward as he stretched out toward Bantos and ended up tapping his sword against Bantos' own. A chuckle echoed from the mouth of the Bandorian king as he shoved Praxus back. A grunt of anger busted from the Lithonia as he went for another strike toward Bantos. The king ducked, only for Praxus to be taken down by a heavy blow. A blow which originated from a war hammer. Bantos nodded with a grin as he looked forward, seeing the wielder of the hammer. A towering figure who stood over the height of three Bandorian soldiers. The hammer itself had to have weighed nearly as one of the Bandorian soldiers.

"Figured you would be here."

"I would do anything for you, my king."

The sound of the battle continued on as Bantos knelt down, checking Praxus' pulse. The Lithonian lives. Bandos sighed as he stood up and sheathed his blade. The hammer wielder looked down at Praxus and raised the hammer.

"Do you wish me to end him?"

"Don't." Bantos said. "No need in killing the boy. Death is too sweet for him to savor. Living will do the job."

Lowering the hammer, the wielder and Bantos looked out toward the ongoing remains of the battle. Allowing the wielder to enter the fight, he moved and quickly decimated the Lithonians and Brithowians with ease. Their combined efforts could not match the strength of the wielder and his hammer. Within minutes of the fight, Bantos' army had appeared to have won. Seeing the dead bodies of Lithonians and

Brithowians on the ground covered in blood. Some without their heads or insides. Bantos saw the day as a victory and rallied his remaining soldiers to return to Bandoria.

Upon their leave, Brithon arose from a pile of bodies with several living soldiers of his own and a few Lithonians who managed to survive.
"Where's Praxus?" Brithon asked. "Where is he?"
Moving through the bodies, they searched the fields for Praxus and were seemly unable to find him. It was as if he vanished from the battlefield without notice. Knowing Praxus is the kind of warrior who would survive the utmost impossible odds, Brithon in his tired state gathered his soldiers and the Lithonians as they agreed to return to his kingdom in hopes of sending out a unit to find Praxus.

Deep in the night, hours after the battle. Praxus awoke and found himself inside of a cave. A cave he was unfamiliar with. In front of him, a fire bellowed. A fire he did not conjure nor make. Attempting to stand on his feet, his back pulsed with pain as he dropped to his knees.
"Do not make a move." said a voice from the darkness of the cave.
"Who's there?" Praxus questioned. "Step into the light and show yourself."
"Is that what you crave?"
"Tell me who you are and why am I here?"
"Very well, Lithonian."
The voice moved from the darkness and into the light. Revealing himself to Praxus. A cloaked being dressed in a violet garb. Yet, like a shadow in his movements. His face unseen, yet a mystic power flowed from his very being. He approached the fire and knelt down in front of it. Siphoning some of the flames into his hands. Transferring the energy of the heat into himself.
"You're a sorcerer." Praxus said.
"Good of you to notice."
"I was taught to abhor those like you. Sorcerers are evil and have only done evil to suit their deeds."
"Such is true for many. Such am I. yet; I will not do the deed of evil

this night. For it is not the time."

Praxus sat up and leaned against the cavern walls. Pressing his back against the rocky walls.

"What are you saying?"

"We were destined to meet this night. It was written thousands of years ago and now, it has come to pass."

"Who are you?"

"I am known as Dakin Maul. A sorcerer who desires this world to be in the hands of my kind."

"I've never heard of you."

"You have now. It is destined for us to be mortal enemies. A man of your barbaric stature could only be a perfect match for a sorcerer like myself. A battle for the ages."

"Then, how come you didn't kill me? Why pull me from the battlefield and bring me here?"

"Because it was not your time to die. Not yet."

"So, was it you who hit me?"

"No. that was Roht. A massive warrior who works under the rulership of King Bantos. He's the one who knocked you unconscious and he sought to kill you, but Bantos spared you. Yet, I already knew of this before it happened."

"Enough of this sorcery talk. Why am I here?"

"To heal. You must return to Brithon to reveal your safe and alive."

"I want Bantos. Where is he?"

"He returned to his kingdom as he should. Don't worry yourself, you'll have your moment with him very soon."

"Answer this for me. Since you know the future, tell me. Do I kill Bantos?"

"Yes," Dakin said with a calm voice.

"Do I kill him soon?"

"I will not say. Just know you indeed kill him and save the kingdoms from the tyrant. When you kill him, I will not reveal."

Praxus leaned his head back and pondered on the thoughts. Dakin knew he was pondering as he showed a faint smirk on his face as it could be seen due to the kindling fire beneath him.

"I need to get going."

"You will remain here for the night. Let your body heal and by the morning light, you shall arise and make your way to Brithon continue your journey."

"And where will you be?"

"I'll be around. It is my destiny to observe you. To learn your skill set for our coming battle. A battle of might versus magic."

"I'll be looking forward to it." Praxus said coldly.

Dakin let out an echoing laugh to Praxus' distaste. A laughter one would deem sinister. A cunning laughter.

"I'm sure you will. As for right now, it is best you sleep."

Dakin reached over and tapped his finger on Praxus' forehead, placing him into a deep sleep.

"We will meet again." Dakin said as he moved back into the darkness of the cave.

CHAPTER IV

The next morning had arisen and Praxus had awoken. Immediately rising to his feet to find Dakin Maul. Hearing no sound within the cave and the fire which was before him had become a shallow pile of burnt wood. The peeking light of the sun touched Praxus' face as he grabbed his sword that was placed against the cavern walls and made his way out. Upon returning to the outside, Praxus stared out into the field of decayed bodies. The remains of the soldiers from the battle before. Their flesh being ripped and torn apart by the Bandorian birds. Feathers as dark as the night. Talons as large as a warrior's boot and beaks sharper than the metal one warrior could wield. There were three of them in the field, yet unaware of Praxus' movements as he stealthy moved past them to avoid a great conflict. One which might bring forth his death if Dakin's words were false.

Praxus took several more steps before he reached the other end of the field. Taking the final step, he pressed into the ground as he paused. His quick pause had slid the dirt under his boot, alerting one of the massive birds. The bird walked toward Praxus as the Lithonia raised up his sword and pointed it toward the creature. The two locked eyes as the bird measured Praxus. In such a close range, the bird stood nearly six feet higher than Praxus. Taking in his scent. Praxus waited for the right moment to strike and the bird raised up its head and let out a small cough before turning away and returning to the dead bodies. Praxus sighed and sheathed his sword, turning away to leave the fields.

Sometime later, King Brithon rested in his castle back in Brithrow. His men moving back and forth from the doors, giving their king details on the remains of his soldiers and the whereabouts of Praxus. Brithon had hoped Praxus indeed survived the battle as he knew the savage Lithonian had the potential to tear down Bantos' tyrannical rule. As one of the soldiers entered the castle, he came with a sense of urgency. Brithon arose from his seat and faced his soldier. He knew what was to come as he stepped forward and walked outside. Looking ahead toward the kingdom's gates, he saw a horse galloping toward him. The rider as he could tell had come from the field. The closer the rider came, the more he knew. A few more inches the rider rode forward and Brithon showed a smile. A smile of relief and hope.

"He's alive."

Praxus stepped from the horse and greeted Brithon and the soldiers who gathered around. Looking at the soldiers, Praxus even saw some of the Lithonian warriors who stood by his side remaining and they saluted one another as brothers-in-arms. With their greetings, Brithon allowed Praxus into the castle to rest up as he could see the tiredness in his eyes, yet his body was full of energy. Entering the king's throne room, the handmaidens had brought the two men wine to drink. Praxus gulped down the drink within seconds and asked for more to the king's pleasure.

"It is good you survived." Brithon said. "Tell me what happened."

"It was simple. I confronted Bantos on the field. Fought him. I believe I had him defeated until I was struck by a heavy blow."

"Struck by who?"

"A warrior called Roht. I was told he was Bantos' right-hand soldier in his rule."

"Who told you this?"

"A sorcerer who aided me without my knowing. A strange fellow. Called himself Dakin Maul."

"Dakin Maul. That's a name I haven't heard in ages. He's still here and around our region."

"I don't know. When I awoke inside the cave, he was gone. Nowhere to be found."

Brithon sighed as he took a sip of the wine, leaning back in his chair.

"Dakin Maul saved you. That's something I've not known him to do. He must have favor in you."

"Said it wasn't my time to die. That he and I have a battle in the future between my strength and his magic."

"Ah. His prophecies speak once more. He's always been the prophetic kind. Telling those of their futures, only for them to come to pass in a way they did not expect."

"So, he was telling the truth? About our battle to come and that I will kill Bantos?"

"What Dakin Maul speaks is the truth in unrighteousness. Only time will unveil what truth will come of it."

Praxus drank more of the wine. Brithon hesitated to tell him to slow down and avoid becoming drunk in his presence. Praxus respected the king's word and took his time. After a while, Brithon informed Praxus of Bantos' return to Bandoria and how he's seeking to rally more soldiers from other lands to take Brithrow from his hands. Praxus lets out his word that he will kill Bantos and he will not wait years to accomplish the goal. Preparing himself to ride out before nightfall that he would arrive in Bandoria to confront Bantos and kill him before the morning broke. Brithon understood Praxus' motivations and agreed with him.

"What do you need me to do?" Brithon asked.

"I cannot allow you to lead yourself and your men into more danger. Bandoria is full of killers who only slaughter for pleasure. I can sneak in alone and deal with whatever forces come my way."

"You can. Meanwhile, myself and a few soldiers of mine will keep the others busy. To give you time to reach Bantos. I heard he speaks a frequent amount of time in his throne room."

Praxus grinned and nodded, extended his arm toward Brithon.

"Then, it's settled."

The two men agreed to the plan and began making moves. Praxus walked outside and gazed upon the sky, seeing the sun reaching west, he left for Bandoria as Brithon and ten of his soldiers each rode out behind Praxus.

Riding out toward the gates of Bandoria by nightfall, Praxus' anger began to bellow within. Brithon looked ahead and saw the guards standing at the gates. He knew if they could take them out, it would give Praxus a better appointee of entering. Praxus agreed to the plan as he made his way toward the gates, sneaking past them by swimming in the moat around. Brithon and his soldiers approached the two guards at the gated entrance.

"Stop. Identity yourselves."

"We come from Brithrow to deliver news to your beloved King Bantos." Brithon spoke.

"And who might you be?"

"The King of Brithrow."

The soldiers paused themselves as their hands dropped down to their swords. Behind them, Praxus arose from the water as his sword moved through the cool air and slashed greatly with his blade, decapitating the soldiers with ease. Impressing even Brithon and his soldiers.

"You move quick."

"We have no choice." Praxus answered. "Otherwise, we'll all be dead."

The soldiers moved to the gate, opening it for Praxus and themselves to enter. The gate opened with a gentle ease as they looked ahead, seeing the city streets clear of civilians and soldiers. Praxus' eyes looked forward toward the massive palace in the distance. He knew Bantos was there and within.

"I'm going for it."

"Be careful, Lithonian." Brithon said. "We'll handle things out here in case it escalates."

Praxus moved through the city, passing by sleeping soldiers and drunken men who relished in the sight of the whores around them. Bantos saw them as a way of keeping the people under his control and he was right. Praxus knew it to be true, seeing the people had no sign of life within their eyes. Their bodies were living , but their souls were drained. Only the faintest sign and taste of pleasure could keep them at bay. No chance of fighting back against Bantos' power. Looking up toward the steps to reach the palace, Praxus ran forward. Nearly thirty steps he reached without fail.

Standing foot on the palace grounds, he moved quietly to avoid the soldiers who patrolled the area. Using the banners and curtains as his way of moving and hiding, Praxus could hear the soldiers talking amongst themselves. Speaking of the battle prior and hw they wished they kill Brithon and took Brithrow for themselves. Continuing his move deeper into the palace as Brithon and the soldiers inched closer to the palace grounds, Praxus moved as he heard the swift sound of a swinging hammer. Hiding behind the wall, he peeked through the curtain and saw Roht standing in the center of the interior garden to the palace.

"You can quit your hiding, Lithonian." Roht spoke. "My king informed me of your arrival would be soon enough."

Praxus stepped from the wall and walked out through the curtain, facing off against Roht. Seeing him in full. A tall brute. His hammer much larger than his sword. Roht scoffed at the sight of Praxus.

"I could've killed you on the field, yet, my king told me not to."

"His foolish decision and his downfall." Praxus said. "All by his own words."

"I think not. This night it will be you falling before his feet after I pummel you with my hammer. The same hammer which knocked you down before."

"What happened before was a cheap blow. This time, I see clearly. Bantos was my only target this night. However, because of your sneak blow, I'll kill you as well."

"Come then." Roht slammed the hammer. "Give your best blow."

Praxus roared, running toward Roht with his sword swinging. Roht deflected the metal with his hammer and kicked Praxus in the abdomen, striking him once more with the top of the hammer, causing him to tremble and fall to the marbled floor. Roht laughed, backing away for Praxus to stand up.

"I will not kill a Lithonian while he's on his back. Stand up and face me once more!"

Praxus gripped his sword and showed a smirk, running toward Roht once more as the brute swung the hammer. Praxus saw the coming attack and slid under the weapon, slashing the left leg of Roht with this sword. The pain shot through his lower body as Praxus elbowed Roht in the chest and kicked him in his abdomen. To his dismay, Roht's flesh felt a similar toughness to a bull. Roht stumbled in his steps, yet maintained his balance.

"Should've worn more armor." Praxus said. "Leaving yourselves bare only give you a weakness."

"Yet, you're barely covered in metal."

"I don't need metal to survive. I'm a Lithonian. All we need is leather, furs, and steel."

Roht raised the hammer above Praxus and went for a pummeling slam. Praxus moved from the hammer's path and threw his sword toward Roht. Straightforward, the blade pierced Roht in his chest. Roht looked at the sword in his chest and pulled it out as the blood oozed from the wound. Throwing the sword to the ground, Roht dropped his hammer and cracked his knuckles.

"Fair play." Praxus said, balling up his fists and stomping his feet.

The two swipe attacks onto one another. Praxus delivering several punches to the face of Roht as the brute snatched Praxus by his hair and dragged him across the garden. Taking his head and shoving it into the dirt of the field. Praxus kicked Roht in the wound of his leg and gasped for air as he rose up from the dirt. Praxus grabbed Roht by his beard and returned the favor, holding his head into the dirt before stomping on the back of his head. Roht rose up, shoving Praxus back as he wiped the dirt from his face and spit onto Praxus' chest. A complete show of disrespect to his own humor. Blood pouring from them both. They clashed once again with punches to the face and kicks to the legs. The sound echoed resembled two beasts clashing in the fields. Praxus slowed down to Roht's pleasure and uppercutted the Lithonian to the ground. Praxus took the moment to catch his breath as he heard the laughter coming from Roht.

"They said Lithonians were savages. Bred for battle. Yet, I look at you and wonder if such a tale is true."

Praxus flipped onto his feet and stared Roht in the eyes with a grin.

"The tales are true. I'm their living embodiment."

Praxus leaped onto Roht and pummeled his face, bringing the brute to his knees. Praxus roared as he kicked Roht in the head, causing him to fall to the floor. Praxus paused and looked down at Roht, seeing he's still breathing. Praxus turned away, looking towards the throne room ahead.

"Where are you going?" Roht said coughing. "You'll have to kill me before you face my king."

"I'm here for him. Not you."

"Either way. You die or we all die."

Praxus looked around and retrieved his sword, sheathing it. Roht screamed continually for Praxus to kill him. Praxus went for his sword and paused. Leaving it be. Instead, he turned to the floor and saw Roht's hammer and lifted the massive weapon to Roht's surprise.

"You cannot be that strong. There is no way."

"Yet, you see it before your very eyes. Your time above this ground is finished. Now, go to your gods. Whomever they be."

Praxus raised the hammer and slammed it atop Roht's head to the sound of a cracking whip. A moment of silence moved through the garden as Praxus looked toward his hands and released the hammer from his hands and turned toward the throne room. Walking slowly as he wiped the blood from his face.

CHAPTER V

Praxus took his steps toward the entrance to the throne room. Hearing the beating sound of distant drums and the flowing sensation of water, Praxus looked around him as he saw several waterfalls on the walls. Facing him was the throne seat and within it was Bantos. A chuckle muffled from his mouth as he rose up and applauded the Lithonian for his arrival.

"I knew it wouldn't take you long to defeat Roht. He was a tough warrior in my ranks. However, I've always known his skill could be outwitted by someone of a much quicker speed."

"Roht was not in my sights to kill. I had to take him out to get to you. You're the reason I'm here this night."

"Well then, savage one. Here I am and a sword I hold in my hand. The question is, will you strike me down before I do the same to you?"

"One of us will meet our god this day and I believe it will be you."

"Let's make it so." Bantos grinned.

Bantos swung with a right swing of his sword, clashing the steel against Praxus' own sword. A smile grew on the Lithonian's face as he shoved off Bantos' sword and sliced down toward the Bandorian's abdomen. Stepping back to look, Praxus let out a quick scoff.

"Are you worried? All men bleed."

"You forget, Lithonian. I am not all men." Bantos glared. "I am above all men!"

"Best to show it than to speak it."

The two clashed their blades once more with a more forceful push from Bantos, stumbling Praxus toward one of the waterfalls. The sound of the flowing waters increased in Praxus' ears as Bantos continued to push him closer. Bantos turned his gaze toward the waterfall and back to Praxus. A thought entered his mind as he let go of Praxus and kicked him into the waterfall. Praxus rose up as the water fell onto him. Stepping forward, Bantos rushed in and grabbed the Lithonian by his neck, holding him down in the water.

"Let's see how long you can live without a moment's breath." Bantos laughed.

Praxus struggled against the might of Bantos. For a man who appeared to be nearly of old age, his strength was of a young man. A peculiar trait in Bandoria. Praxus pushed with his chest, raising up from the water to Bantos' dismay. However, Bantos pressed his boot atop the back of Praxus, shoving him back into the water.

"Just give up." Bantos chuckled. "Accept this death and wander the afterlife with pondering questions of an alternative."

Praxus screamed as the bubbles rose to the surface. With enough strength in him, Praxus shoved off Bantos and arose from the water. His arms stretched and his fists gripped.

"What?" Bantos questioned with fear. "Such strength from a Lithonian is not possible. It is not."

He turned to face Bantos as the Bandorian king went to retrieve his sword from the floor. It was not quick enough as Praxus lunged onto him and pummeled his face in with punches. Praxus continued the blows even as Bantos attempted to block them with his arms and hands. Praxus stood up and kicked Bantos in the chest. Turning back, Praxus went and grabbed his sword and raised it above the neck of Bantos.

"If this is my end, let it be a quick one." Bantos said. "Otherwise, you'll end up dead sooner than I."

"Enough. Your end has come."

Praxus rose up his sword for the kill and setting to make their mark, seven Bandorian soldiers bolted into the throne room with sword sin hand. Without hesitation, they saw their king on the floor and Praxus standing over him with his sword near his neck. The soldiers screamed as they attacked the Lithonian to save their king. Praxus fought back against the soldiers, swinging his sword to their own surprise. The Bandorian soldiers are used to their enemies quickly submitting when there's more than four. However, such was not possible with Praxus. For his is a Lithonian and Lithonians do not fear numbers. They do not fear anything aside from their own failures and dismays. Praxus gripped the hilt of the sword and impaled one soldier into another. Pressing their bodies against the wall as they fell into one of the waterfalls. Turning to the remaining five, Praxus moved with speed, hacking and slashing his blade against their thighs and forearms. It was within a matter of minutes in which Praxus had slaughtered the soldiers. Their bodies lying on the clear marble floor with the blood pouring through like spilled wine.

"Now to finish you off." Praxus said, turning around to face Bantos.

Bantos was gone. No longer was he lying on the floor within his throne room. Praxus turned around and searched the room with haste. No sign of Bantos caused a yell to echo from Praxus. Sounding off throughout the palace and reaching the peek of the city. Even Brithon and his soldiers heard the roar of the Lithonian.

"I wonder if he accomplished the goal." Brithon said to himself.

Praxus looked at the dead soldiers around him as he could hear the running footsteps of more soldiers incoming. Taking the moment to see the throne seat, Praxus carved a mark into the seat as he made his escape just in time before the soldiers arrived. While the soldiers signaled the city to search for the Lithonian, Praxus had returned to the outside where he was greeted by Brithon and his soldiers.

"Did you do it?" Brithon asked.

"I was close. His men were onto me before I could take the strike."

"So, he still lives."

"Yes. But, not for long. He's wounded."

Hearing the bell sounding as the noise of the rustling civilians began to scream, Praxus and Brithon took their leave. Returning to Brithrow. It was only a matter of days when Bantos sent out the decree for all his soldiers to find Praxus and to bring him to the palace for his sentence. A sentence which would only be death under Bantos' rule. Praxus was informed of the decree by several of his Lithonian spies.

"If he wants me, he'll have to find me." Praxus said. "Or, when I find him."

Elsewhere in the far regions of the land, word had spread of a familiar, yet mysterious weapon was discovered near the hills of the Megarian Mountains. Praxus heard the news and grinned with pleasure. Speaking to his Lithonian brethren, Praxus had set out to uncover this mysterious weapon and plotted to use it against Bantos to bring a full end to his tyranny. Praxus had spoken with Brithon concerning the quest as Brithon had begun to warn him of the dangers which rests near the Megarian Mountains. Threats from giant beasts, savage dwellers, mercenaries seeking challengers, and even the legendary Valley of the Lost. All would bring fear upon a normal man, yet, Praxus of Lithonia was not an ordinary man. He is a man of strength, speed, and valor. Loyal to his cause and to his people and allies.

Praxus had prepared himself for the journey as he gathered his equipment and sharpened his sword. Hearing of more powerful threats which may challenge him only gave him the excitement of a fight. The words of Dakin Maul still lingered in his mind. Their meeting was soon to come if the sorcerer's words were deemed true. That is only something Praxus can ponder on until the time comes. The following morning, Praxus had rode out of the Kingdom of Brithrow and set his travels for the Megarian Mountains. His true journey had just begun.

MASSACRE IN THE DUSK

CHAPTER ONE

Bodies piled up in the corners, scattered across the pavements of the alleyway. Lights flickered in the distance as several sirens echoed closer to the alley. Up ahead several police vehicles arrive as the officers move through the alley toward the bodies. They stop in their place, with their guns in hand overlooking the bodies. One of the officers cover their faces to avoid the stench. From there, the coroners were called as they carried the bodies away. The police search the area for any witnesses, only to discover a few homeless people sitting at the edge of the alley. An officer gazed toward them and went to approach. Three of the homeless ran away. Only one had remained, keeping his calm.

"Sir, did you see anything?"

"I saw the blood spill. That I did. I heard the screams. Screams like a banshee. They were echoed in blood. So much blood."

The officer escorted the homeless man to the others as they monitored the coroners. The following day, the news spoke out concerning the murders, calling it a massacre in the dusk. Therefore a manhunt was sent out searching for any suspects which may be related to the victims. While the officers went and searched, they called in a Private Investigator to dive deeper into the murders. An investigator named Luke Cline. Entering the police station was a woman, dressed in casual wear as she began asking for the Commissioner. One officer approached her, seeing her attire and hearing her words.

"You must be the Attorney?"

"I am. I need to speak with the Chief. It's regards this murder case."

"Right this way."

The Attorney went with the officer into the Chief's office. Once she entered, the Chief saw her as he asked for her to sit down. The Attorney reached into her bag, taking out a file and sliding it across the desk.

"You already know why I'm here."

"I do. You have some work concerning this new murder case we're dealing with."

"And I know you called the Investigator. Luke Cline."

"His credentials proved right for this case. He's done these before and has come out with great results."

"I don't think you or anyone in this city understand how Cline does his job. It's not so subtle as one would believe."

"You worked with him before?"

"No. I've studied him. Studied his methods to come the conclusion he is not the one to be called."

"His methods? What about them concerns you?"

"He doesn't follow the strict policies we've laid down. Cline loves to do things on his own term. Granted, he may come in and agree to this case. But, the way he will treat the law is not something one would imply. He's a horror in waiting."

"I see. So, tell me, Attorney Joyce, what would you have me do in this situation?"

"Call Cline and tell him he's no longer necessary for this case. Tell him you have someone else on the job."

"That someone being you?"

"Who else?"

"Ma'am, you're an Attorney. Not a detective. Much less a cop."

She laughed at his words, shaking her head as he slid back the file. Putting it back into her bag, she sighed and gazed around the Chief's office. Her lips smacked.

"You know, I've dealt with a lot of cops in my time. But, there's something different about the ones who operate here. Tell me, what other things have happened since? Before the murders?"

The Chief paused himself, raising up in his seat.

"What are you implying?"

"I'm only asking the serious questions. As an attorney surely would."

"You think you can just plant something on this department? On

404

the officers who do their best here?"

"I don't plant anything. I seek and I find. It's why I'm good at my job."

"Threats don't go well, ma'am. Definitely not in Detroit."

"I'm not threatening you and any officer here. I'm only speaking facts. My truth is this, when I seek out something, I discover it, and I showcase it. A threat is no more than a symbol of one's failure."

"Listen here, you can make up all the threats you want. All the claims you can conjure up in that head of yours. But, I'll tell you this one thing. Cline stays on this case. Whether or not you agree with his motives."

She stared at the Chief and he stared back. Neither one moved from their seats until a knock at the door. The Chief turned his focus, seeing an officer.

"Yes."

"The Investigator is here."

"Tell him to come this way."

The officer went as the Attorney kept her eyes on the Chief. The Chief stood up and walked around the office, looking at photos of his wife and daughter. The Attorney scoffed.

"Sentiment won't be helpful here."

"Who said anything about sentiment?" The Chief asked. "You have a family?"

"I do not."

"Explains a lot."

Footsteps were heard coming closer to the door as the Chief turned around, seeing Cline standing at the door with the officer. The Chef approached Cline and extended his hand.

"Welcome to Detroit."

The Attorney looked back, seeing Cline shaking the Chief's hand. She was immediacy applauded by Cline's preferred style of dress. Black slacks, black shirt and shoes, with a burgundy leather jacket. Cline entered the office and sat down opposite of the Attorney.

"Investigator Cline, this is District Attorney Maria Joyce." The Chief said. "She is also lending a hand on this case. She suggests she's needed."

"Good to know." Cline replied. "Nice to meet you, Attorney."

She looked at his hand and shook. Her eyes locked onto his. However, to Maria's displeasure, Cline was not a pushover. The tension in his eyes moved her as she pulled back her hand and sighed. Standing up from her seat, she took her leave. The Chief told her they will see each other again before the case is solved. She knew the underline motive. Cline and the Chief both spoke on the details surrounding the case. The sudden massacre, the deceased and the contact of their loved ones.

"Is there anything else I should know about before I begin?" Cline asked.

"Um. Yeah. One of the officers managed to speak with someone in the area near the murders. A homeless man. Said he saw something in the alley before the massacre took place."

"In which alley should I be looking?"

"Midtown District. That's where the alleyway is."

Cline nodded, standing up. He shook the Chief's hand before taking his leave.

CHAPTER TWO

Luke had walked toward the alleyway in the Midtown District. What he saw within seconds were the taped surroundings and the dried blood on the concrete. Walking through the tape, he knelt down and glared toward the blood. So much of it. Not even the water which they sprayed was enough to cleanse the alleyway. Hearing scurrying behind him, Luke arose to find a group of homeless people staring at him. One in particular had a keen eye, scouting the tape and the blood.

"Any of you know what happened here?"

"They don't know a thing." One of the homeless men said.

"What about you? You know anything?"

"I know something."

Luke nodded.

"Then tell me what I need to know."

The homeless man nodded and sent off the others as he walked past the tape and toward the blood-covered grounds. He looked at the walls, seeing stains of splattered blood. Shaking his head. The flickering memories began to flood his mind. Snapping himself out of it to the unusual stare by Luke. He nodded slowly and turned around.

"Didn't realize it was this much."

"What do you know about the massacre?" Luke asked.

"I saw it. First-hand I did."

"You saw it happen?"

"Not the start. But the middle and the end. It was, it was something one dare never to witness."

"Tell me what you saw. Details."

"I saw these people grouping together in the alley. Thought they

407

might've been some teenagers looking to get into trouble. They all came into the alley, ran some of us off."

"The homeless used this alley?"

"Before the killings they did. Not too many and not too often."

"What happened next?"

"Screams and cries echoed across the sky. There was nothing I could do. Any of us. We were powerless in the moment."

"Did you see the killer?" Luke questioned.

"The killer?" The homeless man said. "Um, I'm not sure how to describe it."

"The killer. Was it a man or a woman? Race, hair color. Give me something to go on."

"I would, but I'm not certain as to what exactly killed them. It moved with such speed, only within seconds did they scream and went all silent. Like a pen dropping."

Luke took out a notebook and began writing down everything the homeless man told him and more concerning the alley, the other homeless people, and minor details which relate to the alley. Closing the book, Luke looked down and saw a card smeared in blood. Picking it up, he looked seeing the blood on one side. Flipping I over, the card belonged to a club. He showed the card to the homeless man and his eyes widen and his jaw dropped.

"What's with the look?"

"I know that joint!"

"What is it?"

"It's the nightclub down the block. It's not exactly seen as one from the outside. You know. Due to some certain laws."

"I'm not from this city. So, I have no idea what kind of laws you're referring to."

"Oh, my bad. The club. It's where those youngins' came from. They left the club and came to this alley."

"And you saw all of this?"

"I wouldn't be telling you if I didn't."

Luke nodded, placing the card in his jacket pocket. Walking toward the street, the homeless man followed him. Almost like a beggar without the pleading. Luke stopped, turning back toward the homeless man as he only nodded.

"Why are you following me?"

"Because the club's not open."

"Not open?"

"The club doesn't open till past ten. The area gets pretty crowed around nine-ish."

"So, I'll have to make a return trip tonight."

"Yeah."

"Then that is what I will do."

"Anything else I can help you with? Even though I'll still be in the area."

"You never told me your name." Luke replied. "I'm guessing you have one?"

"Call me Stuggs."

"Stuggs?"

"Yeah. I know it's not a common name. But, names are just names."

"As many say, yet none believe. I'll see you around, Stuggs."

CHAPTER THREE

Once night had come, Luke returned to the District to find it crowded with people. A mixed multitude all standing out in front of the entrance to the nightclub. The women dressed in scandalous apparel. Their faces shrouded with makeup to appease the men entering the club. Luke continued walking as he made his way toward the entrance. Skipping the line without giving any of them a look. The bouncer stepped forward, his hand held up like a wall.

"Where are you going?"

"Inside this establishment. I have questions."

"Well get in in line like the rest of them."

"I'm not here to sow my oats. Move aside or else this won't go well."

"You challenging me, boy?"

"A challenge takes skill. This isn't even a test."

The bouncer moved forward with his hand into a fist. Before making an attack, a second bouncer stepped in. calming his associate and permitting Luke inside the nightclub. Luke grinned as he entered with the first bouncer turning toward the other.

"Why you'd let him in?"

"He's law. No need to make a bigger issue."

Luke stepped into the nightclub, the red hue over his head shrouding the club, feeling the beating of the loud music around him. The odor of alcohol and cigars filled the air. Looking over to his left he saw the strippers dancing before an audience of men. To his right was the bar where several men and women sat down drinking. All their eyes glued onto him as he walked through. Their glares had no effect on

Luke. He dusted them off with a smile and a gaze. Stepping toward the bar, he looked at the tender. She looked back at him.

"A guy like you isn't seen in places like this?"

"And how do you know what kind of guy I am?"

"I can tell who's who in this place once they walked through that door."

Luke grinned.

"What can you tell me about this place? Is it this crowed every night?"

"Pretty much. But, tonight is slightly different."

"Different in how?"

"Those men sitting in front of the strippers. they're part of an organization. They come through to collect their shares."

"How do you know of this?"

"I've been here for some time. They talk plainly concerning their affairs."

"Without fear of exposure from the women?"

"Fear is nothing to them but a choice of power."

"Funny how things work. Look here, I'm a Private Investigator. I'm here to speak with the owner of this place. I have questions."

"Questions? What kind of questions?"

"You're aware of the massacre that was discovered down the block?"

"I am. The women here speak about it constantly. Wasn't sure what happened."

"Were any of you outside when it occurred?"

"Some of the women were. They say they heard the screams and ran back inside."

"Can you point me to the women?"

The tender looked up ahead. Her eyes aimed forward with Luke turning around to the strippers. Moving around as they gave the men lap dances with dollars floating in the air. He glanced back at the tender. He was not amused. The tender chuckled.

"You're serious?"

"Yeah. Have to ask them."

"Before I do, one more question. Where were you when the massacre took place?"

"Truth be told. I was in here. Cleaning up the place before my usual clock out."

"I see. Well, best you prepare yourself."

"Prepare for what?"

"Just in case this goes downhill."

Luke stood up from the bar and took a step forward. He stopped, turning back to the tender.

"You never told me your name."

"Why do you want to know?"

"I'm an investigator. Remember."

The tender smiled.

"Madeleine. Madeleine Kay. What's yours?"

"Luke Cline."

"Ah. A strong name. Fits you."

Luke went ahead and stepped down the two-set stairs into the stripper area. Four poles hung from the ceiling as the women danced in front of him. To the men's displeasure, Luke began standing in front of them, nodding toward the women who gave him smiles of pleasure. One of the young men out of the ten stood up, removing his jacket. He tapped Luke on the shoulder.

"What'd you think you're doing?"

"Just getting a nice view."

"Well, get your view somewhere else. You're in our way."

"Oh. Am I?"

"Yeah. Now move."

"I will. Only when I speak with the owner."

A second man sitting down raised his head. He was much older than the first man. Streaks of grey hair covered his face. Staring a hole through Luke.

"The owner? What business you have with him?"

"Law business."

The men stood up from their luxury seats while the strippers moved aside. Nearly all the eyes in the club were on them. Luke held his cool, standing firm as they surrounded him. Each removing their jacket and cracking their knuckles. Luke only grinned while Madeline watched from the bar, taking a drink. The older man stepped forward on Luke.

"Why come in here and start trouble?"

"I haven't started any trouble. From what I see, your buddies are about to start some trouble. I only want to speak with the owner."

"About what? You have a share in this place too?"

"No. About the massacre down the block."

The men held themselves. The older man chuckled while taking a moment to smoke his cigar. The smell of the cigar irritated Luke as he fanned the smoke from his presence.

"Seems this old boy doesn't like the smoke." One of the men joked.

"That's not important." The older man said. "What he's here for is."

"Where is he?" Luke asked.

"He's standing before you, boy." The older man sighed.

Luke's eyes widen as Madeline continued watching. Even the bouncer stood by the door, overlooking the scene while there were others standing outside, banging on the door to have an entry. The owner nodded and told his men to remain at the seats and the strippers to continue their work. He and Luke went and walked toward his office. The music continued as did the strippers. entering the office, Luke sat down as the owner took a stop at his desk. Covering the walls were not posters of women, but landscapes. Mountains, riversides, grassy fields, and deserts. Luke was impressed.

"You taking a gaze ay my wall."

"I am. This place isn't exactly fitting along with the scenery of your club."

"Eh. Well. Not all things are similar in fashion."

The owner laid aside his cigar, taking a seat and measuring Luke's posture. He began to question Luke's reasoning for the visit to Luke's reply was a simple statement of his occupation. The owner was impressed. Having a private investigation inside his club was something he'd never expect. Luke questioned him on the massacre and the owner raised his hands in haste.

"You're not blaming me for the murders, are you?"

"I'm not. I only asked the question."

"Why? Who gave you the idea of coming here and asking?"

Luke reached in his pocket and tossed out the card. The owner saw it and hung his head. Looking at the card, he could see the smeared remains of blood on the opposite end. Throwing the card, he took another moment to enjoy his cigar. Cooling his anger which brew within him. The fact of one of his cards being found at a crime scene struck him. No telling what could've happened if an officer discovered it. His club would've been raided within hours after the bodies were found.

"Where'd you get the card?"

"A homeless guy."

"Homeless?!" The owner yelled. "The fuck did he have one of my cards?!"

"He was near the area when the massacre took place."

"No telling. He's homeless. Of curse he would be out there. Probably heard the screams and all of it."

"Matter of fact, he did."

"See. I was right."

"Said several young people came out of your club and went into the alley. Not sure what they were doing and that is when he heard the screams."

"Young people? Yeah. We get them every so often. You saw the women standing outside before you entered didn't you?"

"I did. Is it like this all the time?"

"Mostly. The club is one of the successful businesses on the District."

"You're sure about that?"

"Damn straight I am. I have the records."

"That's good." Luke said. "By the way, I won't be needing them. No worries."

"Now. That! That is good."

"Your bartender told me several of your strippers were outside when they heard the screams. Said they bolted back inside for safety."

"Bartender? You speak of Madeline?"

"I do."

"Ah. She does her job well. She told you about the strippers?"

"She did."

"Well, I grant you permission to speak with them. And speak only.

No touching."

"No worries from me. I'm here on the job."

"Shit please. Those men sitting out there have said the same thing and look where they're at? Getting their laps bounced by strippers."

Luke nodded with a smile. He arose and left the office and went back out into the environment of the club. Something he noticed was the difference of energies from the office to the club environment. They carried two distinctive notices. Luke kept it to mind as he approached the strippers, interrupting their time with the men.

"I need to have a word with each of you."

"The hell you doing?!"

"Step aside, young man." Luke replied. "I have permission from the owner to speak to these women."

"You're interrupting our fun."

"Oh yeah? Then, speak to the owner. He'll tell you all you need to know."

The young man went for an attack, only to be stopped by his colleagues as they walked toward the bar. One of the older men suggested to the younger to grab a drink. He sighed as he stepped away. Luke turned his attention toward the strippers as he sat them down on the luxury seats and he remained standing. The men stared at the bar, watching him converse with the strippers.

"The tender over there told me you ladies were outside when the murder took place."

"She told you that?"

"Would be the new girl." The red-headed stripper said.

"New girl?" Luke asked.

"She started several days ago. Came in out of nowhere. Boss said she impressed him. Guessing she gave him a blow and he hired her."

"So, you're not familiar with her by any means?"

"No. we went out to get some air and while we were talking amount ourselves, we heard the screams coming from down the block. In fear, we ran back inside."

"You didn't see anything? Nothing that may have caught your gaze?"

"Nothing. We weren't even looking in the direction of the screams.

Before or after."

Luke nodded as he wrote down their words. The blonde stripper stood up, trying to take a look at the notebook to which Luke closed it and stepped back. Pushing him to see, the blonde began shouting at him while the red-head and brunette attempted to hold her back. The men at the bar heard the shouting and the young one took it as an opportunity. Moving with speed, he attached Luke with several punches. Luke retailed with punches of his own, knocking the young man out. The other men watched and took it as an offense. They all rushed against Luke and attacked him in a circle. Luke did his best to block their blows, even going to the point of fighting back. Hitting a few punches along the way. The owner walked back out to the commotion and called for the bouncers to take Luke out. Grabbing a hold of him as he kicked two of the men in the faces, the bouncers struggled to pull him as he fought back against them. Gaining quick shots to their faces before the men teamed up and forced him outside of the club, throwing him out onto the pavement. Luke slowly stood to his feet and brushed himself. He heard a slight chuckle coming from his left side, turning to have a look, he saw Madeline smoking.

"Guess I missed the brawl."

"Wouldn't exactly call it a brawl."

"So, get what you came for?"

"I did. Thanks for the tip. Could've warned me about the blonde one."

"Funny. I thought all men knew the behavior of women. Particularly the blondes."

Luke smiled with a nod as Madeline took another inhale.

"Seems the trippers aren't fond of you working here."

"And I'm not fond of see them shake their asses and juggle their tits in the company of crooked men. But, here we are."

"Crooked men?"

"You didn't notice their stature? Their demeanor? Their look? Ugh, for a private investigator, you clearly have some things to work on."

"What are you talking about? How are those men crooked?"

"They're mafia." Madeline said, exhaling the smoke.

"Mafia. From what area?"

"That's complicated. Not all of them originate from the same organization. Some are from another one that's based on the east coast. Connecticut, I believe. The others? Probably Dixie Mafia. I'm not certain. You can ask."

"Funny. Like that's going to happen. Especially after what's just took place."

The sky above them cracked with the bolt of lightning. Madeline gazed up to catch the streak as she made her way back toward the door.

"Looks like a storm's coming." Madeline said, dropping the cigarette on the concrete."

"Apparently so."

"Guess you need to take cover. But, not inside of course."

"I wouldn't go back in there anyway."

Madeleine went for the door and stopped. She looked at Luke and nodded with a smile.

"You know, for someone who works in the law industry, you're a decent man."

"Not to sound cliché, but, will I ever see you again?"

"Probably. We'll see." She answered, returning inside the club.

The rain began to pour as Luke returned to his car with the thunder rolling across the city.

CHAPTER FOUR

Luke walked into the police department, seeing Maria standing in the front speaking with the Chief. Hearing the footsteps, she turned around to see him and rolled her eyes. Luke paused himself and glared. The Chief shook his head.

"Don't mind her, Cline."

"I wasn't going to otherwise."

"You will if you want to work on this case." Maria said, facing Luke clearly.

"You're not in charge of this facility." Luke replied. "On what orders should I listen to you?"

Maria looked at Luke's face, seeing the scars. Her eyes widen as she stared at him. Questioning the marks with no words spoken. Luke glared at her before realizing she was referring to the scars. His hand rose as he touched the marks and chuckled.

"What's funny about them?"

"Part of the investigation. That's all."

"What happened yesterday that has your face all scratched up?" The Chief questioned. "Where did you go?"

"To the nightclub close to the crime scene."

"Ah!" Maria jolted. "You figured you would find a good time in the middle of an investigation. Tell me, did the women give you a good dance or were they not capable of treating someone like you with a good time?"

"Enough, Joyce." The Chief said. "Let Cline tell us what transpired."

"Before I went to the club, I visited the crime scene. Discovered a homeless man lurking around the block and he informed me of some details. Details which may prove useful in solving this case."

"I have to guess it was the same homeless man who told one of my officers about the scene. Said he was nearby when it happened."

"That's the one." Luke answered. "His name is Stuggs."

"Ugh." Maria said. "What kind of name is Stuggs."

"At least he has a name." The Chief responded. "Anyhow, what else did you find?"

"I found a card at the site. I guess the forensics didn't catch it during their investigation. However, the card came from the nightclub. So, I waited till nightfall and went inside. Spoke with the owner about the murder. A few of his strippers were outside when it happened."

"And their reaction was?" Maria asked.

"They fled. Ran back inside the club for safety."

"And the owner of the club," The Chief said. "What were his words regarding you finding something of his at the site?"

"He requested that he and his club would not become part of the case."

"But, the card is evidence." Maria said. "Therefore, the club is part of the case whether he likes it or not."

"I told him he wouldn't have to worry about it."

"Huh. Funny. Making the rules as you go. Just as I've been told."

"Maria, this is not the time ot draw lines between all of us." The Chief mentioned. "I know you don't like Cline's methods. But I don't give a damn. If he can solve this case, then by all means do what he must do."

"Whatever."

The doors of the department opened, grabbing their attention. Luke looked as he saw Stuggs standing, waving his hand in the air while the other officers look to him with a concerned effort. Luke ran in and calmed the officers down before speaking with Stuggs.

"Must be the homeless guy." Maria said. "Figures."

"Why are you here?" Luke asked.

"I have some more information. About the murder. Figured I would tell you."

Luke turned to the Chief with a nod. The two stepped outside the department while Maria looked on with disgust, turning back to talk with the Chief.

"What have you found?"

"The Mafia."

"Mafia?" Luke said. "What about the Mafia?"

"They are involved. Involved in the murders."

"How do you know this?"

"After you left the scene, this black vehicle drove up in front of the alley. Out of it came four men, dressed in nice suits. Wish I could get one."

"Details, Stuggs."

"Oh right! See, these four men went to the back of the car and took out some gas cans. They sprayed the entire alley. Cleaned up the remaining blood and all. Now, the alley looks like it's never been touched. One couldn't tell that a murder took place there."

"Shit!"

"I knew you wouldn't like it. Told you anyway. Just to be on the safe side."

"You have nothing to worry about." Luke nodded. "Now, where did they go after they left?"

"One of them said they were supposed to have some kind of meeting at one of their residences. I don't know where they might be."

"Leave it to me. I'll figure it out."

"Sure thing. Sure thing." Stuggs nodded. "If I come across anything else, I know where to show up."

"That you do."

Stuggs saluted Luke before walking off. Inside the department, Maria and the Chief watched as Luke reentered and approached them. The Chief nodded to Luke, stating to him a well-down. Luke took the complement with only a nod of his own. The Chief returned to his office while Maria stood next to Luke, measuring him.

"I can smell the homelessness all over you."

"You have something to say to me or can we continue on our business?"

"Business is all we have. Besides that, I have something for you."

"Something like what?"

"No worries. I'm not trying to slow you down. I found something that may interest you."

Maria dug into her bag and took out a note. Handing it to Luke, he opened it and saw an address. His eyes turned to Maria in confusion as he waved the note in her face. She didn't like that notion, but took it well. As professional as she could. She placed her hand over the note to stop him from waving.

"What is this?"

"Um, an address."

"An address to where?"

"To a church." Maria answered.

Luke scoffed.

"Why a church?"

"Because the priest of said church apparently knows something about the case. Something major."

"I'm not understanding any of this. How would a priest of a church have information that connects to the case? There's nothing divine about the murders."

"Well, first thing, this church has nothing to do with the divine. Second, the priest requested you by name."

A paused gesture formed on Luke's face. He took another look at the note and inhaled. A small moment to clear his mind even with all the noise of the department around him. Shaking his head, he placed the note in his pocket and told Maria he would head out and visit the church. She only responded with words of clarity. Before Luke left, he asked her what would be her next move. Only with a smack of her lips did she inform him of a witness to the crime and she would be interviewing them. Unimpressed, Luke waved as he left the department.

CHAPTER FIVE

Luke stood outside in front of the church. His eyes were moving left and right as he shook his head. Taking out the note and looking, just to make sure he was at the right place. Luke knew Maria sent him here not only to annoy him, but because she did not want to come and Luke knew why. The church he stood in front of had an upside down pentagram carved on the double doors. Nine steps to reach them and Luke sighed. Walking up the stairs and once he reached the doors, they creaked. Luke nodded. Entering the church, he saw the decorated details of the interior. Red carpet and red pews. Looked as if the entire church was dipped in blood and left to dry in the heat. Perhaps they were according to Luke's own theories he already conjured up. While the doors closed behind him, the air felt uneasy for Luke. The club's atmosphere was a much better condition for Luke to handle than the church's. in front of him, Luke saw a woman, dressed in all black with a dash of red in her hair.

"Welcome."

"Yes. I'm here to speak to the one in charge." Luke replied. "Are they here?'

"Well, our master isn't here."

"Your master?"

"But, the high priest is here."

Luke nodded slowly. Very slowly.

"I'll speak with him, please."

"Very well. I'll go get him."

The woman turned around as Luke called to her. He asked for her name, telling her he was a private investigator. Her eyes grew big as did her smile after hearing his occupation. She nodded and told him her name. Anastasia. She went to the back and after three minutes, the high priest came from the back. Walking past the podium, he looked ahead, seeing Luke standing in the middle of the aisle. He grinned. Luke watched as the high priest approached him and quickly, an eerie sense moved past him through the air. Unable ot make it out, Luke regained himself and focused. The priest stood before Luke, extending his hand.

"You wanted to see me?"

"I do. I hear you're the one in charge."

"I am. Of this place, yes. Why come here?"

"I'm a private investigator. Someone tip me of this place. Apparently there's something you might know about the murders in the alley."

"I heard about them. Shame souls for fall so quickly. Then, why come here?"

"Wanted to ask some questions. See what someone might know."

"I'll shorten your visit. The nightclub down the block from the alley."

"What about it?" Luke asked.

"The answers you seek are there. Sitting inside waiting for you to discover them."

"I've already been to the club. Spoke with the owner."

"You had words with the Don?"

"The Don? No, I talked with the club owner."

"No. no." The priest said. "The club owner you talked to is the front owner. He's only there to stand in the place of the true owner. The Don."

"Explain this to me." Luke said. "Tell me what you know."

"The Don leads much of the mafia business in the District. Therefore, he must keep close hands on all the businesses which surround said District. In every one of them, he's placed someone he can trust to run those operations while he's often away pursuing other ventures. The man you met at the club is one of those men. Put in a position of power by the Don. You want answers? Then ask for the Don."

Luke continued to ask about this unknown Don. However, the answer he kept receiving was to return to the club and ask for him. The priest informed him once he speaks his name, his men will make themselves known. Thereby, brining him to the Don. Luke asked if it might turn into a fight. The priest grinned.

"You know how clubs operate."

"More than you know."

"Oh I know." The priest replied. "I know many things. I've seen your record."

"My record? How do you know about-"

"My people are everywhere, Mr. Cline. In all forms of business. Finance. Law. Medical. Entertainment. Philanthropy. My people keep me informed with all the doings of the world. It's why we stand. Untouched by the outside world."

"You're not like any priest I've encountered. Nor one I've heard of."

"I am unlike many things you're familiar with. Such as it must be for the work at hand. Although I have been labeled a greater kind."

Luke glanced down. Seeing the time. Catching himself, he extended his hand toward the priest. Stating he had to leave. The priest shook his hand and nodded.

"By the way," Luke said. "Mind if I know your name? For the case records."

"Lance." The priest answered.

"First name or last?"

"Last. First name is Vernon."

Luke nodded as he wrote down the priest's name in his small notepad.

"Vernon Lance, huh."

"That is what they call me."

"Vernon Lance. High Priest of the Satanic Temple."

"You got me." Lance smiled. "Anything else I can help you with?"

"No sir. I have what I need. Thanks for the talk."

"Anytime."

Vernon watched Luke exit the temple and once the doors had closed, Lance questioned why Luke would've made his way to him. What brought him to the church and why. Lance believed there was more to the case than he was let on. From there, he turned back and retreated to the back room, returning to his work.

Within the police department, Maria walked to speak with a supposed witness to the murders. The witness had claimed to seen the suspect before the murders occurred. Maria knew she was out of place to interview the witness, such is not within her jurisdiction. Although, she loved to make certain rules for herself. Anything to solve a case. In her mind, her ways are more professional than Cline's. Maria looked at the witness, a young woman who looked as if she was a college student. She somewhat quickened in her seat.

"Relax." Maria said, calming her down. "You're not in trouble."

The young woman understood with a sense of clarity. Taking out a notepad from her bag, Maria sat down, removing the top from her pen as it touched the cream paper.

"Tell me more about the suspect?" Maria asked. "What did they look like?"

"You won't believe me."

"Trust me, I won't say anything out of the ordinary."

The young woman nodded quickly.

"It was hairy."

"Hairy?"

"All over. Like an animal. Dark fur. I wasn't sure if it was black or brown."

"Yeah. Look, I know it sounds crazy and all, but-"

"You're not lying." Maria nodded. "You're being honest. I can tell."

"I know it wasn't a bear. It walked on two legs."

"Pardon?" Maria paused, putting the pen down. "You mean this thing you saw walked upright? Like a human?"

"Yeah. That's all I know about it. It was hairy and it walked on two legs. I didn't get a good look at it from the front."

"You only caught a glimpse from behind?"

"Yeah. Barely because it was dark and the alley was difficult to see. Only whenever cars would pass by would light enter it."

Maria nodded, writing in the pad and she closed it. Smiling toward the witness. Afterwards, the witness was let go and the Chief visited Maria in the room. He saw something in her eyes. Something pertaining to unawareness. He approached the table, slightly startling her to his amusement, sitting down.

"What's going on?"

"This case is not ordinary."

"What do you mean? the witness said something she wasn't supposed to or?"

"She said the suspect was hairy and walked upright." Maria nodded. "Ever come across something like that? Particularly here in Detroit?"

"Matter of fact, no. We haven't. That's new for us."

"I'm trying to figure out if she saw an animal that looked as if it was walking on two legs. Can't pin-point it."

"What about a bear?"

"She said it wasn't a bear. She was clear on that."

"Then, what other animal could see have saw that night? Only animal I know that could fit the description is a bear. They're able to stand on their hind legs like us and even walk on them. I don't know another animal that could do the same."

"There's monkeys." Maria pointed. "Maybe she saw one of them."

"We don't have wild monkeys roaming around in Detroit." The Chief shook his head.

"Are you certain? Because with the environment, animals can make a change of habit. You know this."

"I do and there is no monkeys in the city. Nor are there gorillas, chimpanzees, or any of those kinds of animals. There's only people and that is that."

Maria leaned in her chair, tapping the pen against the cold steel table. The pen paused.

"Then what did she see that night?"

"Again. I have no idea."

The Chief stood up and approached the door, gazing through the window. He was searching and Maria could tell. She grabbed her notepad, placing it in her bag as she exited the room and the Chief followed her through the moving crowd of officers. The dialing sound of phones echoed as the conversations of the people. The day was indeed a busy one.

"Where are you going now?"

"Back to my residence to do some digging. I want to find out what she meant by this animal. This is becoming very strange. Even for me."

Later in the night, Luke went and took Vernon's words to mind and returned to the nightclub. Packed as it was the night before. He moved past the crowd of men and women who sought entry. Yells and screams of insults moved over Luke's head as he stood in front of the two bouncers. They glanced at him and remembered.

"Why are you here? Again?"

"I'm here to see someone."

"Like who? One of the women inside or the boss?"

"Maybe both. Right now, it is not the time for delays. This is urgent."

"And what comes of it if we let you in? more fighting like last night?"

"I didn't come to fight. Only to speak with someone inside regarding a case I'm working on."

The bouncers turned to each other and nodded with silence. Their gaze turned on Luke as they moved aside for his entry. Inside, Luke saw the place in the same appearance as the night before, only with some missing chairs and slight shards of broken wood on the floor. He knew where they originated from and walked past them. His eyes went first for the bar and he saw a woman tendering to the drinks. Only, it was not Madeline. Sitting at the bar, the tender approached him.

"What can I get you?"

"Only an answer to a question. Do you know where Madeleine is?"

"Madeleine?"

"She was the bartender last night. I came to see her regarding some business."

"Oh. Well, I've been put here as her replacement."

"Replacement?" Luke jolted. "What do you mean by replacement?"

"She was let go this morning. I don't know why. But, on the bright side, she was not bothered by it. More so relieved."

"And you know this how?"

"Because she told me before she left."

427

Luke went and asked for a shot of whiskey, in which he drank with speed. Taking a moment of silence, he nodded to himself and thanked the tender for the drink as he made his leave. Stepping outside, Luke found himself surrounded by ten men all dressed in slick suits. Jewelry layered across their hands and wrists. Some wore necklaces of gold and silver. All of which had their eyes shielded with sunglasses. Luke looked around and saw the bouncers entering the club as the customers who waited had moved aside. Luke took a good look at his surroundings. Outnumbered he knew. He balled up his fists and gave the men a grin before tossing the first punch. The nine remaining men all tackled him to the ground and stomped him into the concrete. Luke went and kicked back, trying to stand up only to be kicked in the side and punched in the head.

"This one has spirit!" One of the men chuckled. "Give him another go-around."

The men stepped back as Luke stood. Wiping the blood from his mouth, he extended is hand toward each of them. Calling for another round. The men grinned, cracking their knuckles as they went to attack him. Luke dodged the first round of punches before kneeing one of the other men, shoving him into another. Luke speared one of the men, slamming him to the ground and pummeling his face with his fists. One of the men, much larger in size than Luke grabbed him by his shoulders and tossed him to the sidewalk. Luke caught himself before falling and jumped back up, punching the man while dodging the coming blows from the interfering others. Luke jumped and kicked the man in the face as he fell to the ground. Nine more remained with Luke doing his best to deflect their attacks and give them his own. The customers standing outside began to circle the fight, each of them taking out dollars and betting on the winner. The bouncers exited the club and stood watch. Luke used many methods to take them on. Aside from the casual punches and kicks and knees, Luke went ahead and uppercutted two of the men before backhanding another. He ducked a haymaker from one of the men before snatching him by his collar and slamming him to the ground. Luke took a moment to catch his breath, wiping more blood from his face.

"Who sent you motherfuckers?!"

"Our boss." One of the men answered, showing his fists. "You've trespassed on business which isn't yours."

The man went for a swing, missing the attack as Luke returned it with a punch of his own. Stumbling in his steps, the man paused, holding his nose and seeing the blood. Luke scoffed. Readying himself for another fight. The man jerked his arms and pulled out a gun. Luke stood calm, raising up his own.

"Enough horseplay." said a voice walking in the street.

Luke turned around and saw an older man approaching him. His style of dress was clean. Highly luxurious than the men and their own suits. His tie glistened like a ruby and the jewelry he wore brought him more attention than he realized. Even the customers were in awe of his fashion choices. Luke didn't care. He just wanted to know who this man was and the possibilities of his identities moved through Luke's thoughts. Connections to the club, the men, maybe even the murder. Luke was unsure to know. But, he had a feeling he would be receiving some answers soon and they were standing only a few feet in front of him. The man stood still, his eyes set on the men in suits. He raised his hand and the suited men each took steps back. They stood to attention and cleaned up their suits. Luke was impressed as the man stood before him, looking him up and down. He scoffed with a faint grin. He eyed his men and nodded.

"You have heart, Luke Cline."

"And you know me how?"

"I know everything which transpires in this city. My city."

Luke nodded with a sense of knowing. The man nodded back. They both knew.

"At least I get the opportunity to see you in person." Luke noticed. "Then, you know why I've been coming to your club these past days."

"I do. You seek to find some answers connected to your little case, right? Believing there will be answers inside. So, have you found anything? Anything which can connect the club to said murder? Besides some fancy card, of course."

"The card is evidence. It's proof your club is involved. Those innocent people were inside your club before they were killed."

"And that proves nothing."

"Nothing? That is something."

"A card. Found covered in blood. Blood that made it untraceable for the forensics when they did their petty search."

"How do you know about-"

"Like I said, kid, I know everything that happens in this city. Your actions here are no different."

Luke nodded with anger, shrugging his shoulders.

"So, what now? You take me out and that's it?"

"No. I'm not going to have you killed. You're proven yourself too valuable to be declared dead."

"Then, what are you going to do about me? Even if you could."

The man scoffed with a hint of laughter, pointing at Luke and looking over to his men. The men chuckled while talking amongst themselves about Luke's behavior.

"Well, I'll be go to hell. I'll tell you what, Like Cline. This is my offer. You return to your little case and get it solved. Once you solve it, you leave my city. Is that clear?"

"I'll leave this city once the case is solved. No matter the time needed."

The man sighed.

"With a voice like yours and the attitude, you're lucky I don't have these men tear you to shreds. But, I'm a decent man. A man of character and I've given you my offer. Besides, you have what you came for or did that Satanic priest tell you otherwise?"

"He told me enough. But, I do have one question."

"What kind of question are you pertaining to ask of me?"

"The bartender who was working your club last night. Madeline. Where is she?"

The man nodded with interest. Stepping closer to Luke, placing his hand on his shoulder. Their eyes locked and Luke could see the answer. He needed no words. The man stepped back and extended his hand. Luke looked.

"You know what to do." The man said. "For your best interest, of course."

Luke went and shook the man's hand. He grinned, signaling his men to leave the area. Nearby, a vehicle drove up in front of the club where the door and exited and opened the back door for the man to enter. Luke stepped forward, calling out to the man.

"Yes?" The man asked.

"It was nice to meet a Don." Luke said. "I'm sure the others are like you or somewhat different."

The Don nodded as he entered the car. Luke looked back at the club before taking his leave.

CHAPTER SIX

Luke entered the department the following morning with Maria entering behind him. She tapped him on the shoulder as he turned around. Quickly, Maria saw the bruises and sighed.

"Again?"

"There's no need for your concern."

"I am not concerned. Only questioning your purpose on this case? Does it only revolve around you coming back here with more bruises or what?"

"I ran into some trouble. That's all."

"Trouble? Like the kind of trouble that follows you pr the kind of trouble you cause wherever you go?"

"Doesn't matter. Can we go and talk with the Chief about the case."

"Well, I'll tell you something while we're on our way."

Luke went ahead and walked with Maria keeping up with is pace. She took out her notepad, showing him. He glanced at the pad once and kept his eyes centered.

"I talked with a witness yesterday."

"A witness?"

"Not your little homeless buddy. Someone else who was there the night it happened. They got a look at the suspect. A decent one it seems."

"Tell me. What did they look like?"

"Hairy and walked upright." Maria answered.

"The hell's that supposed to mean?"

"You said you wanted to know. I just told you."

"You said the witness saw the suspect. What you just describe is not a suspect. That's an animal."

"It's what she said."

"Horseshit." Luke replied. "Try again. Find someone else who might know a thing."

Maria shook her head and saw the bruises on Luke's face. Hesitant to ask, he went ahead and the expression on Luke's face could only give the response she didn't seek. Questioning him about the bruises, Luke went ahead and told her everything. From the club to the men and the Don. Maria wanted to rant as she had done before but held in her composure, stating to Luke she will look into the Mafia which Luke encountered. Luke however suggested he would return the favor by visiting them himself and Maria began to warn him about the Don. From his methods and his power over Detroit. Her words began to linger in Luke's mind. How would Maria know so much about the Don, he asked himself.

"You want to say something, don't you?" Maria spoke.

"Just wondering how you know so much about this Don. You encountered him before in some past case?"

"He's been involved in a lot of cases around here and beyond. His real name is unknown to us. Rarely is spotted in the public eye. The fact you saw him last night is a jewel of an encounter. My first encounter was some years ago when there was talking of some kind of "Apprehension" case being discussed across the border."

"The border? A Canadian case?"

"Yeah. I know my jurisdiction doesn't allow me to work on foreign cases. But, I kept my eye on it when I found out the Don had a hand in it. Not sure if he was deeply involved or just had his foot in the door. He's partnered with a lot of powerful people. A network of society some would call it."

"I still would like ot have a word with him. Man-to-man."

"Leave him be. Unless we find something connecting his organization to the murders, there's no need in bothering him. Especially after what you endured last night."

"His organization is involved. The card. It was laying in the alley covered in blood. The victims came from his club that night. As far as I'm concerned, him and his organization are neck-deep in this case. I can't just move aside and let him be."

"You have no choice, Cline." Maria jolted. "No choice."

"On who's authority? The Chief's? or yours?"

"Don't get me started. I was already on the edge after hearing of your hand on this case. Two days later, where has it gotten you? Bruises and cuts across your face and hell, you look like you've barely slept since you arrived."

"My work is necessary. Other things come second."

"Like your health and all?"

"I can take care of myself."

"I'm sure you can. Just don't die before this case is over, alright."

Luke turned around, heading out. Before he exited, he told Maria he would be returning to his residence to do more work on the case. Meanwhile, Maria gave him a final warning pertaining to the Don and his Mafia. Luke took the words in and buried them deep.

CHAPTER SEVEN

While Luke returned to his residence, he began to feel uneasy. Something in the air, maybe? Luke opened the door and for a moment chose to look down. Which he did and what he saw was an envelope. He picked it up and saw only his name written on the front along with the initials, '*MK*' on the upper corner. His eyes squint, thinking of the initials and who they might belong to. Luke didn't know anyone with those initials or so he thought as he sat down and opened the envelope and found a note. Unfolding the shriveled paper, he began to read it.

"What is this?" He asked himself.

The note described an invitation to a masquerade party being held later that night in the district of Metro Detroit. Luke was familiar with the region, having visited there some time ago on a different case. One much easier than the current. At the bottom of the letter, Luke saw the name Madeline and from there he knew. Folding the letter and placing it in his pocket, he grabbed his keys and left the residence.

Luke returned to the department and found Maria having a conversation with the Chief concerning more potential witnesses. Knocking on the door in a frantic state, Luke ran into the office holding the letter in his hand.

"What's gotten into you?" The Chief asked.

"I've found something." Luke answered. "It's connected to the case."

"And what have you found?" Maria asked. "A note of some kind?"

Luke presented the note on the table, laying it next to the three folders with detailed witnesses. Luke didn't mind them as he was clearly focused on the note. It was his key to finding the source of the case. In his mind as the moment. Whereas Maria and the Chief was confused. Their focus was set on interviewing more witnesses who have stated to have seen something that night around the murder area. From neighboring residences to visitors in the district.

"There's a masquerade party being held ot night. In the Metro district."

"Ok." The Chief said. "So, what does a masquerade party have to do with this case?"

"Potentially everything."

"How are you certain of this?" Maria asked. "Did the homeless guy give this letter to you?"

"No. I found it when I returned to my area. It was slid under the door while I was gone."

"Sill could've been your homeless friend."

"It wasn't." Luke said, pointing toward the name at the bottom. "It was her. Madeleine."

"Madeleine?" The Chief uttered.

"Who's Madeleine?" Maria curiously asked.

"She's the woman who put me on the details at the club. She was there when the murders took place and she knew more. But, didn't converse with me to speak more."

"You're saying she knows something about the case and you're just now telling us about her?" Maria pointed with a sheer sense of irritation.

"I didn't know if what she told me was to be true. Until I had my encounter with the Don and his men."

"Don?" the Chief said. "What's been happening around here the past two days?"

"Cline had a fight with the Don's men. The mafia that is well-known in the shadows of the city. The Don let him go. Probably because Luke held himself steady. Proved himself a capable fighter in the eyes of the Don."

"And you know this how?" the Chief asked.

"As I told Luke, I've had encounters of my own with the Don. Past cases and suchlike."

The Chief sighed, his eyes returning to the witness files and the note. He gave a nod as Luke grabbed the note and returned it into his pocket. Maria wanted to say something regarding the note, but kept it within herself. Something she's not very known to do. Luke looked at the witness files and began to ask of them. The Chief told him they were preparing to speak with more witnesses as to what they saw that night. Luke figured they could be useful, but the party would hold more details to the case. The Chief took his words well and understood them. He couldn't force Luke to remain a the department and speak with the witnesses.

"What time is the party?" Maria asked.

"Why do you want to know?" Cline responded. "You're coming along or something?"

"I am. It's a party and you won't be able to learn everything on your own. You do your thing and I'll do mine."

Luke gave a nod. Maria smiled as Luke left the department.

Within the hour, Maria and the Chief began interviewing the witnesses while Luke traveled throughout the city, searching for a mask to where. He already had a suit in his residence. He brings one wherever he goes in case of a need. The party itself is a need. The witnesses began describing an animal. Just as the first one did. Some said it walked on all fours, comparing it to a bear or a cougar. Others said it walked upright like a human, but its behavior was animalistic. The Chief had hoped one of the witnesses would describe something like a human being, but neither of them did. All were details of a animal that killed the people in the alley that night.

Once the witnesses' interviews were over, Maria took her leave and prepped herself for the party which was being advertised across the city for those who would attend. At his residence, Luke dressed himself in a suit. In his mind, he felt off. His usual clothing fits his personality more than a nice suit. He felt fake within his soul. He had a mask sitting in the car as he headed out.

CHAPTER EIGHT

Stepping into the party, Luke saw himself surrounded by dozens of people. All of them had their faces covered with masks ranging from Halloween-esque figures to the renaissance era. Luke's mask was only a simple doll-like mask, only in black. Walking into the party behind him was Maria, who stood out from among the people with her fiery red Mardi Gras-like mask and dress. The eyes of the many were locked onto her style of fashion. Even Luke gave her a nod.

"You weren't expecting me to show up like this?"

"Figured you would've come here as you were at the department. All business-like."

"Well, we are on business. Just had to blend in. now, where do we start?"

"I figured we should find out who's here exactly. That way we can actually point out whatever it is that we should know."

"Good. I'll take the area over on the left."

"Why?"

"Because I see several men. Their suits are expensive. I believe they may be working with the Don."

"Then, leave them to me."

"Oh no." Maria laughed. "You already had your time with them. I'll handle it this time. Make it smoother to get across."

"And what should I do? Walk around this party like some kind of creep?"

"If you want. But, there is a bar over there. I'm sure you know what to do."

"I'm aware. Keep me posted on your progress." Luke said, walking off.

"Same to you."

While taking his time to reach the bar, a arm grabbed him and pulled him to the wall opposite of the party. Luke stared at the one responsible. Seeing it was a woman as she removed her plague doctor-like mask. Luke saw her face and removed his mask in response.

"Madeleine."

"Surprised to see me here."

"Hold on. Why are you here?"

"I'm on duty."

"Duty? Luke paused. "What are you talking about?"

"It's a long story and I prefer not to waste any more time."

"You have some explaining to do."

"Like what? How I worked at the club that one night, then vanished out of the blue?"

"Yes. Who are you? Truly."

Madeleine sighed as she grabbed a nearby chair from the table and sat down, facing the crowd with Luke leaning against the wall. Crossing his arms as he waited. Madeleine pointed at him. Seeing his demeanor oozing from him. She could only let out a smile. Luke looked at his chest and back.

"What is it?"

"Nothing. Just, the way you're standing there. All manly. I like it."

"Please, explain yourself." Luke responded slowly.

"Ok. I came into the city a week ago on a secret project. Still I do not know the name of the project, but anyways. My first duty was to learn more about the Don. My boss informed me of his works scattered across the country. Eventually, a trail was made that led his busiest operations being held here in Detroit. So, as my first progress, I obtained a job at his club. A bartender. Figured it would be easy. Sure worked on you didn't it?"

"Keep going."

"So, after our meeting at the club and your little tango with those men, I saw the Don entering the club. He went to have a chat with the owner. The man you spoke to that night."

"I see. What else?"

"I was charged with providing them the drinks for their secret meeting. I heard everything I needed to and the next day, I chose to quit. Said the air of the club was too much for a little girl like me."

"And that leads you here? How did you know I would be here?"

"Because I'm the one who left you the note."

"The note was from you?"

"Of course. With the help of Stuggs, too."

'Stuggs knew about this?"

"Yeah. How else was I to find out where you stayed. Stuggs keeps a clear eye on your place. Just in case someone who's not friendly decides to make a move. He may be homeless, but he's got heart. A good one at best."

Luke nodded. Taking a small peek back into the party. His eyes moved through the people in search of Maria. Madeleine noticed it as she glanced out into the field of people.

"So, who's the woman you tagged along with for the night? Some other one you found on your way here?"

"No. she's a district attorney. Working on the same case as me."

"An attorney. That's well to know. I'm guessing she doesn't know about me, does she?"

"Not exactly."

"Perhaps, I should introduce myself to her. See how this all works out."

"No need. Maria and I have everything under control."

"You do? So, have you discovered what the Don has been working on?"

"We have not. That is why Maria is having a conversation with his men." Luke said, pointing.

"Oh. Those aren't his men." Madeleine noticed.

"What do you mean?"

"Well, they are his men. Low ones I mean."

"Then, where are the ones we need to speak with?" Luke asked with a hint of hastiness in his voice.

"You don't find them. They find you."

Taking another look toward Maria, they see three men approach her. She turned around without a notice as two of them grabbed her by her arms and took her elsewhere in the building. Luke went to help, only for Madeleine to hold him back.

"What are you doing?"

"Relax, they aren't going to kill her."

"How would you know?"

"That's not how the Don operates. Right now, what we should do is follow them. Quietly."

"And let them lead us to the Don."

"Yes. You're learning. For a private investigator, you still have some kinks to work out."

"Another time. Let's get moving. They're taking her upstairs."

"Figured he would be up there. Probably staring out of the window like some kind of boss. You know they do that."

Moving through the crowd, their eyes remained on the staircase, seeing Maria being marched upward. She looked out into the crowd and saw Luke staring at her with Madeleine by his side. Her eyes told him a directive. He nodded. Turning to Madeleine to speak, however, she knew what Maria had informed him. To his surprise, Madeleine went ahead toward the stairs with Luke following. Walking up the stars, Luke saw Maria being placed inside a room and sitting at the desk near the window was the Don.

"He's there." Luke said. "In the office."

"As I figured. So, how do we get in there?"

"We wait and listen. See what he tells her. Once, we have enough information, we'll make our mark."

"Understood. But, what about those two?" Madeleine pointed, seeing two guards standing near the double-doors.

Luke looked at them. He measured with his eyes and saw on their right sides a firearm. Nodding his head, he began instructing Madeleine of his plan .she agreed to the plan and quickly made her move. Taking off one of her shoes, she tossed it near them, startling them.

"What was that?" One had asked.

"I don't know. Check it out."

One of the men went and checked to see the cause of the noise. Walking further from the door, Luke went up and choked out the second man while Madeleine went and hit the first man in the head with her other shoe. His body flopped to the floor, causing a small sounding thud. Luke looked up toward her as he was pulling the first man from the door to the wall. Sitting him down as he appeared to be sleeping. Taking his gun for same measures, he told Madeleine to do the same. Grabbing the gun last after she placed her shoes on.

"What's next?" Madeleine asked. "We go in?"

"No. we listen."

"Listen? You're sure we'll be able to hear what they're saying in there?"

"Hush."

"Yes sir." She smiled.

Taking the moment to hear, inside the office, the Don sat at the desk staring at Maria, who was surrounded by the two men who brought her to the room. Maria was not afraid, nor was she concerned. The Don knew it and he wasn't bothered. Familiar with one another. They talked like old colleagues, only with Maria bringing several of his past crimes. He laughed them off while taking a drink of vodka from his glass.

"You're still bummed out about those incidents? Maria, when will you ever grow up and look to the stars."

"I've looked well enough. What you're doing will come out to the public. They always do."

"Not if you own the press."

"Some things have a habit of slipping out."

"And when they do, we will cover them up with an opposite story. A story much more vigorous than the other. The media here is under our control. What the masses see is what we want them to see. The real world, hmm, if they knew what was happening. The truth of the matter, they would revolt. But, such responses to our work, we cannot tolerate it."

"You know what's going on about he case, don't you." Maria asked. "You know who killed those people in the alley."

The Don grinned, standing up from his seat and looking out toward the city.

"Maria, you've encountered all types of criminals in your line of work, correct?"

"I have."

"But, you've never had the chance of seeing a culprit that's beyond human means. Beyond human understanding."

"What are you getting at?"

"I know who killed those young people in the alley that night. I know what it caused. That is why my work is silent on this matter. Why my men have been occupying the club ever since and before."

"What aren't you telling me? Who killed those people? Who is the murderer?"

"Before I speak of this any further, what did those witnesses tell you?"

"How do you know about the witnesses?"

"Like I said. I have eyes everywhere. Even in that department you believe is covered by some form of justice."

"You have some on the inside?"

"I have someone everywhere. This city is under my control. Again, Maria, you know how all of this works. You don't have to be he mayor of a city to control a city's progress. All it takes is money. That money will form a network of very powerful people. Giving one access to much more than they could imagine. Such a network with that kind of money begets power and, you know the rest."

"Just let it out."

"I'm sorry. Let what out?"

"The murderer. Tell me who is it so I can bring them in and close this case."

"It's not so simple. The murderer is not someone you can easily track down and find."

"Give me a name."

"A name." The Don laughed. "And what will you do with a name? trace it in your data mines? Oh no, this culprit you call it, is again, not someone you can easily find."

"Give me a fucking name!" Maria yelled.

"Keep that tone silent before I force it to remain quiet."

"My hands aren't tied. Neither are my feet. Don't make me do something you'll regret, Marquis."

"Using my first name, huh? In front of my men. Such actions are not permitted, Maria. Therefore, I must make an example."

The Don reached into the desk drawer, taking out a pistol and a silencer. Maria jolted from her seat as the two men held her down. She struggled to get free as the Don prepared the firearm. Twisting the silencer. He grinned. Walking over to ward her and leaning against the desk. He held the gun toward her forehead. Maria grunted as he head tapped the muzzle.

"You bright this upon yourself, Maria. Now, what will the people do when they never learn the cause of the massacre."

The door bolted open with Luke and Madeleine standing. Maria looked back, seeing them. She regained control of her arms and elbowed one of the men in his nether regions before knocking the gun from the Don's hand. The other guard pulled out his firearm, only to be shot by Luke. The gunshot had reached the bottom floor and the people began evacuating. Maria jumped from the chair and ran toward Luke and Madeleine as the Don retried his gun and fired back. The three ran back t the floor, being scattered with the people.

"Get yourselves out of here!" Maria yelled. "I'll meet with you later."

"Where are you going? Luke asked.

"To find some answers."

Making their way outside, the two saw Stuggs waiting for them.

"Just in time." Madeleine said.

"What are you doing here?" Luke asked.

"The woman told me to come just in case of a disturbance. I see there was one after all."

"We need to get out of here." Luke said toward Madeleine.

-"Not yet."

"Why not?"

"Because, you see that tunnel there? We need to get in there now."

"Why would we do that?" Luke wondered.

"It's where the Don keeps his research and documents." Stuggs answered.

"How are you aware of this?"

"I spend my time going around the city. I learn things."

"If we can get in there, won't we need a key?"

Madeleine turned around after digging in her dress. She raised up a key to Luke's amusement. Stuggs giggled as they moved toward the tunnel. Several of the Don's men stepped out and searched the grounds, only to see the people running in fear for their lives. Others just stood outside huddling with others.

CHAPTER NINE

Inside the tunnel, Luke looked around. The walls were made of brick. Looked like something from the early 1930s to the 1940s. The stench of alcohol was within the air. Like it might've been soaked into the walls. Stuggs took a sniff and savored it. Madeleine moved through the tunnel, noticing the darkness within growing. Madeleine began wishing she had a torch. Stuggs suggested he go back out and make one with some junk he could find. Luke silenced them and stepped forward, taking out a flashlight from his suit. Madeleine smirked.

"You always carry one with you?"

"I come prepared. No matter the circumstance."

"That's good." Stuggs replied. "Very good. I do the same, you know. With what I have. At best."

"This place must've been used during the prohibition period." Luke noticed.

"You're right about that." Madeleine responded. "That is why the Don chose it as his secret place. Most of the people have forgotten about hidden caverns and likewise."

Continuing their walk for almost another three minutes, they reached a door. Upon the steel structure was an insignia. Something of a triangle mixed with a hexagon. The symbol was unfamiliar to the three of them. Stuggs shrugged his shoulders.

"Is it supposed to be a new shape or something?"

"No." Luke answered. "This is something else. Something not to play around with."

"You're familiar with these kinds of symbols?" Madeleine asked.

"I've had my share of encounters. Being a private investigator brings you into contact with all types of people and the things they believe in."

Taking a closer look at the insignia, Luke noticed the letter 'W' carved into the hexagon, scratching through the triangle. Madeleine placed her hand upon it, her fingers rubbing against the rugged symbol. To her surprise, the insignia was made of a different material than the door. With the door being made of steel, the symbol was made from something else. Something perhaps more durable than steel. However, they did into bother with what mineral was used and she used the key to unlock the door. The door creaked as they stepped forward. Luke had used the flashlight to find a switch and he did, only a few feet from the door against a podium. The light brightened and what they saw in the room gave them a slight startle. Stuggs was amazed at what he saw. Running over to one of the tables, seeing swords and daggers.

"You see all of this?!" Stuggs yelled. "Who knew the mafia was into some medieval shit."

"You see all of this too?" Madeleine asked Luke.

"Yeah. I do."

Luke looked all over the room. Swords, axes, and spears hung against the walls. Paintings of ravaging animals layered across the other wall from wolves, bears, mountain lions, and lynxes. The third wall had a map of the city and the markings upon it had matched previous cases. The smell of alcohol still lingered within the room, yet there was another stench that covered itself under the smell. Luke knew the second stench. Madeleine asked only for Luke to confirm his suspicion.

"Blood."

Taking a closer look toward the map and the markings listen upon it. Luke's understanding, several murders occurred in those marked places. Still staring at the map, Madeleine pointed. One red mark was placed on the alleyway near the club.

"He knew."

From the doorway arrived several of the Don's men. With them were three scientists. The scientists screamed as the shootout took place. Stuggs ducked into a corner while Luke and Madeleine shot fire against the Don's men. Taking several of them out. The remaining ones bolted into the room and returned fire. Stuggs looked out, seeing the men shooting toward Luke and Madeleine. Sitting close to the table, Stuggs raised his head and saw a knife sitting. He grabbed it and with his best effort threw the knife toward the shooter. To his surprise, the knife made its mark, stabbed into the shooter's ankle. Screaming in pain, Luke came from behind the podium and fired the shot. The scientists stood with fear as Luke approached them.

"We're not one of them!"

"Then who are you?!"

"We're scientists! We work with the Don on several projects."

"Why would the Don need scientists to work on his little things?" Madeleine questioned. "What are you helping him with?"

"He didn't have the resources to achieve what he desired." The second scientist said. "So, he contacted us for assistance and with our combined efforts, we achieved what he sought."

"And what did he seek out?" Luke asked.

"Lycanthropy."

"Huh?" Stuggs said, bolting up from the corner.

"He began wondering how he could increase the power of his mafia. Preferably the men who keep his operations protected. He told us having simple humans wasn't enough and he wanted more. Something much more refined for protection. First thing was super soldiers, but they proved unsuccessful. Then the idea of hybridization came into discussions. The Don believed we needed an alpha animal to merge with a human host in order to complete his desired ideas. We tried many operations with a few of his men. Those who trusted him till death. Many died in the trials."

"Yet." The second scientist said. "Only one managed to survive."

"And what happened to one who lived?" Luke asked. "Is he still around? Doing the Don's bidding?"

"He's still around. But, he's not like us anymore."

"He's stronger now." The first scientist said. "Much stronger."

"It makes sense now. Everything he was saying in the office. Everything he told Maria." Luke said. "The Don's been working on something here in secret. Something very-"

"Horrifying." Stuggs said, looking inside a book.

"What are you holding?" Luke asked, looking over toward Stuggs.

"This book. It was laying right here. It was already open."

They went and looked at the book. The pages within were detailed with old writings. Estimating the age of the writings, Luke believed them ot have been written sometime in the late 1800s. Madeleine 's estimate was around the mid-1910s. But, what was drawn on the pages began to cause a stir within them. The drawings were illustrations of a beast. A hairy beast. Sharp fangs and claws. Its red eyes were even detailed to the point, they could be its own eyes engraved on the page.

"Is that a werewolf?" Madeleine questioned.

"I'm afraid it is." Luke answered. "No. this can't be real."

"Then, what do you explain of this? The book? The weapons all over the walls? The smell of blood being covered up by whiskey. Believe it or not, I think we've found the culprit of the massacre."

"I'm sorry to inform you, it's very real." The scientist replied.

"I thought the smell was of gin." Stuggs said. "Guess I was wrong."

Luke took out his phone to dial Maria. Although, the signal was low due to being in the tunnel. Moving with speed. He asked them did they catch a glimpse of the moon before they came into the room. Madeleine said no. Stuggs gave a nod to the question.

"What did it look like?"

"Like it always does."

"No, Stuggs." Madeleine said. "He means how did it look? Crescent, full, new?"

"Oh. It was full. "The second scientist spoke. "You didn't realize how bright it was out there?"

"That wasn't my concern." Luke replied. "Yet, now it seems we have to deal with this now before another killing is committed."

Making his leave, Luke grabbed the book and took it for evidence.

"I'm not sure you can take that, sir." The scientists both said.

Luke turned back with the gun facing them. The scientists paused themselves and startled in their shoes. Both raised their hands in fear. Luke questioned them about the operations and they said their work was finished. Luke waved the gun, allowing the scientists to escape. They ran out of the room like rats. There was no slowing down. Madeleine watched them as they ran and tripped in the darkness of the tunnel.

"You're sure about letting them go?"

"No worries. They'll expose themselves once this is all over. Their hands are all over the operation here."

Madeleine had locked the door in case one of the Don's men would return. Making their way back to the outside, Luke glared up to the clear sky and he saw the moon. In full and shining bright. Madeleine began questioning their next move. Luke responded by informing Maria of the news. He called her.

"Maria, listen, we've found something regarding the case!"

"Get to the alley now!" Maria screamed. "It's here!"

"What's there?!"

"Get here now!"

The call ended with Luke looking around.

"What is it?" Madeleine asked.

"It's out."

CHAPTER TEN

Riding through the streets in Luke's vehicle, they managed to arrive nearby the crime scene with Maria ducked down behind one of the vehicles. The three came to her aid and saw the terror in her eyes. She pointed over to the alley where the bodies were found and Luke was determined.

"What are you doing?" Madeleine asked.

"I'm going to see if this thing is true."

"You already know the answer."

"Make sure you guys are safe. This has to end."

Luke moved with as much quietness he could muster. Reaching clover to the alley, he saw what he knew he would see. A living werewolf. Standing at nearly seven feet in height. The claws shined with the light around the streets and its howling breath gurgled through the air. The wolf knelt and sniffed the concrete. Sensing the blood, it began licking the ground. Luke raised up from behind the vehicle and fired a shot. The wolf jumped, its head turning back and the eyes glaring toward Luke.

"Shit." Luke said. "It's real."

The wolf let out a roar as it ran toward Luke. He fired another shot, the bullets went through the wolf's shoulder. The wolf stumbled. Blood poured from the wound. Luke continued firing more shots, slowing down the beast. The wolf came closer and swiped its claws, tearing down the car Luke stood behind. He moved toward the next one as the wolf continued to destroy the cars with only its claws. The wolf's veins glowed a bright green. Luke had seen something similar in the tunnel. A tube connected to a machine. There was a form of liquid in the tube. A green liquid. Connecting the dots, Luke knew the green material was the power source between the wolf and the man. Luke fired a shot into the veins as the green liquid oozed from the wolf's arm.

"I have you now." Luke said.

The wolf shook off the pain and lunged in the air toward Luke. Taking one aim, Luke fired the shot and the bullet made its mark. Hitting the wolf in the head, causing the body to collapse to the ground. The wolf was now declared dead and Luke stood over it, making sure the creature was truly dead. Unaware as to how the gunshot could've killed the wolf. Maria, Madeleine, and Stuggs approached him. Questioning how one shout could've killed the creature. Maria told him silver bullets were capable of killing werewolves. Luke had checked the rounds of the gun, seeing all the bullets were silver.

"A fail safe?" Luke questioned.

"Probably in case one of his experiments had turned on him. He must've equipped all his men with silver bullets."

"So," Stuggs said. "What's next?"

"We find the Don and bring him in." Maria answered.

The following morning, the police all came out and discovered the Don's men inside the club. They were all arrested, even the owner of the club was taken. The search for the Don continued for several days, only for Maria to discover he made a trip to Europe. Knowing her jurisdiction, she couldn't go after him. She made a phone call to a friend and informed them of the details. A day later, the Don was caught and brought back to the States. The case was officially solved. Yet, the exposing of a werewolf remained a secret between all parties. Luke prepared himself to leave Detroit with Madeleine agreeing to accompany him. Maria had found him outside his residence while Madeleine jumped into the vehicle.

"I see she's going with you to wherever you're off to."

"The case is solved. My time is done here."

"I understand. However, if there is another case to be solved here, perhaps they can call you again."

"It seems you've warmed up to me." Luke grinned.

"For the moment. You proved useful for this case. That's something I can respect."

"I can get behind that."

Luke entered the car as Maria walked toward the door.

"So, what's next for Private Investigator Luke Cline?"

"I'm not certain. I thought this world was only dealing with criminals and drug lords. Now, with this new revelation of werewolves, there must be more out there to discover. To learn. So, that's where I'll be heading."

"To find more werewolves?"

"To learn more about the world." Like nodded. "We have no idea as to what truly dwells among us."

Maria nodded, stepping back from the car. giving her farewell to Luke and his to her. Luke and Madeleine rode off out of Detroit, where a new discovery may very well be set.

AGENT TREVOR

ONE MISSION: A SPY SHORT STORY

The sound of two gunshots echoed through the darkness. The end
of the hallway was difficult to see through without some form of light.
Coming through the dark was a figure. Human-shaped. The figure
continued to grow as it made each step forward.

Walking out of the dark area was a spy agent. Lean-figured, dressed
in a casual suit with no tie. His focus was keen on the mission. The
hallway in front of him had lit up with lights upon the walls and the
rooms are closed. Silent and calm. Coming from around the corner into
the hallway is Trevor moved through the hall with pace. He reaches the
elevator and enters. Going up toward the eighth floor. The agent waited
as the elevator made its move. The steady stop and as the doors slid
open, the Agent saw two well-dressed men standing in the hall,
guarding a room. The Agent has found what he's searching for. He
backed up to avoid being spotted. He reached down toward his side,
revealing his *Ruger LCP*. Raising it slowly, prepared to fire. Before he
continued his act, he glanced over to the wall in front of him, seeing a
fire alarm. He paused. Thinking. He moved swiftly, pulling down the
alarm and setting it off through the hall.

"The hell?" One of the men said.

"What do we do now?" The second man questioned.

"We keep this door secured. Nothing else matters right now."

"You're sure the alarm won't trigger anyone to come up this floor?"

"For what reason would anyone come up here uninvited? They
want to die early?"

From the other rooms on the floor bolted out hotel guests. Many of
them. They make their way toward the stairs and the hallway is
crowded. The Agent took a look, catching the hallway filled and the

two men were still guarding the door. The guards themselves have their hand on their firearms for precaution. The Agent moved through the crowd without a misstep, placing a silencer over the muzzle to his Ruger. The Agent took the first shot before ducking down in midst of the crowd, The shot had killed one of the men as his body fell to the ground in the middle of the moving crowd. His partner turned over to look and noticed he wasn't standing on the other side.

"Where'd you go? We're on duty."

The Agent moved in closer as the hallway showed itself becoming empty. The Agent took the second shot, killing the second guard without fail. The Agent paused. He scouted the hallway, finding no one in sight besides the two dead guards. He nodded and opened the door. He walked into the room with his firearm in hand. Seeing it decorated with shelves of books, candles, and fancy décor. The Agent knew whoever had a room like this had the resources to acquire it. Discovering himself facing who's he come for. The target had been found. There was a man sitting at a desk, drinking a glass of scotch.

"Patrice O'Haire." The Agent said.

Patrice gestured his finger and from both side of the room emerged three more guards. Each with their firearms aimed at the Agent. The Agent glared toward each one of them, showing only an expression of a grin.

"If I only knew you were coming sooner I would've poured you a glass."

"Save yourself the favor. I'll drink after the mission is complete."

Patrice chuckled, laying back in the chair.

"You spies. You're all the same, you know. Always snooping around in others' business. A bit nosy don't you think. Strangely enough, you always wonder why no one wants to take a moment and leave you guys be."

"I'm not here to chat."

"I know. I know." Patrice smiled. "Tell me please, why have you come to see me? What is it this time that has soured those on the opposite sides of the work?"

"You know what you've done." The Agent answered. "No need in repeating past words to rekindle your memory."

Patrice grunted.

"Again with this kind of talk. Do they teach you these words in your training? My goodness! All business and no fun."

"You forget the work of a spy. The mission is always the fun part."

"Sounds depressing." Patrice sighed. "Must be some kind of life, huh?"

"It has its benefits."

"Indeed." Patrice nodded.

Patrice signaled his guards to prepare to fire. The Agent knew the movements well, keeping his eyes locked on Patrice while watching closely the motion of the guards. Six to one. The Agent was confident in his abilities to succeed. Regardless of the numbers.

"Any last words, Patrice?"

"Just a few." Patrice said, turning over to the guards. "Take him."

The Agent gestured his eyes over to the opposite wall, noticing a fire extinguisher. He shot the extinguisher, shrouding the entire room in a fog. From there, he moved with silence throughout the room. The guards scattered themselves searching while Patrice remained at the desk, sitting down with concern.

"Shit!" Patrice yelled with a panic. "Find him! Kill him!"

The guards weren't able to see the Agent, yet he knew through the fog where the guards were placed. The scenery reminded him of target practice. From there, the Agent fired shots toward each of them without a single stop in his step. Only the sounds of thuds were heard through the white fog. Patrice couldn't see a thing, waving his hand in the air. The fog had cleared, Patrice found his desk surrounded by his guards, now dead on the floor, bleeding into the carpet. The Agent however, was standing in front of Patrice over the desk.

"I'm not going to repeat my last words."

Patrice jumped up from the chair, running out of the room toward the door to the hallway. The Agent followed him out. Patrice made a move to the elevator, even though the fire alarm was still buzzing. The Agent watched as Patrice panicked at the elevator with fear. Patrice stood by the elevator, vigorously pressing the button and yet, the elevator doors do not open. Patrice took another look behind, seeing the Agent walking toward him. Patrice fell on his knees, looking down in terror. The Agent removed the silencer

"This was the only way." The Agent said.

The Agent fired the shot, shooting Patrice in the head. Afterwards, the Agent placed his gun into its holster and reached for his phone. He dialed a number. Someone had answered on the other end.

"The mission is done. I'm on my way."

The Agent hung up, leaving the body of Patrice on the floor. The fire alarm had silenced just as the Agent pressed the elevator button and the doors opened. Going down to the first floor. The Agent made his way outside the hotel. He walked toward a silver sports car parked near the entrance. Taking out the keys from his jacket pocket, he entered the car. Driving from the hotel. The Agent drove through the streets, not far out from him was the city of Vancouver. The Agent took a turn, making his way toward the city's airport.

AGENT JOHN TREVOR WILL RETURN.

THE BOOK OF THE ELECT

HAND OF DOLPH

From the eyes I saw nothing but darkness. The cold air rattled me by its cool touch as it swooped in from the doorway. Trying my hardest to lay back to sleep, I could not. Upon deciding to get up from the bed and take a small walk around my home, I began to wonder if I was having an unusual event in my own home. True, I did have my skepticism on the matter of ghosts or spirits. Whichever you prefer to call them. I did hesitate to do a full search of my home because of my thoughts telling me of a burglar in the home. Once that thought entered my mind, I immediately grabbed my sword and walked slowly through my home.

Upon finding nothing inside the home. I took a big exhale and walked back to bed. Few hours later I wake up to the same sight of darkness and the cold air had returned. Now, I wonder if someone really is inside my home. I hear sounds of footsteps coming from the kitchen area. I jumped up and ran toward the kitchen. While I entered it, no one was inside the kitchen. Wiping my head from this strange occurrence, I had no answers to give to these kinds of questions. I started to have a low level of panic inside of my body and rushed back to the bedroom. I later went back to sleep.

I woke up the following morning to the sense of someone in my home. I decided to get dressed and I walked into the front room of the home and I saw no one. But, I could swear I heard someone in the home beside myself and I could hear their voice. It sounded like a elderly woman's voice talking as if she wasn't the only one in the room.

After doing my labor, I returned home and prepared for bed. Though, this time when I entered the home, I saw the elderly woman standing in the hallway, looking towards the kitchen. I called out to her and she didn't make the slightest move. I called to her again and she slowly inched her way toward my sight. She stared at me with cold eyes and I stared back. She gave me a nod and walked down the hall and evaporated in thin air. From that moment on, I knew I wasn't alone in the home and my skepticism had disappeared from my mind as I had witnessed a ghost firsthand.

After witnessing the woman, I began trying to contact her spirit, so I could understand why she would be in the home and not on the Other Side as they like to call it. After a few attempts of practicing with the Ouija Board, I came into contact with the woman. She told me her name was Margaret and she was a former resident of the home during the late 18th Century. I asked her why she was still in the home and she responded by saying that the Endless Ones had kept her here due to her sacrifice of saving her own lover from being murdered by another spirit that once dwelled inside this very home.

Week after week and day after day, I continued to have conversations with Margaret and discussed possible ways to help her leave this realm. She told me that there would be possible ways to help her go into the Other Side, but I would need the tools necessary to accomplish the task. The first tool she told me was knowledge of both this world and the other and how they work and co-exist among each other. The second tool would be faith that I would come out of it alive myself and not lost in the time space as a spirit wandering the earth looking for a way out.

Upon the coming months, I immediately dove my head into many books, accounts, and historical records that contained details of the Other Side to demonology to the Occult and to faith and how it works when facing these kinds of odds. After about four months, I came to the senses that I would be ready to help Margaret enter the Other Side.

One night on sixth day, I sat by myself and began inciting a ritual that would help me conjure up Margaret and send her into the Other Side. While saying the ritual I seen Margaret standing in front of me and as I looked up toward her I noticed a very dark shadow behind her. I felt the same cold air as before when my eyes gazed upon it. From the shadow I could tell it was indeed the same darkness that I saw before. Margaret couldn't say anything, but I could tell that she was in fear and I didn't have a clue how to protect her from that dark shadow. But, from her eyes I could tell that she knew what the dark shadow was, and she was very still not to move away from it or it could've possibly snatched her deeper into the abyss.

From that night on, I continued to study and do a plethora of research to help save her from this house and the dark shadow. Upon doing my due diligence, I uncovered that the land of which the home is built over was once used as a place where the occult would come and perform rituals and sacrifices to a being called The Unheard-Of. Their rituals and sacrifices would first bring out the Endless Ones, which is what Margaret had told me about. After the Endless Ones come and go, they deliver the prayers of the worshippers of The Unheard-Of in hopes of him giving them their prayers and answering them in any part of their lives.

After studying and reading about the Endless Ones and The Unheard-Of, I finally managed to prepare myself physically and spiritually to perform the session. During that night, I managed to conjure up Margaret again and she appeared before me. She appeared and had a small smile on her face. As I continued the session, I once again felt the cold air touch my face and the darkness appeared in my sights. This time it stood directly in front of me. The fears and doubts of failing had started to overcome me due to the shadow in my presence. I could hear Margaret's voice, telling me to fight the shadow with my faith and understanding. I gained my strength and continued to session while the shadow stood there. Eventually, the shadow disappeared, and I witnessed Margaret glow a bright white, a white unlike anything I've seen on this earth. The light emitted from her and she slowly ascended and vanished. Afterwards, I could only feel peace and security, knowing that she is no longer trapped and has moved over onto the Other Side.

To this day, I can still remember that incident and I've also heard countless stories and accounts of others having the same incidents in their own lives. It's been about ten years since the incident and I've learned quite a lot in between those ten years concerning the Other Side, the Endless Ones, and The Unheard-Of. Though, my story isn't the only one that must be told to the world.

I am only known to the people of this world and the elect few as Dolph and I have just presented to you the story of how I became a helping hand into saving a trapped spirit from the darkness that dwells in this world and beyond.

DREAMS AND VISIONS OF LEVI

These are the dreams and visions of Levi, "*The One who Called Them*". These are the words of gratitude and faith of Levi, who prayed and kept faith in the Most High that he would deliver them from the treacherous world where elemental beings were wrecking havoc across the earth. Where no mortal man could find a way in an attempt to stop them. As many people of the earth began to lose faith, Levi held on to his faith and never thought of relinquishing it. The world was as if the tribulation had already taken effect and the world knew of its power and terror. Beings made from the earth, fire, water, air, carbon, ice, sand, and amongst many others were crossing the earth, doing much damage that could be possible to witness.

Blessed is Levi for his great faith. Levi, a young man whose eyes were indeed opened by the Most High, saw a vision of the Holy One on the throne, he saw the heavens and the angels above. Levi knew what he saw was the Messiah sitting on the throne in the future days to come where his Kingdom will come down from Shamayim and will rule for one thousand years on the earth until the Final Battle between the Lawless One and The Most High Yah. Levi had concerned himself for trying to help the earth by fighting against the Elementals, yet he knew that they were sent by the Most High to teach humanity a lesson in humility and for them to truly know their place.

Another night, Levi had fell asleep and was witnessed to another dream where he saw all the Elementals standing near the ocean coast, where he saw above a total of seven beings come down from the sky. He could see their wings and how bright they were. The beings looked as if they were made of some form of metal not known to earth or humans.

Levi understood that the seven beings were a symbol of a force that will come to earth when the time is right. Levi would tell his advising Marshal about his dreams and he was mocked and ridiculed of them as the people of the earth were already giving up and waiting to die to the Elementals. Levi never gave up hope or faith as the majority of the world had given up.

Levi went asleep again and was revisited with another dream, where he saw the seven beings standing before the Elementals and all of humanity. The beings stood above the skyscrapers of the earth and fought against the Elementals, killing them without any pure force. Levi would watch as he witnessed the Elementals being destroyed by the seven beings and he knew it was a sign of good things to come upon the earth. The dreams stayed constant with Levi wherever he would go, the dreams were on his mind and his faith was increasing. Throughout the months, Levi began having visions, where he would see each of the seven beings individually and he would speak to them. He learned their names and their purpose.

In the first vision, Levi found himself in the clouds as he stood in front of the first being, who's revealed its name as Master Titan to Levi. Levi was able to see Master Titan in all of its glory. Master Titan was made of a material not suited for earth, suited for the heavens. Master Titan had told Levi to prepare himself and his allies for their coming, even though they may not listen. They are coming. Levi would tell his Marshal and allies about the dreams and visions. They perceived them to be a fairy tale that Levi was creating in his head.

The second vision had Levi find himself standing before the second being in the clouds, who told Levi its name was Covert Ghost and it told Levi its purpose and also revealed that it was also coming and warned Levi to tell his allies. Levi continued to tell his Marshal and allies about the dreams and visions, and they continued to deny him a word. Levi kept his faith strong and his hope held high towards the Father.

The third being appeared in a dream to Levi, where he saw himself standing in the clouds again facing the third being. The third beings told Levi its name was Iron Cavalier and its purpose was to aid the previous two in the first battle against the Elementals. Stating that they would win the first battle to make a statement to humanity. Levi understood Iron Cavalier very well and was told to warn his allies about their coming. Levi told Cavalier that they would not listen and yet, Cavalier repeatedly told Levi to warn them. Just to give them the warning is all he would have to do.

Levi had given his Marshal and allies the entire warning of the three beings appearing for what they called the *"first battle"*. Levi was laughed at and mocked for his words, he didn't fall short and he gave them the rest of the warnings and left the area. Upon doing so, he witnessed the three beings come down from the sky for everyone to witness. The three beings were Master Titan, Covert Ghost, and Iron Cavalier. They had arrived on the earth and split up in three paths, heading towards the Elementals. Levi knew his faith was answered. The Marshal and his allies came toward him and asked for forgiveness to their ignorance. Levi forgave them as they aligned together with the beings to fight off the Elementals. Though, Levi remembered that he saw a total of seven beings in his dreams and these were only the first three of seven.

After a week, Levi had a vision where he found himself hovering in the air and encountering the fourth being who called itself Skycrush. Skycrush told Levi that he travels through the air and is coming for the "second battle". Levi warned his Marshal and allies about the second battle approaching and they believed him, but still had conjured up thoughts about giving up completely. Levi's faith was still intact, even after the "first battle" was over and won by the first three beings.

In another dream, Levi came into contact and was visited by the fifth being. Levi had seen the being's head as it appeared as a mechanical lion's head with golden eyes. The being told Levi its name was known to earth as Lion Blade and it was coming for the second battle. Levi understood its words and continued to warn the Marshal and his allies about the second battle's coming. Even though, Levi was stuck with his teammates Sheba and Felix as they were tasked with taking down Baal and Moloch for destroying the environment, the beings still ringed a bell in Levi's conscious.

Later, Levi had a vision where he seen the sixth being who called itself Red Slash, for its red coloring. Red Slash had told Levi that the second battle would be more difficult than the first battle due to the increasing power of the Elementals. Levi understood the words of Red Slash and continued to warn everyone that he came into contact with. By that time, the Elementals were stronger than before and most of humanity had completely given up, except for Levi, Sheba, Felix, and his Marshal.

As the second battle had ensured and Levi saw the beings were having a more difficult time with the Elementals than before, he continued to pray for faith and hope that the beings would overcome the Elementals' increasing strength. Levi kept his faith and hope intact as the fight for the earth was becoming more difficult as the days went by. The two men, Baal and Moloch had increased the Elementals' power by polluting most of the earth through cloud spraying and genetically modified crops.

During the days where hope seemed almost lost to many, where the Elementals were apparently winning against the beings because of their increased strength. Levi had another dream and vision where he stood in the midst of the seventh being, who was more powerful than the first six. Levi had noticed something drastically different about the seventh being. The seventh being was covered in the colors of white, gold, and red, all of which shined from its presence. The seventh being had told Levi that his name was Armega Grath and he would save the earth from the most powerful of all Elementals, known as Barawk, an elemental made of lightning. Armega told Levi that he and the six beings were called Vigils and their purpose is to watch over humanity until the time of tribulation and judgment.

"What you see here, Levi, are the days where faith must be restored, and hope shall never be lost." Armega said. "I am now coming to end this battle and bring peace to the earth."

Levi would question Armega Grath about the end of the battle and how the future would be. Armega would only tell him that he would end the battle and would bring peace to humanity for a limited time as there are other beings who exist and are destined to come to earth to prepare for the End Days.

"When you see me come down from the heavens, you will know this great and third fight will be over and the Elect will be protected until the time of tribulation and judgment occurs."

Levi had awoken and found himself on another mission with Sheba and Felix as they were at their final attempt to stop Baal and Moloch. While on their mission, a loud trumpet had sounded from the sky and Levi knew it was Armega Grath and he saw him coming down from sky, glowing and shining in his presence. Armega had aided the remaining Vigils in the third battle against Barawk and Esh, an elemental made of fire. After defeating and killing all of the Elementals, the Vigils revealed themselves to the world and to humanity. Armega looked down and saw Levi. He thanked him for his faith, trust, and hope and vowed that they would return when the next threat makes its presence known to humanity.

These are the dreams and visions of Levi, *"The One who Called Them"*. Blessed be his name as one of The Elect who will inherit the Kingdom of Yah in the days to come upon the earth and upon all of Creation, be it the Father's Will.

DREAM OF THE UNHEARD-OF

Legends have told about a unseen force that works in the shadows. A malevolent force. Some call this force the Devil or ha-Satan as others tend to use other names that appear lower than the previous two such as Lucifer, Mammon, accuser, adversary, Father of Lies, deceiver, old serpent, the dragon, Son of the Morning, or even Son of Perdition. One name that the ancients used was The Unheard-Of. Though, The Unheard-Of has a different description as far as appearances go, but the attitude and character remained the same.

The Unheard-Of is a legendary figure that goes throughout history in many cultures and mythologies. Only mention in a certain few and removed from many in recent memory, The Unheard-Of has a profound history of accounts in which he has been present among the earth and humanity itself. It is said that he is the one who corrupted mankind in order to have them follow in his image and laws. The Unheard-Of is also known for creating the large amounts of war and destruction that have been on the earth and are still continuing at a small, but faster rate. For those who have looked into the tale of The Endless Ones, they have discovered that The Unheard-Of does not work alone and has his soldiers known as The Endless Ones to do his biddings for him. He also has humans on is side as well, giving them promises that they can't deny, yet he delivers some and denies many, thus taking their spirit when they die on the earth and keeping them in his domain of darkness and void.

At one time, an elderly man by the name of Gaius wrote in his own chronicle book of how The Unheard-Of had appeared before him and offered him a chance at immortality and wealth, if he did what he was commanded to do. The Unheard-Of had commanded Gaius to attack his descendants and murder them in cold blood. Gaius, a holy and earthly, but spiritual man declined the offer and rebuked The Unheard-Of, casting him out of his presence. The Unheard-Of is known for appearing before humans that he sees bold enough to take on his offering in exchange for power and wealth. There is even the story of how The Unheard-Of attempted to bride the Messiah into ruling the world and its kingdoms. The Messiah declined the offer and The Unheard-Of disappeared.

Through the numerous accounts of history, The Unheard-Of has been operating in the shadows, just as he does in modern time. If many were to look at the wars, the famines, the desolations, the violence, the purging of many cities, towns, countries, states, provinces, parishes, and even small islands, they would see the foul hands of The Unheard-Of on them. The Unheard-Of would also hand out false lies in order to cause disturbances in many groups that would seem to be untouchable and unbreakable, yet he has managed to break many up and cause grudges among them.

In claims of The Unheard-Of, it is said that he usually appears before humans in a form of the serpent or in the form of a man who appears well-dressed and speaks with flattering, kind words. Though his heart is full of evil, envy, strife, and violence as he seeks to destroy his next victim. History shows how The Unheard-Of was formed and what turned him into the entity that he is in this time. The Unheard-Of was once a servant for the Most High *YAH*, aligned as one of the primary archangels among Shamayim. His name was Abednego, which means shining and servant of light. When the day came that the Most High created the humans, known as Adam and Eve and the Most High told the angels of Shamayim to bow before them since they were created in His image. The angels bowed except for Abednego, who refused to bow due to the Most High creating mankind from dust as he and the angels were created from fire. Abednego's pride began to corrupt him and he set out to dethrone the Most High from his Kingdom and even convinced one third of the angels to aid him in doing so. When the Abednego revealed his true intentions, his allied angels stood beside him and faced the Most High and his angels.

The War in Shamayim took place for a total of seven days in human time as Michael The Archangel battle Abednego and cast him out of Shamayim along with his allied angels. After being cast out, The Most High stated that his days are numbered and there will come a time when he must face his judgment and will be sentenced for eternity. Now, Abednego is known as The Unheard-Of and the rebel angels are known as The Endless Ones, though some human spirits have become Endless Ones as well do to their dark spirit and character.

It is prophesied that in the near future, The Unheard-Of will rise up a man in the earth, a political figure, a man who will be loved by all in the world except by the believers and followers of the Most High. The Unheard-Of calls his leading man Abaddon and he will command The Endless Ones to do his biddings on earth as The Unheard-Of watches over him and applauds his actions in desolating the earth and killing the true believers of the Most High.

During the days before that terrible account, the earth will be filled with nonbelievers and followers of The Unheard-Of. Faith of the Most High will evaporate from many of humanity and will in turn go toward The Unheard-Of. Many humans will end up worshipping themselves and building temples and graven images to themselves in honor of themselves. Their birthdays will become their most celebrated day in the year. To this day, The Unheard-Of still works in his ways, more so than ever as his time is becoming short and he's gathering as many spirits as he can for the coming battle that will take place in the future.

Many say they dream of The Unheard-Of, stating that he's trying to gain their attention in seeking a deal for their spirit. Some accept and some decline, but all will have their answer when the battle occurs on the earth as the sun will be darkened and the moon will turn into blood and the stars will fall out of the sky. The heavens will be shaken, and the earth will rumble as the day is approaching for The Unheard-Of's greatest fall.

THE OLD MAN

In the distant past of mankind, during the days of iniquity and transgression, in a small cabin on the outskirts of the city lived an old man. Though, his name has been lost in history, but what he had accomplished stood the test of time. For the Old Man was a consistent man, a man who did his labor and rested on the seventh day. He was humble and to many people righteous. For people feared him because of his submission to The Most High and he feared the Most High greatly.

One day, when the king known to his land as Ahab, son of Omri arrived at the Old Man's home with his wife Jezebel, the daughter of Ethbaal king of the Zidonians by his side. He walked toward the door and proceeded to knock, but it opened, and the Old Man stood in the presence of a king and his queen.

"It is I Ahab, your king and my great wife and queen, Jezebel." said Ahab.

"For what purpose does thou intend to make by stepping onto my property, King Ahab?" the Old Man replied. "Is there something you wish to take from me? Is there a bounty on my head for a crime that I did not commit? Is there a damsel who has claimed that I laid with her when I did not? For what purpose does thou have by standing at my doorstep?"

"Calm yourself, sir. Thou are not in any trouble. I and my lovely queen here would like to speak with you about a proposal that involves my kingdom and yourself in a pact."

The Old Man stared deeply in Ahab's eyes and didn't bother to even glance into Jezebel's. For he knew what kind of woman she was and he could see how her heart was full of rebellion, jealously, and envy. He allowed Ahab and Jezebel into his home carefully, looking back for any signs of Ahab's soldiers that could be surrounding his home without his knowledge. Though, the Old Man never showed any fear to Ahab or Jezebel. He knew The Most High was with him at all times.

Ahab and Jezebel sat down in his chairs as he approached them at the table, where he had water sitting. Jezebel began to scratch her throat as she glanced over to the water. Ahab noticed her behavior and signaled the Old Man.

"Good sir, my queen appears to be thirsty from the long journey over to your home. Could you care to give her some water."

The Old Man poured some water into a small cup and handed it over to Jezebel, who drank all the water that laid still in the cup. She sat the cup down and smiled at the Old Man, thanking him for the water. He nodded and returned his attention toward Ahab.

Jezebel continued her way of gaining attention in the room by interrupting the conversations between the Old Man and Ahab, suggesting alternative terms and agreements as to what Ahab's offer to the Old Man was about. The Old Man scratched and rubbed his forehead as Jezebel continued to interrupt the conversation. The Old Man raised his hand toward Jezebel, silencing her. Ahab noticed the situation.

"How dare thee decide to raise thou hand toward my queen! You do understand that I could have you in chains if I must be."

"Fear not, King Ahab. For I will not smite your queen. I am a patience man and I would never lay thy hand on a woman. For it is injustice to *YAH* and to His Kingdom."

Ahab shook his head and Jezebel puffed her breath and mumbled in front of the Old Man and Ahab. Ahab tried to relax Jezebel, but his couldn't as she slapped him on his face and caused Ahab to stumble in his seat. The Old Man laid down his head, seeing a woman attack a man in his presence of all in his own home.

"You would never tell me what to do!" Jezebel said. "I am your queen for a purpose and that purpose is to fulfill what is rightfully mine. If I command you to bow down to our Lord, Baal, you would do as much. For I am your queen."

"Ahab, I suggest you get rid of your nail instantly before more harm comes your way. A saucy woman will never do a man any good unless she is fully capable of submitting toward your husband. I would never bow before any false god nor idol. For I am a believer and follower of the Most High and he will protect me."

"You accuse me of not submitting?!" Jezebel yelled. "My king only submits to me! I shall never submit to anyone who walks among this earth."

"Perhaps you do not submit to the Most High. For he is the one who gave you the breath of the spirit of life. He is the one that placed you into this land that you have gained the opportunity of becoming queen. Yet, you throw it all away for more power and destruction. Tell me it isn't so and you can rebuke me."

"I have no need to respond to thou ridiculous questions, old man. I am your queen and you will do what I command thee to do!"

Ahab leaned over toward the Old Man and whispered in his ears before standing up and leaving the home with Jezebel, who continued to rant on about her royalty and good looks. After seeing the king and queen leave his land, the Old Man walked into the center of his home and went down on both knees and prayed to the Most High for forgiveness, in allowing the two royalties into his own home of solitude and set-apart.

"Abba Father, please forgive thee for bringing the iniquity into my home of solitude and peace. Please continue to give me the courage and wisdom while I continue with my earthly life as I know that one day I will be in your presence and will look upon thou face in glory and in peace. Please protect me from the world that stands boldly outside of these walls. Please let your spirit fall onto those who will obey your laws, your statutes, and your commandments. For they will deem themselves as the worthy and Elect in your name and in this world full of evil and wrought. In your glory, AMEN."

The Old Man continued to live in his home that stayed set-apart from Ahab and Jezebel's kingdom and from the world. Many years later, after the downfall of Ahab and Jezebel, the Old Man grew even more weary as he later found himself guiding a young man and his wife. After several more years, the Old Man died, and he gave up the ghost and entered Shamayim to live and dwell among the Most High and the Heavenly Host that stood around him.

THE FAITH OF STEPHANIE

During the late days in the land of Urz, there lived a young woman named Stephanie and she was lovely, respectful, and had great fear for the Most High. Stephanie desired a life full of peace and prosperity. Though, in Urz, she could only gain that peace and prosperity through a man who was fearful of the Most High and followed his laws, statutes, and commandments. Though, there were many men that dwelled in the land of Urz and out of a thousand, not a single man was found to have been worthy of Stephanie's love.

"Oh, my Father in Shamayim, please deliver my praise to find someone who I can truly be with and live among them in your loving sight." Stephanie said.

Stephanie was twenty and two years old when she first went to search for a man who had the qualities of the righteous that lived among the earth. She continued her search throughout the entire land of Urz and still wasn't able to come to terms as to why she couldn't find a man worthy of her presence and love. One day, she left the land of Urz and traveled east toward the kingdom of Akadia and was greeted by her grandmother, Merith, who was fearful of the Most High and was greatly protected by Him.

Merith was one hundred and thirty years old when Stephanie greeted her in the kingdom of Akadia. Stephanie entered her grandmother's home and stayed with her for a number of four nights and four days as she began to learn wise words and knowledge from her grandmother. Merith stated that a man must seek a woman and not the other way around. She began to speak of another woman who was named Beth, she had lived in a land not far from Urz, who seek greatly to find a husband. Merith said that after seven years of wandering and searching, Beth finally found a man worthy of her love in the presence of the Most High. Many men had come before her and did not meet the qualities that she deserved and seek.

"What should I have to do to place myself in the right position or area for a righteous one to stand in front of me and take me as his wife?" Stephanie asked. "What must I do to achieve such a task?"

"I suggest to you, my granddaughter, that you work on yourself first and foremost before going and searching for a husband to cleave onto. I do not want you to make the mistake that many women and men have made over the centuries when it came to this type of discussion. Only a few have listened to words such as this and have succeeded in finding a husband or wife. Many decided to close their ears and ignore the wise council and ended up failing in the process."

Stephanie continued to learn from her grandmother as she stayed in her home for another three night and three days and gained even more knowledge on the discussion and began building up her faith. After the three nights and three days was due, Stephanie left her grandmother's home and left the kingdom of Akadia and returned to her home in the land of Urz, where she dwelled for seven more years, seeking and searching for a husband to cleave onto. During the seven years, she met a man, who spoke with flattering words and impressed Stephanie. They became closer as nights and days went by. Eventually, Stephanie discovered that the man she was seeing had done evil in the sight the Most High and discovered he had been killed in battle against the armies of Isabelle while aiding with Queen Zimmah in the kingdom of Zimmahiah.

Three more years had passed, and Stephanie was only holding onto her own faith in the Most High to give her a husband to cleave onto. During one night, she went down on her knees and prayed loudly for the Most High to hear. She screamed "Oh, *YAH*, I praise in your name and I hope you can hear my voice crying out for your glory. If it is not in your decision to give me a husband, I will understand. For your will be done and I will obey your will and take heed from the evils of this world."

After her prayer, she left the land of Urz and traveled into the kingdom of Dianapolis, where she met Lebbeus, a man who was of heart, praise, and confession. He also trembled in the fear of the Most High. The man had gazed his eyes upon her and could see the love pouring off through her spirit. He approached her as she did him and they set a discussion to speak amongst themselves. After several months of meeting and speaking with one another, the two eventually came to an agreement and married in the kingdom of Dianapolis in the sight of the Most High, who approved the marriage set before them.

Stephanie had finally found peace and prosperity as she submitted herself to her husband as she sold her home in the land of Urz to live with her husband in the kingdom of Dianapolis. After two years, she bares a son, naming him Luke, she said, "He will become a gentle man who will be a shining example of knowledge and wisdom amongst the kingdoms of the earth." She lived with Lebbeus and her son Luke for all the days to come in the kingdom of Dianapolis. One day, she decided to go into a quiet room and give praise to the Most High for her marriage, her son, and her peace that she found on earth. She praised Him in all of His glory. She stated that she began to know her age is catching up to her and prayed that Luke will be a fine man and a servant of the Most High in his days of growth.

She loved her husband. Lebbeus and she loved her son, Luke. But, her ultimate love was toward the Most High, for He was her One True God and her named was written in the book of eternal life as she is one of the Elect.

THE SOUND OF CLARK ZYACK

Clark Zyack was a striving musician and tried his way into becoming a sensational star through music, fame, and glory. He wanted to be praised by millions of people across the world and wanted them all to chant his name in the glory of fame. He desired all the money that he could possibly achieve from his music and hope to gain himself a large mansion where he could live the life of a rock star.

Upon an ultimate opportunity to have his own music tour, he became cocky, arrogant, and selfish. Only looking out for himself in many ways that he could barely keep track of anyone around him that took him for a colleague or a friend. Doing his tours, he became increasingly addicted to alcohol and drug substances. Many of his friends began to abandon him when he couldn't control his behavior and his drinking habits. After months of tours and little breaks, he started losing friends one after the other. Telling himself he didn't care about them in the start, he continued his drinking and continued using numerous amounts of drugs, from cocaine to heroin to even attempting crystal meth during one of his stage shows.

One night, while he was drinking and taking cocaine, he passed out and lost consciousness. He awoke and found himself in a place consumed by darkness. No light shining in any direction, only pure darkness. The purest darkness that could possibly exist among human beings. Much darker than when the lights go out or when a person's head is fully covered. Even with the moon covered up, the darkness wouldn't equal to the pure darkness that Clark felt. He later noticed he could stand up and walk. He couldn't see where he was going, but knew every route of the mysterious location.

He continued to walk until he heard voices ahead of him. The voices were calling unto him to follow them. He told them he couldn't see them. In just a mere nanosecond, Clark's eyes were able to see the location in full detail. Clark looked around and seen that he just exited out of a small prison cell structure. He felt the intense heat burning him from all directions. Suddenly, he could hear loud screams coming from a distance.

He looked at the figures that spoke to him. They wore black cloaks and had their heads covered with hoods to where their faces couldn't be seen. There was a total of three of them that stood in front of Clark.

"Where am I?" Clark asked.

"Come with us and you'll discover it." One cloaked figure said.

The cloak figures gestured their hands toward Clark to follow them. He followed as they were walking through a dense and narrow hallway. He could overhear their conversation. They were making fun of the amount of screams that were heard and one even made fun of Clark's nakedness. Clark looked down at himself and noticed he was completely naked. Though, he had a human body and wondered how the intense heat wasn't burning his flesh. He continued to follow them through the hallway and they stopped. Clark stood behind them as they turned to face him. They each slowly reached to their heads and removed the hoods. They revealed their faces to Clark and he quickly screamed in fear. Their faces were as goblins, though burnt roughly and had very scaly skin as it looked to have been peeling off because of the burns and heat.

"What are you?! Where am I?!" Clark yelled.

"You're with us now, Clark Zyack. Welcome home." The three figures said.

The figures ran over and grabbed Clark. They began stabbing him with knives, blades, and even swords. Clark screamed as the pain was more painful than it would be on earth. As they were stabbing him, one figure grabbed Clark and raised him over their heads and walked toward a lake. The lake was made of fire and the smell of sulfur and brimstone poured off of it immensely. When Clark seen the lake and noticed the millions of people who were in it and screaming in pain, he knew he was in Hell or the Underworld, as many people call it.

"I haven't done anything wrong in my life!" Clark yelled. "Why am I here?! Why am I in this place?!"

They inched themselves closer to the lake, a tall figure emerged from a stack of boulders. The figure had a tail and its body looked as it was made from molten lava that dried. Its eyes glowed red as much as the fire glowed. The large figure stood above Clark and the three figures as if they were like small dogs to him. The figures backed away and left Clark on the ground facing the tall demon.

"Please tell me what I have done to deserve this torment?!" Clark yelled. "Please, I'm begging of you to tell me!"

"You pathetic human!" The large demon said. "You fooled around with alcohol immensely, you played around with drugs that ruined your earthly system. You laid with many damsels that you did not claim for your own and some were married to other men. You treated everyone around you like a sack of shit and you complain about doing everything right. Foolish ones never learn from their mistakes. Instead they hold on to others' mistakes without looking at their own!"

Clark yelled as the large demon snatched him by his head and walked over to the edge of the lake. He allowed Clark to stare into the lake as he saw millions of people who have died over the years burning in eternal torment for what they done with their earthly lives.

"You see all of those wretched souls down there." The large demon said. "They treated their earthly lives like it was a toy to them. They foiled their bodies with toxic chemicals and ignored the truths that were presented to them in their lifetime. Many souls that are down here and those that are yet to come are of souls that were lovers of self, lovers of money, they are boastful, arrogant, revilers, disobedient to their parents, ungrateful, unholy, unloving, irreconcilable, malicious, gossipers, without self-control, brutal, and most of all. Haters of all that was good and beautiful."

"A few of those sound like me."

"No. They are all that you are and because you decided to fool around with meth, you're down here in Gehenna with us."

"No, please. Let me return to earth. I can change my life around for the better. There has to be something that I can do to fix all of my problems."

"If you could do such a task, it will take great sacrifice and I'm not a believer in you to see such a task be accomplished."

"No please!"

"It's time for you to burn, Clark Zyack. For all eternity."

The large demon held Clark up over its giant head. Clark screamed as he tried fighting the demon, but his attacks had no damage to the demon. The demon suddenly freezes, and his body jumped back and crashed onto the boulders. Clark fell to the ground and raised his head. He saw a figure glowing in immense gold reach out toward him with its hand.

"Take my hand." The glow said.

Clark took the hand of the glowing figure and found himself going through a tunnel of light. He felt an immense amount of love and peace. He later continued through the tunnel and saw his life in the past, the present, and what the future could be. While seeing his own life, it starts to dwell on him all the tings his has done wrong in his life. From the alcohol to the fornication to the drugs to the hatred. He starts to cry as he wipes the tears from his face.

"I can change my ways. I know I can."

He continued through the tunnel, until he found himself in a hospital bed. Back in his earthly body, he saw that he was in a hospital and was brought in by some close friends after passing out from the combination of alcohol and cocaine. After a few days, they released him from the hospital and his life was completely changed from the events that he went through. He could still see the figures watching him at all times. He knew he could change his life around for the better and could help others having the same problems that he once had.

Months later, he changed his music format to a much better form of music. His new music was able to affect many people across the world in such a good way, that his new success was even better than his previous success. He was rid of the alcohol, the drugs, the fornication, and the hatred. He was married to a beautiful woman and had two sons with her.

After years of mediating on the event, he knew the glowing figure was the Messiah and had thanked him for saving him. One day, Clark walked outside of his home in his backyard and looked up in the sky. He could see a variety of angels looking down on him. He smiled and nodded as the angels ascended into the clouds. The Sound of Clark Zyack will go on to change many lives for the better for the rest of his days.

THE LOST TEMPLE

The Lost Temple is a legendary and mystical place where people can go and receive knowledge and healing. The temple was always visited by large groups of people on a daily basis. Many came over to the temple to pray and worship. Some came to cause chaos and even attempted to destroy the temple. Throughout the eras of time, many groups of people came to the temple. Those who worshipped pagan gods such as Baalim, Moloch, Tammuz, and Astarte, Queen of Heaven.

A variety of pagan god worshippers would come to the temple to receive knowledge and healing from their pagan gods, only to have caught a disease or even went insane by the vast amount of knowledge that conjured into their minds. During one night, while the worshippers of Astarte laid to rest at the temple, they were attacked and slaughtered by the Eshians or Fireans, the worshippers of the Fire Orb, powered by their god, Megazorah. They were led by Abishag, who proclaimed the temple a place of worship only for the Eshians. After the slaughtering, they took the surviving ones and made the men slaves, they raped and forced the women to be wives, and even molested the children and some even married them under the unction of Megazorah, their god.

"See this land before you, followers of Megazorah!" said Abishag. "We have taken this temple and proclaimed it the Temple of Megazorah, our god!"

The Eshians relished in their ruler ship of the temple and gained its knowledge and healing. The temple began to create witches, wizards, sorcerers, and doctors of the mystic arts. The people began to take pride in themselves with the found power and some started to proclaim themselves as gods. When they would speak of themselves being gods, Abishag would have them sealed to the ground, where he would kill them with their own sword, as they had believed they were above Megazorah and not below him.

A day came to pass when Yirmeyahu, known in modern times as Jeremiah, came across the temple and saw the Eshians bowing before it. He even seen some of his own people, Hebrew Israelites bowing down and drinking wine in front of the temple, praising Megazorah and the Fire Orb. Abishag noticed Yirmeyahu looked in the distant. He approached him and tried to bribe him in joining in. Yirmeyahu declined and said that in the latter days, they would all regret bowing down to idols and worshipping false gods. Yirmeyahu walked away, not looking back at Abishag, the worshippers, or the temple. As he worshipped and praised the Most High above all things.

Within decades, the Eshians found themselves at war with the Qerachians or Iceians, who worshipped the Ice Orb and their god, Steelzorah. The battle lasted eight days in front of the temple itself with both orbs sitting inside the temple on the pedestal. After the eight days, the Qerachians were declared the victors as the remaining Eshians took the Fire Orb and ran into the wilderness from the Qerachians. Four decades pass, until the Qerachians were dethroned from the temple by the Meads and Persians, who took the temple for themselves.

The Persians enjoyed their time with the temple, becoming great people amongst themselves. After they possessed the temple, it was overtaken by the Greeks, and later the Romans. Who completely transformed and defiled the temple. They took what they learned from the temple and its healing powers and began to use it for a sight-seeing location to merchandise the fellow Roman citizens or tourists who were passing through. The Pharisees even one time attempted to deceive the Messiah in entering the temple, which he decided to say, the temple was made of mortal hands and is bound for destruction due to its defilement and sinfulness.

Barbarians had feared the temple's power and refused to enter or even get close to it. After the Resurrection of the Messiah, people began to depart from the temple, causing the Pharisees to lose money and control over the masses. The temple was left abandoned until the 4th Century where the Roman Emperor, Constantine the Great had rediscovered the temple and used it form many of his worshipping ceremonies. He even allowed the pagans to enter the temple to worship their pagan gods. Constantine had noticed a large increase of people in Rome as the temple was the main attraction. He allowed all people to come in and worship their gods within the confinements of the temple.

Many people disapproved of Constantine's motives and ended up succumbing to death. Constantine enjoyed and relished in the celebrations that took place at the temple, from Saturnalia to the birthday worshipping to the people and to their gods. Constantine had made a law declaring that the rights to the temple will be passed down to the Roman Catholic Church, the Vatican.

After Constantine's death, the Vatican took full control of the temple and kept it for use of worship and healing. The knowledge of the temple was kept secret by the Vatican from the masses. From the 4th Century to the 21st Century, the temple is still in use. Though, not as much as it was in the past centuries. People come and go by the temple for healing and prayer, thus not knowing its grueling and profound historical accounts, since they have been kept secret from the public eye. Some information is out in the public for people to search and find the truth.

As it is told in the *Covenant of Ages*, in the Book of Deception and Salvation, the temple will be used as a massive marketing tool to lure people for profit by fooling them that the temple was used by the Messiah in ancient Rome. Many will succumb to the lie as only a few will see the truth in clear sight. The Antichrist will use the temple as the main source of worship in Rome, besides the city of Jerusalem. When the Messiah returns, He will destroy the temple from the earth and its knowledge and healing will be lost from the unbelievers and sinners of the earth.

BEYOND THE STEEP HILL

There is this tale and legend of a hill that appears as one steep and if someone decided to cross over and through the hill, they will find ultimate happiness in the earthly realm. Many have often wondered what could possibly be lying over on the other side of that steep hill. Could it be a city of wondrous prosperity? Could it be a load of gold and silver for one to be rich in the world? Could there be a virtuous woman who happens to live on the other side of the steep hill, waiting for her true lover to come to her? Whatever the case may be, many have decided to attempt crossing the steep hill.

The earliest known event of the hill is where a young man was seeking to please his concubines as he boasted up to go beyond the steep hill and find whatever was lying on the other side. In turn, the young boy didn't cross the hill as a gust of wind had blown him back toward his concubines, where he fell in front of them and was embarrassed of their laughter towards him. He decided to try again the second day and fell again due to the gust of wind. With his temper flurrying, he determined to try again, but this time he had two of his trustworthy allies to join him. The three men climbed the hill as the gust of wind returned, this time they held on by holding close to one another. After the gust vanished, they continue to reach over and suddenly a lightning bolt came down from the heavens and slammed directly in front of the three men. Causing them to fall on their backs towards the ground. The men weren't hurt from the fall and they were so embarrassed and terrified, that they left the hill alone.

The second attempt was during the time and ruler ship of King Liam, where a group of women warriors, led by their leader Queen Zimmah were seeking on discovering a treasure beyond the hill that could be used for warfare and dethroning Liam's kingdom and the kingdom of Queen Diana, the mother of Yisabelle. Queen Zimmah craved the desire of finding a divine weapon hidden behind the hill and sent her warriors to find it. As they climbed the hill, reaching for the top, angels came down from the sky and thwarted them off from the hill. The angels' appearance gave Zimmah the ultimate impression that there was a divine weapon beyond the steep hill, which fed her craving of the hill. Zimmah later tried again, this time with both her men and women warriors. They ran like wild animals towards the hill and Zimmah sought the angels in the sky to come down and deny her of the treasure. This time no angels came down from the sky. Zimmah began to revel in her finding. As the warriors inched closer, a lightning bolt that looked like fire came down and struck the warriors. Burning their armor and flesh until they were no longer walking. Zimmah fled the bottom of the hill with her remaining warriors as they left the burned bodies of their warriors on the hill to rot.

The third attempt took place during the time of the Greeks when the armies of King Mirrannidon sought their way towards the hill on their king's demand. The soldiers in groups of five each walked up the hill. King Mirrannidon was present for the events as described in his counselor, Rilrod's writings. The soldiers took ease as they walked up on the hill. Knowing the history that has unfolded from the hill.

"Nothing can stop us from claiming what is beyond this hill." Mirrannidon said. "We control all of Lelat and we will control the world."

"What if there's something beyond the hill that might cause your kingdom to fall, my lord?" Rilrod said.

"You speak of utter nonsense like a buffoon, Rilrod." Mirrannidon said. "You know how my conquests always end."

The soldiers continued with ease as fireballs began to drop out of the sky in mass. The balls ranged in sizes, some came down small, some came down medium, and some came down large. Mirrannidon fled from the raining fireballs. Commanding his army to fall back as he left the area.

"We shall try it another day. Be it the will of the gods of Eragard!" Mirrannidon boasted. "We will succeed!"

The fourth attempt took place during the days of Rome where a Hebrew soldier known as Arah, who fought for the glory of the Most High had a tragic event. After saying goodbye to his family, he went into battle against the enemies of Yah and was struck by a blow of an arrow fired by a Roman soldier. Arah immediately fell to the ground as the battle continued. He became dazed and suddenly found himself floating in the air. He could see the entire battle taking place below him.

He knew he was in spirit form and his earthly form had died on the battlefield. He noticed that a bright glowing light was in front of him and he reached for it with great strength. After reaching the light, he saw a city made of gold with streets of transparent gold. He knew he was in the physical realm anymore. He was in the midst of Shamayim or the Third Heaven as the modern world knew. As he looked around, trying to maintain his composure, he saw a man approaching him. The man had hair like wool and it was white as snow. His skin looked like bronze that was burnt in a furnace and his eyes looked like they held fire within them. Arah knew that this man was indeed Yahshua Ha-Mashiach or as he's commonly referred to by many in the English tongue, *Jesus Christ*. Arah fell to his knees and his face hit the golden streets.

"Please forgive me of what I have done in my life." Arah said. "I repent for all I have done and sinned on the face of the earth."

Yahshua commanded Arah to stand up and face him. Arah stood up, weeping. Yahshua said that Arah's time on earth was not done and he had to return. Arah shook in his feet as he told Yahshua that he didn't want to return to earth and that he was killed in battle and died a warrior. Jesus stated that his family needed him back and his work for the Most High was not yet done. Arah asked Yahshua what the work was, and he stated that he must do the will of the Father, that he and others who listen will have eternal life. Arah listens to Yahshua's command and is immediately return to earth, where he wakes up on the battlefield with his wound healed. Upon returning home, he came across the hill and knew of its history. He went to climb the him and had reached the peak where he could see over the hill. What Arah saw was unbelievable to his eyes and gave him even more hope in glorifying the Most High. Arah returned home and told his family about the hill and what he saw on the other side.

"There are no words on this earth that can describe what is beyond the steep hill." Arah said. "Not even the thought of a word nor a word created can truly describe what lies beyond it."

Still to this present day, people who know the history of the hill have tried to see what is beyond it and have not even reached the peak as Arah had done nor did they get far enough like the armies of King Mirrannidon nor did they burn like the warriors of Queen Zimmah. Nor were they highly embarrassed as the young man and his two allies. No one living today knows for sure what truly lies beyond the steep hill.

THERE WERE GIANTS IN THOSE DAYS

During the age when the earth was filled with violence and wickedness, there not only existed man among the earth, but giants were also present during the time of wickedness. Chanokh was one to witness the giants of renown enter the earth through the means of the Sons of Yah mingling with the Daughters of Man. Through the intermingling, came forth giants and the men of renown.

The giants fought alongside each other through the earth in those days, whereas even Chanokh knew their existence was not to be created nor to be designed. Giants began to form during the time of Queen Alyssa, whom had a giant build her castle and queendom alongside the men who allied with her, believing her false prophecies that were stated to come in the latter days. The giants were later witnessed by many others whom had come into the earth in those days and had seen the trouble that stood before them.

Harold, a man who had witnessed the galactic war between the Dark Gods and the Cosmics, witnessed the giants being used as tools for both legions against one another after Chanokh was taken from the earth to Shemayim by The Most High. The giants had picked sides, stating the winning side would rule the earth for one thousand years in their lifetime. In which, the Dark Gods won and the giants that sided with them became conquerors over the lands in the earth. Until they were overthrown and defeated by Harold, The Cosmics, and The Most High himself.

The Giants later became more corrupt than before. As they would begin to eat the flesh of man and drink their blood. It was during the days of Dore that the end of the Giants would be completed, and their death would be a civil war amongst each other before the flooding water had covered the lands of the earth. During those days, men fought back against the giants with swords, hammers, bows and arrows. The giants had overcome them in their bloody battles before The Most High spoke to Gabriel to cause them to fight each other until they were all dead.

The giants fought one another in a combat of blood and sweat. Giants slaughtering giants across the lands of the earth. For many had become witness to the great towering battles and foreknew it would be the beginning of the end of their time. The giants later rallied other giants to assist them and the civil war had begun. During the civil war, Dore and his family were preparing their vessel in preparation of the deluge that was coming after the civil war. Mankind in general had become partakers and witnesses to the battles of the giants. Some fed into the fights as a form of entertainment.

The mothers and fathers of the giants were weeping at their children killing and slaughtering each other. The fathers, which were the Sons of Yah, petitioned Chanokh to speak with The Most High in an effort of repentance. But, The Most High had rejected the petitioning and they were left to remain and witness their offspring kill each other in fights of bloodlust and rage. The giants fought for years and years. Generations of man that came before and came during were all witnesses to the war of the Giants. From Chanokh to Dore, the giants waged in a civil war.

Many of the Sons of Yah were taken and bind during the final days of the civil war. Unable to see their offspring again as they were taken into the darkness abyss. During those final years, Dore had preached to mankind, speaking of preparation of the water falling from the sky. Mankind mocked Dore as they went about their lives and continued to watch the war of the Giants as entertainment for their own sakes. Alyssa was gone from the earth, Chanokh was gone from the earth, Harold was gone from the earth, and Dore remained on the earth during the last years of the Giants' war.

Some nights, Dore could hear the roaring and smashing of the giants as they fought night and day constantly without any rest due to the spiritual power of the Archangel Gabriel with his order from The

Most High. The fallen angels bound into eternal prisons until their appointed judgments. They could still hear the sounds of their offspring fighting and dying in slaughters. Dore spoke with Methus, father of Miykael and grandfather to Dore about the coming deluge and the end of the giants' civil war. Methus foreknew that he would leave the earth and enter the spiritual realm after the giants had killed each other in order for the deluge to come across the earth. Dore's three sons, Adad, Samael, and Mordecai were also witnesses to the giants' final days of war.

In those last days of the time of the giants in the days of Dore, the giants were at their last. Constantly full of energy and rage in warfare. Dore and his family were set to enter the vessel before the deluge had come. Methus had prepared himself in entering the spirit world and leaving the natural world.

"The time is almost here, grandson." Methus said to Dore. "Once the abominations have killed themselves on the face of the earth, I will leave this world, allowing the deluge to come and wash the earth of its wickedness.

The giants fought to their last breaths as they all killed each other in warfare. The giants were all dead. Methus had passed on into the spiritual world. Dore and his family were set in the vessel as The Most High had closed the door and the deluge came and washed the earth of its wickedness. Forty nights and forty days the waters stood above the grounds of the earth with the wickedness beneath it, grasping for air.

After the waters had settled and Dore's sons had begat their own children with their own wives, a remnant of the giants was left behind. Though, these giants were in heightening size as of the giants that came before. There were giants in the days of Queen Alyssa, Chanokh, Harold, and Dore. But, the giants that came after were great in stature and powerful, but were nothing like the predecessors before them.

The predecessors however, within them were spirits of their own. Their spirits were of evil and had proceeded from their bodies. The evil spirits of the giants afflicted, oppressed, destroyed, attacked, do battle, and work destruction upon the earth and everyone on it, causing trouble. They take no food, but have an everlasting hunger and thirst, which cause offenses.

The spirits of the giants rose up against the children of men and against the women, because they proceeded from them. The spirits of the giants are what are commonly known as demons.

CETUS

The Cetus, a rare beast that has gone throughout history as one of the world's most terrifying creatures to live underneath the deep seas. The Cetus has its rare cases of destroying ships that sail above the oceans and dragging them and their crew deep beneath the sea to drown and later to eat upon. Those who have seen the Cetus with their own eyes depict the beast as a creature of pure malevolence and evil and its presence of great fear and trembling.

The Cetus is usually associated with the Greek God known as Poseidon, who used the Cetus to attack Ethiopia during the Greek era with Cassiopiea boasted of her daughter, Andromeda's beauty above the Nerieds that lived in the deep waters. In the *Hebrew Scriptures*, the monster is depicted to be the beast who swallowed Jonah. In the *Covenant of Ages*, the individual known as Ohm came into contact with the Cetus and was also swallowed by the beast, only to be freed a few days later. The Cetus is said to have been turned to stone by Perseus during their encounter. There also is a constellation of stars named after the beast itself.

There is one tale that hasn't been spoken about the Cetus that will present itself at this very moment. The time when the battle between the Ostacrean and Magnitran armies in the land of Lelat. During the battle, a warrior who is known as Accladus saw the Cetus with his own eyes before their ships made landfall to face the Ostacrean armies. In Accladus' own words he described the Cetus as a large serpent with eyes that could rip out an individual's soul and throw it deep under the sea until the soul had entered the depths of Hadi, where it would burn for eternity.

"The Cetus' eyes possessed so much darkness that it could suck the soul out of someone's body and throw it deep into the deep sea until it slammed into the ground where it would open, and the soul would be in the dwelling realm of Hadi, who guards the underworld."

There is also the event where the Roman army went into battle with the remaining Greeks and they used the Cetus as a tool for war. Having their soldiers ride on the back of the beast to destroy the Greeks who had ships in the nearby waters. They reveled at the sight of the beast attacking the Greeks and eating their bodies at such quick pace. It even created waves with its body to turn over their ships.

"We can use this creature for our own desires. The creature could possibly help us end this war with those lasting Greeks who continue to thwart our plans of world domination."

The Cetus had later disappeared with many ending tales to its name. People still say they've seen the monster throughout the centuries and decades that have raced over the face of the earth. From the 6th Century to the 19th Century as well into the 20th Century and the 21st Century.

There is also the legend of the Loch Ness Monster, who some believe could very well be the Cetus itself. Though, no evidence has been conclusive enough to determine of the Loch Ness Monster is indeed the Cetus of ancients' old. In the past and present hours, people cling to the idea of a colossal sea monster living beneath the seas that surround the land. People from all parts of the earth come together to tell the stories of their possible encounters with the Cetus while on a ship or near the waters of the sea. There was a quote that an individual said about the Cetus and its future place.

"We will come across the Cetus one day. I know in my heart that we will, and the great legend will be solved once and for all."

The individual continues his search for the Cetus at all parts of the earth where the seas may touch. He seeks the beast and craves its present before his eyes. He also has some companions with him as they all travel together to find the monster and reveal its legendary presence before the modern world. Though, interesting enough, there are tales of the Cetus' return and what its purpose is of returning and its full intent.

"The Cetus will return, and its imposing threat will spread across the globe like a pandemic. People near the seas will regret having their homes placed there as the Cetus will seek to destroy all that they possess. I surely hope they've prepared themselves for the great disaster that awaits them and others who live near the seas' waters."

Some believe the Cetus will be used for good and find a way of saving people trapped at the seas. Others believe that the Cetus is only an animal that has outlived many of its ancient companions and still dwells in the seas of the earth to this day and will do so beyond our time. There are those few who believe that the Cetus will be conjured up from the oceans by an evil force, who will use the beast for its own intended purposes of causing chaos across the globe.

In many books and legends, the Cetus is said to have risen, disappeared, and to return in future days. As sightings of the creature continue to show itself across the globe, many will only wonder if the Cetus will return and cause the chaos that many believe it will or will it return and protect the human race from itself and clean the seas that were once pure of filth and decadence.

"Those of us, who have intelligence and use it wisely, we know that this creature called the Cetus is one of many legends to spread across planet earth. It is our duty and task to find this creature at once before it finds a way to discover us once again and brings about the end of our world."

"Come quickly! The beast has appeared before us in this distressful time we live in. Send the armies to combat the creature as we are in a terrible situation, trapped here in these waters as the beast stares at us. Only

the Most High himself can truly help us overcome the threat we currently face. Send your armies at whatever disposal you can. For if you do not, this monster will come to your waters and destroy them as well. For this creature is not of great miracles and spectacles, but of pure hatred and deep malevolence that it possibly cannot be stopped by mortal men. Only Yah can stop the creature, for it is Him who created the world and it is Him who created the Cetus. Praise Yah. Praise YAH!"

THE ENDLESS ONES

The Endless Ones, many do not understand who they are or where they come from. They have been around since time began and are constantly growing in numbers. Created by The Unheard-Of, the Endless Ones scatter across the universe in a variety of ways. Both physically and spiritually. There have been many reports of the Endless Ones in both modern day and history.

Historical accounts describe the Endless Ones as humanoid beings that appear to be transparent in some parts and fully physical in another. One historical account described in Hebrew mentioned the Endless Ones had once taken over the world through The Unheard-Of, when many people began to consume themselves in violence and sodomy. Upon taking over the land, The Endless Ones were worshipped as gods and granted wishes and miracles to their followers. Many of their followers were misguided spirits who were lost and couldn't find their way to the Other Side. Other human beings who opposed the Endless Ones were either tortured or put to death by them or their followers.

Throughout the latter parts of the historical accounts, it stated that their powers began to fade as many humans turned to another source of faith to guide them in the power of the Christ. Upon losing their powers, The Unheard-Of decided to make himself known and showed himself to a large crowd that surrounded the followers of the Endless Ones and gathered them all, including the followers and took them away from the Earth to never return in their physical form.

After that moment in history, there have been slightly no signs of the Endless Ones on the Earth until the later days of the 14th Century when massive accounts of sighting took place. Many believed that the sightings were a sign that they were returning along with The Unheard-Of to destroy the world. But, that was not the case as the sighting were concluded as misguiding and falsely reported to the general population at that time. In latter centuries, sightings continued to be reported, some even by police, military, and political officials at the time. Though, none were taken seriously to consider a proper investigation and search.

In the early 1800s, there were sightings of the Endless Ones described by the witnesses and were fully detailed in drawings of them. Citing their large and strange humanoid shaped features with their rough burgundy red skin that appeared as if it was burned nearly to a crisp and their piercing and deadly glowing yellow eyes. The eyes resemble that of The Unheard-Of, citing that he has endowed them with some abilities of his own to use to their advantage. The drawings made the front page in news across Europe and later found its way across the globe.

Towards the 1900s, near the first World War, people began to assume that the war was started by the Endless Ones causing a stir in dividing countries from another, thus helping one country fight another with their supernatural help and guidance. Many believed the theory to be subtleness and ignored any possible reference or evidence of the Endless Ones aiding a country in the World War. After the war ended, sightings of the Endless Ones began to fade once again as many people moved on with their lives and their current state in faith. It wasn't until near World War II that many people began to realize that supernatural occurrence were taking place, and many believed it was in the form of Adolf Hitler and the Nazi party.

During the 1930s and 1940s, people were in constant fear of Hitler's rise to power by leading Germany into a new World War with a multitude of countries aligning and opposing each other. During one of Hitler's speeches, people said that they witnessed two humanoid beings enter the offices of the location, which is said where the Nazi party were into to discuss their plans in secret.

When Hitler gave his speeches, people reported seeing the Endless Ones standing beside him as he gave out the speeches declaring his plan to rule the world and create a new race of superhuman beings called the Aryans. Many Germans followed suit to Hitler as he led them into World War II. Many people believed that Hitler was given the idea of concentration camps by the Endless Ones to keep the ones who opposed him in line while he continued his plan of world domination.

After World War II, the Endless Ones began to fade again as the Third Reich collapsed, the Aryan race vanishing, and Hitler disappearing from public and military personnel. Afterwards was the creation of the United Nations, as many saw the opportunity of uniting the countries of the world into one singularity form of government. Some speculated that the Endless Ones were seen again near the Vietnam War and even the Cold War. Sightings of the Endless Ones disappeared with many people who believed they even existed and considered their historical accounts to be fairy tale stories passed down through generations.

Later near the 1980s and 1990s, smaller evidence that indicated the Endless Ones' existence began to give rise to their presence in the world. In the late 1990s, many continue to ignore or even declined information regarding them as they considered it official to be fairy tale stories taken too seriously. Upon the 2000s, as incidents began to occur, few people began to assume that the Endless Ones were making their return to the earth as the faith of a majority of people have died out or faded away over time. In today's time, many begin to believe that they are returning and are preparing the return of The Unheard-Of, who will make his presence known in the world and will claim it for himself.

The sunlight beams through the windows of an office. Inside the office are a young boy and an adult man, dressed in a white shirt and brown slacks, who's reading out of a book. The young boy sits in a chair with his hand on his chin, looking at the adult man reading from the book.

"You're saying that the Endless Ones are walking around us today and they're about the present The Unheard-Of to the world?" The young boy said.

"Son, I'm only reading from this particular book to give you a better way of understanding things. Though, you won't fully understand it until you get much older."

"So, when I'm older, I'll be able to see the Endless Ones and The Unheard-Of with my own eyes?"

The adult man laughed as he closed the book and placed it onto the nearby bookshelf. He walked over the boy and rubbed him on his head. He knelt toward him.

"Only time will tell, my son."

CRIES OF THUNDER IN THE SKIES

In the skies, dark clouds form and the thunder roars tremendously above the ground, striking fear and trembling in the hearts of people. The lightning mostly makes its appearance before the thunder introduces itself to the ears of the world. There are many stories that delve into the power and mystery of thunder and lightning. People would seem to disbelieve or disprove anything that could trace toward the power of thunder and lightning.

When people look up into the skies and they noticed the dark clouds forming above them, getting close together and the first small sound of thunder roars, many run into shelter for protection. The lightning had already made itself known before the thunder roared and yet the people's eyes didn't catch a blink of it. The rain would come falling down from the heavens and onto the earth like a colossal shower taking place. When it comes to rain, the differences between people around the world come together. Some love the rainfall, some hate it, and others really have no care for it other than to clean their material wealth that sits outside.

Legends in the earth tell of a large bird that flies through the air, hidden in the dark clouds causing the thunder and lightning to take place amongst the people and the land they live on. This bird is known as the Thunderbird. A colossal bird of great proportions that when it flies, the sound of thunder follows it with its roar and the lightning presents itself like a lighting show. The Thunderbird also has many names across its long and cryptic track record of existence.

The Thunderbird has been seen by many people throughout time and some say they continue to see the creature to this day.

Though, none have ever had the opportunity to say if they've ever come face to face with the creature or even attempted to capture it for money or glory. Many Native Americans tell the story of the Thunderbird with great detail of its shrouded history. Historians and zoologists have also studied the Thunderbird and could never come up with a solution to its mystery.

"I for one say on this day and time, when the mysterious creature known to us as the Thunderbird makes its presence fully known to the world, that will be the day when all the mysteries of the earth be revealed unto mankind to witness." - Thomas Bradford.

Scientists would usually speculate or throw out the possibility of a Thunderbird existing, let alone flying through the sky creating the sound of thunder and producing lightning from its eyes and wings. They wouldn't believe the possibility of a creature being able to create thunderstorms out of thin air, let alone air that could be filled with dew and possible precipitation. Many of them would say that the individuals or groups that sighted the Thunderbird were only see regular sized birds in large scale due to their binoculars zoomed in or any other theory they could bring up to detest the possibility of the bird's existence.

Some would insist that the Thunderbird was only part of the dinosaur species known as the pterodactyl, due to its appearance and early reports of its sightings in the earth. People have speculated that the Thunderbird could also be an enhanced pterodactyl due to the amount of chemicals in the air or even radiation from the sun or the earth's core.

There is the other theory of there being more than only one Thunderbird living amongst the earth and they travel in various locations, but rarely come together. Many sightings have taken place in Alaska, where people would see the creature flying in the sky above the woodlands. It was usually seen during the winter as it would be searching for prey to consume. There have been other historic legends that regard the Thunderbirds as protectors of the earth that once destroyed reptilian beings that traveled and roamed across the earth.

There are many comparisons between the Thunderbird and the Roc, another colossal bird that is hidden in plain sight. Though, the only sighted Roc would be King Roc that lives not on this earth, but another planet amongst humanoid Roc beings. But, that is for another season to discuss. The Thunderbird and Roc are both large birds with incredible wingspans and able to fly at great speeds.

They can also create hurricane force winds using their wings during flight. Both of the gigantic birds could snatch an elephant or a whale to eat as food whenever they chose to. The Thunderbird is also spoken about as carrying snakes as its travels in the air.

"There will come a day when the legend of the Thunderbird will no longer be a legend, but a reality among people." - Michael Ledford.

Though, when you look at the world, it is filled and shrouded with mysteries since its inception and creation. If the Most High Yah had created the Thunderbird for its use in creating thunderstorms is mainly unknown to the human mind and far too complicated for the human mind to grasp for understanding. Many who have read the Bible know the Most High uses weather to bring humility unto humans in order for them to understand the sense of fear and trembling, in a way of understanding their place on the earth and existing on this side of glory.

It is understandable that the Most High wouldn't have to create a creature such as the Thunderbird to create thunderstorms to bring humility unto His people. If He did create the Thunderbird, as well as all the other strange and mysterious creatures that have been sighted and continue to roam the earth to this very day, He did it for his own pleasure and no argument can be created in order to combat the cause and need.

The Most High has created all things that dwell in the earth and out of the earth. Everything was created for his own pleasure and for his own glory. If the Thunderbird is a true creation of the Most

High, then it is for his glory that the Thunderbird continues to live and stays shrouded in mystery unto the Age of Revelations unfold and all is revealed unto mankind.

THE BAITAL

In this world, there have been many to have encountered the creature known as the Baital. A large shaped creature that has the appearance of a human with brown skin and hair with large bat wings on its back and a goat-like tail. Its eyes frighten whoever lays sight upon it. The Baital attacks its prey vigorously and sometimes kills them without any hesitation or thought. The creature comes from the depths of Hindu Folklore and Mythology and it said to hang itself to trees by its toes, same as the average bats across the world. The name Baital is a variation that comes from the Hindustani word known as "betal". The Baital is said to live in the country of India.

From what is spoken about of The Baital is its skin and facial features. The Baital is said to have a very thin body as if it appeared to be completely stretched across its bones, giving it the impression of an undead body. Old legends have said that its body was near the strength of iron or metal, which would imply that it could not be stopped by any ordinary weapon created by human beings. The Baital possesses either green or red eyes, depending on the area of its location. Its face appeared like a dried-up coconut as some would say. By looking into its eyes, people could tell that there was no life-force within the vessel nor did its eyes ever give off a twinkle of any kind. Within the Indian culture, the color brown is associated with fiends and witches.

The Baital has no blood of its own within its body. Instead it takes over the dead bodies of many who have died and were buried underneath the tree that The Baital possessed and marked as its own territory. Some would believe that The Baital is a vampire of anceitn times, though The Baital does not drink the blood of its victims.

The Baital is also said to tell stories of its history with a king known as King Vikram, who constantly batted with The Baital in ancient times. Vikram had made a promise to a sorcerer that he would capture The Baital. Of course, Vikram had faced many odds and challenges along the way in his process of trying to capture The Baital for the sorcerer. The Baital proved itself as a match for Vikram as tales of riddles would ensue and keep Vikram in a constant trap as The Baital was content in its present state. The countless battle between the two would last through the cycle of capture and release.

"I cannot bear this no longer." Vikram had said concerning the riddles of The Baital. "I must overcome this task of confronting the Baital. I have to."

Vikram's conquest of The Baital lasted for a total of twenty-five times as he returned to The Baital's marked tree and dealt with the riddles and questions thrown upon him to answer. After the situations that erupted during the events of Vikram and The Baital, The Baital itself vanished into the spirit realm. Some accounts have said of The Baital's whereabouts are known to those who seek it.

"If we try hard enough and focus with great concentration and strength, we can find this Baital and the realm where it hides from open eyes. We can use its power to do whatever we so desire."

How can one find The Baital without knowing the proper place and location to seek and search for it? How would one truly know The Baital's intentions in this present world as it is unlike the world of King Vikram. There are many servants of the Most High who see The Baital as an enemy and a servant to the Unheard-Of. The Baital is not of any godly consent nor will it ever be of any godly consent. Judging by its appearance, its stature, and its character, The Baital is a celestial creature that is bent on causing devastations to anyone who attempts to seek its presence.

"We must find a way to capture this creature. How can we know for certain what is taking place amongst the spiritual realm when we have no eyes inside?"

The early tales of The Baital were written in ancient Sanskrit, which is a primary language among Hinduism. The twenty-five events between Vikram and The Baital were written and captured in a book of twenty-five tales and legends, concerning the two battling it out with riddles and questions to be answered amongst each other. The time and date that The Baital had its encounters with King Vikram were recorded in the 1ˢᵗ Century BC and some recordings of the encounters continued into the 11ᵗʰ Century, where all of the recordings were compiled and put together as a complete set.

In today's times, many would wonder where The Baital could be hiding in this present world. The Baital could still be inside its country of origin, India. The Baital could be wandering across the globe, traveling to each country, seeking out a victim of its own to choose and cause madness. Though, it is not said if The Baital would return in the End Days and we do not exclude its theory, for The Baital could be used as one of the Unheard-Of's servants and warriors in the Final Battle at the Land of the Forbidden where the forces of The Unheard-Of collide with the forces of the Most High Yah in a battle that will transformation all of creation as we know it.

The Baital marks its tree of territory and continues to use the corpses that lie underneath its tree for its own purposes. Remember, The Baital is not a vampire by any means or stretch of the imagination, no matter how its outer physical presence may seem to appear in front of your eyes. To this very day, people would still say they've seen The Baital and some may have ultimate proof of their encounter with the creature. They may see an animated corpse that may have risen from The Baital's tree. Whoever shall see The Baital in person and in its full form, they must prepare themselves for an overflow of questions and riddles to be answered and solved.

THE COMING WRAITHS

The planet called earth is surrounded and covered with spiritual beings that travels throughout the universe and the spiritual plane of existence. These spiritual beings are able to shift into human beings, extraterrestrials, animals, or any other source that they can model their shift after. These spiritual beings could be angels, demons, or wraiths. The Wraths are the majority of those that shift into other beings to cause and lead others either astray or lead them to something of great ancient importance. The word Wraith arrives from the ancient Norse word, "*Vordr*", which means "*Guardian*" in the English tongue and translation.

Wraiths would usually appear to those who are near death or even after their death will appear before those who are surrounding the deceased earthly body, leaving them as just empty husks of flesh and blood. Wraiths are ghost-like entities that some would call phantoms, specters, apparitions, manifestations of the dead. Other names for them are Soul-Stealer, since they appear before one's death to enter into the eternal realm of either peace or torment. The primary trait of the Wraiths is to travel amongst the earth with a driven purpose to consume and capture the souls and spirits of humans. Look at today's people and the Wraiths are doing an excellent job in their line of duty.

Many of the Wraiths would possibly confuse the living into doing their own will instead of doing the will of the Eternal One. The Wraiths are able to transform a human spirit and soul into a wraith of its own, therefore it will become simply one of them. A member of the Wraith Clan and under the control of the Unheard-Of.

The majority of Wraiths are under the control of the Unheard-

Of. Just as the Endless Ones are under his control, as well as the Kingdoms of the Earth, so are the majority of the Wraiths.

"What you gaze before you are my Wraiths. They do my biddings to please me for bring humanity to its knees to worship me. For I will be like the Most High and I will ascend to His throne and claim it for myself. I am the Unheard-Of."

The true physical or astral appearance of the Wraiths are mainly all black or mostly a large black fog or cloud that either has a pair of eyes or doesn't have any eyes. Some have mouths and other do not have mouths. The ones with eyes are able to see and the ones without eyes aren't able to see, but are guided by the Unheard-Of through his own vision. The ones with mouths can speak words of a sweet and pleasurable nature, only used to deceive the illiterate ones. The ones without mouths are able to use telepathy to communicate with a human being through their mind and are able to read their thoughts and in near control over their conscious.

They hide in dark, deep caves and forests throughout the twelve hours of the day and rise out of the darkness to torment and to deceive during the twelve hours of the night. The demons take over the day and leave the night to the Wraiths as the demons take time to torment those in their sleep and those who aren't on the right side with the Eternal One. The Wraiths are able to release a loud screech similar to the screech of a banshee. The screech will create and build up fear in the hearts and minds of humans, both male and female.

"The screech became so intensity and unable to bear that I ran out of my home and into the nearest ditch to cover myself from its torturous yell."

The true way of knowing their presence is by the sight of dark clouds. The temperature will drop exponentially, and the Wraith will be known before whosoever is in its presence. Sure, the person might be near freezing due to the fast drop in temperature, but they will surely heat up when their gaze hits the Wraith in its eyes. For surely what would someone do if they came into contact with a Wraith. One question they should ask is why they have come into contact with a Wraith. Have they asked for something greater to seek after in this finite life or have they disobeyed the Eternal One in order to gain something for their self-will and self-indulgence?

I, Michael Ledford have yet to come into contact with a Wraith. I've encountered stupid people amongst all things and yet, I can see the demonic and wicked spirits that live among them and inside them. Once, I was like them, I lived after the manners and pleasures of this wicked world. I desired only what I wanted and what I sought after for my own self. I was all about myself, until I was hit with a spiritual awakening and found myself doing the will of the Eternal One and forsaking all that I had before me.

Now, I am truly a new creature and I no longer do what my own will suggests and throws into my mind. The spiritual awakening brought me closer to the Eternal One and I dearly and truly hope when I see the King coming down from the clouds along with the New Jerusalem out of Shemayim, will the Wraiths finally be put to rest for all eternity with their associates both on earth and in the spiritual realm, and along with their leader, the Unheard-Of when the King and His people rule the earth for one thousand years in peace.

Surely, you're thinking to yourself, this can't all be possible or you're thinking there's no Wraiths or Eternal One and yet, people like you do not bother to do the proper research and study to confirm it for yourself. Neither do you ask the Eternal One for wisdom and understanding. I'm speaking plainly to those who ask questions, but refuse the answers given to the damn questions they asked. The reprobate minded ones. There, that's what they are.

But, to those who truly seek after the will of the Eternal One and continue to do battle within the confounds of spiritual warfare, continue your worship and prayers. For the Wraiths, the Endless Ones, the stupid humans, the demons, and the Unheard-Of will try anything to get your minds off serving and worshiping the true King of the Universe with all diligently.

FORESEEN THE BUNYIP

The Bunyip is a strange creature within the realm of cryptozoology and mythology that is said to lurk within swamps, billabongs, creeks, riverbeds, and waterholes. Some claim the creature to be a water spirit, a spirit that dwells within the Murray River of Australia, its longest river within the Australian Alps. The Moorundi people that live near the Murray River have claimed to see the creature and that it can change its shape and form before the year 1847. Some have claimed the Bunyip to be a gigantic starfish that lives in the Murray River. Others have stated to be in a sense of dread that they can no longer describe its appearance to those who ask of it.

Many newspapers in the 19th Century describe the creature with a crocodile-like head, a dog's face, dark fur, walrus-like horns or tusks, depending on the witness, a duck's bill, flippers, and a horse-like tail. Reports in 1851 indicate that the Bunyip was killed by a spear after it killed an Aboriginal man. Early settlers of Australia claimed to have seen the creature during their arrivals to the continent. Many believed the Bunyip to be a creature that awaited discovery.

Hamilton Hume in 1818 stated to have found large bones. However, did not call them the bones of the Bunyip as some had suggested it to be. Hume and his partner, James Meehan described the bones relating similar to a hippopotamus or manatee. There were fossils found in the Wellington Caves in 1830 by George Rankin, a bushman. Others were later found by Thomas Mitchell. The word *Bunyip* came along in July of 1845. An Australian museum stated to possess the skull of a Bunyip in 1847. William Buckley wrote an account of the creature in his biography in the year of 1852.

In other times after 1852, the Bunyip was said to have been spotted by those who crossed the Australian Alps such as Gabriel Kane, the Monster Hunter and Ufologist during his early studies of becoming a member of the Symbolum Venatores. Kane spoke to his masters of the creature thereafter, only leaving it remaining alive near the Murray River where he witnessed it. Other hunters came across the creature during their studies. Some went to fight, yet lost in the end to the power of the creature.

Many monster hunters made it their mission between 1852 to 1886 to find the Bunyip, yet failed to do so. Others claimed to have seen the creature, but were unable to fight it themselves.

"How can we fight a creature that can change its shape and size? Its form? One minute, it shows itself as a hybrid of many animals that come across the waters of Murray River. Later it appears as if it's an enormous starfish that washed along into the River from the Sea. The next minute it turns itself into some spirit, a water demon perhaps, but not so sure on that matter. In time, Hunters, such as ourselves will confront this creature and then we will have foreseen the Bunyip for what it truly is. Rather it be a natural creature or a spiritual one."

ROAR OF THE WERETIGER

There is a beast that scatters throughout the jungles of Asia with the power and strength of a tiger and the intellect of a human being, which would be great cleverness. This hybrid creature is known to Us as the Weretiger. The Weretiger is spoken about in many ancient folklores and mythologies. They share a great similarity with werewolves and possibly werefoxes and werebears.

The Weretiger goes throughout the day looking like an average human being walking amongst other humans. It is not till nightfall, where it transforms into the Weretiger and begins a bloody massacre by killing anything that comes across its eyesight. The Weretiger has a great thirst for blood in any form possible within the jungles of Asia. Many have come across the beast and only a few have survived the encounter to tell their side of the story when it came across the Weretiger.

There are certain rituals that Asians have taken up to try to transform themselves into Weretigers and scatter the jungles of Asia. Only a few had received the terrible end of the ritual by becoming sick and thrown out into the jungles for the Weretiger to kill and consume. The Weretiger's body is set up as a brute creature with an incredible amount of strength and intelligence. The body of the Weretiger include its long sharp teeth, its slashing long claws, incredible feat of senses with its eyes, nose, ears, and mouth. With its teeth and claws, it can cause deadly bites and devastating slashes. Unlike average tigers, the Weretiger possesses in tail on its body.

The only possible way to transform into a Weretiger is to be bitten by one. Depending on the person who transformers, they either seek revenge on someone or they have an intense craving for power and violence. Maybe the craving for ruling is in there as well.

The Weretiger is said to have started in the areas of India before being spread over into the jungles of Asia, where it currently remains dormant from modern day civilizations. There were a group of explorers and people of adventure who traveled into the deep jungles of Asia to search out the Weretiger and reveal its presence to the world. They were named Gates, Laura, Kenny, Kathy, Rex, and Jude. Gates was the leader of the group as they entered into the jungles.

The jungles is covered with massive trees and slithering insects looking for food and places to rest. Gates finds a location near a large rock where he and his group set their camp for the night. The group place their bags and equipment together at the rock where Rex will stay and watch the cameras during the night with Kathy.

"Ok, Laura will be with me and Kenny, you're with Jude." Gates said.

"Alright then." Kenny said. "Let's get this mission done."

Gates, Laura, Kenny, and Jude walk into the jungles and split up. Two to Two. Gates and Laura went east, and Kenny and Jude went west. All they could see in front of them was pure darkness with the exception of the moonlight shining through the trees. Gates reached into his cargo pants pocket and pulled out some night-vision glasses. He had two in his hand and gave one to Laura.

"Put this on. It should help you watch your steps." Gates said. "The moonlight is shining and yet we can only see darkness in front of us and there's no telling where the Weretiger is at this moment."

"Who knows, Gates, we could come across the beast ourselves and hopefully not be killed."

"We'll see about that once we face the beast."

Kenny and Jude continued walking west on their side of the jungles. Jude noticed some very large footprints on the ground in the muddy dirt. She kneeled down to have a better look at the footprint.

Kenny stopped as he saw her studying the print.

"What did you find?" Kenny said.

"This footprint is larger than any known animal in this jungle. Look at the size of its paw to its nails. This isn't an ordinary tiger we're dealing with here."

"Of course not, lady. We're out here to search and find the legendary beast known as the Weretiger. Which it would be incredible to capture it and reveal it to the world."

"That's if we can capture it. It has the cunningness and intelligence as a human being."

"Sometimes, even human beings are able to be easily fooled and captured by their hunters."

Rex and Kathy sat at the campsite, where they watched on the cameras the majority of the jungles. Nothing was showing itself on the camera and it was dead silent. Rex continued to glance at all four cameras and still nothing was seen.

"Anytime now we should come across something." Rex said. "This jungle is too big not to have some form of movement."

"We still have a few hours of searching and we should come into contact with some kind of animal. Be it a tiger, a panther, or the Weretiger itself." Kathy said.

Gates and Laura kept walking through the darkness with their night-vision glasses on and their small digital cameras in hand through the jungles until they reach what appeared to be a small creek. Gates stopped walking as so did Laura. He scouted the area for any sign of life moving.

"Didn't know there was a creek out here." Gates said.

"It's no telling what you'll find out here, Gates."

They searched around their side of the creek, hearing only the slight sounds of owls hooting in the trees and fish swimming in the creek. Gates looked down and saw the same kind of footprint that Jude saw with Kenny. Laura looked down at the footprint as Gates searched for samples of hair, saliva, or blood.

"Think that's its footprint?" Laura said.

"It could be. Look at the size of it. Unless we're dealing with a fairly enlarged tiger or panther, this could possibly be the footprint of the Weretiger. Which means it's dwelling in this jungle with us tonight."

After Gates took the samples and placed them inside a plastic bag that he put into his shirt pocket, a loud shriek of a roar is heard throughout the jungle. The entire group hears the roars and knows it's not from an ordinary animal. Gates looked around himself and Laura forming a 360 degree circle.

"We have to find the location where that roar came from!" Gates said. "Let's go!"

Gates and Laura ran through the jungle, following the sound of the roar as it can still be heard. Kenny and Jude decide to also track down where the roar was coming from as Rex and Kathy at the campsite were completely glued to the cameras for any sign of movement.

"That roar should've woken up the majority of this jungle's inhabitants." Rex said. "We are about to see a lot of movement taking place."

On the cameras, Rex and Kathy spot several shapes moving past the cameras. They paused one of their cameras and looked to see that it was a pack of orangutans that ran across the camera, going through the trees, away from the roar's location. The other three cameras showed constant movement from animals such as the Silvery Gibbon, the Proboscis Monkey, a Slender Loris, and on the ground, they saw a couple of snakes that slithered past the cameras. But, no sign of the Weretiger was found on the camera.

"No Weretiger, Kathy." Rex said. "Dammit."

After a brief second of silence, they heard a thumping sound that came from nearby their campsite. Rex and Kathy each sat still as the thumping sound inched closer toward them. They sat quietly as the thumping sound turned into a large object that they could see with their own eyes. The object stood still as it stared at Rex and Kathy and gave off a small roar. Rex listened closely and noticed it wasn't the Weretiger and he squinted his eyes and saw it was only a Sumatran Rhinoceros. The Rhinoceros turned its head and continued to walk past the campsite. Rex and Kathy are relieved by the Rhinoceros' appearance.

Back in the jungle, Gates and Laura find themselves deeper in the jungle where the roar is right next to them. They hear rusting in the trees and they turn to see both Kenny and Jude. They all catch their breath.

"Looks like we ran into your zone." Kenny said.

"Just trying to find what is giving off that roar." Gates said. "We have to keep moving."

Gates' communicator sounded off as he answers it. Rex is on the other side of the talkie. Gates answers Rex's call.

"What is it, Rex?"

"We see a large number of animals scattering through the jungle and you have to watch yourselves."

"You're telling us this now instead of earlier?"

"We have a little incident of our own over here with a Sumatran Rhinoceros. We saw a rhinoceros."

"Good call, but did you see anything that could lead toward the Weretiger because that's why we're all out here?"

"No, we didn't capture footage of the Weretiger. Sorry, Gates."

Gates sighed as he turned to Laura, Kenny, and Jude. He told Rex to stay on standby just in case something else would come along. He tells them that they only have about thirty minutes left before sunrise and they have to find the Weretiger before then. Now, all four of them stay together in a group as they quickly search around the jungle for the Weretiger.

Now, with only twenty minutes remaining, the group is becoming more intolerant of the Weretiger's whereabouts. Gates is constantly fighting off the idea of calling off the mission and returning back to camp.

"We have to keep searching with whatever means we can have." Gates said to himself.

Rex communicated back with Gates again through the talkie as Gates responded to his call.

"Anything this time, Rex?"

"Yeah. We just saw something very large walk past the camera and its heading toward your direction."

"What did it look like, Rex?!"

"It looked like a fairly large brute and it didn't look like a friendly type of animal, Gates."

"Thanks, Rex."

"Watch yourselves out there, Gates and company."

They hear the roar again and it appeared to be closer than they originally imagined. Kenny pointed toward the trees in front of them as they began to rustle and shake. The branches of the trees began to break and fall to the ground where the dirt would fly up into the air at mid-range.

They saw a large beast walk out of the trees, with a stick in hand that appeared to be made from the skulls and spines of both a human being and a ram. The beast stood on its hind legs to the estimated height of twelve feet. Its teeth were sharper than any other animal that lived in the jungle and its eyes pierced the group like death on swift wings. The group could only stare in intensely and stay in complete silence as they stared at the beast and its large brute figure. The beast stated at the group and raised its head toward them and gave off a roar. The group had fully recognized that roar and Gates could only believe as the sun began to rise, and he took off his night-vision glasses.

"Guys, this is the Weretiger." Gates said. "This is the roar of the Weretiger."

YAHSHUA AND THE UNHEARD-OF

This is a retelling of the events that described Yahshua the *Machiyach*, Jesus The Christ's time in the wilderness. The time where He was led up by the Spirit to head into the wilderness for the test of being tempted by The Unheard-Of, the Ha-Satan. The story takes place in *Matthew Chapter Four* of the Hebrew Bible, where it describes Yahshua in the wilderness undergoing the trial of overcoming the temptation of the ha-Satan.

The story should be a lesson to anyone of where temptation comes from and how it tries to control, but its up to the individual to overcome it with strength and faith. If Yahshua, the Son of Yah, could overcome the temptation of the ha-Satan, anyone with true believing and living faith can overcome the ha-Satan's temptation and wiles.

The ha-Satan is known for tempting any true believer into doing things they would not exercise in ordinary detail. He's tempted the majority of believers and everyone else on the earth is already overtaken by his temptation and wiles, and they do not see it otherwise. The reason of that is because they are blinded to themselves and refuse to look upon it to see if it's true or false.

The story also confirms the idea of the Unheard-Of beings in control of the earth and controlling all the kingdoms that live upon it. He is called the "god of this world' because the majority of the world worship him in many deceitful ways, ways they have awoken to confront in their lives.

Yahshua had stayed in the wilderness for forty days and forty nights. He fasted thought all the days and through all the nights. He became hungry afterwards as his flesh craved food for his stomach. It was then when the Unheard-Of had brought his presence before Yahshua, to tempt him into eating.

"If you are the Son of Yah, go ahead and command those stones to be made bread for you to consume." The Unheard-Of said.

"It is written, Man shall not live by bread alone, but by every word that proceeded forth out of the mouth of Yah." Yahshua had responded.

"So, he says." The Unheard-Of had said. "Let me take you to another place and show you what you could have."

The Unheard-Of shrugged his shoulders and decided to take Yahshua up into the holy city and had him sit down on a pinnacle of the temple that was placed in the holy city. The Unheard-Of stretched his arm forth with a smile on his face as he showed Yahshua the holy city that was before him.

"If you are the Son of Yah, cast yourself down, for it is written, He shall give his angels charge concerning you and, in their hands,, they shall bear you up, lest at any time you dash your foot against a stone."

Yahshua looked at The Unheard-Of and had responded to his demands of temptation.

"It is written again, you shall not tempt Yahweh thy Elohim." Yahshua had said unto him.

"Very well then. I'll show you something far better than this city and far better than bread."

The Unheard-Of continued his smiling and shrugged his shoulders yet again as he attempted to break Yahshua with one more test of temptation. The Unheard-Of decided to take him up onto an exceeding high mountain, where he showed him all the kingdoms of the earth and the glory of them.

Yahshua looked upon the kingdoms of the earth and turned his attention back toward the Unheard-Of, knowing in full of the test he's undergoing.

"Look at this spectacle! All of these kingdoms, all these things will I give unto you. If you will fall down and worship me above all things." The Unheard-Of said boastfully.

Yahshua stared at the Unheard-Of and knew well in great detail of what was taking place and how to overcome the temptation of the

Unheard-Of.

"Get from hence, Satan, for it is written, you shall worship Yahweh thy Elohim above all things and Him only shall you serve."

"I can't take this anymore!" The Unheard-Of said. "You've proven enough."

The Unheard-Of left the presence of Yahshua as the angels of Yah came down before him and ministered unto him. For he has overcame the temptation of the Devil and his wiles. For Satan, the Created Being attempted to tempt Yahshua, the Creator and yet, the ha-Satan had failed in the process of tempting Him who created him.

HUMANITY'S DECEPTION AND DOWNFALL

In my line of work, I am known as Michael Ledford and I am here to tell you my theory on Humanity. A species that should've never existed nor thought of. A species that proclaims itself above all things in the universe. Humans tend to have an assumption of themselves, both collectively and individually as something superior than what's already been. They say to themselves how unique they are, how perfect they will become. Only to be destroyed by the slightest event that takes place before them.

When something "good" comes their way, they profess that the Most High has given it to them, when in reality, it was only another human benevolence that pleasured them with the "good" that they were given. When something "bad" comes their way, they ball their fist and raise it above themselves while yelling at the Most High for causing the "bad" to occur when in reality, it was only their own actions that brought about the "bad".

The majority of humans profess that they believe in a Higher Being and yet their actions, works, and character follow another being of supernatural origin. Many in reality, worship themselves and see themselves as the Higher Being because they have a lot of material goods, a lot of greenbacks to fill their pockets with, unless they carry it around in briefcases or large gym bags.

The humans come together as collectives, I call them the "collective groups", because of the lack to be individuals. The individuals are no better themselves. Prancing around like boastful children who were given everything they could want. Only for honest people to see them only as spoiled ingrates who hark for attention in any aspect of reality.

The humans always talk of some action they seek to do or have done. Many profess that they will change the world, when in reality, they haven't changed anything, not even themselves or their carnal mind. Sure, when some become upset, thoughts from the spirits and the heart conjure up in their minds, but it is up to them to discern those thoughts and find themselves within them. Many accept all of their thoughts because they believe it's actually them creating the thoughts.

They build, write, sing, dance, play, teach, travel, and do other things that interest them and mostly themselves and call it the life worth living when its only what they perceive as living. They take vacations to foreign lands that they only dream of when people who live in those areas see it as only a city or town, simple and reform.; Unlike the minds of people who travel, calling it a glorious place with nice people when they haven't even spoke with the majority of a people who live in those lands.

They date, they marry, they become one, they conceive children, they raise their children, they watch their children become adults and they just go away. Who can really find a virtuous woman in today's standards of time? Who can find a godly man worthy of a woman's true love and nature? If someone knows the answer to these two questions, speak up and profess your theories and philosophy toward Us who are only asking the questions to questions unanswered by the standard world.

The one thing humans tend not to do is think ahead into the future realm, where things they have done bring about either consequences or rewards. Generously with modern humans, there's more consequences than rewards. Simply because they value their own opinions, their though patterns, they Book of the Law rather than those who have lived longer than they have aged on this earth.

The Bible states that you should not lean to your own understanding, yet ninety-nine percent of this pre-hell world leans to their understanding. It's amazing really, how the currently Unheard-Of had rebelled against Yah for creating the humans. Truly, you can't really blame him because of their flawed nature. Sure, a few will do some good in this physical realm, but the majority will do only evil and they will surely justify it and themselves in the process.

Many of these humans would take the Unheard-Of's side if they listen to him speak with his slithering tongue and flattering words of pleasure. Because they're carnal and worldly in nature. They say you can't be too spiritual, for it will make you no earthly good. Well, what kind of good can you do in these End Days.

If those few humans can balance the spiritual and earthly, maybe there will be some true good walking amongst the earth. But, where will you find them? In reality, you won't. Either you can become them or stay in your carnal mind where everything worldly and materialistic can be your master and savior. I don't use the word "lord" because for those who truly know, lord is Baal. But, that's a whole othe topic to discuss on a later date.

Overall, I seriously suggest the human race think before they ac and speak. Because the tongue is indeed filled with deadly poison and holds life and death in its grasp. Many do not think of the future days nor the present day they live upon. Personally, to me, this race is despicable. They cry out for handouts as in having other humans to do their duty for them and to hand it to them when the labor is completed. Yet, they desire to do no labor of any kind, only desire to sit on their asses and stare at that one-eyed monster that dwells in their living rooms and bedrooms, Yah forbid, there's one in the kitchen and bathrooms.

But, I will state this, the humans will not listen or hearken to any warning that may shout out before them. They will only huddle in their collective groups and mock and laugh at the warnings before their wrath is spread amongst the earth. A few understand that everything they see before them on this earth will soon come to pass, just like their flesh bodies. Which will return to dust as it was created from dust.

This species' deception is currently at hand. If you don't belielieve these words, look outside your dwelling places and check it out. That's correct, I said belielieve instead of "believe", so excuse my choice of words. As their deception takes its toll on them, their downfall will surely follow afterwards.

CALL OF THE REAPER

The Reaper is called upon death
For death brings his presence
As does his heaviness

The Reaper takes the souls
Of those that have left the earth
The Reaper takes the souls

To the other side of glory
Where only the Eternal King
Will be able to sentence them

To a place of peace and comfort
Or to a place of dread and torment
The Reaper knows of his calling

As does his duty in place
For the Reaper will not hinder his work
Nor will he delay on his work

His work is what began at the Garden
Wherefore Adam and Eve disobeyed the one commandment

Thus bringing death into the physical world
Of which we currently live in this day
Before the Fall of Man, death was nonexistent
Eternity ruled over all the physical universe

Until the Lawless One decided
To take matters into his own hands
Causing a civil war in Shamayim

Angels fighting angels above us
Knowing not the outcome of their warfare
Only the Eternal King foresaw the conclusion

The Lawless One is cast out
Thrown into the atmosphere of the Earth
Which is his currently dwelling place

For he persuaded Eve to take the forbidden fruit
Eve gave the fruit to Adam, doing what she done
Causing the Fall of Man in all of Creation

The Lawless One laughs at the sight
Of his mighty work for he aided death
To enter into the earth, so it may destroy

The Reaper was later born
With the power of death in his grasp
For many continue to fear him
He has no strength beyond what he was created for

That was to transfer the souls from earth into Glory
Wherefore does one fear the Reaper

Is it his gaze that troubles many?
Is it his presence that fears those?
What else could it be besides his power of death itself
For whatever the status of it may be
The Reaper continues his sole purpose
To transfer souls in the universe

Without death, the Reaper would cease to exist
Though, there are those who merchandise it
Continuing to do so this day
They say they love the Reaper
But they hate death, despise it
Would rather see life than death

That was a previous generation on the earth
For the current generation has no love
Nor do they have any hate of death

They love the sickening of many
They despise good and embrace evil
When death comes, they laugh instead of mourning

Death shown worldwide across many
They continue their humorous acts
Disrespecting others and not caring

They are this generation we see

The perverse and faithless generation
The last generation of this Age
The Reaper constantly watches
Gazing his eyes over this generation
As deaths strike constantly around us

Without any sense of care
People continue as if nothing happened
Many die and many laugh

Few witness and speak out
They are persecuted and killed
Open for the Reaper to take them

Who will wake up this generation
From their own mistakes and failures
If they do not see them, who will

Overall, we only have a short time
To prepare ourselves and to speak with others
To prepare themselves along the way

Many will laugh and attack the speaker
Plotting deceitful ways to attract the Reaper
Toward them in order to kill them

The Call of the Reaper is fairly simple
One does not completely enjoy the sight of death
Unless they know where the spirit is going afterwards

Many will be sent into eternal hell and damnation

Screaming and clawing toward the heavens
For another opportunity at life on earth

They will be declined and will continue to burn
For their iniquities and transgressions
Which they have wrought unto themselves

When the Reaper came unto them
At the end of their days
They didn't scream nor smile at him
Their faces were like stone
Hard and stiff in structure
Unable to crack or shake off
Until they were transferred into the judgment
Where they stood before the Eternal One
The One who commanded the Reaper to do the duty

They would try to plead
They would try to reason with the One
But, their earthly lives prove all that would be said
Few will be welcomed into eternal peace and loving
Singing and cheering upon one another in the glory of the
Eternal One
Where his light is the sun of all eternity

They will shout the name of the One in glory
Singing praises toward him amongst the angels
The cherubim also sing among them
Their faces will appear as light unseen
The beauty of their spiritual figures beyond human
comprehension
They are as bright as the stars of the night

The Reaper understands his purpose
And his fully aware of his coming end
When death will cease to exist
On that day, death itself will die
The Reaper along with it
Not having any use among the living

The Reaper understands his duty
As well as his takings of souls
The transferring of them fuels him

It gives him the strength he needs
To continue his purpose
The purpose of souls into Glory

The Call of The Reaper
Must be known throughout all the generations of old
Till the generations of today

Unless they decide to ignore the Reaper
And ignore his purpose
They will never understand nor receive understanding

The farther they move
The closer the Reaper comes
For they do not have much time left

There will come a day

When the Reaper himself
Will appear before all of creation

Showing his true form
Not afraid of the outcome
He himself will bow before the King

For it is of the King that created him
And allowed him his purpose in the universe
To move souls to and fro into Glory

Whether it be eternal peace
Whether it be eternal suffering
He knows where they will go

The Reaper sees his calling
As does one with his purpose
For he does not question

If he were to question
He would be in the same position
As many on the earth throughout the ages

The Reaper and death have lost a battle
Before in the ages and they will lose
Again in the coming future

Though, that lost will be their last
That loss will be their final

That loss will end the Call of the Reaper

For it is said
Death is the final one
To be defeated and to be unseen

ABADDON'S RISE TO DESTRUCTION

For the time is near
When the Witnesses of the Most High
Appear before all who live on Earth
They will preach the end days
The future Kingdom will be prophesized

The people of the World
Will grow in hatred and envy
Taking measures into their own hands
To kill and destroy the Witnesses
To end their prophesizing

The Witnesses will be shielded
By The Most High, the Creator of All
Nothing will be able to annihilate them
Nor kill them before their time.
They, themselves will exhale fire from the mouths

Supernatural talks will ensure
People will become petrified by the power
They will stand and watch the Witnesses
Prophesizing of the great things to come
Though the people of the world disbelief

For the Witnesses stand alike olive trees
That cannot be knocked down nor shaken by the might of man
For they can shut Heaven, that it not rain in their days
Powers that can turn water into blood and smite the earth with
plagues
As often as they will during their days

Upon finishing their divine mission on earth
The Beast will ascend out of the bottomless pit
His goal to make war with them and the Most High
He will overcome the Witnesses and kill them
The people of the world will be astonished on earth

For their dead bodies will lie on the ground where they were
smitten
The people of all cultures and creeds will see their dead bodies
For three days and a half, they shall not be buried
For the people of the world will not give them the respect
Of a honorable burial, for they were smitten and suffer graves

The people of the world will rejoice and sing
They will make merry and shall send gifts to one another
Because the two Witnesses, the prophets had tormented them
That dwell on the face of the earth
For Abaddon's Rise has begun will a praise of worship
Abaddon will causeth all to receive a mark
A mark that will allow those to either buy or sell
Those who do not receive the mark are subjected to death
Abaddon's rule is made of an iron forged from the pit
Abaddon's leadership is that of the god of this world

After the three days and a half
The Spirit of life from the Most High will enter
Into the bodies of the Witnesses as they will stand upon their

feet

A great fear will fall upon those who will witness
They will tremble at their presence
A great voice will come from the heavens
Saying, come up here, for they will ascend
Into the heavens in a cloud
Their enemies will beheld them
And tremble at their presence

Within the same hour, an earthquake will shake
Trembling the earth greatly as a tenth of the city shall fall
The earthquake will slay men of seven thousand
The Remnant were affrighted
For they gave glory to the Most High

The second woe has past
For behold to the earth
The third woe cometh
Cometh quickly before the earth
To prepare for the Coming King
Abaddon knows of the time
Abaddon knows of the seasons
Abaddon knows of the Coming
He prepares his army for the time
He prepares his people for the seasons

Abaddon awaits for the Coming
The Coming that confronts his time
The Coming that stumbles his seasons
Abaddon sits for the forty-two months of the seasons

For after the seasons come Abaddon's destruction

SONS OF YAH

Known in the Book of Enoch. For those in the Know.

The Sons of Yah or the Sons of the Elohim as some may prefer to call them are the angels that dwell in Shamayim and that even includes the ones who fell from the divine place after the time of creation. The ones that fell are called Fallen Angels, two hundred of them after which they rebelled alongside the Unheard-Of and after the War in Shamayim, they were cast out of Shamayim and descended onto the summit of Mount Hermon during the days of Jared, the father of Chanokh. They called it Mount Hermon because they had sworn and had bound themselves upon the mountain by mutual imprecations.

The names of the leaders of Sons of Yah are as follows, Shemyaza, their leader, Azazel, Arakiba, Rameel, Kokabiel, Tamiel, Ramiel, Danel, Ezeqeel, Baraqijal, Asael, Armaros, Batarel, Ananel, Zaqiel, Samsapeel, Satarel, Turel, Jomjael, Sariel. For these are their chiefs of the tens.

The Sons of Yah had all together decided to take themselves human wives and they had chosen one for each of themselves, and they began to go in unto them and to defile themselves with them. They later taught them charms and enchantments, and the cutting of roots and had made them acquainted with plants. After a while, the human wives became pregnant and they bare great giants, whose height had reached three thousand ells. The giants had consumed all the acquisitions of men.

When men could not sustain them any longer, the giants turned against them in pure hatred and anger and began to devour mankind. They began to sin against the birds, and beast, and reptiles, and fish, and they devoured one another's flesh and began to drink the blood of them they slaughtered and consumed. Afterwards, the earth had laid in accusation against the lawless ones.

Azazel had taught men how to make swords, and knives, and shields, and breastplates, and made known to them the metals of the earth and the art of working them in warfare. He also taught the women them how to make bracelets, and ornaments, and the use of antimony, and the beautifying of the eyelids, and all kinds of costly stones, and all coloring tinctures. Afterwards, there arose much godlessness and they began to commit fornication with one another and were led astray and became corrupt in all of their ways.

Semjaza had taught them enchantments, and root-cuttings. Armaros taught the resolving of enchantments, Baraqijal had taught them astrology, Kokabel taught the constellations, Ezeqeel taught the knowledge of the clouds, Araqiel taught the signs of the earth, Shamsiel taught the signs of the sun, and Sariel taught the course of the moon. When the men began to perish from the face of the earth, they cried loud and their cries went up to Shamayim.

Then, Michael, Uriel, Raphael, and Gabriel looked down from Shamayim and had saw much blood being shed upon the earth and all the lawlessness being wrought upon the earth. They each said to one another,

"The earth made without inhabitation cries the voice of their crying up to the gates of Shamayim."

"Now to you, the holy ones of Shamayim, the souls of men make their suit, saying, "Bring our cause before the Most High.""

They said toward the Master of the Ages,

"Master of Masters, God of gods, King of Kings, and the Elohim of the Ages, the throne of Your glory standeth unto all generations of the ages, and Your name holy and glorious and blessed unto all the ages! You have made all things and power over all things have You and all things are naked and open in Your sight and all things

You see, and nothing can hide itself from You."

"You see what Azazel has done, who has taught all unrighteousness on the earth and has revealed the eternal secrets which were preserved in Shamayim, which men were striving to learn.

"And Semjaza, to whom You have given authority to bear rule over his associates. For they have gone to the daughters of men upon the earth and have slept with the women and have defiled themselves and have revealed to them all kinds of sins. The women have also borne giants and the whole earth has therefore been filled with blood and unrighteousness."

"And now, behold, the souls of those who have died are crying and making their suit to the gates of Shamayim and their lamentations have ascended and cannot cease because of the complete lawless deeds which are wrought upon the earth. And You knowest all things before they come to pass, and You see these things and You do suffer them and You do not say to us what we are able to do to them in regard to these."

Then said the Most High, the Holy and Great One had spoken, and sent Uriel to the son of Miykael, and said to him,

"Go to Dore and tell him in my name, "Hide himself", and reveal to him the end that is fast approaching. That the whole earth will be destroyed, and a deluge is about to come upon the whole earth and will destroy all that is on it. And now instruct him that he may escape, and his seed may be preserved for all the generations of the world."

Again, the Most High turned and said to Raphael, *"Bind Azazel hand and foot and cast him into the darkness, and make an opening in the desert, which is in Dudael and cast him therein. Place upon him rough and jagged rocks and cover him with darkness and let him abide there forever and cover his face that he may not see light. And on the day of the Great Judgment, he shall be cast into the fire and heal the earth which the angels have corrupted and proclaim the healing of the earth, that they may heal the plague, and that all the children of men may not perish through all the secret things that the Watchers have disclosed and have taught their sons."*

The whole earth had been corrupted through the works that were taught by Azazel and to him ascribe all sin on the face of the earth.

The Most High turned and said to Gabriel, *"Proceed against the bastards and the reprobates, and against the children of fornication, and destroy the children of fornication and the children of the Watchers from amongst men and cause them to go forth and send them one against the other that they may destroy each other in battle. For the length of days shall they not have and no request that they, their fathers, make of them shall be granted unto their fathers on their behalf. For they will hope to live an eternal life and that each one of them will live five hundred years."*

The Most High turned and said to Michael, *"Go and bind Semjaza and his associates who have united themselves with women so as to have defiled themselves with them in all their uncleanness. For when their sons have slain one another in battle and they have seen the destruction of their beloved ones, bind them fast for seventy generations in the valleys of the earth, till the day of their judgment and of their consummation, till the judgment that is for ever and ever is consummated."*

"For in those days, they shall be led off to the abyss of fire and to the torment and the prison in which they shall be confined for ever. Whosoever shall be condemned and destroyed will from thenceforth be bound together with them to the end of all generations. Destroy the spirits of the reprobate and the children of the Watchers, because they have wronged mankind. Destroy all wrong from the face of the earth and let every evil work come to an end and let the plant of righteousness and truth appear, for it shall prove a blessing. The works of righteousness and truth shall be planted in truth and joy for evermore."

"And then shall all the righteous escape and shall live till they beget thousands of children and all the days of their youth and their old age shall they complete in peace. Then shall the whole earth be tilled in righteousness

and shall be planted with trees and will be full of blessing and all desirable trees shall be planted on it and they shall plant vines on it and the vine which they plant thereon shall yield wine in abundance and as for all the seed which is sown thereon each measure of it shall bear a thousand and each measure of olives shall yield ten presses of oil."

"Cleanse the earth from all oppression and from all unrighteousness and from all sin and from all godlessness and all the uncleanness that is wrought upon the earth to destroy from all the earth and all the children of men shall become righteous and all the nations shall offer adoration and shall praise Me and shall worship Me. The earth shall be cleansed from all defilement and from all sin and from all punishment and from all torment and I will never again send them upon it from generation to generation and for ever."

"In those days I will open the store chambers of blessing which are in the Shamayim, so as to send them down upon the earth over the work and labor of the children of men. Truth and peace shall be associated together throughout all the days of the world and throughout all the generations of men."

Behold, all these things Chanokh was hidden and no one of the children of men knew where he was hidden and where he abodes and what had become of him. As his activities had to do with the Watchers and his days were with the holy ones.

IN THE DAYS OF DORE

These days were unlike the days of Adam and Eve, the days of the Lawless One's rebellious act against the Father. Unlike the days of Qayin and Hevel and Seth, the days of Queen Alyssa and the rise and fall of her kingdom known as Bashemath, unlike the days of Chanokh, who walked with the Most High, unlike the days of Harold, who watched the clash between the Dark Gods and Cosmics as the Most High chose him to create a tablet to lock away the Dark God known as Negiter until the End Days where he would be released.

During the days of Dore, known in his time as the Mariner or the One Who Prophesized the Deluge, were truly terrible times. When Dore would enter the sinful cities of Tubal-Qayin and the old remaining cities of Bashemath, the old kingdom of Queen Alyssa, which was destroyed by The Most High for its sinful indulges. Dore would enter the city and begin prophesizing to anyone who would hear him. He spoke loudly about the Deluge that was on its way in a matter of time. The people laughed at Dore, calling him a lunatic, a fool, a weak-minded vessel, a lost spirit.

"He continues to prophesize and yet there hasn't been a drop of rain fall from the sky in three months span." A bystander says to his fellow city people. "This man is a fool and shows it without being shameful."

"You proceed to call me a fool today, yet, when the deluge comes, who will be the fool on that day." Dore said. "Who do you believe will be saved when the waters of the earth rise up and consume the land that you stand upon. Who will the Elohim of this earth protect from the waters that he sent and created to cleanse the earth of the foul beings that sit upon it."

The man would return to his tent, holding his head down in shame as the other bystanders would turn and laugh at him instead of Dore. Dore would continue his preaching before leaving the city.

Dore would ignore those types of comments and continue with his preaching. He would leave the city after preaching, returning to his home out in the wilderness with his wife, Emzarah, and their three sons, Adad, Samael, and Mordecai. The city people were unaware that Dore was building a large vessel to protect himself and his family from the Deluge. Uriel the Archangel would come by and watch as Dore would continue to build nonstop.

While Dore continued building, the city people were celebrating marriages, parties, feasts, and indulging in fornications, orgies, and human sacrifices. After many years of warnings from Dore, the people continued to ignore him and kept their lives going to the fullest. Dore was known as the stranger or the lost one when he would appear into the cities and prophesize.

Dore was never overshadowed by fear of the people or fear of their words and actions. Tubal-Qayin would speak to his people, saying, "Listen not to this stranger that appears among us. For he is a lost one, a child searching for his parents, an animal clinging to its prey's bones." Tubal-Qayin ruled much of the land during the days of Dore, he is also a descendent of a judge that once had a position of power in Queen Alyssa's days.

As the years began to go by, all three hundred and sixty-four days, Dore was coming closer to finishing the colossal vessel, Uriel the Archangel would appear and continue to watch as Dore and his sons were building the vessel.

"He continues, and it shows his faith." Uriel the Archangel had said.

Within the cities, the people began more ruthless and primitive than years' past. The Nephilim that were on the earth in those days, began to slaughter and consume mankind. They would also slaughter the animals and drink their blood. Mankind itself began to rape and murder women, kill the men, and sacrifice the children to their gods known as Negiter and the Dark Gods of old. The Most High grieved in the days of Dore.

"*I will send a deluge upon the earth. Cleansing it of all corruption that mankind has created. Saving only Dore and his family.*" Saith יהוה thy Elohim.

The city people kept up their partying and marriages. Tubal-Qayin never took part in his people's festivities as he only watched them and always looked above at the sky for a sign of the deluge that Dore continued to prophesize about.

"If Dore is right and a deluge is coming, I must speak to him and him alone." Tubal-Qayin said to himself.

Tubal-Qayin had met with Dore a few short days later. They spoke about the deluge as Dore told him of what was coming. Tubal-Qayin believed him, yet were only interested in saving himself and a few of his close allied compensations. He even stated that he would come when the deluge would arrive and bring damsels with him, so he could go into them while inside the vessel. Dore declined that Tubal-Qayin do such a thing, causing a large rift between the two men.

"I hope you're aware of your days, Dore, son of Miykael." Tubal-Qayin said. "For it is only a matter of days that you will be killed and sacrificed before the Dark Gods."

"I will not be a sacrifice to your false gods that lie dormant in the darkness." Dore said. "Me and my family will be protected from your harm and affliction as long as we keep our obedience."

"You talk of obedience and yet you won't allow me and my people to enter into your vessel. Remember, son of Miykael, I am a king on this land and I have an army at my disposal. You only have your family. A wife and three young boys. How would they fare against an army lead by me and me alone?"

"Because we're not alone. He is watching over us as the angels are as well."

Tubal-Qayin shook off the warnings of Dore and himself stood watch for the deluge. The Nephilim had killed off each other in a civil war that was started by Gabriel the Archangel under the Most High's command. After the civil war and the final destruction of the Nephilim, Dore knew that it was time.

When the deluge arrived, Dore and his family were already prepared and sealed in the vessel along with the clean and unclean animals of the earth as the Most High had clarified.

The waters rose up from the seas and burst from the earth, swallowing the city people who were stranded on the ground. Tubal-Qayin had attempted to climb aboard the vessel, but a giant wave knocked him off and dragged him deep under the water where he would drown to death.

Dore and his family survived the deluge and lived long lives of prosperity and happiness. Though, as it is said, *"As it was in the Days of Dore, so shall it become again in the days of the Son of Man."*

DEATH OF A KING

In an ancient kingdom in time past, there was a king of great power and a stature unlike those in the outside kingdoms. The King had fought many battles during his youth until his time of old age. His father and grandfather before him were mighty kings of the lands. They made warfare and combat against any opposing forces that would seek to overthrow the kingdom completely. Some have vowed to witness the end of the kingdom, but have met their own end at the end of the King's sword.

The King's grandfather had one wife that guided him and supported him during his reign. The King's father had two wives, both of whom had supported him during his reign as king. The King during his youth possessed a wife and later a second wife when he became King over the lands.

"I have chosen a second wife, father." The young King said.

"A second wife?" The Father said. "Are you sure you can handle the pressure of two compared to one?"

"If I am able to become your successor in full, father, I must follow in your footsteps."

The father chuckled at his son's words, but understood them completely and he knew how similar they were to his own words to his own father when he became king.

"What is this second wife's name?"

"Her name is Deborah. She lives near the creek in the outskirts of the kingdom."

"The outskirts? So, she's an outsider?"

"An outsider that has vast knowledge of royalty and how a king should rule his kingdom."

"Explain to me, how would this outsider wife of yours know much about ruling a kingdom?"

"She said she had a dream about a righteous king and how he ruled over his kingdom where there was everlasting peace and security."

"Everlasting peace, huh. I would've loved that during my reign as king."

"Do you believe I can give it a shot?"

"I believe you'll take good care of this kingdom, son. Only make sure that no one spits into your ears false ideals and techniques that would see your downfall."

"I will make sure of that, father. I will."

The young King brought Deborah into his chambers and went into her and she became his second wife. Through her, he begat a daughter and from his first wife, two sons.

Several years after the wars amongst the neighboring kingdoms concerning the ways of livestock and ideals, the young King, now in his middle ages sought out a woman from one of the neighboring kingdoms, lost and frightened. Dirty from the ground she walked on. Her face almost unrecognizable from the amount of dirt that covered her face and body. He comforted her and was told that her husband was killed in battle against his army.

"Come back to my kingdom, my lady." The middle age King said. "I will take good care of you there."

"Thank you, your majesty."

He took the woman back to his kingdom and she entered his castle, seeing the amount of treasures that they won through the spoils of war surrounding the castle grounds.

"This place isn't as filthy as the kingdoms in Lelat." The woman said. "What do you do with them, if I may ask of you?"

"We keep them as memories of the wars we've come to face. It reminds us of why we're still walking upright in our days upon this earth."

The maidservants of the King's two wives took the woman to a guest chamber of her own where she cleaned up herself and dressed in modest apparel similar to the maidservants. The King would visit her during the days to see how she was feeling and doing.

"I never got to know your name." The King said.

"My name is Amana."

"Integrity and truth your name stands for."

"How did you know that?"

"Because I can see it in your eyes and hear it in your voice."

"I take it you know of the meaning of names as well."

"I did some learning in my youth. Still learning more as I go about this life."

"You're a different king that the ones that came before."

"So, I've been told."

A few months later, the middle-aged King married Amana and she became his third wife. Through her, he had one son and two daughters. The son looked up to his older half-brothers and the daughters sat at the feet of the mother and their stepmothers, learning the ways of being a woman in life within the kingdom walls.

Several years had passed and another war was waged between the Kingdom and the neighboring kingdoms. The neighboring kingdom brought along men of great stature with them and they stood nearly the height of the trees outside of the kingdom walls. The middle-aged King and his first two sons went into battle with his army and slaughtered the opposing kingdoms within the span of five days. The men of great stature were slain, and their weapons were taken as trophies of the war.

Time slowly began to catch up to the middle-aged King, his body beginning to slow down on him. His great feats on the battlefield were slowly withering away. Near becoming an old man, his first two sons lead the kingdom's army into the battles that came their way. Defeating the likes of the kingdoms of Lelat and Ostacre. The two sons were later killed in their middle ages, after having sons of their own. The near old King wept at the news of his eldest sons' deaths.

"My sons. I know you are in a better land now. With your grandfather and great-grandfather. You're among the family of the dead now. Soon, I will join you and see your faces again once more."

The now old man King had witnessed the death of his first wife and his second wife. Only his third wife remained at his side when he became bedridden.

"Amana, command some of the soldiers, tell them to take me to the trees near the waters. Also call for my daughters to meet me there."

"I will." A middle-aged Amana said.

The soldiers came and took the old King to the tress near the waters, where Amana and his three daughters came to sit with him as he looked out and witnessed the sun setting. His youngest daughter began to weep as she knew what was about to take place. The old King looked at her and grabbed her hand.

"Do not cry over me leaving this world. I am going to a place far better and far peaceful than what this world knows."

The old King looked to Amana with a small tear in his eye. She read the Book of King Liam to him, a king that was a man made after The Most High's own heart. When she finished reading the book to him. He looked out toward the waters and could see two angels standing before him with their hands held out to him.

"It is time." The Angel said.

The King nodded and kissed Amana and said goodbye to his three daughters as he gave up the ghost and entered the spirit world. The King whose name was *Magdiel*, meaning the chosen fruit of The Most High, passed on from the natural world and was engraved in the Book of Rulers for future generations to learn from.

THE HORSEMEN COMETH

The signs have been shown and the world around us having been revealing a large amount of revelations across itself. From the wars, the famines, the pestilence, and the deaths that has consumed this world ever since the Fall of Man. These four occurrences are controlled and ruled by what the world calls the Four Horsemen of the Apocalypse. The ones from the outer depths of space call them the Four Riders of the Universe. The Elect know them as the Four Horsemen of the Forbidden. They have come to this planet to reveal the End Days' arrival and preparation for Abaddon the Antichrist and the return of the Messiah, the One and Only Christ.

There was a series of events that took place within the world, where many witnessed the Horsemen themselves with their own eyes. Some have said their arrival is like a cometh or a presence. They can be felt before they're seen by anyone living within the physical world. They have aided events that have held wars of profound numbers, famines of great losses, pestilences of dire consequences, and deaths of an unspeakable and uncountable number.

The Horsemen of the Forbidden already possess the knowledge of their intended purposes and seek out to fulfill them at any cost, whether anyone living or dead gets in between them and their purpose. The Horsemen guard the field known as the Land of the Forbidden. The Land of the Forbidden is a sacred land where it is said to hold the

Final Battle between the Most High Yah and the Lawless One.

From the time of its inception and purpose, no living human has ever entered into the land and had yet to come out alive only to have their bodies found fully turned to dust. It is documented that only one man made it through the land with some injuries to go along with it. He is known to Us, the Elect as Kenari Clark.

The Horsemen each possess and individual name for themselves. A horse of their kind, a weapon of their choice, and a source of power that they may command at any moment that benefits their purpose. They are sent by the Most High to fulfill his ultimate purpose.

The first Horsemen is known to Us as Bane. Known as the Holder of Pestilence. He is seen wearing an all-white shrugged uniform with a tunic and a cape that both appear to be ripping apart from his body. His face is covered by his white mask, though his cold eyes can be seen. He possesses the weapon known to Us as the Endemic, a bow and arrow that he uses to slaughter the people and bring the diseases into the world. His horse possesses a white hide that many can see within the dark, for hardly no darkness of any kind can cover up the horse. Bane's power is known to go forth into conquest and to conquer by any means necessary. Bane is the first Horsemen of the Forbidden.

The second Horsemen is known to Us as War. Known as the Possessor of Wars. He is seen wearing all armor equipped with black cloth and a blood red cape and hood. The armor has the appearance of looking aged and used for centuries. The cloth is covered with dried blood as the cape and hood have ripped marks and tears across it. He possesses the weapon known to Us as the Redeemer, a longed medium sized blade that can cut and pierce through any form on Earth. His horse possesses a black hide and its mane glistened like the flames of the sun. War's horse can be unseen in the darkness, until its fiery mane makes itself known to the darkness. War's power is known to take peace from the earth and to make the men of the world kill each other in fierce combat to spread their blood across the body and soil of the earth. Their primary task is to kill with the sword that they possess. The modern-day sword would be known as the gun. War is the second Horsemen of the Forbidden.

The third Horsemen is known to Us as Rage. Known as the Bringer of Famines. He is seen wearing gray armor with a helmet with two ram horns on each side. His eyes are seen glowing through the helmet with furious heat. He possesses the weapon known to Us as the *Vehemencer*. A double-sided war hammer used for destruction and fury. A hammer that possesses the double amount of force of an ordinary mortal war hammer that's used for combat. His horse possesses a deep black hide to where not even the darkness itself can find the animal as it buries itself deep within the darkness. Rage's power is known to bring fury upon the earth and to kill with intense torture. Rage is also responsible for the famines of both food and spirit across the earth. Rage is the third Horsemen of the Forbidden.

The fourth and last Horsemen is known to Us as the Reaper. Known as the Entropy of Death. He is seen wearing an all-black cloak with a hood. His face appears as a human skull, though with his white pierced eyes and shivering voice that emit from it. He possesses the weapon known to Us as the Collector, his large scythe with the bladed end that stretches six feet in length from the tip of the blade to the staff it was attached to. The Collector is used to take the souls of the earth and bring them into the spirit world, where they will be judged for their earthy actions and decisions. His horse possesses a pale hide that which many who see the animal shiver and freeze in fear of its appearance. For it appears as a ghost to them that see it and brings them the feeling of death. When his horse appears, people know that many will indeed die. Reaper's power is known to be followed by the powers of Hell, to kill with the scythe that he possesses in his grasps, with famines, diseases, and the beasts that scatter upon the earth. Those are his tools of destruction and desolation to the earth. Reaper is the fourth and final Horsemen of the Forbidden.

The Horsemen are currently guarding the Land of the Forbidden to the time of the Final Battle to take place. The Most High will gather his armies of angels to take battle with the Lawless One and his armies of angels to take battle. It is not sure if the Horsemen themselves will take part in the Final Battle to come, but they will be there to witness it unfold.

VISITATION TO THE ABYSS

There was a time where the entity called by the spiritual realm, Darkous traveled down into the first heaven on Earth. The atmosphere below the second heaven that is outer space or the universe. Darkous had visited Earth on several occasions, whether it was for a small council meeting, bounties, or being a messenger between the Light and the Dark. Darkous understood his role in the spiritual realm and his role within the boundaries of the physical realm.

Darkous had worn his traditional dark violet and black trench coat, though he didn't place the hood of the coat over his head as it laid against the back of the coat.

When Darkous walked down the large hallway that seemed to have no walls on either side except a fall into a bottomless pit into Sheol, which lead toward the entrance door into the atmospheric Abyss, he saw the head of the ha-Satan. Darkous stopped and stood still while facing him as he watched Darkous over the entrance door. The entrance doors themselves were surrounded by demonic spirits and had engraved pentagrams on its front. The ha-Satan's appearance seemed to indicate that he became much taller than he was in previous times, simply indicating that the wickedness taking place in the physical realm is making him much stronger and powerful as the days go by.

"Welcome to my present kingdom, Darkous." ha-Satan said. "I've been expecting your presence here."

"I'm only here on orders, ha-Satan. Not on a friend request. Its business that I speak to you."

"Very well. Enter at will, Darkous."

The large doors opened and flames burst from the doors and

slowly moved toward the side as Darkous walked through them and into the main area of Satan's earthly kingdom. While inside he could see and smell the burning of human flesh as he witnessed people burning and screaming in the flame of eternal torment down in Sheol, each spirit having a traumatizing remembrance of their sins that occurred in their earthly lives. The screaming of the spirits was loud enough to cause a human to go insane and possibly would injure their ear drums.

"Please help me!!!!" A female spirit yelled toward Darkous.

"Sir, please!!! Let me tell my family about this place of torment! Let me warn them." A male spirit yelled.

Darkous stopped and looked at the spirit, seeing it was a male and he was in great torment.

"They have the writings of *Mosheh* and the Prophets." Darkous said to the spirit. "They even have the letters of the apostles. That should be enough."

"They won't believe them!!!!"

"Very well, if someone were to rise out of the grave and the pit of Hell, they wouldn't believe them either. I'm truly sorry for your natural family."

Darkous walked past them as he approached ha-Satan standing before him, a figure that stood at the approximate height of eighteen to twenty-three feet. He still possessed a form of his wings and had a burned look upon his body as it once shined brightly. Ha-Satan grinned at Darkous while rubbing his hands together.

"Don't get any ideas in here." Darkous said. "You know what will happen."

"You know I won't, believe you me. Now, let's discuss this business that you spoke of at the entrance door."

"The business that I speak of is about what's currently taking place on this planet Earth. You of all angels know how this place operates and how much wickedness and darkness consumes it because of your rebellion."

"I chose to rebel for a purpose that neither you or any of the angels could understand. I want to be like the Most High and I shall become like the Most High."

Darkous laughed quietly to himself as he listened to ha-Satan speak.

"Do you hear yourself, Lucifer? You already know the outcome. You already have control of the earth until the end of this Sixth Day."

"Silence your tongue! Don't speak of the day when my kingdom will fall. Of course, I know that I will be defeated and bind by chains into the eternal darkness that awaits me. You, Darkous are unlike the other entities that appeared after my rebellious act. You were only created by Him to have watchful eyes and ears over the darkness in the cosmos. Five days have passed since my rebellion and we're approaching the end of the six. I dread the Seventh Day and what it will bring toward me."

"Because you understand that during the Seventh Day, you will be in darkness for one thousand years in time and space."

"So, you say, though it will feel like twelve to twenty-four hours to me and I will be released yet again before my final end."

Darkous glanced down at the ground of earth. He could see the humans dwelling on it in mass. From his view, he could see nearly an entire continent if not two and the people living on them. He could also look further down at the tormented spirits of Sheol that scream in agony in the eternal lake of fire. Ha-Satan rubs his chin as he sits back in his throne chair made of molten rock and burned flesh.

"You never spoke of the business you claim here to make."

"The business I came to discuss involves this planet Earth and the humans that live upon it."

"What of them? You want me to stop the violence and desolation? I will not do such a thing, Darkous. The violence and desolation have a purpose of being on this planet because the humans put it there"

"By your deceitful speech toward Eve when you led her through temptation to sin and cause the Fall of Man to take place by the hand of Adam. I witnessed it happen along with the angels above."

Ha-Satan laughs off Darkous' sentence and shakes his head while laughing hysterically. Darkous only stared at the ha-Satan with his arms crossed.

"You got me on that one, Darkous. I can give you that one for once. But, you know I will not cease those actions, so why bother asking me about them."

"I know you will not. You're doing what you chose to do. I speak of the humans that are fighting and destroying your kingdom on earth."

"Those saints of the Most High. I have them on my list to deceive and destroy in due time."

"How can you destroy them when they are protected by Elohim? You know you cannot and it drives you mad at times doesn't it. You want the Elect to transgress the Law, so it can open the door for you to enter and bring destruction upon them and boast in yourself at doing so."

"Sometimes you sound like Michael to me."

"At least he doesn't go around and boast about himself and what he did and what he can do. He could've rebuked you about the body of Mosheh, yet he did not."

"Just like you boast in your victories whether they're against your mystical adversaries or your successes on the humankind front."

"At least few of humankind is aiding us in destroying your kingdom until Elohim takes care of it in full."

"All in good time. But, from what I can understand and take curiously from your last mission, my servant Kabra surely did a move on you and your precious Beauty. Though, that Malach HaMavet proved to be a worthy foe against my kingdom. Though their deaths will not come yet, but it surely will take place by my command."

"Kabra will receive what he deserves and so will Mazakala and Desolation. While you sit by at times and watch what's ongoing, I and my allies, both on the spiritual and physical sides will continue to destroy your kingdom and end your wickedness."

"Sit by?! You've gone mad, Darkous! I roam the earth to and fro and walk up and down in it. I roamed the earth when Adam and Eve left the Garden of Eden and I continue to roam this day. I stand where my servants do their work and justify it to themselves in order to please me."

"Well, contact me when you do show up on the earthly grounds again. Because I want to see you there and maybe I and the Elect can show you what we're capable of on earthly grounds."

"Don't worry yourself and get anxious, Darkous. You will see me on the earth in due time and it will be at the right time."

"I look forward to seeing you around, ha-Satan."

"I want you to see me around, Darkous or Doctor Dark, as humankind calls you. I will look forward to murdering you and your allies and leaving your blood on the ground for the earth to drink as it did Abel."

Darkous walked away and looked back at the ha-Satan and gave him a smile.

"I'm sure you want to see that. Funny how neither one of us know when it will take place and that makes it interesting to meditate on."

Darkous walks out of the atmospheric kingdom of Satan as the entrance doors closed behind him, sounding like an earthquake had gone through the air. The ha-Satan stayed sitting on his throne, smirking.

"In due time, Darkous. All in due time."

INSTINCTS ARE A CALLING

Preston Maddox, a homicide detective and Marshal of the United States goes into a mission that concerns the rise of Satanism. Maddox studied the case alongside his partner, Emily Weston. Both of whom, sit inside the office of their Chief, Eldon Ross, discussing the case and reading over the files.

"I didn't know it went this far." Emily said.

"It was meant to come." Preston said. "Just the question is how far it will go before it consumes all of the world."

"I believe it already has accomplished that, Preston." Eldon said as he walked into his office.

Eldon sat behind his desk as they talked about the case.

"Now, Preston I know you love this kind of stuff deep down, ever since your encounter with the Spirit after being shot. So, you will go on this case."

"I certainly will, and Emily has decided to tag along with me or it."

Eldon turned over to Emily. Discerning her facial expression, seeing how she's thrilled, but concerned about her well-being of being out in that area.

"You'll be fine, Emily. Trust me, Preston's got your back. Especially on a case like this he should."

Preston grabbed his coat and turns to Emily, who places the file back on Eldon's desk. She looked at him with a cautious face, Preston only smiled back toward her.

"You're ready for this?" Preston said to Emily.

"Ready when you are."

Preston and Emily had left the office and traveled through New Haven, Connecticut to find the newly built Satanic Church. The church is known for having secret human and animal sacrifices taking place in an underground area that the church itself is built over. Preston speeds down the street, as if he's racing to get to the church first.

"You ever heard of slowing down?" Emily said.

"This is an important case, Emily." Preston said. "Not just for us, but for everyone in the world. This kind of stuff can't be left alone to continue."

After a few stops and turns, they arrived at the Satanic Church. They exited the car and started walking up the stairs of the church that appeared to be made of burnt stone, possibly stones from an erupted volcano.

"These steps look as if they've been burnt by something." Emily said. "What do you think, Preston?"

"Its just something they had to build up the suspense of the damn place."

Upon reaching the top step and facing the front entrance, they noticed a variety of small statues that stood in front of the church. The statues consist of gargoyles, dragons, serpents, and a small bronze statue of Baphomet. Preston glanced upon them and spat on them.

"I hope no one saw what you just did." Emily said.

"Who gives a shit."

They opened the doors and entered the church. Inside the church, it appeared to be any ordinary church. Pews on both sides with a podium in the front at the center, though behind the podium was a large bronze statue of Baphomet that its height nearly reached the ceiling of the church. Preston stared with disgust brewing in him.

"This kind of stuff is sick I tell you."

Emily notices a priest, wearing a black and scarlet robe walking toward them. Emily grab Preston's attention as the priest approached them and they stood in front of the podium that sat in front of the statue of Baphomet.

"Welcome to our church." The priest said. "May I ask why you are here this day?"

"Preston Maddox, United States Marshal and Homicide Detective. This is my partner, Emily Weston, United States Marshal and Homicide Detective. We're here to speak with a Mr. Vernon Lance."

"Ah, our top priest. Well, he is here, but he's downstairs at the moment. Whatever you have to tell him, tell me and I will pass it along over to him."

"We need to speak with him in person, if you don't mind." Emily said. "Just call him up and we'll be out of your hair soon enough."

"Very well then, Marshals."

The priest walked back behind the back doors and Preston noticed he went down a flight of stairs. Emily glanced over to see what Preston was looking at.

"What do you see?"

"He just went down some stairs. I take it we'll be seeing Mr. Lance soon enough."

"Hopefully, because I can't stand being in this place. Something just doesn't feel right." Emily said.

"I understand what you're saying." Preston said. "I mean, who in the hell, no pun intended, would sit in a place where there's a statue of that caliber sitting and facing you."

"Most churches have statues facing them. Made either from wood or stone."

"Idolatry at its finest."

They hear some voices coming from the back of the church doors. They recognize one to be the voice of the priest, though the second one doesn't sound familiar to them. They see the back doors opening and the priest coming out first and behind him another man, with long wavy black hair that surpassed his shoulders, he wore a black trench coat that went down near his ankles, and he wore all black clothing with black fingernails. His pupils were the color of fire purging.

"What in the hell are we dealing with here." Preston said.

"We're about to find out."

The Priest and the man confront Preston and Emily. They stand their ground while facing the two individuals.

"Here's Mr. Vernon Lance, detectives." The priest said. "I will leave him to you."

The priest walked away, leaving Lance facing Preston and Emily. Lance let out a smile and extended his hand toward them.

"Excuse my manners, I am Vernon Lance. The Satanic Church's High Priest."

Preston shook his hand and stared Lance in the eyes intensely. Emily continued to watch on as the two started for about a minute.

"Preston Maddox, United States Marshal and Homicide Detective."

"I know who you are, and I know your partner as well. Ms. Emily Weston to be exact. I know a lot about the people of this city and the people of the world."

"If you don't mind me asking, Mr. Lance. But, are you the Satanic Priest that was talked about being discovered in an old abandoned church by a Dr. Galen Donovan and that Spirit-Seeker guy?"

"I cannot say. I would never forget of having a confrontation with Mr. Travis Vail. Though, if I did, I do not remember the event."

"We'll look into it for more information." Emily said.

"I'm sure you will, my lady. Now, why are the two of you here today?"

"We're here to discuss information that concerning of animal and human sacrifices taking place underneath this church."

"Sacrifices you speak of." Lance said. "If we were doing those things, we would obviously send out invitations for people to come and see and if need be, partake in them."

"What kind of person would say something like that?" Emily said.

"A greater kind."

"What kind of "greater kind" are you talking about, Mr.

Lance?" Preston said. "I'm just curious about what you're saying."

"All will be revealed in good time, but there are no sacrifices taking place here. I can assure you of that."

Lance glanced down at his watch and faced Preston and Emily.

"Now if you'll both excuse me, I have a meeting I need to get back to in my office. Nice speaking with you both. I hope to see you two sooner than later."

"We're sure, Mr. Lance." Preston said. "Twisted ass clown."

Preston and Emily left the church and returned to the Marshal office. They spoke with Eldon about what they saw and what Lance had told them. Eldon was still curious about the place and was uncertain of Lance's actions.

"You two can decide if you want further investigation on this case. If not, I'll just send Leon and Darius on it." Eldon said.

"We can take this case, Chief." Preston said. "You can count on it."

"Alright then, Preston. Hope you do the job well and not cause any casualties this time."

"Unless its necessary."

"Pretty much." Eldon said. "You're right on that."

Preston and Emily left the office. As they exited the elevator downstairs, Preston felt uncertainty entering into his mind. Emily noticed it by how Preston moved and walked.

"What's wrong?" Emily said.

"I feel there's something much greater taking place at that church and it won't bring any good."

"Maybe your instincts are calling out to you about the place and it doesn't seem to look good."

Later that night at the church, underground, Lance and five other priests are conducting an animal sacrifice with a goat. Lance reads from a book, where he later slashes the goat's through as it blood drained down a line which entered into a statue of *Baphomet*. The statue's eyes light up like fire, releasing a low toned growl as Lance smiles and bows before it.

"Take this offer, my master." Lance said. "For we here, serve you and your kingdom of eternal hell."

THE NEW AGE AND THE FUTURE KINGDOM

The time we are all living in is the End Time. The Sixth Day of the Seven. Wickedness is growing at a constant rate across the world. Morality is vanishing amongst humanity. Good is called evil and evil is called good. The faith of many are falling away, returning to a life of sin and unbelief. The confederate leaders of the world are preparing for the Man of Sin to make his grand entrance and proclaim himself to be God reincarnated.

The entire world will be pulled into the lying signs and wonders performed by the Man of Sin and will ultimately believe he is God. He will cause all both great and small to receive a mark on their forehead or their right hand. During his reign, the world will love what he presents. The Saints of The Most High will stay amongst themselves, away from those of the world. The Dragon, Satan himself, embodied in the flesh as the Man of Sin will make every attempt at finding the Saints, who are in hiding from the world in a prepared place in the wilderness.

The prophets of Old proclaimed these events to take place and they will take place. The signs of their coming have already presented themselves to the people of the world and many refuse to look and accept it for what it is. Riotous living will continue to grow as many become stacked up in the population centers called cities. Woe to the women who are with children or pregnant during these coming days. The coming days we live in are the ones the prophets wished to witness. The return of Egypt and Sodom in spirit.

During those days, the angels will blow their trumpets in sevens. Two witnesses will appear and prophesy a thousand two hundred and sixty days. They will stand upright as of two olive trees and candlesticks. The people who attempt to harm them will be consumed with fire from their mouths, which will devour them. They will possess the power to shut heaven, blocking the rain coming from the filled clouds in those days. They will possess the power to turn water into blood and smite the earth with the plagues that derived from the time of the Exodus in Moses' day.

In their final days of prophesy, the Beast, Satan himself will make war against them and he will overcome them and kill them. Their dead bodies will not be buried and will remain in the streets of the trodden down Jerusalem, where Jesus was crucified on a tree. Those days will the people of the world celebrate with gifts and rejoicings. They rejoiced because the two prophets had tormented them in those days on the earth. When three days and a half pass by, the Spirit of Life will enter them and they will rise up on their feet and great fear will fall onto the people of the world that witnessed their prophesying.

"Come up here." A voice from heaven will say to them.

The two witnesses will ascend to heaven in a cloud and their enemies will watch this all take place before their very eyes. The world will witness this event take place. Within that same hour, a great earthquake will tremble the earth and a tenth portion of the city will fall. the earthquake will take the lives of seven thousand people. The remnant of The Most High will be frightened and will give glory and praise to The Most High.

That will be the second woe passing away and the third woe will come quickly after that.

The nations of the world will make war with The Most High and his remnant with Satan as their leader. They will make way to Harmegiddo, the land where they declare war against The Most High and his remnant. The Returning Messiah will come down and kill the armies of the nations with the Word of The Most High and will destroy their city of Babylon within one hour. For within that one hour, the kings of the nations and their partakers all lost everything.

Babylon, the great harlot and mother of harlots and the abominations of the earth will fall by the hand of The Most High and His remnant will rejoice over her defeat. After the Great Tribulation, the Messiah will return from out of the clouds with a white horse and a vesture dipped in blood. His eyes were like the flame of fire. On his head were many crowns and a name that only Himself knew. The armies of heaven that followed him will be dressed in white linen, white and clean, and will be riding on white horses.

From His mouth will go a sharp sword, which will be use to smite the nations of the world and he will rule over them with a rod of iron. On his vesture and thigh will be a name written that says, King of Kings and Master of Masters. His name is called The Word of Yah. Satan will be bound in the abyss for one thousand years during the reining of the Messiah. The remnant that did not bow to the Beast nor received his mark will live and reign with the Messiah in the New Kingdom for a thousand years.

Within the Kingdom, the remnant will have ruler ship over the nations and the nations will be their servants and wine dressers. They will lick the dust from the remnant's feet. The people will visit the Messiah three times in a year during His feast days. Within the end of those thousand years, Satan will be released to cause more to fall way from The Most High and after the thousand years are completed, Satan himself will be placed into the eternal flames of hell along with his angels that sided with him in the beginning. The old heaven and the old earth will pass away and The Most High will create the new heaven and new earth in their place to remain for all the righteous to dwell for all eternity.

We are nearer today than the prophets were thousands of years ago. The end of the Sixth Day is at hand and the Seventh Day is approaching faster than many will come to notice. Repent of your sins and be transformed by the renewing of your mind. Separate yourselves from the world to determine what is of The Most High and become one of the few that will enter New Jerusalem.

THE VIRTUOUS AND THE WICKED

Throughout the centuries of the world's existence, there have been women of those that were considered virtuous and those that were considered wicked. Here, will be a small discussion on the lives of those that were virtuous and those that were of the wicked. From Hawwah, the second wife of Adam to Yessica, we receive those of the virtuous. From Lilith, the proposed first wife of Adam to Carissa, we receive those of the wicked.

The first of this brief document will be the wicked ones. Starting with Lilith, the proposed first wife of Adam. Little is known Lilith, it is said that she was created alongside Adam during the days of Creation by the Most High, Yahweh. It is said that Lilith didn't agree with Adam for being on the bottom during sexual intercourse and she yelled the secret name of Yahweh and vanished into the atmosphere where she is still roaming to this day with her ally and possible husband in theory, the ha-Satan.

The second in this brief document is Queen Alyssa, the dominant queen of the queendom she called Bashemath. The daughter of Qayin and Awan. Alyssa was physically beautiful and seductive toward men and women through the flesh. She became queen during her days of leading both men and women astray as she commanded them to build her a kingdom of her own, where she could rule over those who would appear and would see fit to live there. Alyssa knew of the existence of Yahweh due to her father receiving the Mark. Alyssa grew with a respect and honor toward the Most High until her queendom was built and she began to see herself as a goddess amongst man of the earth.

It wasn't until she committed secret sodomy with a whore named Seba, that she was frequently visited by Uriel the Archangel, who gave Alyssa warnings to turn from her wicked ways and start focusing her whole attention on Yahweh by first banishing a homosexual from the queendom.

Alyssa agreed and started to do so until impatience took its course over the years and her heart was hardened. Her people began to worship her and even built monuments and images in her image. She later took place in many murders during the final years of her queendom until she had one more visit from Uriel, who told her that her queendom's demise would take place the next day and it did. Fire rained down from the heavens upon Bashemath, killing all who remained in the city. Alyssa was last to escape as she watched her queendom burn and turn into ash. The rise and fall of Queen Alyssa took place within a time span of thirty years. Alyssa later died in the wilderness at the age of seventy years old.

The third one that will be spoken of in brief detail is Ivah. The first wife of Dore during his younger years. The name Ivah means *iniquity* and that is what she brought upon him. They had no children together due to Ivah being barren, which hardened her heart toward Dore and toward Yahweh. Dore eventually sent Ivah away and nothing else is known of her till this day beside her actions toward Dore and Yah and the origin of her name.

The next wicked one to come across the earth was Jezebel, the wife of Ahab, who was the King of Israel during his day. The rebellious and stubborn woman who adorn makeup to attract those by the lust of the flesh. Jezebel continued to manipulate her weak husband into doing things her way, including to kill Elijah. After time made its course,

Jezebel was killed when she was tossed out of a window and consumed by the dogs that awaited her fall.

The following wicked one is Queen Zimmah, the forceful queen who over through Queen Diana of her kingdom and took over it for a period of twenty-seven years until Diana's daughter, Yisabelle took back the kingdom by killing Zimmah and her daughter, Zimmariah. Queen Zimmah was known for being a queen that desired to over through King Liam of his kingdom, known in spirit as Israel. She is also known for trying to search what was beyond the steep hill until her army fell at the hands of a supernatural power beyond earthly comprehension.

There is one wicked woman to come in the latter days and she is only known as Death. Referred to by some as the Hallucination of Sin and the Seductive Princess, nothing much is known of Death besides being the sister of Negiter, the dark god. She has played a frequent role on earth and will play even a larger part that concerns a man who is one of Us and who is the one to carry the Sword of the Elohim at this time. He and Death will be known throughout eternity as archenemies. A yin to a yang.

One of the final wicked ones to come across in the near future will be named Carissa, derived from Queen Alyssa and will be her successor in the future days ahead. Carissa will be a queen over a kingdom not yet given and her power will surpass the other nations in that period. Her rule will be like a lion stalking its prey until it has it by the jaws with blood pouring out to satisfy its hunger.

Carissa is a woman who will look pleasurable after the flesh, but rotten in the spirit as her ambition will always be to please the ha-Satan. Her ultimate goal will be to convince the entire world to love Satan and to cause them to receive his mark in order to live in this earth. Carissa has an opponent in the last days known as Yessica who will be spoken about in the virtuous section of this document.

Now, we head into those of the virtuous. Starting with Hawwah, the second wife of Adam. Hawwah, known as Eve to many became the wife of Adam after Yahweh had taken the rib from Adam and formed her from it, thus the woman became the help meet of the man in this earth for its existence. Even though Hawwah is responsible for eating the forbidden fruit first before Adam, the woman is known as the weaker vessel or the meekness and gentleness of Yah. Therefore, was the serpent able to easily manipulate her into doing so and in convincing Adam to eat thereof and bring sin from the outside world into the physical realm. After a while, hardly much is spoken of about Hawwah besides giving birth to her three sons Qayin, Hevel, and Seth and her two daughters Awan and Aclima.

Emzarah is the next virtuous woman to be spoken of in this document. The second wife of Dore during his middle years. Dore married Emzarah when he was five hundred years old and they had three sons together. Adad, Samael, and Mordecai. Emzarah was later greatly helpful in helping her sons find themselves wives before the deluge would come upon the earth and drown it. After the deluge and the chaos that followed, Emzarah lived a happy life with Dore and she died in her old age.

The next woman is Moriah, the wife of Adad, elder son of Dore and Emzarah. Moriah was chosen to be Adad's wife by Dore and Emzarah during the search for wives for their three sons. Moriah showed great character and humility toward them that they knew she was the one for Adad. Moriah married Adad and after the deluge they had children of their own, which the seed of the righteous had later come through into the world.

The woman Stephanie is another virtuous woman who endured patience of over seven years for Yah to send her a husband worthy of her submissiveness and humility. During the seven years, Stephanie had sought guidance and counsel from her grandmother, Merith. After which one man came to her and was discovered to be the wrong kind of man for her and within a short time, Lebbeus came into her life and they were married and had a son named Luke, who later became a warrior for Yah and His People.

The next woman is Beth, who had a somewhat situation similar to Stephanie's own. Beth was an attractive woman who had come from another nation where she had searched across the various nations of the earth at that time to find a husband to cover her. After a few years, Beth was led by the widow Naomi into the nation of Yah's People where she met her husband and married. After certain number of years, they had three children named Samael, Andro, and Krutis.

Yisabelle is the next one in this lineup who was deemed virtuous by her character and her actions toward Yah and His People. The mother of Yisabelle, Queen Diana had no where to look for guidance during the sacking of her nation by Queen Zimmah. Yisabelle sought to seek guidance from King Liam, where she later found herself being tested, proven, and tried by not only Liam, but of Yah as well. Yisabelle overcame the trials and tests where she confronted Zimmah with the aid of Liam as she defeated Zimmah and Zimmariah in combat to win back her mother's nation. Yisabelle later moved from her mother's nation and moved into Liam's nation where she remained until her death.

Zora is one virtuous woman who will appear into the world during the days when the United States loses its democracy and becomes a third-world country. Zora will grow up in a dictatorial United States with Lucef Lukas as its leader and who was the one to have killed Zora's father, Theos. Zora will come to her true purpose on this earth and over through Lukas to bring back some prosperity into the people's hearts.

The final woman to be spoken of in this document is Yessica, highly called, the Virtuous Woman. Yessica will be the antithesis of Carissa, the Wicked Woman. Unlike Carissa, who will grow up with the ambition to please Satan, Yessica will have the ambition to please Yah as she will live in the world. It will not be a long one before Yessica and Carissa cross paths as they will battle to the death in the days of the Great Tribulation with Yessica defeating Carissa and killing her.

"These are primary a few of the important ones of the Virtuous and the Wicked. There are countless others on both sides that have lived in times past and will exist in times future. For the young women living today on this side of glory, I, Michael Ledford ask of you to take a look at your life and what you're currently trying to seek and to make sure that you're on the right path and that path is the strait and narrow way into the Kingdom of Heaven."

SINGLENESS

Many call themselves single to feel more preserved about their own well-being. The society that we currently live in has an uncanny ability to look down on those that have no mate. Whether man or woman, they are looked down upon. Some are even caused names because of their singleness. Yet, when you see those individuals' lifestyles and how they treat their mate, it becomes clear that they desire to have your place in the life of singleness rather than being cling to someone they have no love towards.

The tale of singleness goes far beyond the years before this present moment. Many have lived in this world without a mate, later find one and fall asleep, returning to the earth as they were formed. Some goes through the earth with a mate and create a family amongst themselves, seeking and hoping their offspring enter the same form of agreement when they come to the age of knowing. You also have the ones who were assigned to be with certain mates. Depending on how the relationship is started and built in the process, one cannot fully tell how it will turn out. Some spit out their theories and emotions on another one's relationship, only to have destroyed it with their foul tongues.

For the Elect know that the tongue is an unruly evil and filled with deadly poison and holds life and death in one's mouth when they speak of others and amongst others. The tongue is almost equal to the heart of a person. For no one knows the heart, for it is also evil and neither one man nor woman on earth knows their own heart to discern it. When it comes to this subject, people automatically throw out their own feelings and emotions without even concerning the one who is either with a mate or potentially going to be with one.

For not everyone is destined a mate, nor are they destined to have offspring. There are those parents that have the possessive dream of their offspring creating their own children, granting them grandchildren. There are barren women that walk among us and are mocked because of their symptom. There are men who are unable to produce enough seed to create an offspring, yet, they are mocked as well amongst the barren women, but with greater feeling.

They say that men are programmed to crave an offspring at certain ages in their lifespan. There are those that crave it at an early age, those that crave it once they reach adulthood, and those who will never crave it. There are those today who constantly crave a child and yet have no sustainability to take care of it, let alone take care of themselves to have a child. They never take heed the warnings that are given to them by elders and friends and end up having the child and witness their lives turning into a living hell.

"Yet, who's to blame but the one that didn't take heed. For they mocked and scalded the ones who warned them and now they suffer greatly."

Some live their lives and continue with their mates. Living a prosperous life. Some end with death, with separation, with fornication, with adultery. Yet, today, these are taken as extras into what the world calls marriage. Yea, they have no knowledge and understanding when they become married and are granted a marriage license by their government. Not realizing that they have entered into a third-party agreement with the State.

"For why should one possess a piece of paper to proclaim their marriage to another. For it is nonsensical to one's eye such as mine."

The ones that are currently single and trying to discover their purpose in the world. Continue to do so. Do not bother with the poison that people will spit at you to cause you to have doubts and conjure up depressive thoughts and feelings to make you feel bad because they want you in something that they can't possess themselves. Though, there will be those who will speak kind words of encouragement and will not try to shove you into their perception of reality of how to live and breathe on this side of glory.

"If one should speak kindly to another, it will give them great inspiration and thought of how they should go out and do what they intend to do."

There is this notion of a Gift of Singleness that has been said to exist. Containing the notion of singleness grants an individual the ability to focus on more important things rather than their own personal lives. Be it selfish or selfless, they have the knowledge of working on bigger things than themselves and are humble enough to admit it to themselves and to others.

What these people should do is stay focus on achieving the bigger tasks at hand in this earth. For many have lived this life single and have had a greater purpose. Jeremiah was directly told by the Most High that he should remain single for his purpose on earth. Daniel was single due to his incredible hold on his faith toward the Most High. The apostle, Paul was single and wished that every man would be like him when it came to singleness. Because it gave him more time and energy to do the work of the Most High through the Messiah. Even the Messiah himself was a single man when he was on this earth.

"There will be those who marry, because they work better as a team rather than individuals. There will be those who do not marry, and work better because of their individuality."

The ones that marry, will marry and a few of them will live a long and prosperous life. The others will end up in chaos and separate from one another, hoping the next one will be the "One" for them. There will be those who will marry, and the Angel of Death will have come and taken their mate, leaving them a widow on the earth. There will be those who will never marry, because of symptoms or their individuality. Either way, they know their purpose.

"For if one knows they should marry, marry so that you can be happy. For those that know they should remain single, for their work is a greater task than having a mate, continue on with your work, for it will help many along the way and inspire those who are going through these circumstances."

The Gift of Singleness is given to those who possess the ability to achieve great tasks and are able to have more time to give thanks to the Most High and do the work of Him to spread it across the earth for the Elect to see and hear.

ONE SOUL

The fortune of knowing one's soul is very distant and unconscious to the conscious mind of society. Many in this present hour neither seek or find what one's soul truly is and how it could bring prosperity to someone life. Even their own lives if they desired to seek it. How can the people today study how a soul works if they don't have the desire to seek it themselves? In this current time space, people no longer have the belief in a soul. They only believe in a flesh body walking on top of concrete, dirt, grass, and whatever else lies beneath their feet.

If one should go out into a public location and ask the question, "Do souls exist and do we possess one soul?", the majority of the people would be astonished by the words that were spoken in the question and secondly, they wouldn't know how to answer. You'll get some yes answers, no answers, and those indifferent ones that only gravitate towards another's answer to fit in amongst the crowd. If you're currently reading this text amongst the other text in this Book of the Elect, you're sure to find more later on as you go in life until your time on this side of glory ends.

In this book, you've read the accounts of many who have in reality, lived centuries before this time period and some who are currently living amongst us still in their human bodies. The ones of the past centuries, such as Stephanie, Lebbeus, Luke, the Old Man, Ahab,

Jezebel, Abishag, Dore, Paul, and amongst the others have gone onto the other side beyond this realm we currently inhabit. The ones who are living amongst us today in this realm are Dolph, Clark Zyack, Levi, Preston Maddox, the father who read to his son about the Unheard-Of, as well as those whose name appeared briefly in the other texts are still living amongst us and yet, you're probably wondering where do you fit in all of this.

The answer is really simple. You fit amongst all of us in this realm. There are those such as the Elect who are the Most High's chosen people and are currently scattered abroad the world and will be reunited with each other in full when the Messiah returns and places his Kingdom on this earth to rule for one thousand years. For one to know their place and where they fit in this colossal universe, you just simply follow the Most High's laws, statutes, and commandments and obey his Word above all things. If you choose not to follow him, enjoy your life here in this realm and be happy with it and try to bring as much happiness in your life as you can.

Sometimes, people like me wonder about those who have come in the past and have left, where are they and what are they currently doing in the other realms. Both Shamayim and Geyhinnom, as some would call them, Heaven and Hell or Sheol. What could they possibly be doing. They have no earthly body of any kind, nor the thoughts that they conjured while they were here. Its best that you protect your soul at all cost. Guard your heart and mind greatly from the corruptions in this realm.

For we, the Elect know that we do not fight against flesh and blood, but the principalities, the rulers, and the darkness of this decadent world. For we know that the Unheard-Of or the ha-Satan is the god of this world and his image is shown before the world in monuments, stickers, logos, and anything that can be thought of as an image. As the Bible says in *2 Timothy 2:15*, Study and show yourself approved unto Yah. By doing that you will have a sense of reality in your mind about how you should operate before jumping on others for their characteristics and lifestyle.

We must stand strong and fight the battle that is currently taking place all around us. For angels are battling demons on a daily basis and yet we have no sight of it, because the fight is taking place in the spiritual realm and in the near future it will be in the physical realm, where we will all see it unfold. The battle between good and evil in all its detail. Many will be frightened of the tribulation unfolding and yet they should build up faith in the Most High to protect them and shield them from His wrath upon the earth.

For we the Elect understand that we have only one soul and we determine where that soul will go once we leave this side of glory. We determine if we will be dwelling with the Most High in his Kingdom of peace and love or if we will be dwelling with the Unheard-Of in his kingdom of fire and sulfur. For those who will understand this small text, hopefully they will get the full picture soon as possible, with obedience to the Father and studying his Word.

I am aware that standing up for the Most High that I will have a slew of enemies from all sides of the earth and they will do whatever in their power to tear us down and annihilate us from this earth. Yet, as the ones of old such as Chanokh, Harold Vosloo, Dore, the Old Man, and those who live today, Levi, Maddox, Zyack, we understand that in the end of all of this, we will prevail. For we obey the Father and keep his commandments and laws.

Before this is finished, I must say that there is an age coming of perpetual revelations that will be unfolded for the world to witness.

Those living today and those being born today are going to witness events that the ancients have not yet seen. For those who truly believe will see the signs around them and those who do not believe, will continue to live their lives happily as they can. I end this with a final statement. We all have one soul and it is up to us to determine our fate in this life and the next.

My name is Thomas Bradford and I say to you. *Shalom.*

AGE OF REVELATIONS

Allow me to properly introduce myself
My name is the Dragon of the Wilderness
I understand something apparently
Since I have existed on this earth
I have done some horrible things to many people

There is an event upon the horizon
An event that has reached afar in the minds
Of many in the world
The event has legendary proportions from its prophecies
The Age of Revelations

Humans, have you ever taken the time to see me for how I
really am?
I am the Way into the cities of Babylon
I am the Way into eternal pleasure and pain
I am the Way to go among the lost beyond the time
I STAND!

I see the fire, I see the will
I can look into your own spirit
And I can honestly say
you honestly believe you can defeat Me

At Har Megiddo

Liar. Liar! You are a liar!
You built this Kingdom all around us
And your foolish pride allows you to prey upon the weak
And fill them up with all this… hope. But the hope is dead.
As will be your Kingdom

YOU should have been more careful of what you've wished for
When I take center at Har Megiddo, you then will realize
That I am the most powerful entity
That has ever stepped foot
On this earth

Just remember this.
You're the one with everything to lose
When I come through and destroy
Who will be there for you
When I take it all away?!

You've sealed your own fate
When you decided to rebel and destroy
There's no escaping what will happen at Har Megiddo
You will be desolated
You will be punished

I have broken Your Saints.
I HAVE BROKEN YOUR SAINTS!!!
My sword has left a scar on their souls
A scar so deep and open
That can never heal

But you listen to Me now
The eternal flames after Har Megiddo
For you, your angels, and your nations
Will be the eternal punishment
For you all

You know this
Just as much as the angels in Shamayim
Just as much as your saints
Just as much as my kingdoms of the earth
I am already punished

The pain waiting on you after Har Megiddo
Will last for eternity as you,
Your angels, your nations
And your kingdoms
Will be the most pain of all

Humans, wake up, wake up,
WAKE UP!
Wake yourselves up and take a look around
Look at this world you're living in
Look at this world you're living in Man

I will open up the gates of Shamayim
And I will unleash a fury
A fury of which no mortal man
Throughout all of earth's history
Has never been seen

At Har Megiddo
Is the time and the place

Among your creations
Your beautiful creation of all
Is when reality sets itself in

At Har Megiddo
You will be defeated
You will be left alone
You will be judged
You will be rebuked and punished

Open your eyes, generations of Man.

YAH IS ONE

A word by Kenari Clark

O' Yah
Save your remnant from this untoward generation
We await your coming with patience
With fear and tremble we stand
We await

Abba Father,
Be merciful toward your children
We may fall at times in this life
But we get back up to continue moving forward
Be merciful

O' Yah
Throughout all the days of my life
Will I worship and praise you
You brought me out of the world
And showed me your marvelous light

I thank you for your mercy
You formed me before I was in the womb
You knew me before the earth was created
You know all of us better than we know ourselves
We praise Your Name

You showed us the way of truth and life
Through your son, Jesus Christ
Who sacrificed himself for us
To wash away our sins
To cleanse us for a better day

We are becoming new
The old man is passing away
And the new man is being born
The new man will praise you
The new man will worship you

We renew our minds
We learn Your ways and abandon our ways
We guard Your Law with our hearts
We keep it within us to be in remembrance
We remember your promises

When Noah built the ark
He was counted as righteous
When Abraham had walked in faith
He was considered righteous
We strive for righteousness

With righteousness
We inherit your Kingdom
A Kingdom made by Your power
A Kingdom that will come down from the sky
A New Jerusalem

O' Yah

We know the day is near
We know the time is close
We see the prophecies coming to pass
We know to prepare

Both our hearts and minds
We are to prepare
Our enemies will seek to stumble us
But, we will stand firm
We will trust You

We will have faith in You
We seek Your Kingdom
As this earth passes away
And everything that dwells upon it
We strive

YOU ARE ONE

COMPLETE THE COLLECTION

ABOUT THE AUTHOR

Ty'Ron W. C. Robinson II is the author of several works of fiction. Including the *Dark Titan Universe Saga*, *The Haunted City Saga*, EverWar Universe, Symbolum Venatores, Frightened!, Instincts, and others. More information pertaining to the author and stories can be found at darktitanentertainment.com.

Twitter: @TyronRobinsonII

Twitter: @DarkTitan_
Instagram: @darktitanentertainment
Facebook: @DarkTitanEnt
Pinterest: @darktitanentertainment
YouTube: Dark Titan Entertainment

CPSIA information can be obtained
at www.ICGtesting.com
Printed in the USA
LVHW090755040222
709971LV00022B/1311

9 798985 110